FAIRY BOND

THE KEY TO EMBRALIA
BOOK 2

FRANCES RUIZ

HINTERLAND SKY PRES

First Edition: 2010

Second Edition: 2026

Hinterland Sky Press, HinterlandSky.com

Second Edition

Print ISBN-10: 0-9818880-8-9

Print ISBN-13: 978-0-9818880-8-8

EBook ISBN-10: 0-9818880-9-7

EBook ISBN-13: 978-0-9818880-9-5

 Formatted with Vellum

1

AWAKENING

Kelly rubbed her eraser against the paper, trying to erase the last hints of the lopsided trapezoid she had drawn. The two bases were supposed to be horizontal, not vertical. She glanced up at the clock. Still thirty minutes left, and only two more questions. It was the first day of ninth grade and her first class at the new high school. She was taking a diagnostic math test for Intro to Chemistry. She didn't understand why geometry was relevant to chemistry, but these were the problems on the test. She rubbed the crook in her neck, then attempted to draw a neater trapezoid.

A sudden flurry of activity by the door caught her attention. She looked around to see if anyone else had noticed the commotion. No, of course they hadn't. All the other students were scribbling furiously on their papers, unaware that Kelly's fairy friend Bubbles had just flown into the classroom in his transparent, invisible-to-humans form. Kelly could see him because she was a fadaman — half-human, half-fairy, a fact she had unceremoniously discovered after she caught Bubbles stealing her fourteenth birthday cake only two months before. As his ghostlike form flew towards her desk, Kelly's eyes narrowed. He'd better have a good explanation for showing up here.

"Kelly, Kelly!" Bubbles panted breathlessly as he plopped himself down on the side of her desk. Clearly, he had rushed over here from somewhere. Beads of sweat swelled on his forehead and his hefty belly jiggled up and down as he tried to catch his breath. "Kelly, you won't believe it!"

I can't talk now, I'm in class. Kelly scribbled the words on her scratch paper, then pointed so that Bubbles could read them.

He frowned. "Stupid human classes, not worth anything. I have something to tell you."

It'll have to wait. I told you, you can't bother me at school.

Kelly was not pleased that Bubbles had already broken his promise of not disturbing her at school. It was only day one, for crying out loud. Bubbles was not pleased either. He crossed his arms and pouted, then wiped his forehead with a handkerchief from his shoulder bag. Kelly went back to redrawing her trapezoid while Bubbles fidgeted impatiently. After a few minutes he was swinging his legs back and forth off the edge of her desk so much that the desk shook.

She shot Bubbles a stern look and put her index finger up to her lips. When she realized Mrs. Jenkins was scrutinizing her from the front of the room, she quickly looked back down at her paper. Bubbles sat still for almost a minute. Then he started singing. No one else in the room could hear him, but to Kelly's ears he came through loud and clear.

"I'm flying through the forest, it's a beautiful day. The birds and bees and mice they best get out of my way. The branches and the leaves and trees oh my how they swaaaay—"

Stop it! Kelly scribbled on her paper. Bubbles sang louder and higher, his voice cracking as he reached outside of his range. "My good friend Kelly dear, isn't list'ning to me. I'm sad, so very sad, like when I sprained my knee..."

Kelly rolled her eyes and did her best to ignore Bubbles.

When he saw that the singing tactic wasn't going to work, he tried another. He pulled out his wand, a human toothpick, and pointed it at Kelly. "Come outside so we can talk right now, or you'll be sorry," he said.

We talked about this. I can't leave during school. GO AWAY!

"Fine then. Just remember, I did ask nicely first." With a quick twist of the wrist he flicked his wand. A bright spark shot from its tip and onto the center of Kelly's paper. A tiny flame burst forth and started to burn a hole in Kelly's test. She hurriedly blew on the flame to extinguish it.

"Is everything all right, Miss Brennan?" Kelly jumped at the sound of Mrs. Jenkins's unamused voice.

"Yes, ma'am," Kelly answered, blushing as all the other students turned their eyes on her.

Bubbles smirked and repositioned his wand for a second strike. The next spark hit Kelly on her shirt sleeve, and she clapped her hand over it before it could form a flame. Then Bubbles took aim at her leg. *That's it,* Kelly thought. In a flash she reached out and snatched Bubbles's toothpick out of his hand, tossed it to the floor, grabbed him with both hands and pinned his arms to his sides.

"Let me go!" Bubbles shouted.

Kelly struggled to maintain her grip as Bubbles squirmed. The girl sitting next to Kelly was staring, open mouthed. *She must think I'm crazy,* Kelly thought. She couldn't blame her. After all, from the girl's point of view it would just look like Kelly was holding an imaginary ball and shaking it. *Great, the first day of high school and I'm already going to be labeled a freak.* Bubbles broke free of her grasp and scrambled to retrieve his wand.

Kelly raised her hand.

"What is it, Miss Brennan?" Mrs. Jenkins asked.

"I'm not feeling very well. May I go get a drink of water?"

"Are you finished with your test?"

Kelly looked down at her unfinished test, then at Bubbles, who had regained his wand. He extended it, scowling, waiting to see what she would tell her teacher.

"Yes, I'm done," Kelly said. She would have to take the hit on the last couple of questions. She brought the test to the front and handed it to Mrs. Jenkins. Mrs. Jenkins handed her the wooden hall pass. As Kelly stormed out the door, she heard a few snickers from her classmates.

She burst into the bathroom down the hall with Bubbles close behind. She swirled to face him. "Are you happy now? I can't believe this! You promised you wouldn't bother me at school." Kelly struggled to keep her voice shy of a full shout.

"I'm sorry, but you didn't have to grab me. That was uncalled for." Bubbles rubbed an elbow as he fluttered in the air.

"Oh yeah? Was burning a hole in my test called for?"

"I suppose you have a point there," Bubbles admitted. "But don't you want to hear what I have to tell you?" His eyes gleamed with childlike excitement.

Kelly sighed. "Fine, what is it?"

"Thomas's mother and the rest of his family just arrived in Glendenland. There's going to be a feast tonight, a feast like never before! And Thomas wants us all to be there. Well, he wants us to meet him for a private royal dinner, but it will still be a feast just like the big feast." Bubbles performed a somersault with delight, then cocked his head to the side and squinted at the automatic paper towel dispenser.

"You barged into the middle of my class to tell me that?"

He didn't answer. He was too intrigued by the dispenser. He flew past the sensor and a paper towel rolled down. He giggled. He flew past the sensor again.

"Bubbles? Did you hear me?"

"Oh, yes, sorry." He flew back over to her. "You said I could interrupt you for important things. So, I did."

"Important things would be stuff like my house burning down, an earthquake, or Miasmos and his minions attacking Glendenland. Not Thomas's relatives arriving. That could easily have waited until school let out."

Bubbles's face fell. "I thought you'd be excited."

I would have been, if you'd told me after school. But now I'm upset because you interrupted my class. You made me look like an idiot on the first day of high school."

Bubbles rolled his eyes. "Why do you care about those morons anyway? Why don't you just come live in Glendenland?"

"You know I can't just abandon my mother. And besides, in spite of how foreign it seems to you, I like my human life."

Bubbles pouted.

"Listen, I know you don't understand why school is important, but it is really important to me. So would you please go away now?"

"Fine."

Kelly walked back into the hall and headed for her classroom. Bubbles flew along for a few paces.

"So, are you going to come to the feast tonight?" he asked.

"Maybe."

Bubbles grinned, satisfied. "Be there by nine!"

A FEW HOURS later Kelly stepped into the high school cafeteria for the first time. It was much bigger than the middle school one, which made sense because it had to fit all the graduates from three neighboring middle schools, not to mention the upperclassmen, who for the most part moved about as if the freshmen didn't exist. Kelly saw many new faces as she waited in the lunch line.

The lunch choices weren't much different from the middle

school choices. There was pizza, a salad bar with brown iceberg lettuce and unripe tomatoes, cheeseburgers, and some sort of casserole. Kelly opted for the pizza. After she paid, she spotted her best friend Stephanie waving at her from the end of a table in the middle of the room.

"How's your first day going?" Stephanie asked as Kelly sat down across from her.

Kelly glanced around to make sure no one else was within earshot before telling Stephanie how Bubbles had shown up in the middle of her test. Stephanie was the only human who knew Kelly was a fadaman, and she had accompanied Kelly when she first went to Glendenland to hide from the evil Miasmos and his fadaman son Marcos Witherings.

"Bubbles has absolutely no emotional intelligence," Stephanie said when Kelly had finished recounting his visit. "We are going to go tonight though, right?"

Kelly smiled at her friend's enthusiasm. Stephanie jumped at every chance to don her prosthetic wings and be shrunk to fairy size with fairy dust. "I suppose," Kelly answered.

"Good." Stephanie took a bite of her mystery casserole and grimaced. "I should have gone with the pizza."

Kelly shrugged. "I'm not sure about that. It's soggy."

Stephanie wrinkled her nose, then she perked up. "Eye candy alert, six o'clock!" she said.

Kelly turned around to see a tall blond boy bending down to retrieve a soda from the soda machine. His tight black t-shirt rose up slightly and Kelly could see the small of his back. It was toned. She'd never seen him before. "Maybe he's from another middle school," she said.

Stephanie shook her head. "No, he's an upperclassman."

"How do you know?"

"Can't you tell? It's all in how he carries himself. With confidence."

The boy turned around and Kelly saw he had a pleasing

face to match his pleasing frame, with startling ice-blue eyes. He tossed his soda can high up in the air. It swirled around four times before he caught it with one hand and made his way over to sit with a large group of guys in varsity t-shirts. Popular kids.

"He's so dreamy," Stephanie sighed.

"He's out of your league."

"I always like a challenge."

"Judging by the company he keeps, he's probably a jerk."

"He might be nice."

"Give me a break," Kelly said. "When was the last time you met a nice jock?"

"There's a first time for everything," Stephanie answered. "Besides, you shouldn't stereotype people."

"Whatever."

The boy said something and all of his companions burst into hysterical laughter.

"Hey, Pixie Chick." Kelly heard Tommy Thompson's voice behind her. *Just who I was hoping to see,* she groaned internally. Tommy Thompson was always making fun of her unusually pointed ears. He had no idea how close some of his nicknames came to describing Kelly's true identity.

"How was your summer?" Tommy continued, taking a seat beside her. "I heard you spent it making Christmas tree ornaments with your mommy. I guess I shouldn't be surprised; that's suitable work for an elf." He chuckled at his own cleverness. Stephanie and Kelly just looked at him. "Suitable work for an elf, get it?" He waited for them to laugh. They didn't.

"What do you want?" Kelly asked finally.

"Who, me? I don't want anything. I was just saying hi." He stood up. "Hey, when did you start wearing jewelry?" He eyed Kelly's fairy sense necklace, and then the emerald heart necklace she had been awarded by Thomas, the king of Glendenland, for her role in the battle against Miasmos and his son.

"Why do you care if I wear jewelry?" Kelly snapped.

Tommy shrugged, reminding Kelly of a stubborn English bulldog. "Just curious. See you in German class, Elfie."

"How does he know you're in the same German class as he is?" Stephanie asked once he was out of earshot.

"We had our first class this morning. Plus, he saw me registering last year in homeroom. He probably signed up just to torment me."

"Well, don't worry about it. If he pisses you off you can get Bubbles to set one of his tests on fire," Stephanie said.

Kelly laughed. Maybe that wasn't such a bad idea.

HALF AN HOUR later Kelly and Stephanie sat down for their Algebra I class, the only class they had together. Instead of individual desks, there were several long tables arranged in rows, each with four chairs behind them. When they arrived, the prime real estate in the back of the room had already been claimed, and the teacher's pets had already taken up position in the front row. So they sat in an empty table in the middle of the room.

The teacher was a huge man who looked like a bodybuilder on steroids, but he had bright white hair and must have been at least sixty years old. He paced back and forth in front of the whiteboard, waiting for the seats to fill. It was still a few minutes before the bell and students filed in one by one. Kelly recognized about half of them from her middle school, and she assumed the other half were from other middle schools, since mostly freshmen took algebra. Soon almost all of the seats were taken, except for the seat to the left of Stephanie, where she had rested her backpack. A very skinny boy with long black hair, eyeliner, and black nail polish sat down next to Kelly. Moments later, in walked the cute boy from lunch. He paused just inside the door, scanning the room for an empty seat. Kelly poked Stephanie. Stephanie quickly moved her book bag off the seat beside her and flashed a smile at the boy. He came over and sat down beside them.

"Hi, I'm Stephanie. This is my friend Kelly," Stephanie said to him. Kelly nodded. She hoped Stephanie didn't say anything too embarrassing.

"Dmitri," he mumbled, before reaching into his bag for his notebook.

"Are you new here?" Stephanie asked.

"Huh?" His reaction was delayed, as if he hadn't immediately realized that she was talking to him.

"No, I'm a sophomore."

"Then what are you doing in Algebra I?" Stephanie asked.

"I failed this class last year," he answered, his face turning pink.

The bell rang. "Good afternoon, class," the teacher began. "I hope you like where you are sitting, because these will be your assigned seats for the entire semester."

Stephanie broke into a wide grin at these words.

"My name is Mr. Patterson. Let's begin by going over the class rules." Mr. Patterson launched into a long speech about respect and dedication, which lasted almost the entire period. When the bell finally rang to announce the end of class, Dmitri got up quickly and raced from the room without saying anything to anybody.

"Can you believe he's in our class?" Stephanie asked. "This year is going to be great. I can feel it."

THAT AFTERNOON on the metro ride home Kelly thought about her first day of high school. Not much seemed different about being back in the classroom, which surprised her. She had been expecting everything to feel dull and strange after her exciting summer. In the last two months she had found out she was half-fairy, learned her absent father (who was a fairy!) might still be alive, started magic lessons, and helped defeat Miasmos and his fadaman son, Marcos Witherings. She shivered to think of how Witherings, who before his fateful duel with Kelly had been running for US president, now lay in a crazed stupor in the jail bubble of Glendenland. Kelly had driven him crazy by causing him to experience all the pain and suffering he had ever caused anyone else. Kelly knew he had deserved it, but she still felt guilty. Her attack had only worked because Witherings had still possessed some remnants of a conscience. The same technique wouldn't have worked on his father, who didn't have even a shred of a conscience anymore, if he'd ever had one to begin with. Kelly's heart fluttered. Miasmos had escaped the battle — weakened but far from dead. She dreaded what could happen if he regained his strength before Thomas's forces tracked him down.

Almost no thoughts about fairies had crossed her mind during the school day, however. Except for when Bubbles barged into her class, of course. At school everything had seemed like it had been before. She still cared about the same things, like not wanting to look like a freak. Intellectually she knew she shouldn't care, but she did.

When she got home Kelly found her mother Mindy in the kitchen, busy making dinner. "How was your day, sweetie?" Mindy asked.

"Okay. How was yours?" Mindy was an elementary school teacher, so today was also her first day with a new class.

"It was great. My kids are such a good group. I'm very excited," Mindy answered happily.

"Do you need help with dinner?" Kelly asked.

"No, you just go relax. I've got everything under control." Mindy started chopping carrots for a salad.

"All right. By the way, can Stephanie come over later and spend the night?"

"On a weeknight?"

"All of our teachers gave us a lot of homework," Kelly ventured. "We think they did it to drive home the fact that high school is going to be harder than middle school. I thought it would be easier if we worked on the homework in the same place so we could compare answers and help each other. But, there's so much of it that it will probably be pretty late by the time we're done. Too late to ask her dad to come pick her up."

Mindy nodded knowingly. "In that case, of course she can stay the night."

"Thanks, Mom." Kelly retreated upstairs to her bedroom. She was already tired, but she resisted the urge to lie down. She had to finish her homework before Stephanie arrived. While she had been lying to Mindy about why Stephanie was going to come over, she hadn't been lying about having a lot of homework.

About two hours later Stephanie rang the doorbell. She and Kelly quickly ate dinner with Mindy (but only small portions to leave room for the feast), and then they went up to Kelly's room. Mindy was always trying to give Kelly 'her space,' so the girls weren't worried about their true plans for the night being discovered.

As the door to Kelly's room closed behind them, Stephanie flung her backpack down onto Kelly's bed. "So, what are you going to wear?" she asked.

"I don't know." Kelly hadn't given it much thought.

Stephanie had. "Look at what I'm wearing." She reached into her backpack and pulled out a bright red dress.

"Wow, that's bright."

"Of course it is," Stephanie replied. "We have to look good. It isn't every day that previously exiled royal families return to fairy kingdoms. Besides, who knows what kind of cute cousins Thomas might have?"

While Kelly stood and looked through her closet for something suitable to wear, Stephanie changed into her red dress and applied vibrant red lipstick to match. Finally, Kelly decided to wear black dress pants and a light blue blouse.

"You're wearing that?" Stephanie asked disapprovingly. "What about that shiny silver dress?" She pointed to the bright dress in Kelly's closet that Mindy had insisted she buy for a neighbor's wedding.

"That would look silly with my wings," Kelly answered. In fairy form Kelly had light purple wings with bright silver lines running through them, like the veins of a leaf. Wearing a silver dress would look quite tacky.

"I suppose you're right. Well, at least put on some makeup." Stephanie extended a tube of mascara to Kelly.

"No, thanks. I'll just stick to my strawberry flavored lip gloss."

Stephanie shrugged. "Suit yourself. But hurry up, it's already 8:30."

"Oh no. We're going to be late!" Kelly hastily changed into her chosen outfit. Glendenland was a thirty-minute flight away, so they had no time to spare. "Where's your fairy dust?"

Stephanie pulled a tiny jar, about a half-inch tall, from her backpack. It was filled with a fine and shiny silver powder — fairy dust. "Get over here and dust me."

Kelly closed her eyes and willed herself to change into her fairy form. The transformation was now second nature to her, and it only took about a second. Once in fairy form, Kelly flew over to Stephanie, took the fairy dust jar, opened it, and poured a generous amount of the dust onto Stephanie's head.

Stephanie rapidly shrunk to fairy size, ending up about one foot tall. Next Stephanie handed Kelly her prosthetic wing bundle, a ball of jumbled wires. Kelly pulled on two of the wires and the wing skeleton sprung into shape. She held the wings up to Stephanie's back and pressed the attach button. The wings instantly attached directly into Stephanie's back. After stretching brown fibrous wing covers over the wing skeleton, they finished off Stephanie's getup by attaching her prosthetic ear tips. Most of the fairies in Glendenland didn't know Stephanie was actually a human, and Thomas preferred to keep it that way, since anti-human sentiment was far from uncommon amongst the general fairy population.

After Stephanie tested her wings by flying around the room a few times, they both put on the fairy shoulder bags they had bought in Glendenland during the summer. They were ready. Together they pushed the window open and flew out into the night.

They knew the way to Glendenland by heart. Within thirty-minutes they had reached the small park on the shore of the Potomac river that contained their usual entrance to Glendenland — a statue of a sitting lion, right by the water. As they approached they realized there was a problem. A human couple sat on a nearby bench, mere feet from the statue. Since Kelly could only make herself half-invisible to humans, seeing as she was only half-fairy, and Stephanie couldn't make herself even a little bit invisible, they would have to enter Glendenland another way. Through the water.

"But I don't want my makeup to get messed up," Stephanie complained.

"Don't worry, it'll be fine," Kelly said.

They pulled their underwater breathing masks from their bags, put them on, and dove into the water. Kelly could see Glendenland's large expanse of interconnected underwater bubbles below them. They emanated a faint glow that made them visible to fairies at night. Stephanie followed Kelly closely, not able to see Glendenland from above, due to the invisibility charms that kept humans from spotting it. Kelly located the bubble she wanted and headed towards it.

They came through the ceiling of a bubble hallway just outside the entrance to the king's royal quarters.

"What are we doing here?" Stephanie asked, touching down on the ground. She pulled a compact mirror out of her bag to check her makeup. Luckily, makeup was the only thing to worry about; their clothes and hair had been dried automatically when they passed through the charmed bubble membrane. "Shouldn't we be in the Great Hall, or the mess hall?" Stephanie added.

"No. I'm sure they must have had an official welcoming ceremony earlier. Bubbles said that Thomas wanted us to join him for a private dinner, and to be there by nine."

Stephanie looked down at her watch, a pretty mechanical one she had bought from the fairy market, since fairies didn't have digital watches. "That's in three minutes."

Kelly put her hand up to the middle of the shaded semicircle that marked the entrance to the royal quarters. She heard the expected series of chimes announcing their presence just before a familiar mechanical voice spoke.

"State your names, fairies," the voice commanded.

"Kelly Brennan and Stephanie Portersfield," Kelly answered.

"State your business, fairies."

"We are here to see Thomas," Stephanie said.

"Invalid business. Please rephrase."

"They really need to reprogram this thing," Stephanie whispered to Kelly. The gatekeeper seemed only to accept a set series of requests phrased in flowery language, and they always had to try several times to get it right.

"We are here at the request of his Grace the just, loyal, unwavering, and wise Thomas Penadas," Kelly said.

"Valid business. Please pass through the archway and wait for further instructions."

When Kelly and Stephanie walked through the archway, they were greeted by the portly fairy attendant Flimsly, who was presently dressed in his best red jacket and white pants.

"You're just in time. Follow me," he said.

They followed Flimsly through the archway that led to the royal dining hall. Inside, the royal dining table stretched before them, and the enormous chandelier hanging from the bubble's ceiling shone brightly as it shifted back and forth with the water movements above them. The fireplace at the far side of the room was also lit, but the decorative fire didn't give off any heat.

Thomas sat at the head of the table. His long brown hair hung loose over his shoulders, as was the traditional style for formal occasions. His ornate golden crown sparkled atop his head. Kelly knew the crown's presence was due to the formality of the occasion as well, since Thomas hated to wear the delicate vine of golden leaves unless he had to. Unfortunately for him, he'd already needed to wear it several times in the past two and a half weeks since he became king.

Thomas's gold-streaked blue wings were currently folded behind his back, as were the wings of the other guests. To his right sat his wife Carmina, who looked stunning in a flowing lavender dress that perfectly complemented her glistening yellow wings.

Continuing down the table on Thomas's right were fairies Kelly knew well: Prince Venuto, who had been looking much happier since being appointed first advisor to Thomas instead of being forced to take the crown after his father King Glenden's death; Petania, Venuto's girlfriend, who had been warming up to Kelly and Stephanie after realizing they weren't competition for Venuto's affections; Dimpleton, tireless friend of Thomas who had been promoted to advisor when Thomas returned to Glendenland; and Bubbles and his sister Beatrix. Bubbles waved excitedly to Kelly. She nodded to him curtly, still not fully forgiving him for his antics earlier in the day.

Flimsly guided Kelly and Stephanie to the two empty seats that completed that side of the table. Once seated, Kelly took in the fairies across from her.

On Thomas's immediate left was an older fairy woman. She sat with a very straight spine. Kelly could see the resemblance between her and Thomas. She had the same color hair, the same blue eyes, and the same bone structure. Her face was starting to become lined with time, but it was still very striking. Kelly couldn't see her wings because they were folded down, but she was curious as to their color. To the woman's left sat a male fairy, who looked to be about the same age as Kelly. His dark black hair was a tousled mess of curls. Beside him sat three other male fairies, who looked closer to Thomas's age.

"Welcome," Thomas said, smiling at the newest arrivals. "Mother," he continued, looking to the female fairy on his left, "these are my friends Kelly and Stephanie. Kelly and Stephanie, my mother Reynalda."

"Nice to meet you," Kelly said.

"I've heard a lot about you," Reynalda replied, not changing her expression. Her stoic manner reminded Kelly a bit of Glendenland's last king, King Glenden, who had rarely ever showed his emotions.

"And this is my cousin, Blaine," Thomas indicated the next fairy. "He is my late Aunt Mimi's son."

Blaine flashed them a wide smile, and his curls bobbed around his forehead. Looking more closely, Kelly noticed that his brown eyes were so dark she couldn't see where his pupils separated from his irises. She also noticed his strong jaw and well-balanced cheekbones. He was very handsome. Kelly avoided making direct eye contact and hoped she wasn't blushing.

"And those three are also cousins. Gerald, Peramino, and Mustino."

The last three fairies nodded politely.

Before Thomas could say anything further, Blaine broke in excitedly. "Kelly, Thomas was just telling us how you beat Marcos Witherings all alone. That's amazing."

"It was just luck really," Kelly said. Being showered with praise, especially from someone as good looking as Blaine, made her uncomfortable.

"She's just being modest," Stephanie said. "He didn't stand a chance against her."

Blaine looked impressed. But no matter what anyone else thought, Kelly knew it had just been luck.

Flimsly, with the help of another attendant, laid an appetizer of cranberry herb soup before them. It smelled delicious.

"So, how was the trip here?" Kelly asked, trying to change the subject before Blaine could ask her more about Witherings.

Blaine opened his mouth to answer but Reynalda beat him to it. "It was fine," she said flatly.

"And how do you find Glendenland so far?" Kelly asked.

"It's great," Blaine said. "They had a ceremony for us in the Great Hall followed by fireworks in the underwater park. It was incredible. And everyone is being so nice to us."

Reynalda let out a harsh breath that might have been a laugh, but Kelly couldn't be sure. "Just remember those fairies that are being so nice to you now are the same ones who caused you to go into exile for thirteen years."

"Mother," Thomas said.

"Don't *Mother* me Thomas," she snapped. "Making you king and having a party doesn't erase the past."

"No one is trying to erase it," Venuto said quietly. "We are just trying to make amends."

Reynalda turned her eyes to him. They flashed with a fierce

intensity that made Kelly glad she wasn't the recipient. Venuto gazed back calmly.

"Amends?" she asked, incredulous. "This coming from the son of the man responsible for our expulsion from our own kingdom!"

"My father did the best he could with the information he had at the time," Venuto answered, his voice shaking ever so slightly. Kelly knew that the death of his father was still fresh in his mind. She saw Petania reach for his hand under the table. No one had yet touched their soup.

"He did not do his best," Reynalda said. "He let his grief for the loss of his wife cloud his judgment."

"Mother," Thomas said again, putting his hand on her forearm.

"Let me speak!" She pulled her arm away. "What his father did to this family is horrible. My poor nieces and nephews, having to grow up like free fairies, without a band, without a home, scarred for life."

"I don't think I'm scarred for life," Blaine said.

"You just say that because you don't know what your life would have been like otherwise. You don't know what you've lost. Nothing any of you can do now can make up for those thirteen years." Her eyes were back on Venuto. Now the emotion was clearly written on her face. Everyone sat uncomfortably for a few moments. Venuto looked like he didn't know what to say.

Finally, Dimpleton, who had been sitting still as a statue and just as quiet up until that point, broke the silence. "What happened happened, and there isn't anything we can do to change it. All we can do is try to make the best out of the future that we have."

"Well put," Thomas said.

Venuto nodded. Reynalda still had a surly scowl on her face, but she didn't say anything back, perhaps because she knew how hard Dimpleton had worked to try and clear

Thomas's name. Maybe his actions deserved her respect. Or maybe she just couldn't think of a smart reply.

"So, Kelly, how was your first day of school?" Carmina asked. Kelly was grateful for the change in conversation, as were the others. Soon Kelly and Stephanie were busy answering questions, mostly from Blaine, about what human school was like. This topic kept the conversation going through the main course of fish and creamed corn mush, and it carried on about halfway through their dessert of strawberry lime ice cream. But then the conversation topic finally shifted.

"One thing I don't understand," Blaine said, "is how you two expect to fight Miasmos when you're still in school?"

Kelly and Stephanie just looked at each other, unsure of what to say.

"There isn't much anyone can do about Miasmos at the moment," Thomas said. "We are trying, but we can't really hope to sense his location given his expert ability to hide himself."

"But, can't we be out there, actively searching for him?" Blaine asked.

Thomas raised an eyebrow. "And where would we start?"

Blaine frowned.

"Exactly my point."

"It just feels, wrong. To sit here and do nothing," Blaine said with a sigh.

"Sometimes in life you just have to wait," Venuto said. "Although while you're waiting you should work to make yourself ready for when the time comes."

"When will the time come?" Blaine asked.

"You'll know when it does," Venuto said.

Blaine's frown deepened.

By the time Flimsly took away their dessert bowls it was after 11pm. Kelly and Stephanie politely excused themselves, knowing they would have to get up very early for school the next morning. As they walked down the hall away from the royal quarters, they heard a set of quick footsteps run up behind them. Kelly turned to see Blaine approaching.

"Wait, I want to ask you something," he called out.

"What is it?" Stephanie asked once he'd caught up.

"Will you take me to see him?"

"To see who?" Kelly asked.

"Marcos Witherings," Blaine replied in a hushed whisper.

"Why are you asking me? Ask Thomas," Kelly said.

"He's so busy. I don't want to bother him."

"Are you sure you aren't just worried he'll say no?"

He bristled. "No, I just don't want to bother him. Like I said."

"Why do you want to see Marcos Witherings?" Stephanie asked.

"I'm curious."

"Why?" Kelly asked.

"I've never seen a crazy, evil half-fairy before, that's why." At first Kelly thought he might be joking, but on second glance she realized he'd meant exactly what he'd said. A boyish, naive interest shone from his eyes.

"What makes you think I have authority to go and see him?" Kelly asked.

He looked surprised by the question. "Fairy law, of course." The girls stared blankly at him. "Whoever captures a prisoner has visitation rights," he explained.

"That's weird. What if whoever captured a prisoner had a grudge against them?" Kelly asked, thinking of how many people might want to take personal revenge on someone they had captured.

"Obviously if the visitor tried to hurt the prisoner they would be stopped by the guards and not be allowed in after that," Blaine answered.

"How do you know so much about fairy law if you spent most of your life outside of Glendenland?" Stephanie asked.

"My Aunt Reynalda made sure of it. I probably know more about Glendenland than most people who've been here all their lives do. So, will you take me to see him?"

"I don't know. It's late, and I'm not sure Thomas would approve," Kelly said.

"What would it take for you to say yes?" Blaine asked.

Kelly wasn't sure what he was getting at, but Stephanie's response made it clear that she and Blaine spoke the same language.

"A jar of high quality fairy dust should do the job, don't you think?"

Kelly frowned.

Blaine nodded his agreement to the terms. "Kelly, do you accept?"

Kelly didn't like it much, but Stephanie was staring at her with her famous puppy dog eyes, and she supposed it couldn't really be such a big deal. Witherings was harmless, after all, and they would be quickly in and out. Plus, Thomas had never expressly said anything about not going to visit him, so if he were to get upset then she could just say she didn't know it would bother him. "All right," Kelly acquiesced.

"Yes!" Blaine jumped up and down.

"Really, I don't see what you are so excited about," Kelly said.

They walked to the nearest transport bubble and Kelly examined the map of Glendenland on the podium in the center of the room. She quickly located the transport bubble closest to the jail bubble complex. Though she had never been there, she knew the complex was situated on the outskirts of Glendenland, past the far edge of the underwater park. She pressed on the red circle representing the transport bubble closest to the jail, and the shadow archway on their right turned from its inactive opaque gray to its active bright blue. Kelly, Stephanie, and Blaine walked through the portal.

They exited the transport bubble on the other side and proceeded down the hall until they reached a nondescript, unlabelled shadow archway. Despite the absence of identifying markings, Kelly could sense that this archway was the entrance to the jail complex. Using her developing fairy senses was still a strange feeling. She didn't visually see what was on the other side of the archway; she just somehow *knew* it was the entrance to the jail bubble.

Kelly put her hand up and touched the middle of the archway. There was a series of chimes. She noticed Blaine looking at her with a strange expression.

"What is it?"

"I just had the strangest feeling," he said. "You seem so familiar to me. Almost like we've met before."

"Uh, we've never met. I think both of us would have remembered." She couldn't tell if he had intended his comment to be some sort of a pickup line or not. Either way, it was odd.

They waited a few moments at the archway, but when no disembodied voice came forth to ask about their business, they took that to mean they were allowed to enter. They walked through unimpeded. On the other side, a long hallway stretched before them, and a middle-aged male fairy sat in a small wooden chair just inside the entrance. He was sound asleep, and snoring blissfully.

"Excuse us," Kelly said.

The fairy just snorted, still asleep.

"Excuse me, sir?" Kelly repeated. No response.

Blaine walked up to the sleeping fairy and tapped him on the shoulder. The fairy jumped from his seat, unfurling bright red wings in a quick motion. He pulled a small wooden wand from his pocket, disoriented and startled. "What, who goes there?" he asked, facing away from them.

Blaine cleared his throat. The man spun around to face them, panic in his eyes. When he realized they weren't menacing, he lowered his wand slowly. "Sorry, er, I'm the warden. How can I help you?" He tucked his wand back in his pocket and refolded his wings.

"We want to see a prisoner," Kelly said.

"Marcos Witherings?" the warden asked.

"How did you know?"

"He's the only prisoner we've got, besides old Ricketer."

"Ricketer?"

"Yep," the warden answered. "And no one besides young Venuto has ever been here to see that old chap, at least not in the twenty years I've worked here."

"Wow, twenty years. What's he in for?" Blaine asked.

"Nobody knows."

"What do you mean nobody knows?" Stephanie asked.

"He was put in prison some sixty years ago, before even our dear late King Glenden's reign, may he rest in peace. And the reason for his imprisonment was a secret. Only the king and a few others knew why. All I know is that it's a life sentence."

"But how do you know he deserves a life sentence if you don't know what he's in for?" Kelly asked.

The warden shrugged. "What's your name?"

"Kelly Brennan."

The warden nodded. "Very good. You're only allowed to bring in one guest with you per visit, however."

"I'll stay here," Stephanie said. "I don't really want to see him anyways. The idea gives me the creeps."

"As you wish. You two follow me."

Kelly and Blaine followed the warden down the hallway. It was very long and twisty, and there were shadow archways spaced evenly along it — one about every six paces.

"There're certainly a lot of cells here for only two prisoners," Kelly commented. Blaine nodded in agreement.

Finally, they rounded a corner and Kelly could see two guards standing in the hall, one on either side of an archway about three archways down from their position. The presence of the guards, who stood facing the archway, implied that the cell was occupied.

Kelly expected the warden to stop at the guarded cell, having assumed it was Witherings's, but when they reached it he just kept walking. Even so, Kelly couldn't help but pause for a moment from curiosity outside of the cell. The archway astonished her; it was transparent. She had never seen one like it before. It was clear, but flickering rivers of bright pink and purple glistened over its surface, like colors over the outside of a soap bubble. Kelly guessed it made sense for prisoners' archways to be transparent when occupied, so that the guards could see if the prisoner inside made any sort of unexpected movements.

She squinted to see through the archway. She could make out a small cot with someone sitting cross-legged on top of it, eyes closed in deep meditation. It was a very old fairy with a long gray beard. He seemed to feel Kelly's stare. His eyes opened. Kelly gasped at their startling purple color — and their intensity. She felt as though his gaze was penetrating to the very core of her being, scrutinizing her. It would probably be a good idea to look away, she thought, but for some reason she didn't.

"Let's go." The warden's voice jerked Kelly's attention away from the prisoner. She moved to follow the warden, glancing back quickly over her shoulder. The old man was again sitting with closed eyes, like a statue, and for a second Kelly wondered if he had really even opened his eyes at all. She hurried to catch up with the warden and Blaine.

A few archways later they came upon another see-through archway with guards. Kelly looked at the guards, wondering something. "Are there guards stationed outside in the water too?" she asked the warden.

"There's no need," he replied. "The prison bubbles are non-pervious, save for the entrances, so it's impossible to exit through the top of them into the river like you can do with other bubbles."

"I see." Through the glistening wall Kelly saw a small cot. A form lay on top, covered almost entirely by a blanket: Marcos Witherings.

"You can have fifteen minutes," the warden said. He placed his hand on the archway and a series of chimes tinkled to indicate that it was now unlocked. "I'll be back when your time is up."

Kelly and Blaine walked into the cell. Once they were inside the chimes rang again behind them.

"He didn't say he was going to lock us in," Kelly said. "I don't like the idea of being locked in a room with Witherings, even if he is in a coma."

Glendenland's head healer, Margretta, had said that Witherings might never come out of his coma. All the same, Kelly felt very uneasy in his presence. He hadn't made any motions when she and Blaine had entered, but she still hung back as Blaine approached the edge of the cot. He pulled down the blanket to reveal Witherings's face.

Just as she remembered from the last time she had seen him, Witherings stared unseeingly into the air, drooling and trembling slightly.

"Whoa," Blaine said. "You made him this way?"

Kelly nodded.

"Wicked," he said appreciatively.

"I don't think it's anything to feel proud of," she answered. "Actually, I feel horrible."

"What? Why?"

"Just, seeing him like that. Knowing I'm responsible."

"He's the only one responsible. He did bad things and all you did was turn them back on him. You should be happy about it."

"I just feel bad because the only reason it worked is because he still had some of a conscience left."

"The key words there are 'some of a conscience,'" Blaine said. "He was evil and he got what was coming to him."

"I know, but I still feel a little sorry for him. I can't help it." She looked down at her watch. They'd only been in the cell for two minutes. Thirteen more to go.

"You know, everyone else still thinks you had help bringing down Witherings," Blaine said. "Thomas said I'm not allowed to tell anyone you're a fadaman. But you know, if the rest of the fairies knew you took him down all alone, you'd be really famous around here."

"I don't want to be famous. Please don't tell anyone."

"Don't worry. It's just an idea. You should think about it, though." He leaned over Witherings, examining the comatose fadaman's face intently. "I wonder why his father hasn't tried to break him out of here."

"It's too dangerous when everybody is looking for him, I suppose," Kelly said.

"Yeah, everybody is looking for him, but nobody can find him."

Nobody can find Witherings's father, Kelly thought. *Like no one can find my father.* In spite of their best efforts, she, Venuto, and Thomas had gotten nowhere. Mindy was no help either; she didn't even remember how she'd become pregnant, and Thomas believed a powerful fairy had erased her memory for as-yet-unknown reasons. *Miasmos once said he knew my father.* Kelly's eyes narrowed on the huddled form of Marcos Witherings. *And if Miasmos knew him, then maybe Witherings did to.*

What if she could ask him — would he tell her? She felt an impulse creeping into her mind. Not sure exactly what she was doing, she approached Witherings. It was ridiculous, thinking that she could ask him. He was in a coma, cut off from everything, wasn't he? Then it came to her — fairy senses. She knew it was possible to connect telepathically to another's mind, although she had yet to receive the training. She had talked mind-to-mind with Witherings before, twice in fact. What was it he had said? That he had sent her a 'mental invitation,' and that she had accepted. Now it was her turn. She would send *him* an invitation.

She wasn't sure what to do, but as she reached his bedside she felt a sudden urge to touch his forehead. She extended her hand downwards.

"What are you doing?" Blaine asked.

She didn't answer him, nor did she notice the apprehensive look he was giving her. Her hand made contact with Witherings' forehead. She closed her eyes. *Tell me who my father is,* she thought towards him. She concentrated very hard and repeated the thought, imagining it travel through her hand and into his mind. At first nothing happened, but then she felt a hint of heat in the center of her palm. She couldn't tell if the heat was coming from her hand or from Witherings. After a moment the heat intensified so much that it almost burned. A thick fog overtook her mind's eye. Shapes appeared in the mist — flashes of haggard, ghoulish faces, one after another. Dizziness gripped her as she was sucked deeper and deeper into the fog.

She tried to pull her hand away, but it was stuck. The heat moved, and she realized that it was coming from her. All of the energy in her body was rushing into her hand, then out through her palm and into Witherings. A creeping chill spread through her, down to the bone. When there was almost no heat left, suddenly the transfer stopped. With the connection severed, she fell to the ground. She blinked, and the fogginess receded. She looked up to see Witherings still lying on the bed. He didn't appear to have moved an inch.

"Are you all right?" Blaine asked, kneeling over her.

"I'm tired," Kelly said. She was so sleepy that it was all she could do to keep her eyes open. Blaine felt her forehead and a worried look formed on his face. He started to get up, but just at that moment one of Witherings's fingers twitched. A strong puff of air flew from it and struck Blaine in the head. He dropped to the ground beside Kelly, unconscious.

Marcos Witherings sat up. Kelly strained every muscle, trying to move, but she couldn't. She vaguely heard chimes at the archway — the guards were coming in to stop him. But then there were two more bursts of air, followed by dull thuds as the guards fell to the ground. Kelly looked on, gripped by terror, as Witherings swung his feet off the cot and stood up. He stepped towards her. She expected the worst, but she wasn't going to give him the satisfaction of pleading with him. She squeezed her eyes shut, expecting the deadly strike at any moment.

It didn't come. After what seemed like an hour, but was probably only a few seconds, she cautiously opened one of her eyes. Witherings looked down at her with an odd expression on his face, one like a person might have after smelling spoiled milk.

"Never touch someone you view as an enemy on the forehead, Kelly," he said. "Not unless you know what you're doing, and you are certain your enemy does not."

With those words he turned and walked towards the archway — slowly, deliberately, and unimpeded by the downed guards. Kelly felt a wave of relief, followed by perplexity, before she gave in to a deep, dreamless sleep.

2

BOMIN ANARENA

Kelly opened her eyes. The undulating ceiling of the hospital bubble loomed far overhead. The smell of ginger and allspice met her nose, and she spotted the source — a cup of healing tea in the hands of Bubbles, who sat on the edge of her bed. He stared down at the tea morosely.

"Bubbles?"

He jumped up, startled, and the teacup went flying three full arm lengths, spraying its contents all over the floor. He didn't even give it a glance; he was too focused on Kelly. "She's awake! Kelly's awake!"

Several sets of footsteps rushed over from across the room. Soon Thomas, Stephanie, and the warden stood around Kelly's bed. The warden looked positively furious.

"Where's Blaine?" Kelly asked, hoping he wasn't dead.

"He's still unconscious," Thomas said. "What happened?"

"Blaine asked me to take him to see Marcos Witherings. And...he woke up."

"We know that part," the warden hissed.

"Did you catch him?" Kelly asked.

Thomas shook his head. "Venuto and some guards went in pursuit, but they will not likely find him."

"We need to know how he woke up," the warden said.

Kelly groaned. It was all her fault. "I put my hand on his forehead," she admitted.

"You did what? How could you be so stupid?" The warden was practically shouting.

"Kelly's not stupid!" Stephanie said, stepping in between the bed and the warden. "Besides, it's your fault Witherings escaped." She jabbed him in the chest with an index finger. "Are you only capable of controlling your prisoners if they're comatose or older than time?"

"Why you insolent little—"

Thomas put up a commanding hand for silence. The warden complied, though the vein bulging from his neck betrayed the effort it was costing him.

"Why did you touch his forehead, Kelly?" Thomas asked.

"I'm not sure. I started to think that maybe since Miasmos knew who my father was, that Witherings would too. I was trying to read his mind."

"That was very dangerous," Thomas said. "When you made mental contact with him he was able to retouch reality again, and to suck almost all of the energy out of you in the process. Making direct contact in that way is only to be done by the most skilled fairies."

"I didn't know anything like that could happen," Kelly said.

"The mystery is why he didn't suck all the energy out of her," Bubbles said. "He could have easily killed her." He patted her arm, visibly shaken by the idea.

Thomas was silent for a while, turning the thought over in his mind. "Did Witherings say anything to you? A message perhaps?"

"Just that I shouldn't touch the foreheads of my enemies."

No one seemed to know what to make of that. Bubbles twisted his face in a lopsided grimace that Kelly knew meant he was deep in thought. Stephanie looked mad, the warden glared, and Thomas was very quiet.

"You and Venuto need to resume your magic lessons. There is still much you need to learn," Thomas said finally.

He signaled the warden and turned to leave. The warden followed, but paused just long enough to shoot Kelly one last stony glare.

"My fairy sense necklace never got so hot before. You are lucky," Bubbles said.

"I know."

Bubbles's eyes widened suddenly, and a look of horror overtook his face. "Oh no!"

Kelly's stomach dropped. "What is it? Did you sense something?"

He ignored her. "Oh no. Oh no," he muttered, flapping his wings in agitation.

"Bubbles, what's going on?" Stephanie asked, grabbing him by the shoulders.

"I spilt Kelly's tea! Margretta made it special."

Kelly sighed in relief. "Don't scare me like that, Bubbles. I thought something serious had happened."

His lower lip trembled like he was going to cry. "It could be serious. You need your medicine."

"I feel much better already. Don't worry."

"If that's so," Stephanie said, "then we should be going. I don't want to rush you, but it's almost six in the morning. Your mom is probably planning on waking us up at six-thirty, so we have time to eat her special pancake breakfast."

Drat! Kelly thought. She couldn't believe she'd been out for almost six hours. They had to get back right away, unless they wanted to have to try and explain their absence to Mindy. Kelly sat up, and a wave of dizziness hit her. She lay back down on her pillow with a groan.

"Are you okay?" Stephanie asked.

"I can do it," Kelly said, sitting up again. This time she did so more slowly.

"Maybe I should come along too. Just in case you pass out half-way there," Bubbles said. "Plus, I could go for some pancakes."

The three of them pulled out their underwater breathing masks, sprang into the air, and approached the ceiling. They had almost reached the top when Kelly spotted the healer Margretta enter the room below them.

"Where do you think you're going, young lady?" Margretta shouted. "You need to stay in bed for at least two days!"

"I can't. I have to be at school in less than two hours," Kelly called back. Just before she passed through the ceiling, she glimpsed Margretta shaking her head in exasperation before turning her attention to a bed down the line — a bed where Blaine was stretched out, still unconscious. Kelly hoped he would be all right.

~

THEY MADE it back in the nick of time. Stephanie's latest re-pinch of fairy dust had only just worn off when Mindy knocked on Kelly's door, inviting them downstairs for chocolate chip pancakes.

During breakfast, Bubbles, in invisible form, gorged himself on the pancake chunks Kelly placed on the side of her plate when Mindy's back was turned. Kelly only managed to eat two bites, because her stomach was queasy.

On the way to school, she fell asleep on the metro and would have missed her stop if Stephanie hadn't been there to wake her. She could barely keep her eyes open during the first periods of the day. She was grateful for the chance to down a coke at lunch, but the caffeine didn't help very much. Before algebra class, Stephanie wanted to check her makeup, so Kelly walked from the cafeteria to the classroom alone. Once at her seat, she put her head down on her desk to rest for a moment — and promptly fell asleep. She awoke with a start when someone tapped her shoulder.

It was Dmitri. "Mr. Patterson's staring at you," he whispered with a sly grin.

"Oh, thanks," Kelly mumbled.

"Rough night?"

"You could say that."

"Partying on a Monday night." He shook his head in mock admonishment. "You should know better."

Kelly couldn't keep a little bit of a smile from escaping her lips. *You have no idea,* she thought.

Stephanie walked into the room a moment later, her bright red lipstick freshly reapplied. "Hi, Dmitri!" she said.

"Hey," he answered, suddenly very interested in his algebra book.

"How're classes going?" she asked him, unfazed.

"Fine." He turned a page and furrowed his brow.

Stephanie waited for a moment, as though expecting him to reciprocate the question. When he didn't, she shrugged and turned to Kelly. "I think he's warming up to me," she whispered. Kelly gave Stephanie an incredulous look. The bell rang.

"Hello, class. Please pass your homework up to the front of the room," Mr. Patterson said. Then he promptly began his lecture in his high-pitched yet paradoxically droning, monotonous, and oddly calming voice. Kelly struggled to keep her eyes open, and Stephanie had to keep poking her with a pencil when her head started to go down. Finally, the bell rang again to indicate the class was over. Kelly groggily put her book in her backpack, dimly aware of other students doing the same around her. Dmitri was one of the quickest. He was up and out of his seat in no time, but he paused on the other side of the table in front of Kelly on his way out.

"Try to get some sleep tonight," Dmitri said to Kelly with a wink, before turning and briskly exiting the room.

"What was that all about?" Stephanie asked.

"I guess he noticed I was tired?" Kelly said.

"Maybe." Stephanie frowned. "Well, try not to fall asleep in your next class, okay?"

"I'll try."

WHEN KELLY GOT HOME after school, she went straight upstairs to her room and fell asleep in her bed, still wearing her shoes. It only felt like a few minutes had passed when her mother's excited voice roused her.

"Kelly, come downstairs. You have to see this!" Mindy said from Kelly's doorway before sprinting away. Kelly hadn't ever heard her mother's feet pound so fast down the stairs before. Her curiosity getting the better or her tiredness, she staggered out of bed and down to the living room. Her mother sat on the couch, eyes glued to the TV, which was still on commercial break. Kelly sat down beside her mother.

"What is it?" Kelly asked.

"You'll see."

The commercial ended and a view of the Lincoln Memorial came onscreen. A large crowd had gathered around an impressive speaking podium on the stairs. The camera panned to a familiar, overly made-up face. "Good afternoon, this is Melanie Johnson reporting. We're waiting for democratic presidential candidate Marcos Witherings to address the crowd. This morning, after nearly four weeks missing, he released a statement in which he said only that 'circumstances outside of his control' kept him away, and that he would reveal more in tonight's announcement. Let's see what Senator Greg Allen, who seemed sure to get the party's nomination with Witherings out of the picture, had to say earlier today."

The view cut to a visibly shaken Greg Allen. "This news is most unexpected, and I decline to comment further until we know the facts behind it. But if Mr. Witherings is now back in the race, I welcome the competition. I trust the American people to use their best judgment in the primaries." The senator clearly meant his statement to sound confident, but his voice shook with each word. Kelly could tell he wasn't happy. She didn't blame him, considering how Witherings had been trouncing him in the polls before he disappeared.

The view cut back to Melanie, who raised her right hand to her earpiece and paused. "We've just received word he is about to come out. Now we are going to uninterrupted coverage of Marcos Witherings himself."

The screen cut to another camera, one placed closer to the speaking podium. Some clapping could be heard here and there, but most of the crowd waited in silent anticipation as Witherings walked out onto the stage. He looked skinnier, but then Kelly remembered he always looked skinnier in his human form. When he reached the podium he stood behind it silently for a moment, surveying the crowd. He was letting the tension build. Kelly noticed that Witherings's old fairy side-kicks, Murk and Lurk, who previously never left their master's side, were nowhere to be seen. She wondered where they were. Maybe he'd fired them for their cowardice; Murk had run away after Kelly had injured Lurk in a fight, instead of standing his ground to face her.

"Good afternoon," Witherings began. He didn't appear to be reading from the teleprompter. "As you all know, my whereabouts have been unknown for the last several weeks, causing many to speculate that I had withdrawn from the presidential race. Let me assure you, I am still very much in the race. I was not absent by choice." He paused, letting the audience absorb this information. He seemed to enjoy the suspense he was creating.

Kelly chanced a look at Mindy to see that her mother was still staring raptly at the TV. Kelly hadn't really considered that Witherings would get back in the race now that he was free, but it made sense. His winning the presidency would give him and his father unprecedented power. She rubbed her arms, suddenly feeling a chill.

"You see," Witherings continued, "I was kidnapped by domestic terrorists who did not want me in the race. They were afraid of change. They did not want to see the end of partisan politics. They did not want to see us move forward as a nation, with both sides of the aisle working together for progress and prosperity. But they did not succeed. I was able to escape them and now I am back, more determined than ever. It will take a lot more to stop me, because I represent the will of the American people. Together we are strong. Together we are unstoppable."

The crowd erupted into cheers. Tears formed in Mindy's eyes. Kelly frowned.

"Mr. Witherings, does this mean you will be participating in the upcoming debate?" a reporter asked.

"Of course," he answered. "Now, I'm afraid I won't be able to take any more questions at this time. Thank you all for coming, and God bless America."

The view went back to Melanie. "You just saw democratic presidential candidate Marcos Witherings, announcing his comeback to the presidential race after being held captive by domestic terrorists. Now we are joined by chief political analyst, James Brewer, for his thoughts on this startling development."

Mindy muted the TV just as James Brewer's lopsided toupee appeared on screen.

"Can you believe it?" Mindy asked. "It's incredible. I knew he didn't just disappear. Terrorists, and homegrown ones at that." She shook her head.

"Mom, you aren't going to vote for him, are you?" Kelly asked.

"Of course I am," Mindy laughed. "You couldn't possibly have thought I'd vote for Allen, did you?"

Kelly's chest tightened. She wished she could tell her mother the truth about Witherings, but she had promised Thomas and Venuto that she wouldn't tell her mother anything. Not until they could figure out how and why Mindy's memory of Kelly's origins had been erased. Kelly sighed. "But, how do you know his story is the truth? He could have been doing anything for those weeks. The story of domestic terrorists is a bit far-fetched."

"Kelly, just because something is farfetched, doesn't mean that it isn't true. Besides, I'm sure he'll give evidence. Now, how about some dinner?"

Two days later Kelly sat nervously in the secret room near the back of Glendenland's library, where she had her magic lessons with Venuto. He was late, which was uncharacteristic of him. At last he joined her.

"Sorry I'm late. I was trying to calm down a dispute between Reynalda and a fairy she overheard 'disrespecting' the Penadas name." Venuto sighed and eased himself down on the square blue mat next to Kelly's. He looked tired.

"She has a serious chip on her shoulder," Kelly said.

Venuto raised an eyebrow, not understanding the human expression.

"That means she won't let her anger about the past go," Kelly explained, although she was not quite satisfied with that explanation.

Venuto nodded in agreement. "You are quite right. And this 'chip' she has is causing me much grief. Now, let's get started. Thomas tells me you tried to read Witherings's mind."

"Yes," she admitted.

"You realize now that was a bad idea." It was phrased more like a statement than a question.

"I'm sorry," Kelly said. "I didn't mean for it to happen. It's my fault he escaped." She put her head in her hands.

"It isn't entirely your fault."

"It isn't?"

He sighed. "It's partly my fault. I didn't think you were ready for more advanced control of fairy senses, which is why I never warned you. You instinctually did something very advanced — you did the motions required for reading someone's mind, but you were unprepared. Even I wouldn't have attempted what you did on someone like Marcos Witherings. A weak-minded fairy, yes, but not a strong-minded fairy, and never a fadaman."

"Why not?"

"Because in order to read someone's mind you have to connect your mind closely to theirs. If you are not careful or strong enough, then the other person can get into your mind instead. You opened up a direct channel, making it easy to transfer mental contents and energy. When he felt your healthy mind and body in contact with his, your mind actually shook his mind, and his mind was able to overcome its sickness, aided by him sucking almost all of your energy out of you."

"How would I have avoided that?" Kelly asked.

"You would have had to be consciously shielding your body and mind, while at the same time targeting his. It is a very difficult and a delicate process. We will not get into it now. It is still way beyond your ability and I don't want you attempting it on anyone else."

"But what if someone does it to me?"

"You must try to avoid getting into the position of physical contact, especially palm-to-forehead contact. It is possible for fairies to steal energy from you without touching you, but not to the same degree, and they can't see directly into your mind without physical contact."

"What if it did happen? How exactly do you block your mind? What elements do you use?"

Venuto furrowed his brow, like he wasn't quite sure how to reply. "It's very difficult to teach, because it is subtle. You must use your intention. All more advanced, or more subtle magic is based on intention. Really, you are still using the elements, in different combinations, to influence the mind and matter around you. But it is in such a complex way that it can't be thought of directly in amounts to be balanced and measured. Instead, with your intention, you 'will' things to happen, and if your intention is strong enough then the elements obey."

"So, I would just 'will' that my mind be shielded?" Kelly asked, frowning.

"Yes."

It sounded too simple to be true. "And when you shrink humans without fairy dust, it's the same thing? You just 'will' it to happen?"

Venuto laughed. "Yes and no. When you say you 'just' will it to happen, that makes it sound like it's easy. In order for your mental desire to manifest physically, you must have a subconscious command of the elements on a deep level. When I 'will' a human to shrink, firstly the human has to be open to it, and then I have to concentrate very hard, and though I don't know intellectually exactly what is happening, my intention is strong enough that it creates vibrations that travel to the human and change the elements within the human's body, until I again focus my intention to reverse the effect."

"So if I tried it now, would it work?" Kelly asked.

Venuto chuckled. "Doubtful."

Kelly didn't find this discussion amusing. Not when Miasmos and Witherings were out there.

Venuto seemed to notice her troubled expression. "I know you want quick results, but it usually takes many years, and much dedication, to reach such a stage. The majority of fairies never reach that point. Most never even develop their fairy senses past being able to sense the vague location of other fairies they know well, or having occasional dream flashes. For instance, there are probably less than a few thousand fairies in North America capable of true telepathic communication."

"Witherings is capable," Kelly said, thinking of when he had contacted her telepathically when he wanted a duel. "Will you teach me?"

"Of course, but not today. Unfortunately I have to cut our lesson short because I'm needed in the Great Hall."

WHEN KELLY WALKED out of the library she found herself face to face with Blaine. "Glad to see you are on your two feet again," Kelly said.

"Oh, that was nothing." He waved a hand dismissively. "Visiting Witherings was way more awesome than I expected. Much more action than just a drooling comatose guy."

"Are you being serious?"

"What do you mean?"

"You thought it was exciting when Witherings escaped?"

"Yeah," he answered. "But, of course it was bad too, that's a given," he added upon seeing her dark expression.

Kelly headed for the nearest transport bubble, from which

she would go to the lion statue and then back home. She was beginning to like Blaine less and less. He seemed immature.

He fell into step beside her. "How was your lesson?"

"How did you know I was having a lesson?"

"Bubbles told me. You finished just in time for the ceremony. I was about to go without you."

"What ceremony?"

"Bubbles didn't tell you about it?"

"No."

"He must have assumed you already knew about it. Who doesn't? It's only the most important ceremony of the year."

"Well, I don't know about it," Kelly answered, feeling a bit out of the loop. This ceremony must be why Venuto was needed in the Great Hall. He probably assumed she knew about it too.

"Sorry. It's the Bomin Anarena ceremony. It celebrates the origin of fairies."

"Why didn't anyone say anything about it before? I would have thought there would be some excitement leading up to something that big," Kelly said.

"Why talk about it if everyone knows about it?" Blaine responded.

They made their way to the Great Hall. When they arrived, the large space was already about three-quarters full. Fairies flew about excitedly, and the air buzzed with thousands of voices. Many fairies were dressed all in white, with little wreaths around their heads made from flower stems.

"Does white have a particular significance?" Kelly asked Blaine.

"It represents birth."

"And the hats?"

Blaine shrugged. "Not sure. Just a tradition."

As they walked towards some empty seats, Kelly looked around but didn't see Bubbles or any of her other fairy friends.

However, she did see that some fairies pointed at her as she walked by, whispering to each other.

"I guess it's gotten around that Marcos Witherings escaped because of me," she said.

"They don't know the details," Blaine answered. "They just know you were there. They've been talking about me too. It's kind of cool." He waved at a little girl who had just pointed at him. She giggled. Clearly Blaine relished all the attention.

"Hey, Blaine!" a voice called from a few rows above them. Kelly looked up at the speaker, and saw one of her least favorite fairies in Glendenland. The two had never been properly introduced, but she didn't want to be. He was the teenaged pink-winged fairy who had been skeptical about Miasmos's existence and called Glenden an old fool behind his back. He had also been so excited when Kelly and Stephanie had been hit by a giant ball of freezing mist that he had urged her to tell him what it felt like. Somehow she wasn't surprised that this fairy and Blaine might be friends.

"Hey, Skip, how goes it?" Blaine asked the pink-winged fairy.

"Great. Why don't you come sit up here with me?"

Kelly kept scanning the hall for her friends, hoping to avoid sitting with Skip. Finally, she spotted Bubbles and Beatrix on the far side of the hall, along with Bubbles's girlfriend Bamblelina and Dimpleton's brothers Wimpleton and Pimpleton. "I'm going to go sit with Bubbles and Beatrix," Kelly said, not making any effort to address Skip.

"Okay, we'll come too," Blaine said. Skip hopped down to their level.

Great, Kelly thought. "Suit yourselves," she mumbled.

They lifted up in the air to fly to the other side of the hall.

"Blaine told me about what *really* happened, Kelly," Skip said as they flew. "That is wicked how you tried to read his mind. Really daring, especially since he's a fadaman. I mean, no fairy I've known has ever attempted that." Skip had a tinge of genuine admiration in his voice. While she didn't appreciate Blaine telling Skip the details of that night, she was at least glad he had kept his mouth shut about her being a fadaman. "I can't believe you didn't die," Skip continued. "That's wicked. And you saw inside the madman's mind. Even wickeder."

"Whatever," Kelly said. The word 'wicked' seemed to be Skip's favorite word. It was already getting old.

"Hey, Blaine," Skip said. "Do you have that stuff you were going to get me?"

"Of course." Blaine retrieved a small black pouch from his pocket and handed it to Skip. Skip grinned and tossed Blaine a small blue pouch in return. As Blaine caught Skip's pouch there was a soft jingling sound, indicating that it contained glitterons. Kelly raised an eyebrow at the exchange, but she wasn't curious enough to ask them about it.

They were almost to the other side. Bubbles spotted them. "Kelly, Kelly, over here!" he shouted and waved his arms in the air. "You guys are late, it's about to start."

Kelly sat in the empty seat on Bubbles's left, and Blaine and Skip sat to the left of her.

"How was your lesson?" Bubbles asked.

"Fine," Kelly said. "You know, Stephanie's going to be mad she didn't know about this ceremony. Why didn't you tell us? You always talk about everything."

"It slipped my mind. I've been busy," he whispered, leaning in closer. "I'm getting ready to propose to Bamblelina, and I'm trying to write a poem." He glanced furtively to his right, but Bamblelina was immersed in conversation with Beatrix.

"Seriously? That's great," Kelly said. Although a bit soon, she thought, considering Bubbles and Bamblelina had only met two months before.

"Will you read it when it is done?" Bubbles asked.

"Sure."

"Kelly, will you be staying for the feast after the ceremony?" Bamblelina asked from the other side of Bubbles. Bubbles's shoulders jerked and his face flushed a bright red.

"It depends on how late it gets," Kelly replied. "My mother will worry if I stay too long."

A few minutes later an expectant hush fell over the crowd. Kelly looked to the speaking platform, on which the usual three thrones sat. Flimsly walked on stage, followed by four other musicians. As Flimsly stood front and center, his four companions broke off in twos, one pair moving to stage left, and the other pair to stage right. Instead of his typical red jacket, Flimsly was dressed all in white, as were the others. After the musicians played a long fanfare on the instruments, the royal bodyguards entered and took their places behind the thrones.

"Welcome," Flimsly said with a grand flourish. "Please stand for his Grace the just, loyal, unwavering, and wise Thomas Penadas; his wife, her Grace the intelligent and fair Carmina Penadas; and esteemed head advisor, our prince, the brave and honest Venuto Grand."

They all stood as Thomas, Carmina, and Venuto came into the Great Hall, all dressed in identical flowing white robes. Thomas wore his crown, yet again. Before they sat down they unfurled their dragon-like wings, giving them a majestic appearance.

"Please be seated," Venuto said to the crowd. The spectators took their seats.

After a moment of silence, Thomas gave an almost imperceptible nod of his head. With that signal, Flimsly and company quietly left the speaking platform. Seconds later a group of fairies from the front row flew up into the air in unison and positioned themselves in an airborne line just in front of the speaking platform. The group consisted of eleven beautiful female fairies, all with tan or brown wings, except for the one fairy in the middle, who had light purple wings. The two fairies on either end of the line held little flutes, and they started to play a lilting, slow, yet bewitching melody. It was atonal yet somehow catchy at the same time. Everyone watched with rapt attention.

As the music played, the other fairies moved their arms in practiced movements, reminding Kelly of traditional Hawaiian dances. She didn't know what the motions meant, but it was clear they were telling a story. There were wide gestures up to the sky, followed by wave-like motions pointing downwards. As the performance progressed, the gesturing became faster and faster. Until suddenly the dancing stopped — but the music continued. The fairy in the middle moved forward and the other fairies held their hands facing her back. Faint streams of mist emanated from their hands to the center fairy. They were sending her energy from their own bodies so that she would have more strength.

The lead fairy put her right hand up, palm outward, and began to paint a picture in the air out of flames. First she made a cluster of human-like figures, without wings, about half the size of real-life fairies. The cluster of human-like figures stayed in place, flickering. It must be taking an immense amount of energy to shape the fire like that, let alone to maintain the shapes. Next the fairy created a small group of flying animal shapes that looked like bats. These bat shapes flew around in a cluster beside the human-like forms.

The fairy raised her right hand dramatically in a fist, then opened her palm. A tight ball of blue fire zoomed from her hand and smashed into the human-like figures and bat-like creatures. The contact created a dazzling burst of multi-colored sparks and sizzling sounds. The figures swirled around each other, writhing as if possessed. The audience watched in silent reverence, which Kelly found odd, since fairies would normally be ooh-ing and aah-ing appreciatively at such a display. After a while the shapes started to merge into each other — the bat forms each found a human form and blended with it, creating a new group of winged hominoid forms. These forms flew out over the audience before bursting overhead into a bunch of firework-type sparks. As the last sparks dissipated and the music came to an end, the fairies finally broke their silence. They stood up and cheered. Many threw their wreaths in the air.

The performing fairies curtsied politely and returned to their seats. Thomas stood up. "Unt asi nenné anfegte," he said.

"What did he just say?" Kelly whispered to Bubbles.

"He said: 'and so we began,' in the ancient fairy language."

"Oh."

"Now," Thomas continued, "please enjoy the feast in the mess hall."

After Thomas, Carmina, and Venuto left the stage, the fairies began to file out of the room.

"They did such a good job this year!" Bubbles said. "Dimpleton will be sad he missed it."

"Where is Dimpleton anyway?" Kelly asked.

"On assignment," Bubbles said. In addition to his new role as advisor, Dimpleton had a diplomatic job, consisting of formal trips to other fairy bands. At least, that was the story. Kelly suspected he was a spy, although she hadn't had a chance to ask him about it directly; he was hardly ever around, and the only time she'd seen him since Thomas became king was the dinner with Thomas and his relatives.

"I don't know how great it was, Bubbles," Blaine said. "The sparks could have been more colorful."

"Why don't you try to make sparks with that many colors and see what happens," Bubbles said.

"Whether or not I could do it isn't the issue. It matters whether or not the people actually doing it do it correctly," Blaine said.

"Whatever. What's taking so long? I'm hungry!" Bubbles stood on his tiptoes, trying to see why the crowd was moving so slowly. It didn't look like there was any particular reason, except for the fact that the other fairies didn't seem as anxious as he was to get to the feast. They all chatted and laughed as they moved forward in a relaxed manner. Bubbles bit his fingernails.

"Did the performance represent the origin of the fairy race?" Kelly asked him, hoping to distract him from his impatience.

He nodded.

"It looked sort of like humans were mixed with bats," Kelly said in a low voice, not wanting any of the surrounding fairies to overhear.

At this comment Bubbles burst into hysterical laughter. "Not humans, and not bats!" He managed to gasp out before laughing some more. "You see, a long, long time ago, there existed humans and also their sister race, the falila. The falila were similar to humans, but not exactly the same."

"Neanderthals?" Kelly asked.

Bubbles wrinkled his nose. "Huh? What in the flapping grasshopper wing is a Neandy-thal?"

"Never mind. There were humans and their sister race. Go on."

"And there was a flying reptile-creature, the anari. No one knows what it looked like exactly, just that it could fly and it had scales. One day a horrible plague came upon the land of the gods. They knew their time was short, so they came down to earth hoping to pass on some of their powers and knowledge to one of the races. But they realized none of the existing races were suitable, so they merged the falila with the anari, to create a new race, the fairies."

"How can gods be sick and die?" Kelly asked. "Aren't they supposed to be immortal and all-powerful?"

"The gods had the power of creation and magic, and lived many ages. But they weren't immortal," Bubbles said.

Kelly found the fairy myth intriguing. On the surface, the fairies seemed very secular, down to earth, and non-religious. But every once in a while their deep-seated cultural beliefs would appear out of nowhere. Like when, before the battle with Miasmos, she had been invited to a queimada, a ceremony in which her fairy friends had called on the traces of their lost ancestors to help them in the battle. Such events made Kelly feel like she had still only barely scratched the surface of what it meant to be a fairy. It was frustrating, considering she was half-fairy herself.

A sudden shaking from her pocket startled Kelly. She realized she had forgotten to turn her cell phone off. She hastily reached into her pocket and silenced it; it was only on vibrate, but it still made a dull buzzing sound.

"What was that?" Bubbles asked.

"My cell phone," Kelly whispered, looking around to see if anyone else had heard it. Thankfully, no one seemed to have noticed. Blaine and Skip were closest to them, but they were joking with each other about who had made the biggest fireball in their life.

"Why did you bring your phone here?" Bubbles asked. "You know fairies don't have cell phones."

"I know. I forgot I had it with me. Besides, I never thought it would actually work when shrunk."

"Of course it would. Stephanie works when shrunk, doesn't she?"

"Stephanie isn't an electronic device," Kelly said.

"Well, we're lucky it didn't make noises during the ceremony," Bubbles said.

Kelly grimaced at the thought. "Yes, that would have been very bad." She resisted the urge to take out the phone to see who had called her. She supposed it had been Stephanie or her mother. Either way, she should get going. She hadn't planned to be gone more than a few hours, and Mindy was expecting her to be home by dinnertime. She pulled out her underwater breathing mask.

Bubbles's face fell. "You aren't staying for the feast?"

"Unfortunately, no. I really have to go now. I'm late getting home." She waved a quick good-bye to her fairy friends and headed for the ceiling.

3

A NAME

Once back in human form and taking the metro home, Kelly pulled out her phone. The missed call was from a number she didn't recognize, and there was no message. *Great, maybe I could have stayed longer,* she thought grumpily.

Dinner was already on the table when Kelly walked into the house.

"Hi, honey, how was your day?" Mindy asked as Kelly took a seat.

"Fine."

"And studying with Stephanie? Did you get all your homework done?"

Kelly groaned mentally at Mindy's reference to her cover story. She hadn't even started her homework yet. She would be lucky to be in bed by midnight. "Almost done," she lied. "I still have a few math problems left."

"You poor thing. Have some tuna casserole. It will make you feel better." Mindy plopped a huge scoop of tuna casserole onto Kelly's plate.

"Thanks." The casserole was a bit on the salty side, but still very tasty. Before Kelly could take a second bite her cell phone rang. It was the same number as before. Kelly squinted at it.

"Are you going to get that, dear?" Mindy asked.

"Oh, yes." She tapped the screen and brought the phone to her ear. "Hello?"

"Hello, Kelly," a scratchy voice answered. Kelly nearly dropped the phone. She would recognize that voice anywhere. It was Marcos Witherings.

Kelly's change in demeanor was not lost on her mother, because Mindy scrutinized her daughter's face curiously.

"What do you want?" Kelly asked, trying to sound nonchalant. Her voice shook anyway.

"I want you to meet with me."

Why would he want to meet? She gulped. "What makes you think I would agree to that?" She chose her words carefully, since Mindy was still watching with interest. Luckily the volume on the cell phone was too low for her mother to actually hear Witherings's side of the conversation.

"I want to meet with you so I can tell you something," he said.

Kelly was silent, thinking. Was this a trap? Did he want to finish her off? That wouldn't make sense, because he hadn't killed her before when he had the chance.

After a few seconds, Witherings spoke again. "I want to tell you something," he repeated. "About your father."

Her father? Kelly reflexively looked at Mindy, but then looked away quickly as their eyes met. "I don't understand. Why do you want to tell me?"

"That's complicated," he answered. "I will explain when we meet. What do you say?"

"Why can't you just tell me over the phone?"

"Because I want to give you something too."

Kelly snorted. "Like what? A fireball to the face?"

Mindy raised an eyebrow.

Witherings chuckled. "Not quite. But I don't wish to discuss it on the phone. What do you say? Do you want to hear what I have to say about your father or not?"

Kelly's heart skipped a beat when he mentioned her father again. She knew she couldn't trust him, but she needed to hear what he had to say. She would just have to be careful. "Where do you propose?" she asked.

"In the lobby of the Museum of the American Indian, Monday, 4pm. In your human form, of course. And I suppose I don't really have to mention it, but don't tell any of your fairy friends about this. If I sense them I won't show."

"Agreed," Kelly said. Her fairy friends would not want her to meet Witherings anyway, so it was best to tell them after the fact, if at all.

"Good. See you then." He hung up.

Kelly put the phone down, trying to appear casual. Her stomach twisted in knots. She took a tiny bite of her casserole. Mindy just sat and watched her, as if expecting her to say something.

"What?" Kelly asked.

"I was just wondering what that was all about."

"It was my project mate for our history project," Kelly lied.

Mindy shook her head. "They certainly are keeping you busy."

They ate in silence. After a few minutes Mindy put her fork down with a sigh. "Kelly, we need to talk."

Kelly shifted uncomfortably in response to her mother's serious tone. "Uh...okay."

"Is there anything bothering you?"

Kelly laughed nervously. "No. Why to you think that?"

"It's just, after what happened this summer you've seemed preoccupied, like your mind is always somewhere else."

"I'm fine, Mom. I've just been thinking a lot about high school. You know it's a big change in my life from middle school to high school."

"Are you sure that's all? You never talked about the time you were kidnapped. They say healing doesn't start until you talk about the trauma."

"Mom, it wasn't that traumatic, okay? I just got mistaken for someone else and locked up by the authorities for a couple days. Then I hid out in my friend's basement for a few weeks. It's no big deal. I didn't get as much of a tan as I would have liked this summer, but I'm fine. I'm over it."

Mindy didn't look convinced. Kelly felt a twinge of guilt. She wished she could share what really happened with her mother. Then again, knowing the truth would only give Mindy much more reason to worry. Perhaps the summer had been harder on Mindy than Kelly realized. Maybe her mother was the one who was traumatized.

"Look, Mom, I really am fine. I think the best thing for us is to leave the past in the past and not dwell on it, okay?"

"I suppose you're right, sweetie." But for the rest of dinner Mindy just pushed her casserole around on her plate with her fork. Clearly she was still bothered, and the tone of Kelly's phone conversation probably hadn't helped much.

KELLY LOOKED AT HER WATCH. It was 9am, on Monday. Only seven hours until 4pm — and her meeting with Witherings. The feeling of anticipation she had woken up with that morning got worse with each minute. Her palms were slick with sweat as she flipped her German book to page twenty-five, to the partner exercises for the day.

"Now I want you all to switch partners," Frau Steinberg

instructed. "Work with someone you've never worked with before."

Kelly was slow to react and remained seated whilst her usual partner, a quiet girl named Sarah with blonde hair and thick black glasses, got up and left for the other side of the room. Kelly was just looking up from her book for a new partner when the seat next to her was once again filled.

Tommy Thompson shot her a toothy grin. "Hiya, Spock. I thought I'd try the air up here on your home planet. What's it called again?"

"Earth, knucklehead," Kelly blurted out. In seven hours she'd be face to face with her archenemy. She really wasn't in the mood for Tommy's games.

"Sheesh, I thought vulcans were supposed to lack emotions. I guess Star Trek got that detail wrong," he said smugly. Kelly thought he looked pleased to have gotten such a rise out of her.

"Auf Deutsch!" Frau Steinberg's voice reverberated through the room. Giggles and English whispers were replaced with halting, mumbled, and self-conscious attempts from the students to perform the exercises.

"Was machst du heute nachmittags?" Kelly asked Tommy Thompson.

"Ich, er, ich arbet, arbeite," he answered, the tips of his ears turning red.

"Machst du deine Hausaufgabe, oder?" Kelly asked, knowing her German was much superior to his and feeling good about demonstrating that fact to him.

"Um..." Tommy shifted in his seat, and the redness spread from the tips of his ears to his cheeks. He hadn't understood.

"Machst..du..deine..Hausaufgabe, oder?" Kelly repeated, speaking exaggeratedly slowly, as if to a small and stupid child.

"What's Hausaufgabe"

"It's in the book, Tommy. Look it up."

Tommy flipped to the back of his book and searched for 'Hausaufgabe,' while Kelly tapped her fingers on her desk.

"Oh, homework," he said. "Ja, ich mache mein Hausaufgabe."

"*Meine* Hausaufgabe," Kelly corrected.

"Right, that's what I meant," he said, shifting uncomfortably. His expression of abject dejection brought a startling thought to Kelly's mind. Could Tommy Thompson have a crush on her? Was his teasing over the last few years an awkward attempt at making a connection? *No, that's ridiculous,* she thought. In fact, the idea was so preposterous that she started to laugh. She put her hand over her mouth to try and curtail it, but she couldn't stop laughing. Maybe it was her anxiety about that afternoon bursting forth in a fit of giggles.

"Why are you laughing at me?" Tommy asked. Kelly just laughed harder. Soon Frau Steinberg was standing over her, and Tommy was near tears.

"Was ist lustig, Fraülein Brennan?"

"Nothing," Kelly said.

"You mean 'nichts,'" Frau Steinberg replied stiffly before returning to the front of the room. "That's all for the pair exercises. Please return to your normal seats."

Tommy raced to his seat, head down. Kelly felt sorry for him, but didn't dwell on his hurt feelings. In less than a minute her mind was already back on what might happen that afternoon.

KELLY AND STEPHANIE were heading across the schoolyard when Bubbles's voice rang out behind them. "Kelly, Kelly!"

This is just what we need, Kelly thought with a groan. She kept walking as Bubbles caught up to them. She hadn't seen any of her fairy friends since the Bomin Anarena ceremony and she was hoping that she wouldn't see any of them before she met with Witherings. That way she wouldn't have to lie to any of them directly. And now, just as she and Stephanie were on their way to the meeting, Bubbles had decided to show up. Did he have a sixth sense for the absolutely worst times to come around?

"What is it?" Stephanie asked, not having heard Bubbles's voice. She must have noticed the sudden stiffening of Kelly's back, however.

"Bubbles is here," Kelly answered.

"Oh, hi, Bubbles," Stephanie said to the empty air in front of her, looking nowhere in the actual direction of where Bubbles was flying in his invisible-to-humans form over Kelly's right shoulder.

"I finished it. I finished it!" Bubbles exclaimed.

"You finished what?" Stephanie asked, this time having heard him. Although Bubbles had to stay in his invisible form when other humans were about, he was in the habit of letting his voice be audible to humans, as long as no one besides Stephanie was close enough to overhear.

"My poem! The one I wrote to ask Bamblelina to marry me. I want to know what you think." He pulled a bunch of disordered papers out of his pocket.

"That's great, Bubbles," Kelly said. "And I really would love to hear it, but Stephanie and I have to go to an important meeting for school."

"So? I'll recite it to you on the way over there."

"We need to go alone," Stephanie said. "We have to discuss some things before we get there."

Bubbles squinted suspiciously. "If you have a meeting for the school, then why aren't you meeting at the school?"

"We're meeting at our project partner's house, because her dad knows the topic and we are going to ask him for ideas," Stephanie answered.

"You told me you only have math class together. What kind of projects do they give in math class?"

"Lots of projects," Stephanie replied easily. "Our teacher subscribes to the theory of social mathematics."

Kelly was glad Stephanie was so good at making up believable lies, well, lies that were believable to Bubbles at least.

Bubbles scrunched up his nose like he was confused, but then he shrugged. "Silly human professors. It does wound me, however, to see how much more important your school is to you than your friends." He gave an exaggerated sniffle.

Stephanie rolled her eyes.

"You know that isn't true, Bubbles," Kelly said. "We want to be sure we absorb your poem without distractions, so we can give you good feedback. We can't listen to it now because we're too preoccupied with the meeting. Wouldn't you prefer our full attention?"

"Well, I guess that makes sense," Bubbles admitted. "When will you be done with your meeting?"

"I don't know. Why don't you just go wait at my house? My mom baked banana bread." Kelly hoped the promise of banana bread would cause Bubbles to race to her house immediately, thus decreasing the probability that he would follow them out of curiosity.

Bubbles perked up in an instant. "With nuts?"

Kelly smiled. "Of course."

Bubbles stuffed the papers back into his pocket and zoomed off, giving a quick wave over his shoulder. Kelly watched him go.

"Is he gone?" Stephanie asked.

Kelly nodded.

"Good. That was close."

They hurried to the metro station and walked down the stairs to the tracks. The blood pulsed in Kelly's ears. Stephanie gave her a reassuring smile. Witherings had said not to bring any fairy friends; he hadn't said anything about human friends. Kelly closed her eyes and hoped Bubbles wouldn't be able to sense her location, just in case he got his fill of banana bread and got bored. She had hidden herself from his senses once before, and she hoped she could do it again.

KELLY FELT the surrealistic feeling of being an outsider in her own environment when she walked into the lobby of the Museum of the American Indian. Parents with their children milled about, and a group of young boys scrutinized the large canoe that filled up the central floor space of the lobby. Others leaned their heads over the ledges of the spiraling upper floors, looking down on the happenings below. Everyone was carefree, innocent. Everyone except for Kelly and Stephanie.

"Do you see him?" Stephanie asked.

"Not yet."

They sat down on a bench by the sidewall and waited, trying not to look too out of place. A few minutes later Marcos Witherings walked in. At first Kelly just felt his entrance — a cool burst of air on her face along with the almost intangible feeling of being watched. She looked to the doorway and saw the figure of a tall, skinny man in jeans and a hooded sweatshirt. His hands were stuffed in his pockets and he chomped on a piece of gum. If Kelly hadn't known any better, she would have thought a sixteen-year old teenager had just walked into the room, not a thirty-six year old man. Kelly poked Stephanie with her elbow and Stephanie jerked to attention. The figure in the hooded sweatshirt approached. He sat down beside Kelly, but stared straight ahead.

"I thought I told you to come alone," he whispered.

Kelly realized that the nervousness she had felt up until a few moments ago had all but disappeared. Instead, she almost felt...exhilarated. Like she was in a spy movie. "You said not to bring any of my *fairy* friends, and I didn't." Out of the corner of her eye, Kelly saw the edges of Witherings's mouth inch upwards into the faintest of smiles. She didn't have to look at Stephanie on her other side to know that her friend had fixed Witherings with a harsh glare.

Kelly cut right to the chase. "So, what do you have to say about my father?"

"I want to tell you what I know about him."

"And that would be?" Kelly asked.

"Not much, I'm afraid. All I know is his name, status, and his fairy band."

Her heart fluttered. That wasn't much — but it was all she needed. It would be enough to find him.

"Well, what are you waiting for?" Stephanie asked. "Tell her already."

Witherings gave an almost imperceptible nod. "As you wish. His name is Darindian. He is second-born prince of the Ardagali, a secluded fairy band in the West, in what the humans call Yellowstone National Park. To the fairies it is known as 'Forpifudo peni dis Po Ardagalassa,' which in the ancient language means 'Land of the Terrible Ones.'"

Darindian. She knew his name. It sounded dignified, and mysterious. And she knew where he was. She fought the urge to drop everything and rush to Yellowstone that very instant.

Stephanie didn't seem as convinced. "How do we know you're telling the truth? You're the enemy. Kelly has every reason to change to her fairy form and kill you right now."

Witherings was silent for a moment. He took a deep breath. "I do not deny that I have done many bad things. But I have realized the pain I have caused, and I do not wish to act in such a way any longer. Giving Kelly this information is a small token of my gratitude to her."

"Gratitude?" Stephanie asked, shock written on her face.

"For awakening me from my sleep."

"Uh, you do remember that I put you in the coma in the first place, right?" Kelly asked.

"I'm not referring to that sleep. I'm referring to the waking sleep I was in before, when I blindly followed my father's will, unaware of the full weight of my own actions. When Kelly fought me, she showed me my errors, and in my coma I realized many painful truths."

Kelly examined the little she could see of Witherings's face underneath his hood. He sounded sincere, but was he? Could this be part of another trap? Was it some twisted plan of his father's? She could only assume that Miasmos still wanted her dead, so if Witherings was sticking to his father's plans, why hadn't he killed her when he'd had the chance? "Does that mean you aren't helping your father anymore?" she asked.

"I didn't say that," Witherings snapped. "I do not agree with all my father's methods, but his ideas are not wrong. Humans are destroying the earth. Maybe they need a shepherd."

Stephanie snorted. "You can't be serious. You're talking about taking over the world. You do realize that, don't you?"

"Of course. I'm no imbecile. But if there is a choice between taking the world over and watching it be destroyed, I choose to take it over."

"Taking over the world would amount to the same thing as destroying it," Kelly said.

Witherings's shoulders tensed. "That is an opinion, not a fact," he said. "I'll tell you what is a fact: nothing will stop my father. Would you rather I let him do things his way, or would you have me stay with him and minimize the damage he does along the way?"

"You can't say nothing will stop him," Kelly said. "No one is undefeatable." She remembered how her strength combined with that of Venuto, Thomas, and the late King Glenden had overpowered Miasmos in the battle of the underground tunnels. *Yet he still managed to escape,* she thought. Doubt crept into her mind, but she pushed it away.

"Kelly's right. And if you joined us, we could stop him," Stephanie said.

"I will not betray him. He is still my father!" Witherings nearly shouted, drawing the bewildered gaze of a nearby girl who looked to be about six years old. "I don't wish to discuss this topic any further," he added in a quieter tone. After a brief and awkward silence, he pulled something out of his pocket and extended it to Kelly. "Now, I want to give you this."

Kelly looked down at the silver ring resting in his palm. It possessed a black oval stone, which was flat and smooth, like a mirror, and about the size of a dime. Kelly took the ring and examined it. When she looked into the stone, she was surprised to see no reflection from its shiny surface. "What is it?"

"It is called the spy ring, so named for its special properties. You will need it if you journey to the Land of the Terrible Ones, because the Ardagali do not like strangers. This ring will warn you if you are being watched, or if you are in danger. The person that means you harm will appear in the stone. It will also help you sense others. If you think of them you will be able to see them in the stone, but only until they realize you are watching them. If they sense they are being watched they will be able to block you."

"If the ring really does all you say, it must be very valuable," Kelly said. "Why would you give it to me?"

Witherings shrugged. "My fairy senses are strong enough that I do not need its assistance."

"How do we know it doesn't have some sort of spell on it that will spy on *us*?" Stephanie asked.

"You don't. Although I suppose you could ask one of your fairy friends to examine it. I would suggest against that, however, since if the Glendenians see that you have the ring they will most likely take it from you."

"Why would they do that?"

"Because it is one of the ten curtains."

"The what?"

"You've never heard of them?" Witherings asked.

"No."

"Well I suppose they aren't exactly common knowledge. But you do know that my father seeks the Key to Embralia, the stone guarded by Thomas, yes?"

Kelly rolled her eyes. "Of course."

"He also needs something else; once he has the Key, he needs to know where Embralia is."

"I thought everyone knew where Embralia was," Stephanie said.

He shook his head. "No. We only know that it was somewhere in the ancient lands, meaning, across the sea. But it could be anywhere. The city was hidden by the great avalanche, and the king of the city, Carlo, decided to obscure its vibrations so that no one could find it. The vibrations were so strong that he couldn't diminish them by normal means, so he counterbalanced the vibrations by positioning powerful objects from the city in secret places throughout the globe. In this way the vibration was spread out all over, shielding the city's true location. Only if all of the objects are found and cleansed of their vibrations, will Embralia's location be revealed."

"How could an entire city be hidden?" Stephanie asked. "Didn't other people know where it was back when Carlo hid it?"

"Yes, but only a few, and Carlo used his powerful fairy senses to find them and to erase their memories of the location. At least, that is how the story goes. To this day, even the guardians of the Key to Embralia do not know where Embralia lies."

"So this ring was one of the objects hiding Embralia?" Kelly asked.

"Yes. My father has found three so far. When he finds the others, the only thing stopping him from gaining Embralia's powers will be the Key."

"How easy are these objects to find?" Kelly asked.

"Difficult. It took him twenty years to find the first, but only five to find the others. Each one you find makes the next easier to find. So it won't be long now."

Kelly shivered. "Why are you telling us all this? Wouldn't Miasmos be mad you're letting us know his progress?"

Witherings chuckled. "It's not like you knowing he's found some of the objects will stop him from finding the others."

"In other words, we're too insignificant to be considered a threat," Kelly said.

Witherings just smirked.

"Do the other objects have power like this ring?" Stephanie asked Witherings.

"Yes. Some have quite strange powers, hidden powers. My father gave me another one to figure out what it is for. I have had it for three years, but I have yet to discover its purpose."

"What is it?" Stephanie asked.

Witherings looked around to make sure no one was paying them any attention. Once satisfied, he raised the left leg of his jeans to reveal a small tattoo on his ankle. It was an abstract, almost calligraphic brushing, suggesting the shape of a bird. Witherings waved his palm over the tattoo, and the tattoo began to swirl. After a few moments it floated away from his leg like smoke. The smoke settled into his palm. He squeezed his fist around it, and when he opened his hand again a small, perfectly round stone lay in his palm. It was about the size of a marble, black, but with an almost imperceptible blue tint.

"Cool," Stephanie said.

"Definitely," Witherings agreed. "But besides its being 'cool,' I have yet to unlock its secret."

"Are you sure it has one?" Stephanie asked.

"It must. Carlo only picked objects of great power. It must do something." Witherings leaned down and pressed the stone against his now unmarked leg. He let go, and it dissolved into a swirl of dark blue mist before settling down once again on his skin as the birdlike tattoo. "Well, that concludes our business," Witherings said. "I enjoyed our little talk, but I am still my father's son, remember that. I hope we will not have to oppose each other again in battle. I would protect my father." A hint of the old iciness returned to his voice with that warning. He stood up. "Good day." He inclined his head, then sauntered from the museum in his imitation of a teenager's gangling gait.

Kelly and Stephanie sat in silence for a few minutes. Kelly examined the ring. She wondered what her mother was up to, and suddenly a tiny image of Mindy chopping zucchini for dinner formed on the face of the stone.

"That's awesome," Stephanie said, seeing the image over Kelly's shoulder. "Can I hold it?"

Kelly handed the ring to Stephanie and returned to her thoughts, which were racing at a mile a minute. She believed that Witherings had meant the things he had said. He had really changed, at least a little bit, but his continued allegiance to his father worried her. If he spent any time with Miasmos, it might only be a matter of weeks before his mind was poisoned completely again. And what about her father? Was he really a member of a secluded fairy band? If that was true, how did he ever end up meeting her mother? Had Mindy ever even been to Yellowstone National Park? Was her father still there? And what of the past between her father and Miasmos? Miasmos had once referred to her father as a 'joke.' What had happened between them? Why did they even know each other? She would find out. She would go to this Land of the Terrible Ones and find her father. She would get answers.

But when could she go? She couldn't afford a plane ticket right now. She only had about sixty dollars saved up. Plus if she missed school her mom would know about it. That meant she would have to wait until Thanksgiving vacation, which was over two months away. She put her head in her hands. Two months! The wait would be torture. She really couldn't see any way to go earlier, though — she needed time to save the money.

"Whoa, check this out!" Stephanie's voice jerked Kelly out of her swirling thoughts.

Kelly looked at the spy ring in Stephanie's hand and saw the tiny figure of Dmitri. Apparently humans could use the spy ring too. *Of course, if Stephanie had to pick someone to spy on it would be Dmitri*, Kelly thought. She noticed that Dmitri held the hand of a blond boy, who must have been about five or six years old. Then she recognized the canoe from the museum. Dmitri was here! She looked up and saw him and the little boy standing by the canoe, only a few yards away.

"Give it back," Kelly said. Stephanie handed Kelly the ring. Kelly slid it onto the third finger of her left hand, twisting the stone so that it was hidden on the underside of her fingers. By the time she had finished putting on the ring she realized that Stephanie was already striding towards Dmitri and his companion.

Kelly got up to follow, knowing it was useless to try and stop her friend. She just hoped the experience wouldn't be too embarrassing.

"Hi, Dmitri," Stephanie said loudly to Dmitri's back. He jumped almost three inches in the air at the sound of his name. He turned around.

"Hello, Stephanie," he said politely. He noticed Kelly and smiled broadly. "Hi, Kelly."

"Hi."

"This is my little brother Dominic," Dmitri said. "Dominic, these are my classmates, Stephanie and Kelly."

"I'm not little," Dominic protested, pulling his hand out of

Dmitri's grasp and shoving it into the pocket of his tattered jeans.

"What brings you here?" Stephanie asked.

"My brother likes museums," Dmitri answered.

"Of course." Stephanie giggled nervously.

"Well, it was nice to see you—" Dmitri began, only to be cut off by Stephanie's brazen invitation.

"Would you like to go for some coffee? There's a little café over there."

"Thank you, but we should be going."

"But I'm thirsty, Dima," Dmitri's brother said with hopeful, big blue eyes.

"There's a water fountain over there," Dmitri told him.

"I want a soda. Please, please can I have a soda?"

Dmitri shrugged, a gesture which caused Dominic to break into a large grin and run for the café.

"Your little brother is so cute," Stephanie said.

"Thanks," Dmitri mumbled.

"I don't have any siblings. I always wished I had a brother or a sister," Stephanie continued.

They reached the café and ordered at the counter. Dmitri ordered a coke for Dominic and just a glass of tap water for himself. Stephanie chose a sugary coffee and whipped cream concoction, and Kelly bought a bottle of apple juice. While Stephanie stayed at the counter to watch her coffee drink being blended, Kelly and Dmitri followed Dominic to a small round table with four chairs around it.

"So, you and Stephanie like museums?" Dmitri asked.

"Sure, but we were just looking for some information," Kelly answered.

"Doing a report for school?"

"Something like that."

"You seem to be a very secretive girl," he said.

"Why do you say that?"

"I don't know. Just a feeling, I guess."

Little Dominic let out a loud burp, having downed more than half of his soda in under five seconds.

"Don't drink so fast," Dmitri said. "Kelly, do you have any siblings?"

"No, I'm an only child."

"Really? I wouldn't have thought you were an only child. You don't seem spoiled."

"Not all only children are spoiled," Kelly said. "Only if they have bad parents."

"So you have good parents then."

"A good mother. I don't know my father." She stopped just short of adding 'yet.'

"I don't know my father either," Dominic piped in, in the innocent way children have of saying things.

"He left when my mother was pregnant with Dominic," Dmitri explained.

"I'm sorry," Kelly said.

"Don't be. I'm not."

Just then Stephanie joined them.

"Wow, that's humongous," Dominic said, eyeing the four-inch tall whipped cream mound topping off Stephanie's drink.

"That's how I like 'em," Stephanie said with a wink. "So, Dmitri, what do you think of Mr. Patterson's class?" Kelly rolled her eyes. What a dumb question.

"It's all right I guess," Dmitri replied.

"I think it's boring," Stephanie said. "His voice is like a lullaby or something."

There was a silence. Kelly thought about what Dmitri had said; if he wasn't sorry his father had left, then his father must not have been very nice. She could tell that Dmitri really cared about his brother, but it must be hard to take on the father figure role when he himself was still a teenager.

"So, you like sports?" Stephanie asked Dmitri next.

"Yes. In the fall and winter I do cross country, and then in the spring and summer I do track. I used to do football, too, but I like running better."

Stephanie's jaw dropped. "You like running better than football? But football players get all the attention."

Dmitri chuckled. "I don't like so much attention."

"Really?" Stephanie asked, eyes wide in disbelief.

"Really."

Kelly understood where he was coming from. She hated it when all the fairies stared at her in Glendenland, knowing she was the one who captured Witherings, and also the one who let him escape.

Dominic tugged on his older brother's sleeve. "I have to pee, Dima.'

"Okay." Dmitri stood up, gathering his and Dominic's cups. "I guess I'll see you two tomorrow in class. Say goodbye, Dominic."

"Bye-bye," Dominic said.

"Bye," Stephanie and Kelly answered in unison.

After Dmitri and his brother had gone, Kelly and Stephanie headed back to the metro station. "Wow, who would have thought we'd run into Dmitri at the museum? What are the chances!" Stephanie asked as they walked.

Kelly shrugged.

"Do you think he likes me?" Stephanie continued.

"Really, Stephanie? Marcos Witherings just told me where I can find my father, and you're worried about whether Dmitri likes you?"

"Sorry. We just saw Dmitri, so it's fresh in my mind. But of course I care about your father. He's a prince! That means you're a princess."

"I guess so." Kelly hadn't thought about it like that. She found the idea quite strange.

A twinkle came into Stephanie's eyes. "I bet he has jewels

and diamonds. Maybe he'll give you some. Then if you wear them and change to human form, they'll grow too, and we'll be rich."

"Don't count your chickens before they hatch, Steph. For all we know, the Ardagali's currency might be poppy seed or something. Not every fairy band is like Glendenland."

"You're right, sorry. I get carried away sometimes."

Kelly laughed. "That's an understatement."

4

FSP

When they got to Kelly's house, Mindy was preparing dinner. Bubbles whizzed around her in invisible form.

"Hi, girls. Dinner will be ready in twenty minutes," Mindy said. Bubbles grabbed a stray corn kernel from the counter and raced over to Kelly and Stephanie.

"Will you listen to the poem now?" he whispered.

Kelly nodded. "Mom, we'll be upstairs."

"Sure, dear."

Bubbles could barely contain his excitement on the way up to Kelly's room. He waved his crumpled bunch of papers around and flapped his wings in impatient agitation as Kelly and Stephanie positioned themselves on the side of Kelly's bed.

"Are you ready?" he asked.

"Let's see what you've got," Stephanie answered. Bubbles cleared his throat and recited:

> *Oh, the pasture of my heart was barren,*
> *And brittle was the grass that grew there,*
> *Ere I met the young and charming maiden,*

Bamblelina, sunny, jolly and fair.

Now the pasture of my heart is lively,
Green and bright is the grass that grows there,
And now it's full of flowers so lovely,
Because of Bamblelina's patient care.

The days we go collect wild berries,
Make me forget the world is full of strife,
I would be the happiest of fairies,
If my Bamblelina would be my wife.

The tips of Bubbles's ears were red. Suddenly self-conscious, he crinkled the papers into a tight ball and shoved them in his pocket. He stared down at the floor.

"I think it's beautiful," Kelly said. "I'm sure she'll like it." She hoped she sounded convincing. In truth she thought the poem was cheesy, especially the part about wild berries.

He looked up hopefully. "You really think so?"

"Yes. Don't you, Stephanie?"

"Oh yes. I think it's masterful. But, it would probably be better if you memorized it."

Bubbles's eyes widened. "Memorize it?"

"You know, when you commit something to memory so you don't need to read it," Stephanie explained.

Bubbles rolled his eyes. "I know what memorize means, silly. It's just hard, and I'm so nervous."

"Well, think about it," Stephanie said.

"When are you going to propose?" Kelly asked.

"Um, soon, soon," Bubbles said. "But I don't know exactly when yet."

"I see." Kelly wondered if he would manage to work up the nerve before the school year ended.

~

KELLY LAY IN BED, turning the spy ring over and over in her hands. Bubbles had stayed until late in the night, trying to decide on the best time to ask Bamblelina to marry him, so Stephanie had needed to leave before they had a chance to talk any more about Kelly's father. Finally alone with her thoughts, Kelly reviewed the day's events. Witherings had seemed different — less scary, but she couldn't be sure it wasn't just an act, or a temporary change. Would he soon regret their meeting and come back looking for the spy ring?

She held the ring up to the light from her beside lamp. The surface of the stone glinted, as if bragging about its gifts. The idea of spying on Witherings with the ring crossed her mind, but she suspected he would notice, seeing as he used to own the spy ring himself. Instead, she wondered what her mother was doing. In a flash, a tiny view of Mindy reading a book in the kitchen took over the ring's surface.

Next Kelly wished for her father to appear in the ring — but after her mother's image disappeared, the ring returned to its smooth dark surface. Why couldn't she see him? Did that mean he was dead? She shivered. No, it must just be because she didn't know what he looked like.

After that, she thought of Venuto. She brought the ring nearer her face for a closer look at the image that appeared. The prince was in the library, looking quite tired. He sat cross-legged on the floor with a bunch of very old, tattered pages scattered out on the floor around him. He examined the papers with deep thought. Kelly squinted but she couldn't make out what was written on the pages. A few seconds later, Venuto perked up and looked over his shoulder like he felt someone watching him. Kelly quickly pressed her thumb over the ring stone, hoping he hadn't sensed her. Venuto had very strong fairy senses. Kelly made a mental note not to spy on him again.

Better to stick with humans for the time being. She thought of Stephanie, who was sleeping in her bed, hugging a pillow. Next she thought of her algebra teacher. Unfortunately, she got a glimpse of him singing in the shower — completely naked. She dropped the ring at the sight. *Ew! This thing should come with a warning!* Maybe it should be called the 'Peeping Tom' ring, not the spy ring. She shuddered, unable to wipe the image of her teacher's bare behind from her mind. As she thought of other private situations in which she wouldn't want to see her acquaintances, she decided it was probably best to only use the ring if she had a very good reason to, not just out of curiosity.

Would it work on Miasmos, she wondered? That certainly qualified as a good reason. She picked up the ring and again focused on the stone. At first there was nothing, but then she saw a dark outline emerge. It was tinted blue; Miasmos's surroundings possessed little light, and his luminous wings provided the sole illumination. He was kneeling, concentrating on the ground. He used a small trowel to free something from the dirt. Whatever it was, it was almost free. He put down the trowel and lifted a small object up from the ground. He blew on it gently to remove the clinging bits of earth. His wings glowed a more intense blue, indicating excitement, but before Kelly could get a look at what he was holding, he stood up and looked around. He knew he was being watched. Kelly covered up the ring just as he spun around and glared right out from its surface. She cursed herself for spying on him for so long. She had been so curious to see what the object was that she had been careless. What *had* it been? Was it one of the ten curtains? She hoped not, because that would bring him one step closer to finding the location of Embralia. But, what else would he have been digging for in the dark?

~

THE NEXT DAY in algebra Dmitri gave Stephanie a polite nod in response to her energetic smile, but he flashed Kelly a wide grin, which she returned.

Mr. Patterson began passing back their most recent homework.

"Man, I only got a 75," Stephanie said when she received hers. "What did you get, Dmitri?"

"72," he said, looking deflated. "What about you, Kelly? How did you do?"

"I did okay," Kelly said, not wanting to make Dmitri feel bad.

Unfortunately, Stephanie knew her too well. "What she means is she got a one hundred, as always."

Dmitri's eyes widened. "A one hundred? Really? Wow, you must be really good at math."

"I'm all right," Kelly answered modestly.

"Attention please," Mr. Patterson said. "Some of you performed disappointingly on your most recent homework. So, today we are going to review. Flip to page 39, please." He turned to write something on the board, and Kelly stared down at her book, trying to push away the icky image of him naked in the shower that kept popping into her head.

Kelly's mind began to wander. Soon she had completely tuned out the lecture. She felt an urge to use the spy ring again, in spite of its pitfalls. Still, she didn't want to risk any of the other students nearby looking at the ring and seeing the moving images. So instead she just thought about what she might need on her trip to look for her father. Definitely maps and a compass. What else? A tent? She had never even been camping before, let alone trekking through uncharted wilderness. Would there be bears? Her stomach churned, but it would take a lot more than bears to dissuade her. Besides, maybe Margretta had some sort of sleeping potion for bears. Or, she could always throw fairy dust on them so they would shrink to fairy size. She stifled a giggle at the thought of a fairy-sized grizzly bear.

Kelly jerked back to attention when Stephanie tapped her on the shoulder. "Hey space cadet, class is over."

"Oh." Kelly started to put her books away. "So, you're coming over tonight for dinner and homework right?" she asked Stephanie.

"Of course. I might be a little late though."

"Why?"

"You'll see," Stephanie replied with a cryptic grin. "It's a surprise."

WHEN STEPHANIE ARRIVED at Kelly's house, she still had a cryptic grin on her face and she refused to say a word about the surprise until they were safe in Kelly's room after dinner.

"So, what is this surprise you were talking about?" Kelly asked, by this point dying to know.

"We have to shrink first," Stephanie said.

"Why?"

"Because what I have to show you doesn't change size when we do. It's special like my prosthetic wings."

"Okay." Kelly transformed and Stephanie sprinkled herself with some fairy dust from a tiny salt shaker she had recently created, so that she could do it herself. Once shrunk, Stephanie pulled a small black pouch from her bag. Kelly's eyes narrowed. It looked just like the pouch Blaine had tossed to Skip at the Bomin Anarena ceremony. "Where did you get that?" she asked suspiciously.

"Blaine gave it to me."

"He *gave* it to you?"

"Well, technically I bought it from him."

"When? You haven't been to Glendenland since Thomas's family arrived."

Stephanie rolled her eyes. "It isn't like I don't ever go there without you. You go there by yourself, don't you?"

"I...I suppose." It hadn't occurred to Kelly that Stephanie would ever go to Glendenland without her.

"That doesn't bother you or something, does it?" Stephanie asked.

"No, of course not," Kelly lied.

"Good. So, are you ready to see?"

Kelly eyed the pouch uneasily. She didn't have a good feeling about this. "All right."

Stephanie opened the pouch to reveal a black powder speckled with tiny silver flecks. She set the pouch down on the bed between them.

"What is it?" Kelly asked.

"Fairy sense powder, also known as FSP."

Kelly frowned. "It looks like a drug."

"It is. It gives you a fairy senses experience, like a vision."

"Is it illegal?"

"How can it be illegal if it's a fairy drug? Human police wouldn't know about it."

"You know what I mean, Stephanie. Is it illegal for fairies?"

"Blaine said that it is frowned upon, but it isn't illegal. You can possess as much as you want, but you aren't supposed to sell it. Blaine said he doesn't usually sell it to just anyone, but since I was complaining about how I don't have fairy senses, obviously, since I'm not a fairy, he said I should try it. He thinks it will temporarily give me fairy senses." Stephanie's eyes gleamed at the prospect.

"He *thinks* it will? So, you haven't tried it yet?"

"No. I wanted to wait to do it with you," Stephanie said.

"Thanks...I guess."

Stephanie made a move to pick up the pouch, but Kelly put a hand on her shoulder.

"Wait. What if it has strange effects on fadamen, or humans? It might not be safe."

"Blaine said it would be safe."

Kelly rolled her eyes. "That's a relief."

"What's that supposed to mean?"

"I don't trust him."

"Why not?"

"He's very immature," Kelly answered.

"No way. He's really deep. You just don't understand him."

Kelly's jaw dropped. "Wait, you don't *like* him, do you?"

"Maybe a little bit," Stephanie admitted.

"I thought you liked Dmitri."

Stephanie laughed. "I do. But a girl's got to keep her options open." She waved a hand dismissively. "Enough boy talk. Do you want to try it or not?"

"I don't think so. You know how I feel about drugs."

"Look, Kelly, you worry too much. It's not addictive or illegal. It's not like human drugs."

Maybe Stephanie did have a point, Kelly thought. She said fairies could have as much of it as they wanted. It wasn't illegal. And it was supposed to enhance one's fairy senses. Would it enable her to glimpse her father? Her future? What Miasmos had found in the dirt when she spied on him in the ring? "What kind of vision will it give you?" she asked.

"Blaine said it can't be predicted, but they can be quite powerful. In the olden days great rulers used FSP before battles, or when they were sworn in."

"All right. Maybe it wouldn't hurt to try it just once."

"Yes! I knew you would do it, Kelly. Here, you have to put a little bit on your palm and then sniff it up through your nose."

"Snort it? Are you serious? That sounds like hard drugs. I thought we'd just sprinkle it on ourselves like fairy dust."

"Listen, it's harmless, okay?" Stephanie held out the pouch, waiting for Kelly to take a pinch.

"No. I changed my mind. I don't want it."

"Come on, take it." Stephanie pushed the pouch closer. "Don't be a wimp."

"I said no!" Kelly shoved Stephanie's arm away. Startled, Stephanie dropped the pouch. A cloud of the fine powder drifted into the air.

Stephanie groaned, leaning down to retrieve the bag. "You wasted almost half of it." She sneezed, and even more of the dust rose into the air as her shoulders jerked.

Before Kelly thought to hold her breath, she felt a sharp tickling as the powder flew up her nose and into her sinus cavities. It brought with it the smell of burnt carbon, like the odor after a match has been blown out. A bitter, sour taste formed in the back of her mouth. "I think I breathed some in," she said.

"Do you feel anything weird?" Stephanie asked.

"Not yet." But just after she said it, she felt a vertiginous feeling — like the twirling sensation she got sometimes just before dropping off to sleep. It felt like her whole body was spinning. Then it seemed like she was floating. She looked down on herself and Stephanie. *Weird.* After lingering there for a moment, she, or rather her mind's eye, floated unimpeded through the ceiling. She raced very fast over the city. Before long she was outside of the city, moving over the mountains. As she flew, the sunlight came and went, fast like a blinking strobe light as her fairy senses took her mind into the future. She realized she had reached a big city. There was water. The Statue of Liberty loomed beside her. Then, in a sudden nose dive, she flew down into a building and hovered over a young business-woman in an office. The woman held a paper in her hand. She folded it and put it in an envelope. As the woman leaned forward to lick the envelope, Kelly's view shifted and she was no longer watching the woman; she was looking out through

the woman's eyes. She tasted the glue from the envelope as if she herself had licked it. The muffled sound of a phone ringing in the next office came through the wall.

Almost immediately after the phone rang there was an odd sound — low and rumbling, like far-off thunder. The woman got up and walked to the window. Kelly felt her high heels pinching her feet. Outside the window, a wall of water headed straight towards her. It crashed around the buildings in the distance as it made its way closer and closer. Cars and buses were tossed around like toys. A strangled scream escaped the woman's mouth, but she seemed frozen in place. Instead of trying to escape the impending deluge, she just stood there, staring at the water. A panic rose up within Kelly. The rumble was now a rushing roar, so loud it overpowered the woman's screams. It was odd to feel like she was screaming at the top of her lungs, but to hear no voice.

The water was there. It smacked into the window, and for a second it seemed as if the glass would hold. Time stood still for a moment — and then the glass shattered. The frigid water hit with immense force, but somehow Kelly, or rather, the woman in her vision, was not unconscious. Shards of broken glass dragged over her skin, and little clouds of the woman's blood floated into the water. She struggled to move to the window, but she couldn't. The water had pinned her back to the wall. It churned with such strength that it rushed its way into her nose and mouth with unstoppable force.

With a jolt Kelly was back in her room. She took several deep breaths, reassuring herself that she had not in fact drowned. She coughed uncontrollably, feeling as though she had swallowed water the wrong way — a lot of it. In spite of the noise Kelly was making, Stephanie didn't move. She sat with her eyes closed, a serene expression on her face. *She must be having a nice vision,* Kelly thought. Not like mine. Kelly had never felt anything so horrible in her life, not even when

Miasmos had used painful dark magic on her. But what had she actually seen? Who was that woman? Had she glimpsed the future? If so, how far in the future? She tried to remember how many days had flashed by in the vision, but she couldn't remember. A tsunami in New York City? Should she warn someone? *Don't be ridiculous,* she thought. *There couldn't be a tsunami in New York.* Or could there? She tried to reassure herself that visions of the future were only one of many possible occurrences, and besides, the black powder could have just been playing tricks.

"So, how was it for you?" Stephanie asked, having stirred.

"Awful. You should flush the rest of that stuff down the toilet. It's dangerous."

"Oh no. What did you see?"

Kelly told Stephanie about her vision.

"I'm sorry. Mine was nothing like that. I was in some kind of a big blue ball of energy, and I was traveling over the ocean. It was really fun, and peaceful. And then I landed on a beach somewhere, and when I walked out I pointed to a palm tree and a bolt of electricity shot right out of my hand. It set the tree on fire! It felt so cool. If that's what it feels like to use magic, I'm even more jealous than I already am." She tied up the top of the pouch, then tucked it into her pocket. "I'm actually a little glad you don't like it, because now I can have all the rest to myself."

"I really don't think you should use it, Stephanie. I know you don't think it's bad, because it's from fairies, but it's dangerous. It's a real drug, like LSD or something. You wouldn't take LSD, would you?"

"Of course I wouldn't take LSD. But FSP is totally different."

"I don't think so," Kelly said.

"I do. If it were dangerous, it would be illegal. So relax. I liked my vision and I'm definitely going to do it again."

Kelly shook her head, feeling her chest tighten again at the

memory of her own vision. "Suit yourself. But I think it's a very bad idea."

TWO DAYS later Kelly entered the Great Library of Glendenland before her next magic lesson. She walked towards the secret room, but she paused just outside of it, realizing she still had the spy ring on her finger. She took it off and put it in her pocket.

Venuto was already waiting inside. He sat quietly on one of the room's blue square mats. He gestured for Kelly to sit on the mat across from him.

"How are you doing, Kelly?" he asked once Kelly was seated.

"I'm doing all right."

"Good. Should we get started then?"

"I have a question, first, if you don't mind."

"Of course."

"Have you ever heard of a fairy band called the Ardagali?" She hoped she had sounded nonchalant.

Venuto nodded. "Yes, I have heard of them, but I have never been there myself. Nor have I met any of the Ardagali. They are one of the most secretive bands in the world, and they jealously guard themselves against outsiders. Although, now that you mention them, I seem to remember that our band had dealings with them in the time of my grandfather. I believe it was trade in rare potion ingredients. But those ties were broken when my father was still a child. Why do you ask?"

"Well..." she let her voice trail off, unsure of what to say. She had planned to give him a line about having heard some fairies telling scary campfire stories about the Ardagali, but now that she was here, that line sounded very silly. And Venuto was looking at her with trusting eyes. He didn't expect her to lie. It would be the farthest thing from his mind. "Marcos Witherings said my father is from there," she blurted out.

Venuto's eyebrows pulled together. "When? When he escaped?"

"No. I kind of...met him in person a few days ago."

"What?!?"

"He called me and said he wanted to tell me who my father was. I knew it was dangerous, but I met him in a public place, in human form. Please don't be mad."

Venuto sighed. "I wish you would have told me before taking such a risk."

"Would you have let me meet him?"

Venuto hesitated, thinking it over.

"See? You aren't sure. That's why I didn't tell you beforehand."

"I suppose you have a point. Next you'll want to take yet another risk: going to see the Ardagali, I presume."

"How did you know?" she asked suspiciously. "Did you read my mind?"

A faint smile played on Venuto's lips. "I don't need to be a mind reader to figure that out. But I am puzzled. The Ardagali would be the last band I would have expected your father to come from. It is practically inconceivable that one of them would have made a fadaman with a human."

Kelly's spirits fell. "Do you think Marcos was lying, then?"

"I don't know. Did he say why he wanted to meet with you?"

"He said it was a token of gratitude for my having put him in a coma, which is weird. But he said he learned from his mistakes and that I'm to thank for that."

Venuto looked thoughtful. "Then he may have told you the truth, at least, what he believes the truth to be. I won't even try to stop you from going to the Ardagali, but I must counsel you not to go alone. You must at least bring a member of the royal guard with you, if one can be spared. When do you plan to go?"

"On Thanksgiving break, in late November."

"I see. I will discuss the matter with Thomas. Normally I would also suggest sending a messenger to the Ardagali in advance, but the messenger we sent to invite them to the council meeting this past summer was not able to make contact. They attacked him without asking any questions and he barely escaped. I do hope they will be able to sense that their blood runs through your veins. Perhaps that fact will make them more hospitable."

"Thank you," Kelly said. She was relieved to have met with so little resistance. Venuto probably knew that the only way he could really stop her from going to find her father would be to lock her up in the jail bubble, which luckily wasn't something he seemed willing to do.

"Now, let's get to the lesson, shall we?" Venuto asked. "I think we should start with trying to hone your ability to sense the location of others."

Kelly leaned forward, most intrigued.

"First, let me ask a question," Venuto began. "Do you know why it's so hard for fairies to sense fadamen?"

Kelly shook her head no.

"It's because fadamen have a rare vibration that is unfamiliar to fairies. Of course every living being has its own individual vibration, but each being also has the overlying vibration of its species. Fairies can sense humans pretty easily not because human vibrations are anything like their own, but merely because there are so many humans around, and over time a fairy that lives near humans becomes adept at recognizing and distinguishing human vibrations. There are so few fadamen, however, that most fairies have much trouble sensing them."

"But if my vibrations are so different, how come no one has noticed that I'm a fadaman when I walk into a room?"

"Good question. At a close range the vibrations seem very

similar, if you are not paying special attention. Also, vibrations of nearby fairies can mask your vibration. Since you have been in Glendenland, surrounded by thousands of fairies in close proximity, most fairies will not have strong enough senses to pick up on the difference in your vibrations. Just like they won't notice Stephanie is really human, especially since her vibrations become more fairylike when she's under the influence of fairy dust."

"It sounds very difficult," Kelly said. "I don't even know what anything's, or anyone's vibrations feel like."

"Have you ever been alone in a room, and then suddenly you felt like you weren't alone anymore? Then you turned around to realize that someone else had just entered the room?"

"Yes," Kelly said.

"In that case, you actually felt that person's vibrations as they entered into the room."

"I did? It seems so subtle."

Venuto nodded in agreement.

Kelly sighed. "Once I can sense someone, how do I form a mental connection to talk with them telepathically?"

Venuto smiled. "You are getting ahead of yourself. You have to be able to sense them first." Just then Venuto got a vacant look in his eyes. "One moment, Kelly." Someone was contacting him mind to mind. After about a minute his eyes refocused on her. "I'm sorry. I completely forgot that I have to go to a meeting with Thomas to plan his mother's birthday party. We have to make sure it is a very elaborate affair, one befitting her 'status.' Even so, I'm sure she'll find something wrong with it."

"Maybe she'll come around?" Kelly said.

"I doubt it. Her chip runs deep."

THE NEXT DAY at school Kelly was on her way to her last class when she heard a familiar voice calling her name from a few feet behind her, but she couldn't quite put her finger on it. She turned around to see who it was.

"Hi, Kelly," Dmitri said. "I'm glad I caught you. Listen, I want to ask you something." He paused, waiting for her permission to continue.

"Go ahead."

"You know our first math test is coming up next Friday, right? Well, obviously you know, and I was wondering if you would help me study. Um, because I'm really having trouble with the material and you know it really well."

"Sure. Stephanie and I are going to study next Thursday night if you want to join us."

Dmitri grimaced. "I was kind of hoping we could meet alone. I mean, without your friend. She seems nice and all, but, I don't think we would get much work done if she was there. She'd be hitting on me the whole time."

Kelly laughed out loud. She hadn't expected Dmitri to be so straightforward about his awareness of Stephanie's crush. His directness was refreshing. Plus, he was probably right. Stephanie wouldn't be able to concentrate with him there. Kelly didn't think Stephanie would be happy about her meeting Dmitri alone, but he needed help. She couldn't just turn him down, especially since most guys would have been too embarrassed to ask for help in the first place.

"All right, we can meet alone. Maybe sometime over the weekend?"

"Great, here's my cell number." He handed her a piece of paper with his number written on it. "Call me tonight." He started to walk away. "Oh, and don't tell your friend, okay?"

Kelly put his phone number in her pocket, thinking about what he'd just said. Maybe it was better to keep it a secret from Stephanie. Then again, maybe not. If Stephanie found out about it some other way, she would be really mad Kelly had kept it from her. She would think Kelly had wanted to be alone with him or something, which wasn't the case. She'd best get it over with and tell Stephanie the truth — that Dmitri didn't want her to be there. She just hoped Stephanie wouldn't take it too hard.

~

"He what?" Stephanie exclaimed. They were sitting in Kelly's room that afternoon, waiting for Bubbles and Beatrix to get there to help Kelly practice sensing people. Kelly had just broken the news about Dmitri. "Like heck I'm not coming," Stephanie continued.

"Steph, he knows you like him, and he doesn't want you to hit on him. Don't you think it would be awkward if all of us were there?"

"Okay, maybe a little. But how could you say yes? Why didn't you tell him you'd only help him if I came too?" Stephanie pouted.

"Because he needs help. He already failed the class once. I don't want him to fail it again."

Stephanie sighed. "All right, fine. But say nice things about me so that he sees how cool I am. And then you can invite him to do something else, because you'll be like official acquaintances. Then of course you will also invite me, and voilà , sparks will fly between us!"

"Don't take this the wrong way, Steph, but maybe you should just accept the fact he isn't interested?"

"Are you kidding? No one is not interested in me. He's interested — he just doesn't know it yet. Oh, and I have dibs, you know that right?" Stephanie asked.

Kelly found herself pausing a second before giving an

answer. She was actually relieved when Bubbles and his sister whizzed into the room at that very moment.

"Your mom opened the door to go check the mail and we flew in!" Bubbles said.

"Sowawesupzdto?" Beatrix said.

"Hold on, Beatrix. You're talking too fast again," Kelly said. She transformed herself into fairy form so she could better understand Beatrix's lightning-fast speech. "What did you say?"

"I asked: so what are we supposed to do?" Beatrix said.

"I thought maybe I can sit here with my eyes closed and then all of you can go into the hall, and then one of you can come back in and I can try and sense who it is. What do you think?"

"That's a good idea, don't you think, Bubbles?" Beatrix asked her brother.

"Sure. Let's get started." He zoomed out of the room, and Beatrix and Stephanie followed.

"Okay, ready," Kelly called out. She squeezed her eyes shut and concentrated on the space around her, trying to sense her surroundings. She waited, and waited. Nothing.

"Boo!" Bubbles shouted right beside her ear. Kelly jumped. "That wasn't too good," Bubbles said. "Maybe we should announce when someone is coming into the room?"

"All right," Kelly agreed. She closed her eyes again.

"Someone's coming in!" Bubbles announced from the hall. Kelly focused her attention on the door and thought she could just sense a presence — a slightly more 'dense' feeling in the center of the doorway, but she couldn't tell who it was.

"Um, Beatrix?" Kelly guessed.

Beatrix giggled hysterically from outside the doorway.

"No, it's me again, silly," Bubbles said. "Can't you tell I'm more solid than she is?"

"No," Kelly replied, frustrated. This was even more difficult than she'd thought it would be.

"Bubbles, what if both you and Beatrix came in at the same time?" Stephanie suggested. "Then she could try to differentiate between the two of you."

This time Kelly thought she sensed two presences in the doorway. She tried to look more deeply at the globs in her mind's eye. One was heavier, weightier, but not lethargic. It seemed to hold a potential energy inside, just barely contained by its outer lines. The other presence was more fluid, full of motion although it wasn't moving. That had to be Beatrix.

"I think Bubbles is there." Kelly pointed without opening her eyes. "And Beatrix is there."

"Right!" Bubbles said.

"Stephanie, will you walk in now?" Kelly asked.

Stephanie stepped into the doorway and Kelly could feel a clear difference; her underlying vibrations were not the same as the fairy vibrations. It was like the frequencies were slower or something — she seemed more syrupy than the other two.

"Let's try one at a time again," Kelly said.

This time the doorway was empty, and empty and empty. "Did someone come in yet?" Kelly asked.

"Not yet," Stephanie's voice said from the hallway.

After another few minutes, Kelly finally felt the more fast and fluid presence enter the doorway. "Beatrix?"

"Correct!" Beatrix answered.

Then came Stephanie, then Bubbles. They kept practicing for about thirty minutes. By the end, Kelly was able to identify them all consistently, although she occasionally got confused if two entered at the same time without telling her first.

"You did great," Bubbles said when they stopped practicing. He flopped himself down on her bed.

"Maybe for you three," Kelly said. "But I know you already. Plus, I have to concentrate really hard and you're only a few yards away. How would I sense you from far away, with all of the other vibrations of everyone else in between?"

Beatrix shrugged. "We don't know. It's kind of automatic for us, since we learned as kids. You just ignore the other people."

"Give it time," Bubbles said. "You'll get better in a flash, you'll see."

"I hope so."

"Hey, don't act so sad," Stephanie said. "I'll never be able to do it. I can't even sense people when I use FSP." She looked forlorn.

Bubbles perked up. "FSP? The dream dust? Where did you get it?"

"From a friend."

"How much did it cost?" he asked. "And where can this friend be found?"

"Bubbles, you don't need to be on FSP," Beatrix cut in. "You know it is only for special ceremonies, and you can't trust the stuff you buy from any old person."

"I was just curious," Bubbles said.

"Curiosity killed the grasshopper. You'd best remember that," Beatrix answered, uncharacteristically serious.

"Thanks for the advice, Mother," Bubbles said sarcastically.

"You little twerp!" Beatrix chased Bubbles around the room. They wrestled in the air as Stephanie and Kelly laughed at them.

"Oh, I should call Dmitri," Kelly said, remembering she needed to set up their study session.

"Can I have his number?" Stephanie asked.

"No. He didn't want me to tell you I was going to tutor him, so do you think he would want me to give you his number?"

"Fine. Don't get all testy. I just thought I'd ask."

Kelly got her cell phone and entered Dmitri's number. He answered on the second ring.

"Hello?"

"Hi, Dmitri, this is Kelly."

"Hi, Kelly. So, when do you want to meet this weekend to study?"

He got right to the point. Kelly appreciated that. She hated small talk. "Are you free Saturday?" she asked.

"Sure, does three o'clock work for you?"

"Yeah, that works. Where do you want to meet?"

"I could come by your place if you want. I would suggest mine but I don't think my little brother would leave us alone," Dmitri said.

"My place is fine," she said. She explained where it was to Dmitri and then they said goodbye. Kelly felt a little tingle as she put down the phone. She explained it away as a shiver.

"Who was that?" Bubbles asked.

"Someone from school. I'm going to help him study for a test."

Bubbles shook his head in bewilderment. "Stupid human school."

Stephanie pouted. "If only I was the one who was good at math."

Kelly grinned. "Well, now you have a reason to brush up."

5

OLD MAN RICKETER

The wall of water crashed into the window. In the pause before the window broke, Kelly felt the anticipation of the cold water running up her nose. The pause seemed like an eternity. Waiting for what was to come was almost worse than the actual experience.

Kelly woke up, coughing uncontrollably again. Cursed FSP. The vision had been in her thoughts several times over the last few days. She lay staring at the ceiling, waiting for the residual feelings of panic from the dream to subside, and for her heartbeat to return to normal. The streetlights shone their light in through the blinds in her window, making it only half-dark in the room. Somehow the indistinct patterns of shadow that outlined the objects in her room were comforting, not scary.

After a few minutes her heartbeat slowed, and the prickling feeling in her chest from imagined water being breathed in went away. But now she felt a new, disturbing sensation. It felt like she was being watched. Was someone trying to sense her location? She lifted the spy ring to her face, hoping to see who it was. She saw nothing. She closed her eyes and attempted to sense who was contacting her, but before she could even tell if she was making progress, the feeling vanished. Whoever had been sensing her had gone. She wondered who it could have been.

~

WHEN KELLY finally made it downstairs the next day, Saturday, it was close to noon. Mindy was in the kitchen, leaning over a recipe for pound cake.

"Mom," Kelly said with a groan. "I thought I told you not to make a fuss when Dmitri comes over."

Mindy winked. "I'm not making a fuss. You two will need something to eat while you study. It's good for your brain."

"Fine. Just, promise not to embarrass me, all right? Don't go pulling out my baby pictures."

"Not to worry. I'll save those for the second time he comes over," Mindy joked.

At exactly three o'clock the doorbell rang. Dmitri wore blue jeans and a dark blue T-shirt that brought out the color of his eyes. His backpack was slung over his right shoulder. He smiled. "Hey, Kelly." He seemed relaxed, more so than at school or in the museum. Maybe it was because Stephanie wasn't there.

"This way." Kelly led him to the living room, where her math book waited on the table. As they sat down on the couch, Mindy appeared in the doorway, wiping her hands on the old-fashioned apron she always liked to wear when baking. Little white patches of flour clung to the apron around her hips.

"You must be Dmitri." Mindy grinned.

"Yes," he answered. Mindy vigorously shook his hand, bouncing it up and down more than four times and squeezing very hard. "So nice to meet you." She finally released his hand. "I'll be in the kitchen. The pound cake is almost ready." She left the room, humming jollily to herself, after bestowing another wide smile on Dmitri.

"Your mother seems nice," Dmitri said.

Kelly noticed he was massaging his hand where Mindy had gripped it so tightly. "I hope you like pound cake," she said.

"Actually, I hate it," Dmitri whispered, glancing furtively towards the kitchen. Kelly laughed, and almost told him not to worry because Bubbles would probably show up at some point and eat it all. Luckily she caught herself just in time. *Weird,* she thought. She had never felt the urge to let something slip about fairies to any of her human friends, besides Stephanie of course. She would have to be careful.

"So, should we get started?" Dmitri asked.

"Sure. Did you do the practice test?"

"Yeah, but I got half of the questions wrong. I don't know why I just don't get this stuff."

"Well, Mr. Patterson isn't really that great of a teacher. He only ever explains things one way. Remember last week when Stephanie asked him to explain multiplying exponents again, and he just repeated word for word exactly how he had explained it before?"

"Exactly! And his explanation was just what the book said already."

"I know. It's ridiculous," Kelly said. "Really, a lot of this stuff is quite simple once it's explained in a different way."

"How did you figure out the other ways to explain it?" Dmitri asked.

"If I don't understand something, I look it up on the internet."

Dmitri tucked his pencil behind his ear. "I'm not really that good with using the internet."

"Really? I've been using it as long as I can remember."

"We didn't even have a computer until two years ago," Dmitri explained, looking down at his hands.

"Well, it doesn't matter. Should we go over the first one you got wrong?"

Kelly was surprised by how fast Dmitri understood the concepts, once she explained them in a different way. She had been expecting him to be slow or something, since he had already failed the class once, but she realized that he just thought in the completely opposite way as Mr. Patterson. He approached the problems from another angle, so with only the book's and Mr. Patterson's uncreative explanations, he didn't have a prayer of understanding them before.

"Wow, I can't believe I never thought of that," Dmitri said with respect to one problem. "You're a lifesaver," he added.

Kelly blushed. "Don't thank me. Thank the internet."

"You're too modest."

"Sounds like things are going well," Mindy said from the doorway. She was holding the pound cake. She brought it over and set it on the side of the table, along with two little plates, forks, and a knife.

"Thanks, Mom," Kelly said.

Mindy stood there, looking at them adoringly.

"Thanks, Mom," Kelly repeated, raising her eyebrows and giving her mother a pointed look.

"Oh, right. Enjoy, and let me know if you need anything to drink," Mindy said, going back to the kitchen. "Will you be staying for dinner?" she asked Dmitri, poking her head back into the room.

"I would love to, but I need to get back before then."

Mindy looked crestfallen, but she tried to camouflage her disappointment with a smile. "Well, you're more than welcome to stay if you change your mind."

Once Mindy was out of earshot, Kelly turned to Dmitri. "Would you like some pound cake?" she asked with a sly grin.

"Yes! Yes! Yes!" Bubbles's voice from over her shoulder made Kelly jump. She did her best to dissimulate. If there wasn't already something called 'dessert senses,' there was now. Bubbles had a knack for showing up just when anything tasty was out of the oven. He hovered over the cake excitedly in his invisible-to-humans form.

"Are you okay?" Dmitri asked.

"Sorry, just a shiver. I got cold for a second, but now I'm fine."

"I don't really want any pound cake," Dmitri whispered.

"Don't worry. I'll sprinkle a few crumbs on your plate so my mom thinks you ate it. Do you want something else though? Like fruit or something?"

"No, thanks."

"Are you going to talk all day, or are you going to cut the cake?" Bubbles said. "You better hurry up before I can't help myself."

Kelly shot the fairy an admonishing look and cut a fat slice of cake. She sprinkled a few crumbs off the side of it onto Dmitri's plate before depositing it on her own plate. She broke off a piece and tasted it, then broke off another little piece and pushed it to the side of the plate. Dmitri looked back at his paper and Bubbles scarfed up the little piece on the side.

"When are you going to be done with this human concentrating?" Bubbles asked. "There's a big game of tag later at the underwater park. You shouldn't miss it."

Kelly shrugged to Bubbles, and he took another big bite of the cake, after glancing at Dmitri to make sure he wasn't looking in their direction. Dmitri wouldn't have been able to see Bubbles, of course, but he would have been able to see part of the cake suddenly disappear.

Bubbles glared at Dmitri. "Why are you wasting time with this human anyway?"

"Did you hear me, Kelly?" Dmitri asked.

"Oh, sorry. I spaced out for a second. What was that?"

"Is the y-intercept three or negative three?"

"Good question. I'm not sure, let me see." Kelly slid the paper over to look at the problem.

"Y-intercept?" Bubbles asked. "What kind of burnt and blistery poppy seed is that?"

"It should be negative three," Kelly said.

"Oh, right, of course." Dmitri's eyes fell to her plate. "Wow, you ate that pound cake really fast! I hardly even noticed you were eating it."

Kelly realized that her plate was now completely empty. Bubbles burped. She chuckled nervously. "Well, I guess you were concentrating so hard on the math problems that you didn't notice."

"I'm still hungry!" Bubbles said.

Kelly cut another fat piece. *Dmitri is going to think I'm such a pig,* she thought. But it was better than trying to deny Bubbles access to the cake. She didn't want him to get feisty and set their study papers on fire.

"I don't think I'll eat any more after this," Kelly said pointedly, looking at Bubbles.

"Oh, we'll see about that," the fairy answered, grabbing a fistful and stuffing it into his mouth.

A few minutes later, as they were nearing the end of the practice test, there was a spectacular clang as Kelly's fork fell to the floor. Dmitri nearly jumped out of his skin.

"Oops," Bubbles said, giggling.

Kelly bent to pick up the fork. "So, what is it that you like about cross-country?" she asked, trying to smooth over the falling fork incident.

Dmitri leaned back and stretched out his arms a bit, wiggling his wrist to relax it after holding his pencil so much. "I like it because it's peaceful. When I am running all of my troubles kind of fade away into the background, and I can just run. I can *be* running. I don't know if that makes any sense," he said, looking a bit self-conscious.

"I haven't experienced it, but I think I sort of know what you mean," Kelly answered.

"Please, just 'be' running?" Bubbles rolled his eyes. "That's ridiculous."

Dmitri looked at his watch. "Well, I guess I should be going. I have to watch my brother. I think I understand the last problem, it's just like the one before it."

"All right. Let me know if you have any more questions before the test. I'd be glad to help."

"Thanks, I really appreciate it. I'm feeling a lot more confident than before." Dmitri packed up his bag and stood up.

"I guess my mom will want to say goodbye," Kelly said. "Mom, Dmitri's leaving!"

Mindy rushed into the room so quickly that Kelly wondered if she had been standing right inside the kitchen door the whole time, eavesdropping on them.

"It was so nice having you over, dear," Mindy said to Dmitri, giving his hand another vigorous handshake.

"Thank you, Mrs. Brennan. And thank you for making the pound cake. It was very thoughtful of you." Dmitri winked at Kelly. Kelly tried not to grin too widely as her mother chuckled good-naturedly in response to Dmitri's words.

"Anytime, anytime," Mindy said.

"See you at school, Kelly," Dmitri said before leaving.

"He's so cute," Mindy said after the door closed. "Just remember, sex kills."

"Mom! That's just uncalled for. He's only a guy from my class. He isn't even really my friend yet, and certainly not my boyfriend! Besides, if he were, that's still just such an inappropriate thing for you to say."

"Sorry. You've never had a guy come over before, that's all."

"And maybe I won't ever have one over here again if you keep saying things like that. Geez. I'm going to my room now."

Kelly stormed up to her room with Bubbles flying after her.

She flung herself down onto her bed. Bubbles plopped down beside her. "What's sex?" he asked.

Kelly rolled over to face him. "You can't be serious. Fairies have sex don't they? How else do they have babies?"

Bubbles's eyes widened in sudden understanding. "Oooh, you mean 'amorous relations.' I always wondered if humans called it the same thing."

"I'm very surprised that you didn't hear it before, considering all the other things you know about humans. And you guys speak the exact same language as we do."

"You mean, as *they* do," Bubbles said.

"Right. That's what I meant." Kelly shifted uncomfortably.

"Anyways, I'm going to go play tag now," he said. "Are you going to come or not?"

When they arrived at the underwater park, Bamblelina, Beatrix, Wimpleton and Pimpleton were already there. So was Stephanie. She rushed over the moment she saw Kelly.

"So?" Stephanie asked.

"So what?"

Stephanie gave her an exasperated look. "How was it today with Dmitri? Did you tell him how cool I am?"

"Oh sorry, um, actually I forgot. You didn't come up in conversation at all."

"What? How could you forget? You weren't too busy flirting with him yourself, were you?" Stephanie asked.

"No, of course not," Kelly answered, perhaps too quickly.

"Well, at least you guys are friends now," Stephanie said. "You need to have a party or something and invite both of us."

"Do you ever stop scheming?" Kelly asked.

"Come on, it's me we're talking about here." Stephanie winked.

"You're it!" Bubbles squealed as he flew by in a blur, tapping Kelly on the shoulder as he blew past. Kelly sprang into the air after him and the conversation with Stephanie was momentarily forgotten.

KELLY SANK into bed that night tired from the game of tag, but feeling less stressed than she had in days. Before she could fall asleep, however, something began to tug on her mind — a temptation. She wondered what Dmitri was doing. She rolled over. *No, I decided not to use the spy ring without a good reason.* She tossed and turned, the urge to look in the ring getting stronger and stronger. Finally, she reached for her bedside lamp. She looked at the spy ring's stone and thought of Dmitri. His image appeared. She had expected to see him at a party or something, because it was a Saturday night. That was what all of the popular guys did on Saturday nights, wasn't it? Instead, Dmitri sat beside his little brother on a couch, apparently watching a children's movie. Dominic laughed as he threw pieces of popcorn at his older brother. Dmitri playfully tossed the popcorn pieces back to Dominic. They were alone in the room. She wondered where Dmitri's mother was.

IT WAS PITCH BLACK; Kelly couldn't make out her surroundings. All she could tell was that she was sitting cross-legged on a stone floor. She sensed another presence in the room, a few feet away from her. It didn't feel threatening; rather, it was old and calm, like an oak tree with deep roots. There was a slight hissing sound, followed by a bright flash, and then a ball of bright flame floated in the air above them. Kelly finally laid eyes on her companion. It was the old fairy from the jail, Ricketer. He sat there, cross-legged before her, still as a

statue, staring at her with his blazing purple eyes. Kelly could only hold their gaze for a few seconds before she had to look away.

The subway came to a halt. It was Kelly's stop. *Strange,* she thought. She had closed her eyes for a moment, so she must have dozed off. Yet, it hadn't felt like a dream. It was too real. Had it been a mental communication? Or a vision of the future? She got off the subway and walked towards the edge of the river where the lion statue entrance to Glendenland sat. She looked around furtively, but luckily no one was around to see her transform into fairy form and touch the lion statue on the nose, or to see when the lion statue opened up its mouth for Kelly to crawl inside.

Venuto was already waiting when Kelly arrived at the secret room in the library. They'd scheduled a makeup lesson, since their last two lessons had been cut short. Venuto looked tired.

"Rough day?" she asked.

"Sorry?"

"You look tired, like you've had a rough day."

Venuto sighed. "Ah yes, we've run into a bit of a snag with Reynalda's party. The peacock feathers we ordered from the Pixelori might not arrive in time."

"Peacock feathers?"

"For decoration. We were going to line the entire circumference of the Great Hall with them for the ceremony, but the Pixelori say they are having trouble finding enough peacocks. Those Pixelori are not very dependable. I never thought we should deal with them, but they are the only band offering large amounts of peacock feathers, and since they're Thomas's mother's favorite bird..." Venuto's voice trailed off.

"I'm sure it will work out," Kelly said, although she didn't think her voice sounded very confident. She was really thinking that it would be nearly impossible to please Reynalda. No matter what they did, no matter how fancy, Thomas's mother would no doubt have complaints.

"Well, enough about that, shall we begin?" Venuto asked.

Kelly nodded.

"Today we can try telepathic communication. Are you ready?"

Kelly grinned. "Definitely."

"Good. First I want you to work on receiving, because that is easier. You've received communications in the past subconsciously. I'm going to reach out to you with my mind, and you should accept the connection, but only partially."

"Okay."

They sat with their backs facing each other, about three feet apart. Kelly looked at the wall across from her and tried to clear her mind. After a moment she felt like she was being watched, and this time she noticed that the feeling also brought with it a sense of Venuto's vibrations, which reminded her of evergreen needles and honey. Kelly accepted the connection. As she did so her vision went black and suddenly she was seeing Venuto from the other side of the room — and she could see herself slumped over on the floor behind him. She had passed out.

Venuto smiled good-naturedly. *You accepted the connection with your entire mind. That's why you fell over. Let's try that again. This time, imagine as if we are talking on a human telephone. Don't try to see me, just imagine that you are picking up the phone, nothing more. Concentrate on being present too, in your body. Pay attention to the feeling of the floor on your legs for example, to keep you rooted in your body.*

The connection was broken by Venuto, and Kelly, now seeing from her own eyes again, sat up. She focused on the feeling of the floor beneath her. This time when she felt the tug on her mind, she followed Venuto's suggestions. At first she thought she hadn't succeeded, but then she felt his presence against her mind, but not inside it; she wasn't reading his thoughts, and he wasn't reading hers. It was more like a channel had been opened between them.

"Good," she heard Venuto's voice inside her mind. It vibrated in her head, feeling almost like the sensation one feels when they themselves say something.

"Wow, I can't believe it worked," Kelly thought, sending the words towards Venuto. *"Will you be able to hear everything I think?"* she asked, a little paranoid.

"No, just what you want me to hear. This is a surface connection, nothing more. Now, would you like to try to initiate the contact?"

This time, Kelly reached out with her mind to feel for Venuto's vibrations. When she had found his location in her mind's eye, she thought: *"Venuto?"* Just as she did so, she felt the probing push of his mind connecting to hers, and again the channel was established. *"Wow, this is really cool!"* she thought.

"Strange, I feel no change in temperature," Venuto answered.

"No, not 'cool' as in 'cold.' It's an expression. Another way of saying that something is neat, or interesting."

"Oh."

After they broke contact, Kelly was reminded of the vision of Ricketer she had experienced on the subway ride. She summarized it for Venuto.

"It didn't seem quite like a dream, you say?" the fairy prince asked.

"No, it was different, but not exactly like a mental connection either."

"Curious. Let's go ask him," Venuto said.

"What?"

"Let's go ask him why he was contacting you."

"I'm not so sure he was really contacting me."

"All the more reason to get to the bottom of things," Venuto said. He was already on his feet and almost at the secret archway. "Aren't you coming?"

"Oh, sure," Kelly mumbled, scrambling to her feet. For some reason the idea of seeing Ricketer again face to face, this time with no cell archway between them, filled her with anxiety. Her heart raced as she followed Venuto down the corridors that led to the jail bubble. Venuto's bodyguard, who had been standing guard outside the room during their lesson, followed at a respectful distance. Kelly wondered why Venuto was so quick to suggest they go see Ricketer.

When the warden saw Kelly, his face contorted into an unmistakable expression of distaste, but after receiving a stern look from Venuto his expression reduced to a surly frown.

"You've come to see Old Ricketer?" he said gruffly, more with the inflection of a statement than a question.

"Correct," Venuto said.

The warden turned and walked down the cellblock without another word. They followed. When they reached the guarded cell, Kelly could see Ricketer inside, sitting cross-legged with his eyes closed. He made no movement as the warden opened the archway.

"Just let me know when you're ready to come out," the warden said after Kelly, Venuto and his bodyguard had stepped into the cell. Then the warden locked the archway and disappeared from view.

"No fifteen-minute limit?" Kelly asked.

"We can stay as long as we need to," Venuto said. He walked up to the bed and stood directly in front of Ricketer. Kelly hung back by the archway.

The old fairy remained in his meditative posture, without any visible indication that he had recognized their entry into the room.

"I have been very patient with you, old man, but you are starting to try my patience," Venuto began in a steely tone that Kelly had never heard from the gentle Venuto. "Why did you contact Kelly?" the prince demanded.

Kelly felt the tendril of a mental invitation from Ricketer, as he continued to sit still on the bed. She had almost instinctively opened her mind to receive the communication when Venuto interrupted. "If you have something to say to her you will say it in front of me," he said.

The old fairy opened his purple eyes calmly and focused them on Venuto. "What I have to say is for her ears alone."

"Then it shall not be heard. Don't try contacting her again. I'll be listening."

"You are overconfident in your sensing powers," Ricketer said with a slight smile.

Venuto's face twisted in frustration. He turned from Ricketer and stormed to the archway. "Come on, Kelly. We're wasting our time here."

Once the warden unlocked the archway for them, Kelly looked over her shoulder to see Ricketer was again meditating serenely. Venuto walked down the hall without saying anything, visibly angry.

"May I ask why he is in prison?" Kelly said. "And why he makes you so mad?"

"He stole something that could be the key to defeating Miasmos, and he refuses to say where it is," Venuto said. "Yet he claims to be a wise man. It infuriates me. The longer the item he stole is out of our hands, the more likely it could fall into Miasmos's. Then we will have little chance of fighting against him if he succeeds in unlocking Embralia's power."

"But, you don't think...I mean, Miasmos won't succeed, will he? Even if he finds the location of Embralia, he could never get the Key from Thomas. Could he?"

Venuto sighed. "Anything is possible. I never thought Miasmos could kill my father. But he did."

They continued down the corridor in silence for a few moments.

"What did Ricketer steal?" Kelly asked.

"I hope you don't mind terribly, Kelly, but I'd rather not say. It is a secret and it should stay that way. If Miasmos does not know of it, then the fewer others who find out about it, the better."

"I wouldn't tell him."

"I know, but if he ever captured you then he could make you."

Kelly shivered at the thought. Venuto was right, she supposed. He had to conceive of all potentialities, even the unlikely ones. But she was curious. What could Ricketer have stolen? And why did the old fairy want to talk to her? Because of her connection to Witherings? Because she was a fadaman? Was Ricketer evil? She didn't know why, but she strongly felt he was not. Yet if he had good intentions, then why wouldn't he trust Venuto?

KELLY GROANED INTERNALLY. It was Thursday, but it felt like a Friday. Why did Mr. Patterson's class have to be so boring? At least it gave Kelly time to practice her fairy senses. As his voice droned on, giving a final review before the next day's test, Kelly tried to feel the different presences of everyone else in the room. The goth boy beside her felt cool and almost 'silvery,' if she had been forced to try and describe the feeling in words. Mr. Patterson was somewhat like molasses, and Dmitri reminded her of pine trees. She felt confident when sensing all of the students inside the room, and whenever a student left the room with a hall pass she tried to follow their vibrations as they walked away down the hall. She still wasn't very good at extending her reach that far, unfortunately. After she'd sensed all the students in the room several times, Kelly had the urge to look at the spy ring, to see what her mother was doing, or what famous people were doing. She just barely managed to resist. It was too risky to use the ring in class.

Still bored, Kelly decided to see if she could make mental

contact with Bubbles from afar. First she mentally envisioned his essence in her mind, trying to remember exactly what it felt like. Then she let her awareness spread outwards. Everything was a bit fuzzy, as she allowed the vibrations she wasn't interested in to sort of blur together. To her utter astonishment, after only a few seconds she thought she could feel Bubbles hovering inside the school cafeteria, near the ice cream machine. She concentrated and mentally thought: *"Bubbles. Bubbles?"* At first nothing happened, but soon she thought she felt a pressure pushing back on her mind. Excited, she didn't remember not to open herself up completely to the connection, and black dots appeared along the edges of her vision and rapidly moved inward. All went black for a second, and then in her mind's eye she was standing beside Bubbles in the school cafeteria.

"You sensed me. You sensed me, that's awesome!" Bubbles said. "But what are you doing over here? You opened your mind up all the way."

"Oh no. I better get back! I'm probably sitting with my head on my desk or something."

"All right. See you later."

Bubbles broke the connection and Kelly's awareness was abruptly back in her classroom. It was worse than she'd expected. Instead of just slouching over onto her desk, she had actually fallen out of her seat. She looked up to see Stephanie's and Dmitri's worried faces, and Mr. Patterson's soon followed. Kelly hastily sat up, amidst the stares and suppressed chuckles of the other students in the class.

"Are you all right?" Dmitri asked.

"I'm fine."

He didn't look too convinced.

"Miss Brennan, I think you should go to the nurse to get checked out,' Mr. Patterson said.

"No, really, I'm fine," Kelly protested.

"I must insist."

Kelly packed her backpack, knowing that arguing at this point would simply make the situation worse.

"Don't you think someone should go with her in case she passes out again on the way there?" Stephanie suggested.

Mr. Patterson considered for a moment. "All right, but you come straight back after you drop her off."

When they got out into the hall, Stephanie asked about what really happened. "Did Witherings contact you again? Or Miasmos?"

"No. I sensed Bubbles and I apparently reached out to him successfully with my mind, but then I put my entire mind into it again."

"Oh. Well, that's good though, right? I mean, the part where you sensed him."

"I guess so. But he was just in the cafeteria, so it wasn't really that far away."

"You have to start somewhere," Stephanie said. "All right, we're here. I hope you drank enough water at lunch so that you can fill the little cup."

"Why would they take my urine?"

"Because they'll probably think you're on drugs or something," Stephanie said.

"Great, that's just the reputation I need."

"It would do you good to lose some of your good girl reputation, if you ask me."

"Have you thought about what you're going to take with you?"

Stephanie asked. They sat in Kelly's room that afternoon, quizzing each other in a last-minute preparation for the next day's test.

"Take with me where?" Kelly asked.

"When you go to find your father."

"I try not to think about it. If I do I get impatient. I still have to wait two months."

"I understand, but you should still think about it a little. You might need to bring some things — things that might take a while to get."

"What do you mean?"

"I don't know. Maybe there are certain items the Ardagali really like or something, hard to get things. If you bring something like that with you as an offering, then they might not attack you. We should ask Blaine for ideas."

Kelly closed her algebra book. "Blaine? Why would we ask him?"

"He knows the Ardagali. He's never been to their kingdom directly, but, they make the key ingredient of FSP."

"How do you know that?"

"Naturally, I wanted to know where the FSP I'm taking comes from."

"I see. Well, I don't want Blaine to know that I'm going there. So it's best not to ask him anything about the Ardagali."

Stephanie suddenly grew very interested in punching numbers into her calculator.

"What is it?" Kelly asked.

"Nothing."

Kelly's eyes narrowed. "You told him already, didn't you?"

"Um, it sort of just slipped out. But I didn't say why you were going there."

"I can't believe this! How could you just let something that important slip?"

Stephanie pursed her lips, trying to figure out what to say.

"And not only that," Kelly continued, "to someone like him?"

"What do you mean, someone like him?" Stephanie glared at her.

"Seriously, Stephanie, he thought it was fun when Witherings almost sucked the life out of me."

"Don't be so quick to judge people." Stephanie crossed her arms. "He's intelligent and funny. And caring."

Kelly stared at her friend, struck by how childish she looked at the moment. Her sour expression was like one a spoiled little kid might wear right before a tantrum. How could Stephanie trust Blaine, of all people? That in itself was a serious lapse of judgment in Kelly's book. Furthermore, Stephanie never should have told him anything without checking with her best friend first. "I think we've studied enough," Kelly said.

"I agree," Stephanie answered, picking up her books. "Don't bother accompanying me to the door. I know my way out."

"Don't worry. I wasn't planning to."

KELLY SAT down at an empty table, on the other side of the cafeteria from where she and Stephanie usually sat. She didn't spot Stephanie anywhere; maybe she had also decided to find a new place to sit on the day after their fight. Kelly looked down at her sloppy joe and her stomach did a little twist. She didn't have much of an appetite.

"Is this seat taken?"

Kelly looked up to see Dmitri standing on the other side of the table. "No, go ahead."

"Thanks." Dmitri sat down. "I see that you aren't sitting with your friend Stephanie today."

"We had a fight."

Dmitri raised his eyebrows in a concerned manner and waited.

"I don't want to talk about it," Kelly said.

"I see. Well, I'm sorry you guys had a fight, but I'm not sorry you aren't sitting together. You guys always seem so deep in conversation that I never want to interrupt. And then there's always the 'not feeling like being stared at by Stephanie while I eat' aspect."

Kelly laughed. "Won't your sports friends miss you?" She inclined her head slightly in the direction of the table where Dmitri usually sat. The sports boys were all laughing and talking amongst themselves as usual.

"Nah," Dmitri said.

"So, are you ready for the test?" Kelly asked.

Dmitri slathered a French fry with ketchup. "I feel good about it, thanks to you."

Kelly hoped she wasn't blushing. She picked up her sloppy joe and attempted to take a neat bite out of it, but in spite of her attempt some of the meat slid down her chin and onto her plate. She quickly brought her napkin up to her face. "Sorry," she mumbled.

"No worries. They're called sloppy joe's for a reason. They're impossible to eat without making a mess, unless of course you eat them with a knife and fork." With those words Dmitri picked up a plastic knife and fork from the side of his tray and cut a little piece off his sloppy joe.

"You eat sloppy joe's with a knife and fork?"

"Sure, and hamburgers sometimes too, if they are really tall with lots of toppings."

"But they're sandwiches."

"So?"

"I just never would have thought of that, I guess," Kelly said. "People eat sandwiches with their hands. It would be strange to eat one with a knife and fork. People might laugh or stare."

"Knives and forks are just tools to make eating easier. Why not use them to eat sandwiches? Who cares what other people think? If they are shallow enough to think less of you for eating a hamburger with a knife and a fork, then they really aren't even worth wasting any thoughts on, don't you think?"

"You have a point," Kelly said, standing up.

"Where are you going?"

"To get myself a knife and fork. I don't want to walk around school the rest of the day with an orange face like a baby who eats spaghetti with its fingers."

"Good point. Although I think the sloppy joe sauce is a bit browner than tomato sauce," Dmitri said in a mock-scientist tone, before placing another small forkful of sloppy joe into his mouth.

WHEN KELLY and Dmitri walked into algebra class together, Stephanie shot Kelly an ice-cold accusing look, before trying to appear unaffected by opening her book and flipping through the chapter the test was on. She didn't look up when Dmitri and Kelly sat down on either side of her.

Mr. Patterson rushed into the room a moment later, just before the bell rang to start class. He carried a thick stack of papers and appeared flustered. He must have just finished copying the tests, Kelly thought. Her thinking was confirmed after they put their books away and Mr. Patterson passed out the tests. Hers was still warm from the copy machine.

"Good luck, Kelly," Dmitri whispered.

"Thanks, you too."

"You too, Stephanie," Dmitri added.

"Hmpf," Stephanie acknowledged, with a tone that could have been interpreted in many ways.

Kelly's pencil had barely touched the paper when she felt the now more easily-identifiable feeling that someone was reaching out to her telepathically. The instant she thought to accept the connection, she realized too late that she hadn't grounded herself in her body by feeling her connection to her chair. Instead she'd reflexively fully opened up again. Her vision blackened before she found herself in a new place.

It was pitch black. She sat cross-legged on a stone floor, aware of another presence in the room, a few feet away from her. It was old and calm, like an oak tree with deep roots. A hissing sound started overhead, and then a bright flame floated in the air above her and her companion. The light danced off of Ricketer's face.

"Thank you for answering my invitation," the old fairy said.

"How come I'm not seeing you in jail? Did you escape?"

Ricketer smiled. "This is a secure mental 'location' that is out of Venuto's sight," he answered. "I thought it better to meet here than in my cell."

"Oh no. I was just about to start my math test. I have to go back!" Kelly said, fearing she'd fallen out of her chair again. She attempted to break the mental connection, but she found an unexpected barrier.

"I must talk with you first."

"Let me go," Kelly said.

"I'm not stopping you. Subconsciously you must want to hear what I have to say."

Kelly wasn't sure she believed that, but looking at Ricketer's calm face, she didn't think arguing would make a difference. The best approach would be to avoid antagonizing him and to just try and keep it quick. Besides, she was curious, she realized. "Why did you contact me?"

The old fairy's purple eyes flickered unnervingly. "When I saw you in the hallway when you came to visit the demented one's son, I knew you had the power."

"The power?"

"The power to unlock the memory stone."

Kelly just stared at him. The memory stone? What was he talking about?

Seeming to sense her confusion, Ricketer explained. "The Gods brought three stones with them from their home beyond the stars. The sister stones. One stone, the key stone, which is commonly known as the Key to Embralia, is the key to the power of the Gods. The second stone, the memory stone, is the store of the Gods' memories. The third stone, is the bearer. You have seen this last stone before."

"I have?"

"Marcos Witherings is its master. I am the master of the memory stone." Ricketer lifted his left pant leg up a bit to reveal a tattoo identical to the one that Kelly had seen on Witherings's leg. Ricketer waved his hand over the tattoo and it transformed into a small stone, just as Witherings's had. But this stone was tinted with a hint of purple instead of blue.

Kelly stared at it, not sure what to make of what was happening. "I don't understand. Why do you say I have 'the power'?"

"The Gods soon realized that their children were not as full of good qualities as they had hoped, and the lesser aspects of their natures like greed and selfishness were still strong, too strong for them to be entrusted with such a great power as that commanded by the key stone. So they locked up the power and hid the key stone deep in the forsaken forest, where it should have remained. But, as you know, King Betardany caused it to be found before it was meant to be found. The Gods had sealed the secrets of their past in the memory stone, and they planned for the key stone to remain hidden until one day when time ripened and their children had matured enough. When that day came, one with the power would open the memory stone, and then they would have instructions on how to use the key stone and the power it commanded for the greater good."

"There's no way we are mature enough to use the key stone's power for good," said Kelly, thinking of Miasmos and of how others would surely rise up to fight for it if such power became available.

Ricketer nodded. "You are right, but there is a great danger now. Our only hope if Miasmos succeeds may be opening the memory stone, and of all the people I have met who may have the power, it lies the strongest in you. When I saw you the stone spoke to me. It recognized you."

Ricketer spoke knowingly. It was clear that he was very wise, and Kelly found herself trusting him. But she found it impossible to believe she had some sort of strong power. "You must be mistaken, my fairy senses aren't very good at all," she said.

"Fairy senses are not the power of which I speak. The power of which I speak is something else, but you would not understand if I attempted to explain."

"I think you should attempt anyway."

Ricketer's only reply was a patient smile.

Kelly sighed. "At least tell me why you are contacting me now."

"I will soon die. I feel my time is coming. I have but a few weeks left. Before I am gone you must come to me alone and take the memory stone."

"I can't come alone. The warden wouldn't let me anywhere near you."

"You will find a way. If you do not, when I am gone it may fall into the wrong hands, as it nearly did sixty years ago when I realized what it was, hidden in the depths of Glendenland's store rooms, forgotten by the Grands, those who were meant to be its guardians — those who had been charged with keeping it safe until time ripened. They had forgotten their duty over the years, and they thought of the stone as a curious trifle, nothing more. The secret would have been lost for good if I had not found the ancient documents in the corner of the library, where the most full accounts of the arrival of the Gods are kept, although even the most full accounts leave much to be inferred."

"Is that why you are in jail?"

"Yes. I took the stone and was accused of theft. But I didn't return it because I knew it would not be safe. And so here I have been, locked up until I reveal where it is. I have not, of course, and so I am here still."

"How could you stand spending so many years in jail? Why didn't you just tell them you had it with you the entire time?"

"Because I knew the risk of it falling into the wrong hands. It *takes little to turn the minds of most, and I felt a premonition that someone would soon arrive more determined than even the evil Venalaz of old was to find the Key to Embralia and unlock its secrets. If he who seeks the key stone finds it, terrible things will come to pass. I sense that you have already glimpsed the killer wave."*

Kelly gasped. "That was real?"

"I'm afraid so. If Miasmos were to get the key stone and also the memory stone, I fear that our chances of defeating him are nothing. The memory stone has all of the ancient knowledge of the Gods inside. Our hopes of defeating him may lie in its depths."

"Do Venuto and Thomas know why you're in jail?"

"They believe that I stole an artifact of great value to Glendenland and would not return it. But they do not know what it is. Although, I do suspect the young Venuto may be getting close to discovering its true purpose."

"Why don't you tell them? They can be trusted."

"Perhaps. But the power does not lie in them. The stone must pass directly only to the one with the power. You must come see me. You must."

With that he was gone and Kelly found herself lying on a stretcher, being rolled down the hallway of the high school by two paramedics.

This is just great, Kelly thought sarcastically. She must have been talking with Ricketer much longer than it had felt like.

"She opened her eyes," the paramedic on her right, a young man with a greasy ponytail said.

"Kelly, can you hear me? Do you know where you are?" The paramedic on her left, a middle-aged yet fit blonde woman with a buzz cut asked her in an overly loud voice.

"Yes, I know where I am. And I'm fine, this is completely unnecessary." Kelly attempted to sit up but realized she was strapped down on the stretcher.

"We're taking you to the hospital to run some tests," the

blonde paramedic replied. "You were out for over fifteen minutes."

Fifteen minutes? She was overcome by a wave of embarrassment. She had passed out yet again in math class, twice in as many days.

"I feel fine, really," Kelly insisted.

The paramedics exchanged knowing looks. *They must think I'm on drugs,* Kelly thought.

"Your teacher said this isn't the first time you've passed out in class," the greasy-haired ponytail paramedic said. "Your heart rate dropped to only 45 beats per minute and you were unresponsive to pain stimulus. You need to get checked out."

The ride got bumpy as the paramedics pushed her over the main entrance of the high-school, then rolled her down the zigzagging wheelchair ramp.

Bubbles appeared over Kelly's head just as the paramedics lifted her into the back of the ambulance. "Kelly! What happened, are you all right?" he asked, concerned.

Buzz Cut went to drive the ambulance and Greasy Ponytail stayed in the back with Kelly. He checked her pulse and made notes on a clipboard.

Kelly carefully reached out her mind to Bubbles. *"I fully accepted a mental connection again in class, so it looked like I passed out. Well, technically I guess I did pass out."*

Bubbles wrinkled his nose. *"I thought you were getting better at controlling that."*

"Apparently not good enough. How come you are here?"

"I sensed when that math boy got all concerned about you, so even though my fairy sense necklace didn't heat up I thought I'd come and check things out."

Dmitri had gotten concerned enough for Bubbles to sense? That was...sweet.

"How many fingers am I holding up?" Greasy Ponytail interrupted.

Bubbles giggled. *"They really hold up their fingers and say that? I thought that was only on the moving picture box. Who was contacting you, anyways?"*

"Three," Kelly answered Greasy Ponytail, attempting not to roll her eyes too obviously at Bubbles. *"Do you know Old Ricketer?"*

Bubbles nodded. *"I've heard of him."*

"It was him. He seems to think I have some sort of power."

"Like fairy senses?"

"No, something else."

"What day is it?" Greasy Ponytail asked.

"Friday." Kelly sighed. Then a perturbing thought struck her. "Did you guys call my mom?"

"Yes. She's going to meet you at the hospital."

Kelly groaned. *"Oh no, what am I going to tell her?"* she thought to Bubbles.

Bubbles shrugged. *"I hope she brings cookies."*

"Who's the president?"

Kelly gave the paramedic a *you've-got-to-be-kidding-me* look.

"Sorry, I have to ask," he said.

"Whatever. John Pontamarino."

"So what kind of power besides fairy senses?" Bubbles asked.

"He said I have the power to open some ancient artifact." Bubbles looked thoroughly puzzled by that. "Listen, could I at least sit up?" Kelly asked Greasy Ponytail. "I don't see why I have to be strapped to this gurney."

"It's best we keep your neck immobilized, just until we can verify you didn't hit it on the way down."

"What ancient artifact?" Bubbles asked.

"He said it was one of the three stones the Gods brought with them. The sister stones."

Bubbles's brow furrowed. *"The only stone like that I've ever heard of is the Key to Embralia, and you'd be hard-pressed to find a fairy who's heard of any more. They do say Old Ricketer's got burnt pollen for brains, you know. He's no spring squirrel."*

Kelly laughed out loud, having just had a ridiculous mental image of a squirrel skipping joyously through a meadow of spring flowers.

"What's so funny?" Greasy Ponytail asked, taking a pause from scribbling notes on his clipboard.

"Nothing, I just remembered something funny my friend said earlier today."

"What was that?"

"He's annoying. And nosy," Bubbles said.

"You don't have to tell me," Kelly replied.

"What did your friend say?" the paramedic repeated.

"She said it to *me*. It was for my ears alone," Kelly answered tersely. Greasy Ponytail's mouth twisted into a tight-lipped frown.

"Wow, you really 'told' him, didn't you?" Bubbles laughed.

"Are you trying to learn human slang?"

"Maybe. How am I doing?"

"Not too bad."

"When did you last eat?" Greasy Ponytail asked.

"At lunch."

"What time was that?"

"Twelve, and I had a sloppy joe with fries. How many more questions are there?"

"Just a couple. Are you on any medications?"

Just a couple questions meant twenty or so. They ranged from how often she exercised, her medical history, and if she used drugs or alcohol. Clear doubt was expressed on his face when she said she didn't use drugs or alcohol, and he said "uh-huh," in that drawn out punctuated way that implies: *yeah, I don't believe that for a second.* When the ambulance finally pulled to a stop outside of the hospital, Kelly felt relieved.

Buzz Cut got out of the front and opened the back doors,

and she and her partner wheeled Kelly into the hospital. Bubbles sat on top of Kelly's stomach for the ride. When they came to a stop in an examination room where her mother was already waiting, Kelly couldn't believe Mindy had beaten the ambulance to the hospital.

"Kelly!" Mindy jumped up from the plastic chair she had been sitting in. Bubbles flew straight to Mindy's purse on the ground, searching inside for sweets.

"Are you all right? How do you feel?" Mindy put her hand on Kelly's forehead.

"I'm fine, Mom."

"I'm getting really worried. You might have stood up too fast last time, when you blacked out for a moment in class, but this time you were unconscious for fifteen minutes!"

Kelly didn't know what to say.

"Are you on drugs?" Mindy asked.

That was quick. "Of course not."

"If you are, I won't judge you. I understand why you might have gotten into them after what you went through this summer. But if you are, you need help."

Kelly bit her tongue. It would have been so much easier if Mindy knew the truth, but if she started talking about fairies her mother would definitely think she was on drugs. Besides, since Mindy's memory of Kelly's father had been erased, Venuto and Thomas said it could cause damage to reveal the existence of fairies without the proper precautions.

"Look, I'm not on drugs, Mom. Like I already told you, this summer was more traumatic for you than it was for me."

Mindy's lower lip trembled like she was about to cry.

"I hate to interrupt this, uh, heart-ful discussion," Bubbles said, *"but there are no sweets. So I'll be going. I'm supposed to meet Bamblelina in about half an hour."*

"Okay, I appreciate you coming to check on me. By the way, have you asked Bamblelina to marry you yet?"

Bubbles blushed. *"No,"* he admitted.

"Well, you should. It isn't going to get any easier, you know."

Bubbles flew out of the room. Mindy still looked like she was about to cry. "Listen, Mom, I don't know what, if anything, is wrong with me, but I feel fine right now. So please don't worry. They are going to do some tests. Whatever it is, they'll get to the bottom of it, okay?"

Mindy sniffled and nodded. Kelly hoped the tests wouldn't be too uncomfortable.

~

THE DOCTORS COULDN'T FIGURE out what had happened, of course, since she was unconscious much longer than people normally are from fainting, and she hadn't exhibited the expected symptoms of a seizure. Therefore, they suggested she see neurologist for a consult in two weeks.

When Mindy and Kelly got home, Mindy made Kelly lie down on the couch in the living room so she could keep an eye on her. Kelly stared at the ceiling, listening to the sounds of her mom bustling around in the kitchen making dinner. Her cell phone rang. Her stomach flip-flopped when she saw the caller ID on the screen. It said Dmitri.

Kelly cleared her throat. "Hello?"

"Hey, Kelly." Dmitri paused as if he was unsure what to say. Kelly didn't know what to say either. "How are you?" he finally asked.

"I'm fine. The doctors said it was nothing serious."

"It didn't seem like nothing serious," Dmitri said.

"They said it was just dehydration. I didn't drink much all day." She felt a wave of guilt at lying to Dmitri. Maybe it was just her general aversion to lying, but she was surprised that she felt almost as guilty lying to him as she did about having to lie to her mom.

"Anyways. How was the test?" she asked.

"Mr. Patterson postponed it until next class, since you caused so much commotion. You're a hero." Kelly could hear the hint of a playful smile in Dmitri's voice.

"So, I'm not a complete laughing stock? I thought they would have come up with a nickname for me already, like Droppy Kelly or something."

"Someone did call you Fallgirl. I think it has a nice ring to it."

"Great." Kelly didn't feel as mortified as she had expected, although going into school on Monday might be a different story. She wondered if Stephanie was worried. Probably. But the anger she felt about Stephanie telling Blaine about her plans to visit the Ardagali was still quite fresh. She didn't feel like talking to her friend yet.

"You still there?" Dmitri asked.

"Sorry, yeah."

"You sure you're okay? You don't need anything?" He sounded really worried.

"Really, Dmitri, I'm fine."

"Okay." There was another long pause. "Well, I guess I was just calling to make sure you were all right."

"Thanks. I appreciate it."

"I'll see you Monday then, I guess," he said.

"Yeah, see you Monday."

Kelly closed her eyes. Her mind swam with the details of the conversation with Ricketer, and with thoughts of the mysterious memory stone. Bubbles didn't know what this power was. Venuto might know, but she couldn't ask him. Dimpleton might know, too, but he was such good friends with Thomas and Venuto that she wasn't sure he would keep the fact she was in communication with Ricketer quiet, and he was still off on a secret assignment anyway. That didn't really leave anyone she could talk to. Unless...no, that was a bad idea. Witherings still couldn't be trusted. But he did have a stone too. Would he know about the power?

She looked down at the spy ring on her finger. Maybe it wouldn't hurt just to see what Witherings was up to. She would only take a quick look. When Witherings's image appeared in the ring, he was sitting in human form in an office with a big glass window. The view that the spy ring had chosen showed him from the front, with his back towards the window. Kelly couldn't quite figure out which view the ring chose and why — sometimes it showed people from the back, other times from the front. Witherings turned something over in his right hand. The picture in the spy ring was of course very small, but Kelly was certain he was examining his stone, the one Ricketer had referred to as 'the bearer.' After a few seconds he started to look up. Kelly hastily covered the ring, hoping he hadn't sensed her presence.

6

PREPARATIONS

"Look who it is. Hiya, Fallgirl!"

Kelly slammed her locker door. "Shut up, Tommy."

Tommy grinned, probably glad she hadn't just ignored him. "As you wish. Auf wiedersehen!"

Kelly rolled her eyes as Tommy pranced off down the hall.

"It looks like you have a secret admirer. Or maybe, not so secret."

Kelly jumped at the sudden voice behind her. She turned around to see Dmitri leaning against the locker next to hers.

"Who, Tommy?"

Dmitri nodded with a spark of amusement in his eyes.

Kelly shrugged. "I don't know. If that's the case he has a weird way of showing it."

Dmitri chuckled. "That's true." Then his expression grew serious. "How are you feeling?"

"I'm fine."

"Are you sure?"

"Yes."

He frowned.

"Really, I'm fine," Kelly insisted. "And you'd better stop asking before you remind me of my mother."

Dmitri laughed. "I bet she's really worried."

"That's putting it mildly. She hovered over me all weekend. I only got to Gle— I mean, I only got away once the entire weekend." She kicked herself internally — she couldn't believe she'd almost just let the name Glendenland slip out. She felt a twinge of guilt for having been so hard on Stephanie for making a similar mistake, but Stephanie really should have been able to stop herself. "Anyways, I should get to homeroom," Kelly added, hoping Dmitri wouldn't inquire as to where she had gotten away to. She started walking down the hall.

Dmitri fell into step beside her. "Are you ready to take the test again?"

"Sure. Are you?"

"I think so. Assuming I didn't forget any of the stuff we went over."

"Don't worry. You'll be fine," Kelly said.

A skinny boy Kelly didn't even recognize passed by them. Over his shoulder he snickered: "Fallgirl."

"Oh, come on. Does everybody in the school know?" Kelly asked.

"Just ignore them," Dmitri said. "They'll get tired of it soon. Unless you pass out again, of course."

Kelly groaned. "Let's not waste any more words on that subject. How's Dominic?"

Dmitri smiled at the mention of his younger brother. "He's fine."

"Did you go to any museums lately?"

"Actually, the other day we went to the Natural History Museum. He really liked the dinosaurs."

"Those were always my favorite, too," Kelly replied. "I liked the ones that moved around like they were alive."

"They didn't scare you?"

"I knew they weren't *really* alive."

"I knew that too, but they scared the heck out of me until I was like, eleven," Dmitri confessed.

"Really?"

"Yep."

Kelly stopped outside of the next doorway. "This is me," she said. "I guess I'll see you later?"

He touched her elbow. "Wait a second. I've been meaning to ask you something."

Her stomach fluttered. "Okay."

"I wanted to know if you, uh...would like to go to the movies with me."

She blinked. Had she heard right?

"Or, we could go to a museum, if you prefer."

Kelly couldn't help but let a completely girlish giggle escape her mouth. "I think I'd prefer a movie."

"How about Friday night?"

"Sounds good," Kelly said.

Dmitri grinned. "Great. I was worried you were going to say no because of your friend."

"We're still fighting." Kelly knew full well that Stephanie would be mad. On the other hand, it wasn't fair for Stephanie to monopolize guys who weren't even interested in her.

"Lucky for me," Dmitri said. "Does that mean you won't be sitting with her at lunch?"

"That's pretty safe to say."

"That's good for me too." He winked. "See you later."

Five minutes into homeroom an announcement came over the PA system. "Kelly Brennan, please report to the principal's office." The smile that had been lingering on her face since seeing Dmitri promptly disappeared. *Uh-oh,* she thought. No doubt the principal wanted to discuss the fact that an ambulance had been called to the school because of her. Her classmates gawked at her as she stood up to leave.

When Kelly reached the outer room of the administrative offices, the secretary seated behind the front desk didn't even look up. She was too busy touching up her makeup with the aid of a handheld mirror.

"Excuse me, I got called on the intercom," Kelly said.

The secretary set the mirror down on her desk and looked Kelly up and down with eyes like a hawk.

Kelly grew uncomfortable under the intense gaze. "Um...the principal wanted to see me?"

"Yes, you're the lucky one, aren't you? He didn't want to hear my opinions, which is just beyond me. He just wants to talk to you, and you're too young to vote!"

"I'm sorry?"

The secretary waved a dismissive hand. "Well, don't just stand there. Go on in."

What's wrong with her? Kelly thought. The secretary was usually cheerful and warm, smiling at everyone she passed in the hallway. *Maybe she's just having a bad day.*

When Kelly put her hand on the doorknob to the principal's office, a strange feeling washed over her. It was like ice on a frozen lake. She shook the feeling off and walked inside. Once she did so, the secretary's demeanor finally made sense. Instead of the balding principal, sitting at the desk was none other than presidential candidate Marcos Witherings.

"Hello, Kelly," he said politely. "Please sit."

"What are you doing here?"

Witherings smirked. "The principal supports my campaign. I told him I needed to talk to some students because I wanted to know what younger audiences think about my candidacy."

"Is that why you're really here?"

A rasping chuckle escaped his lips. "Hardly." He gestured again for her to sit.

She hesitated for a moment, but then she closed the door behind her. If he'd been planning to attack her there were many better ways to go about it. Besides, in human form neither of them could use any magic other than their sensing abilities.

She sat down across from him. "You could have just contacted me telepathically and saved yourself the trip," she said.

He brought a hand to his chest with an exaggerated gasp. "But how would I live with myself if you had been riding a bike? Or heaven forbid, swimming in the river, or maybe—"

"You can stop that now," Kelly snapped. "I get the point."

He smiled, looking quite pleased with himself. "Very well. I like the new nickname, by the way."

Kelly's face flushed with embarrassment. "I don't. So don't even think about using it."

"Fair enough."

"What is it you really want to talk to me about?" Kelly asked.

"I was about to ask you the same thing," he replied.

"What do you mean?"

"I know you were watching me in the spy ring last night."

She looked down at her knees. "I was hoping you hadn't noticed." She was sure her cheeks must be beet red by now.

Witherings let out another rasping chuckle. "I did give you the spy ring, remember? I am at least mildly aware of its properties."

"I guess I should have known better."

"Quite right. But when you were peeking in on me, I sensed you wanted to ask me something. So, here I am."

Well, she *had* wondered if he knew anything about the power Ricketer had mentioned. But Miasmos would surely want to get his hands on the memory stone if he knew about it. "Um, I didn't have anything to ask. I was just curious about how you were doing."

His eyes narrowed. "That was not very convincing, Kelly.

You are concerned that I will tell my father anything you say, aren't you?"

"Can you blame me?"

"I suppose not." He pensively ran his right fingertips back and forth over the knuckles of his left hand. "Would it help if I promised not to tell my father?"

"I hope you won't be offended if I don't take you at your word."

"I see," Witherings said. "We are at an impasse, then?"

Kelly thought about it. Maybe she *could* ask him about the power, as long as she didn't mention the stone. "I suppose it wouldn't hurt to ask you a few general questions."

Witherings waited.

"I was wondering if you might know what powers there are besides fairy senses."

"An interesting question indeed. Why do you ask?"

He was already fishing for more information. She had to be careful. "No reason."

He snorted. "There has to be a reason. Otherwise you wouldn't be asking."

"Fine. Someone might have said that he thought I had such a power, but he said I wouldn't understand if he tried to explain it to me."

Witherings leaned forward almost imperceptibly, but his interest was apparent in the tone of his voice. "By any chance was this power a power over a particular object?"

"No one said anything about an object," Kelly said quickly.

Witherings leaned back in his chair, a smug smirk returning to his face. "Just as I thought. It is an object."

Apparently she was a very bad liar.

"Don't look so shocked, Kelly. I used to interrogate fairy prisoners all the time for my father. I'm quite good at spotting lies, even from those who tell them frequently. And you obviously don't."

Kelly sighed.

"Besides, your question only confirms my suspicions. My father told me I had a power too, a power to discover the purpose of the stone he gave me. I suspect it has something to do with my being a fadaman. Since you are also a fadaman, you might have a similar power. Furthermore, I've heard a rumor that a certain fairy, Old Ricketer, has a strange tattoo. No one else seems to know what that means, but, since I have one just like it, well, it leads me to draw certain conclusions."

"You mean, you already know about the memory stone?" Kelly asked.

"Is that what it's called? I didn't know it by name. I just assumed it must be another stone like mine."

"Yours has a name too." The words slipped out so easily. *Shut up, Kelly!* she thought. Why was she telling him so much? Why did she feel so comfortable sitting in the same room with him? She had to remind herself that his father was still planning to take over the world — and despite the fact that Witherings didn't want her dead anymore, he was still on his father's side.

"Are you going to tell me what my stone's name is?" Witherings asked.

She frowned, considering keeping the name from him. But she'd opened the door by mentioning it. Besides, what harm was there in the name? He already had the stone. Plus, he'd told her about her father. She wouldn't go so far as to say she owed him anything, but perhaps telling him the name of his stone was only fair. "Ricketer called it the bearer," she said finally.

Witherings got a faraway look in his eyes. "Interesting. Very interesting."

After a surprisingly un-awkward silence, Kelly spoke up. "I am confused about something. If you and Miasmos already know Ricketer has a stone like yours, why haven't you tried to get it from him?"

"Assuming I could get into the jail bubble without anyone in Glendenland sensing the disturbance and calling the royal guard, I would never go against Ricketer. Even with my fadaman shielding advantage, it would be too risky. Surely you sensed how powerful he is?"

Kelly considered it. Sure, Ricketer had seemed powerful, she supposed, but not obviously so. As if he was reading her mind, Witherings said: "Power doesn't always feel the same as physical strength or force. The deeper, quieter expanse is the most powerful. Like water behind a dam — still and serene, but ready to rush forward with incredible force."

Kelly nodded in understanding. His explanation had sounded just like something Venuto would have said in one of her lessons. She found it disconcerting, that Witherings had reminded her of her mentor.

"Now, I'm not sure Ricketer is so strong that he could take my father and myself together," Witherings continued, "but, it would still be a risk. As long as the memory stone is with him, and as long as he's in jail, then it stays with him." He hesitated.

She realized he was looking at her with the same strange expression of discomfort he'd had on his face the night he'd escaped the jail bubble. "Is there something you'd like to add?" she prodded.

His eyes glinted icily. "Yes. If my father found out that someone else, like you, for example, had the stone instead, well, it would be quite easy for him to get his hands on it."

Kelly gulped. "Is that a threat?"

"Consider it a word of caution. My father won't go up against Ricketer, but he's not afraid of you."

A shiver ran down Kelly's spine. Witherings suspected that Ricketer wanted to give her the stone. If she took it, would it be worth the risk? Her thoughts were interrupted by the shrill bell signifying the end of homeroom. "I should go," Kelly said.

"Very well."

She headed for the door.

"Kelly?"

She paused, hand on the doorknob. "Yes?"

"Take care of yourself."

He'd sounded sincere, but she couldn't be sure if the look in his eyes was real concern for her wellbeing, or just an imitation of it. She might not be a very good liar, but he was one of the best. "You take care too," she replied, not quite sure if she really meant it.

DMITRI AND KELLY spent most of lunch reviewing for the test. Stephanie glared at them from across the cafeteria. During class, she didn't say a word to them, and the stony silence weighed heavily on Kelly. But she wasn't about to make the first move; even though Stephanie's slip was unintentional, and possibly even understandable, Stephanie still owed her an apology.

When school finally let out for the day, Kelly headed straight for Glendenland. Margretta hadn't blinked an eye when Kelly had asked her over the weekend if she could help out in the medicine storage and creation bubble. She'd told Margretta she was interested in earning a partial glitteron stipend and that she missed learning about fairy medicines. The truth, however, was not so innocent.

The worktables at the front of the bubble were covered with a pale blue powder and dried grasshopper legs. Margretta leaned over a boiling cauldron off to the side, intent on her latest concoction.

A tendril of green smoke reached Kelly's nostrils. She gagged at the acrid smell, which fell somewhere between rotten banana peels and spoiled fish. "What is that?" she asked, taking short and shallow breaths.

"Hello, dear!" Margretta spun around and waved the wooden spoon she was holding in an energetic arc. Chunks of yellowish slime flew off it and spattered against the wall. Margretta laughed heartily. "I can tell by your grimacing that you don't yet appreciate the smell of halcyontonica. Don't worry. It grows on you. I find it most marvelous." She guided some of the vapors to her nose with her hand. She breathed in deeply. "Wondrous."

Kelly doubted that she would ever find this stench pleasant. "What is it?"

"Halcyontonica? It's a very special calming poultice, dear. I'm making it for our dear King's mother."

Why am I not surprised? Kelly thought. "Do you want me to help you with it?"

"If you'd like."

"Maybe...maybe instead you would prefer if I helped you find expired products in the inventory?" Kelly suggested. "Last time I looked at the shelves, I noticed some bottles were past their due dates."

"What a brilliant idea, Kelly. Go on back."

Kelly tried not to look too gleeful as she grabbed a chair and made her way to the back shelves. She didn't want Margretta to get suspicious. Kelly stood on the chair to get a view of the topmost inventory items. Most medicines were stored in dark glass jars and bottles of various sizes, sealed with either wooden corks or twisty metal tops. Every so often, stuffed between the bottles, were brown cloth bags containing dried ingredients. These bags were labeled with yellowing papers tied on with tattered strings.

Kelly picked up the first bottle and wiped away the dust that obscured the label. Margretta's faded script appeared: *Heart of Aye-aye. Willingly donated. Keep away from intense heat.* Kelly grimaced. She was thankful the bottle's glass was too dark for her to see inside. There was no expiration date. She picked up the next bottle. Its label read: *Roly Poly Legs In Vinegar. For energy stimulating tonics. Best if rinsed before use.* Kelly sighed. Due to Margretta's organization, or rather, her lack thereof, it might take weeks for Kelly to find anything useful.

Nearly two hours later, Kelly's shoulders ached, and her tired eyes were finding it hard to decipher Margretta's hand-written labels. Thus, she stared down at the small bottle in her hands for more than a minute before she realized it could be the answer. The label read: *Stun Pellets. For patients who become too violently agitated to be safely controlled by conventional means. Use only from a distance.*

Bingo. Kelly glanced over her shoulder to make sure Margretta was still puttering about in the workspace. Satisfied she wasn't being watched, she popped the cork off the bottle to find dozens of little pearly beads inside. Margretta would never notice if a couple went missing. Kelly hastily poured five of the pellets into her hand and then stuffed them into her pocket. She had only just put the jar back in its place when she heard Margretta's footsteps approaching.

Kelly tried to act normal. She picked up the cloth bag beside the bottle and pretended to read its label.

"How is it going?" Margretta asked.

"Fine."

"Well, you'll have to stop now.'

Kelly's heart skipped a beat. "Why is that?"

"If my senses are correct, you have an appointment."

"I do?"

Before Margretta could give an answer, Milak, towering

head officer of the royal guard, stormed into the bubble. His footsteps pounded as he made his way to their location in the shelves. "You, I've come to fetch you!" he growled, jabbing a finger at Kelly.

Kelly hoped she wasn't visibly shaking. "What for?"

"The king wants a word."

"About what?"

"You ask too many questions." He swirled around and marched back to the work area, where he waited with crossed arms.

"Milak, dear," Margretta said as she joined him in the work area. "Would you take some of this poultice for the Lady Reynalda?"

She calls Milak 'dear'? Kelly thought. *Maybe she should look 'dear' up in the dictionary.* Milak wrinkled his nose at the pouch Margretta extended to him. The lower lid of his good eye twitched.

"I'll take it to her," Kelly offered.

"Thank you, sweet. You are so helpful."

Kelly held the stinking poultice at arms length as she struggled to keep up with Milak's long strides.

When they reached the waiting area just inside the royal quarters, Kelly was struck by how much more elaborately decorated the room was compared to the last time she'd been there. The understated potted plants along the walls had been replaced by intricate vines of blooming blue and purple flowers, and dazzling embroidered pillows with golden threads were stacked so high on the chairs that it would have been difficult to sit down comfortably. No doubt the newfound opulence was Reynalda's doing.

Thomas himself came out to meet them.

"Where's Flimsly?" Kelly asked.

"He's otherwise occupied — my mother," the king said, as

though that explained everything. "Please, join me in my study."

Kelly had never been in Thomas's study before. It was a moderately sized bubble, sparsely furnished with the bare essentials: two wide bookshelves and a big wooden desk, and three chairs. Milak declined to sit in the chair Thomas offered him. Instead he stood off to the side of the desk where he had a good vantage of the door. Ingrained habits of a royal bodyguard, Kelly supposed. As Kelly sat down in the chair Thomas offered her, little plumes of dust rose up from the armrests.

"Sorry about the dust," Thomas said. "I don't actually use this room very much, but to go anywhere more comfortable we would risk running into my mother." He put his head in his hands.

"I'm sorry," Kelly said. "Oh, that reminds me. This is for her."

"Thank you. I'll see that she gets it." Thomas took the pouch and set it on his desk. He straightened up. "I hope you don't think poorly of my mother, Kelly. She can be difficult, but she is still very bitter about having been exiled. I can understand, that, in principle. Yet I realized years ago it does no good to feel bitter."

"I suppose that's easier said than done," Kelly said.

"Wise words, Kelly." Thomas smiled approvingly. "Now, Venuto tells me your lessons are going well."

"He's very generous to say that. I always wonder how he doesn't get impatient with me."

"You have very high expectations of yourself. It can be detrimental to your progress if you worry so much about how you think you should be doing, instead of just accepting how you are actually doing."

"Wise words, your highness."

Thomas chuckled. "Why, thank you."

Milak cleared his throat loudly.

"Forgive our small talk, Milak," Thomas said. "Let me get to the point. Kelly, I want to talk to you about your plan to travel to the Land of the Terrible Ones."

"I hope you're not going to try and talk me out of it."

"No. But I'd prefer you go on the journey in as safe a manner as possible, instead of doing something desperate or reckless due to lack of support. So, I've assigned Milak to travel there with you."

Milak scowled. He looked just about as unhappy about his assignment as Kelly felt. "He isn't busy with his duties?" she asked hopefully.

"His vacation guard will take over when he accompanies you."

"I see. Well, thank you, Milak," she said.

"Hmpf," Milak replied. "Don't thank me until we get there."

"Speaking of getting there," Kelly said. "Do you have any ideas for peace offerings? You know, special things that the Ardagali might like to receive as presents?"

"If I'd known of any trinkets that'd strike their fancy then maybe I'd still have two eyes," Milak said.

Kelly's stomach dropped. "I thought you lost your eye in a meteor shower."

"I did. But the meteor didn't just decide to fall into my eye all by itself. Do you know how unlikely that would be?"

"Virtually zero," Thomas supplied.

Suddenly the endeavor actually seemed dangerous. Up until this point, Kelly had taken comfort in Venuto's hypothesis — that maybe the Ardagali would sense that their blood ran in her veins. But what if he was wrong? Or, what if they didn't care?

"What general items should she bring, in your judgment?" Thomas asked Milak.

"A good dagger wouldn't hurt, fairy dust is a requirement,

and in case we get separated, that ring she has in her pocket could prove useful in the case of an ambush."

The ring? How did he know about the ring? She was trying to decide whether or not she should deny having it when Thomas spoke up.

"Thank you, Milak. That will be all for now."

Milak gave a curt nod to Thomas and strode out of the room without acknowledging Kelly.

"Um, the ring—" Kelly began.

"Yes, the spy ring," Thomas said.

"You know about it?"

"Why yes. Venuto told me."

"He knows about it?"

Thomas chuckled. "Of course. He sensed it the first day you brought it here. After you told him you'd met with Marcos Witherings, he put two and two together as to how you got it."

Kelly felt her cheeks grow hot. The fact that they had known about it and hadn't said anything made her feel like hiding under a rock. "Why didn't Venuto say anything?"

"He thought you would reveal it when you were ready. And it doesn't seem to pose any immediate danger, although I must caution you against using it too frequently."

"Why is that?"

"You might get addicted to it, for one. Secondly, you might start depending on it more than on your fairy senses, which could stunt your progress, and three, with sensing comes responsibility. To artificially enhance your abilities is not a good idea."

Kelly thought about it. Every time she'd used the spy ring, she had felt like using it more.

"Why didn't you tell us about it?" Thomas asked.

"I'm sorry. I just thought...I thought you might take it away from me."

"You see now that you were wrong. We won't take it away, as long as you use it wisely."

"Thanks."

Thomas reached out and gave her right hand a squeeze. "Kelly, I want you to trust us."

"I do."

"I want you to feel like you can tell me anything. Anything at all."

He waited, like he expected her to tell him something. Did he know about Ricketer? Did he know she'd stolen stun pellets from Margretta? "Er...thanks," she mumbled. "I'll keep that in mind."

Thomas seemed satisfied with that reply. "Good," he said. "Oh, and one more thing before you go. Have you told any of your other fairy friends about your trip?"

"Not yet. I'm sure Bubbles will want to come, but I've been waiting to tell him. I'm worried he will insist on following me around twenty four seven to protect me when he hears I found out about the Ardagali from Witherings."

"I'm glad to hear it. Since, it is best you don't tell him at all. You and Milak will make two, which will be less threatening than a larger group of fairies showing up. And you'd best not take Stephanie either."

"Why not?"

"It would not be safe for her. If they found out she was a human I have no doubt that the Ardagali would kill her. Any human that dares stray too close to their territory meets with death. Luckily most of their charms keep human hikers away from their areas. The few who have gotten past them have never been heard from again. That is why it is so strange that your mother had a relationship with one of them. It is most unusual."

Kelly frowned. "If they hate humans so much, why don't they attack human cities?"

"They don't mind humans as long as they can live far removed from them, with no contact whatsoever and with no visible effects. But they might be starting to realize that the humans are damaging the Earth, and I do not know how much longer they will be content to live in the shadows."

"Do you really think they would move against humans?"

"There are some rumors going around." He shrugged. "But then again there always are."

"I hope they are just that. Rumors, I mean."

"Please, don't worry yourself with such things, Kelly. That's for me to worry about, seeing as I'm the king."

He sounded tired. "I see now why Venuto was so happy he didn't have to take the job," Kelly said.

Thomas smiled ruefully. "To use a human expression, being king isn't all it's cracked up to be. Of course it is my duty, and I accept it gladly, but the responsibility does weigh heavily on me sometimes. However...I shouldn't be burdening you with that, either."

"It's all right, Thomas. Everyone needs to get things off their chest sometimes."

"I appreciate that. I suppose I should get back to my duties now. You will be here for my mother's birthday party, on Thursday?"

"Yes."

"Good. I will be away until then. I'm leaving this afternoon to get the last of the peacock feathers from the Pixelori."

"You're going? Isn't that a task for, I don't know, for someone other than the king?"

Thomas laughed good-naturedly. "Usually you would be correct. But it's the only way to ensure they are to my mother's liking."

"Can't you just make a portal and go there? Wouldn't that be faster?"

"Portals, especially temporary ones, can't be made over

such long distances. I can only make them for about 15 miles, at least with my abilities." Thomas stood up. "But no worries. Honestly, I'm quite looking forward to the break. And I do love flying on human planes."

"You go in a human plane?"

He smiled, seeming amused at her surprise. "Yes, most fairies would never dream of it, but I find it fun. And it affords me a great opportunity to study human psychology."

"What can you really learn from watching people sleep and play games on their cell phones?" Kelly asked.

"You'd be surprised."

Kelly followed him back into the waiting room. "I suppose I should say, enjoy your trip," she said.

"Thank you." Thomas turned away to walk back inside his study.

"Oh, Thomas?"

"Yes?"

"Do you have any idea where I might find Blaine?"

Thomas closed his eyes for a second, then opened them. "He's at the underwater park at the moment."

"Thanks."

KELLY EASILY SPOTTED Blaine when she entered the underwater park. He was playing a game of very rough tag with a group of other fairies, a group that of course included Skip. At least Stephanie wasn't there.

Blaine spotted her and signaled a time-out, then swooped down to greet her. Skip was by his side.

"What brings you here, Kelly?" Blaine asked.

"I wanted to ask you something."

"Shoot," Blaine said.

Kelly looked pointedly at Skip, who was standing there

eagerly. Blaine gave an exaggerated nod in understanding. "Skip, why don't you guys keep the game going while I take a little walk with Kelly?"

"What? But..." Then Skip's eyes grew wide like he'd realized something. "Oooh, I see. Sure, no problem." He winked and gave Blaine an energetic slap on the back before he jumped into the air to rejoin the others.

Great, he probably thinks I'm interested in Blaine or something, Kelly thought.

"I'm so glad you came to see me Kelly," Blaine said. "How are you? Stephanie mentioned the other day that you were going to go see the Ardagali. That's wicked. You are fearless."

"That's actually what I've come to ask you about. Stephanie mentioned that you've had some dealings with the Ardagali before."

"Shhh, keep your voice down." Blaine's eyes darted around nervously.

"Illegal dealings, I take it."

"No comment. But yes, I've made the acquaintance of members of the Ardagali before."

"No one else seems to know anything about them, so that makes you somewhat of an expert. What can you tell me about them?"

"I could tell you a couple of things," he said.

"Such as?" Kelly waited.

"I *could* tell you," he repeated, "but you know, with all the cultural differences, such things can be subtle. For instance, you might think you are giving someone a compliment when in fact you are insulting them. So, I could tell you, but, it would be much better if I just came with you."

"What?"

"I've been meaning to go there in person for a long time, just, the opportunity didn't present itself. Now, since you're going, you'll need someone to watch your back."

"Milak is going to be watching my back."

Blaine's eyes widened. "Really? He's going? A high ranking member of the royal guard? Wicked. But, the word is, his past encounter with the Ardagali didn't go very well. You'll still need a cultural guide."

The idea of spending a week with Milak was bad enough. Spending a week with both him and Blaine? While she might be willing to ask Blaine a few questions, having him come along as a guide was several steps outside her comfort zone.

"Can't you just tell me the most important things?" Kelly asked. "Like, if they like certain dishes?"

"Sure. I don't think it would do you much good though, if you can't talk to them."

"That doesn't make any sense. Why wouldn't I be able to talk to them?"

"They don't speak English, Kelly. They speak Ardagali, and there's probably less than ten fairies in their entire band who speak anything else."

"Are you serious?" She couldn't believe it. Her father might not even speak English? Then how could he have spoken with her mother? "Isn't there some way to translate, like with fairy dust?"

Blaine laughed. "Any fairy who invented something like that would be swimming in glitterons."

"I don't believe you. Fairies can do all sorts of incredible feats of magic and you're telling me they can't use their intention to communicate with fairies who speak different languages than they do?"

"I didn't say it was impossible, just, to do that you'd have to be pretty good. Better than you, for sure."

She squared her shoulders and glared at him. "You don't know my powers."

He put his hands up defensively. "Hey, don't get touchy. It would be beyond my powers too."

"I bet it wouldn't be beyond Milak's."

"Perhaps, but a connection like that would require both parties to concentrate on the same goal, which might be a little hard when the other guy is trying to kill you. The Ardagali aren't exactly going to stop and open their minds to you when they are shooting at you with arrows."

Kelly hated to admit it, but he did have a point. After all, Milak had gotten a meteor to the eye. "Fine, I'll consider it," she said.

"Yes. I knew you'd agree!"

"I didn't say that. I said I'd *consider* it."

"Right. Well, don't 'consider' for too long. If something more exciting comes up, then I might not be available."

Something more exciting? Yeah, right. She tried not to roll her eyes too obviously. "Assuming I did say yes, how would you explain to Thomas how you know so much about the Ardagali?"

"Um...I'll just tell him I had a friend from there when I was exiled. It's not so hard to believe. It also happens to be true."

"If you say so." She pulled her underwater breathing mask from her shoulder bag. Blaine flew back to his friends. Looking down on them from the ceiling, Kelly saw that Blaine was getting high-fives from all the other fairies. *Boys,* Kelly thought, shaking her head.

WHEN KELLY GOT HOME she found her mother in the living room, eyes glued to the television set. "What's going on?" Kelly asked.

"It's a debate between Senator Allen and Marcos Witherings," Mindy answered, not taking her eyes off the screen for even a second.

"Isn't it a little early for a debate?"

"The first primaries are in three months," Mindy replied with a shrug. "Oh, I'm keeping some lasagna warm for you in the oven," she added.

"Thanks."

In the kitchen Kelly came across Bubbles. He tugged furiously on the oven door, without success. "Kelly, I'm so glad you're here. I'm starving, but the door is too heavy for me!"

"If you're so hungry, why didn't you just eat in Glendenland? They have great stuff over there all the time."

"Have you ever tasted your mother's lasagna?"

Kelly laughed and retrieved the lasagna from the oven. As she set it down on the counter, she expected Bubbles to rush forward for a taste, but instead he hovered in the air, squinting at her curiously.

"What's bothering you?" he asked.

"Nothing," she said, perhaps too quickly.

"My fairy senses tell me otherwise."

Sometimes she hated how Bubbles had such sharp fairy senses. "Really, it's nothing. I am just a little stressed out because I had a fight with Stephanie."

"Ah. That's a shame. You should make up."

"Maybe after she apologizes."

"Maybe you should apologize first. Sometimes when I fight with Beatrix, I apologize even if it isn't my fault. That makes me the more mature one." He puffed his chest out with pride.

"That's nice, but I don't think I will."

Bubbles sat down on the countertop and sniffed the lasagna. "Why don't you tell me what happened? Then I can advise you if you should say you're sorry or not."

"That's sweet, Bubbles, but I don't want to talk about it." She grabbed a spatula and cut a piece of lasagna for herself. Then she cut a larger piece for bubbles and transferred them both to the same plate. She opened the oven door to put the rest of the lasagna back inside.

"Why are you doing that for?" Bubbles protested.

"I know better than to leave it out. If you ate it all when I watched the debate with my mother, how would I explain that?"

"Mice, of course!"

Kelly laughed. "Nice try, Bubbles. But don't worry, I'll come back for seconds if you're still hungry."

"Thanks, Kelly. You're the best."

When she and Bubbles sat down on the couch, Kelly asked her mother who was winning.

"Shhhh..." Mindy replied.

Bubbles clapped his hands. He hadn't yet tasted his lasagna. Kelly raised an eyebrow and established a mental connection with him. *"I didn't think you'd be so excited to see a human political debate."*

"I don't care about that. I just want to see what that waste of space Witherings is up to. And I can't wait to try and distract him by sending him mental insults."

"Don't distract him like that. Just because you don't like him doesn't mean you should play dirty. And...he's not a waste of space."

Bubbles nearly fell off the sofa. *"Huh? Who are you and what did you do with Kelly? He almost killed you. Twice!"*

"Only the first time was on purpose."

"Hmpf. Like that's an excuse." Bubbles scrunched his eyebrows together and stared at Kelly, perplexed. But when she still hadn't said anything after a moment, he shrugged and dug into the lasagna. *"Yummy!"*

Kelly cut the mental connection with Bubbles and finally focused on the TV screen. The debate looked like it had been arranged to resemble a pleasant encounter; instead of facing off behind podiums, Witherings and his opponent were seated side by side at a shiny, black oval table across from the moderator, a man who seemed capable of only one facial expression, likely due to an overuse of botox. Witherings looked very dignified in a dark blue suit with a red tie. His opponent, Senator Allen, was dressed in a similar fashion, but his suit jacket was too tight. Kelly felt a sense of relief as the senator stuttered his way through an awkward response to the moderator's latest question. *What's wrong with me?* she thought. *Even though I don't hate Witherings anymore, I don't want him to win. Not if he's still helping his father.*

Now it was Witherings's turn to answer the question that had posed such a problem for the senator. "Mr. Witherings, what do you think the American people are looking for?"

Witherings flashed a disarming smile. "Well, James, as a nation we are facing challenges that generations before us never faced. The war on terror, the economy, and above all, the peril our planet faces from increasing pollution and environmental devastation. What America needs is a shepherd, a guide who is firm and steadfast in his ideals. It won't be easy; difficult choices and sacrifices will have to be made. That is why I ask the American people to put their faith in me."

A shepherd? Kelly thought. How arrogant. But her mother was eating it up. Mindy stared adoringly at the vision of Marcos Witherings on the television. Judging from her mother's reaction, Kelly thought there was a very high possibility Witherings would win the democratic nomination. Of course, there were always the republicans and the independents to oppose him, but Kelly doubted whoever went up against the fadaman would be able to hold their own, no matter what their political affiliation. Witherings was only thirty-six years old, he had never held any public office, and yet people were flocking to him in droves.

Bubbles burped. Kelly looked down at her plate to see that both pieces of lasagna had disappeared, and Bubbles had licked the plate so clean that it looked like it had come fresh out of the dishwasher. Luckily Mindy was too absorbed in the debate to notice Kelly hadn't taken one bite herself. "I'm bored," Bubbles complained. "Can we talk about something?"

Kelly established a new mental connection with Bubbles. *"What do you want to talk about?"*

"Maybe your secret."

"I don't have a secret."

"Fine then, be that way." Bubbles crossed his arms and pouted.

Her chest tightened. It hurt to lie to him, but Thomas had been very clear about the dangers of bringing too many fairies along to see the Ardagali. *"Have you asked Bamblelina to marry you yet?"* she asked, hoping to change the subject.

"No," Bubbles said, looking down at the empty plate that had held their lasagna. Then he patted his large stomach. *"I wanted to go on a diet first, so that I was in good form."*

Bubbles? On a diet? She stifled a chuckle. *"Bamblelina already likes you just how you are. Are you sure you aren't just putting it off because you're nervous?"*

"No way. I want to be healthy and dapper for her. That's why I'm on a diet."

"But Bubbles, you just ate more than half your body weight in lasagna."

"Yes, but I'm only having one dinner."

"What?"

"Usually when I eat at your place, I still go eat again at the mess hall, and then sometimes also at home, if Beatrix cooks something."

"I see. Well, with only one dinner instead of three, I'm sure you'll be 'dapper' in no time, then."

Bubbles grinned, not having picked up on the touch of incredulity in her statement. *"You're a good friend to say that, Kelly. I hope you're right. Now, how about some dessert? I'm only having one of those too, so, let's make it count."*

Mr. Patterson didn't grade their tests until Thursday. Not only that, he refused to hand them out until the very end of class.

When Dmitri finally got his test paper, his eyes lit up. "I got a 92!"

"That's great," Kelly said. "I knew you'd do well."

Stephanie rolled her eyes.

"How about you, Stephanie?" Dmitri asked.

She shrugged. "Like you care."

Dmitri raised an eyebrow. "That bad, huh?"

The bell rang, and Stephanie rushed from the room. Kelly shot an apologetic look at Dmitri and ran out after her friend.

She caught up to Stephanie outside the doorway.

"Stephanie, can we at least talk about this?"

Stephanie kept walking, ignoring Kelly.

"Listen, it's been almost a week now," Kelly said. "Are we going to stay mad at each other forever?"

Stephanie walked faster. "Maybe."

"Is that what you want?"

"Maybe."

"Gosh, Stephanie, you're so difficult. Listen, I forgive you for telling Blaine. Are you happy now?"

Stephanie moved to the side of the wall and came to a stop. She glared at Kelly. "You're so full of it."

"What's that supposed to mean?"

"Blaine just told me you asked him to come with you!"

"He what? That's not what happened at all."

"Yeah right. It's not enough that you're trying to steal Dmitri, now you want Blaine too?"

"That's ridiculous. I don't like Blaine. And I'm not stealing anyone. I only agreed to go out with Dmitri tomorrow once it was blatantly obvious he didn't like you. It's not fair for you to 'claim' him when he doesn't like you."

Stephanie brought a hand up to her face like she'd been slapped. "He asked you out?"

Kelly nodded.

For a second Stephanie looked like she might cry. Then she just let out a bitter laugh. "Figures. Of course he's interested in you. You're the special one."

"That's not true. You're special too."

"Whatever. I have to get to class. I hope you and Dmitri are happy together."

7

OF PEACOCK FEATHERS
AND MISSING KINGS

"Come on, Bubbles, give me a hint," Kelly protested as she followed her fairy friend down the hallway leading to his living quarters.

"Nope. Just wait and you'll see!"

After school, Bubbles had appeared on the metro demanding Kelly come over to his place before Reynalda's birthday celebration. When she'd asked him what was so important, he would only say cryptically that he and Beatrix had a surprise for her.

"This had better be good, Bubbles. I was hoping to change into something nicer before the party."

Bubbles swirled around and looked her up and down. "Don't worry. You look nice." He continued down the hall.

"Are you sure?" she asked.

"Of course. Besides, you can borrow a dress from Beatrix if you must."

After a few more minutes of walking, Bubbles paused dramatically at the shadow archway leading to his home. He placed his hand up to the wall and the soft series of unlocking chimes reached their ears. "Are you ready?"

growing sense of uneasiness in the pit of her stomach. Dimpleton had looked very upset when Venuto had summoned him. She had a very bad feeling that whatever Venuto needed Dimpleton for, it was almost certainly much more than *nothing*.

~

NEARLY AN HOUR LATER, after an appetizer of Beatrix's soup, Kelly, Beatrix, and Bubbles made their way to the Great Hall. When they arrived it was already jam-packed with expectant revelers. The new arrivals stopped short just inside the entrance to take in the impressive decorations. The entire interior surface of the gigantic bubble had been painted with intricate floral patterns in shimmering, metallic colors. The backs of all the chairs had been draped with lace. The speaking podium was a site to behold: a delicate layer of moss covered the floor, and the most beautiful miniature blue flowers were arranged around the borders.

Bubbles let out a low whistle. "They certainly spared no expense."

Kelly nodded in agreement, but she noticed one key element was missing. "Where are the peacock feathers?"

"What peacock feathers?" Beatrix asked.

"The ones Thomas went to fetch himself from the Pixelori."

"Maybe they weren't to his mother's liking," Beatrix said. "look, there's Bamblelina!" They flew over to Bubbles's friend, who was seated in one of the middle rows on the side of the Great Hall. Bamblelina told Bubbles he like he was losing weight. He beamed and planted a big her cheek. Once they were settled into their seats, otted Stephanie in the very first row, directly in front eaking platform. And she was sitting right next to

Kelly rolled her eyes and brushed past him. She had barely made it through the wall membrane when she felt a pair of skinny but strong arms hoist her up into the air. Dimpleton laughed as he swung her around in a big circle. "Kelly! It's so good to see you."

"You too. But I'm getting dizzy."

"Sorry." He put her down. Kelly blinked, waiting for the room to stop spinning.

"Do you like the surprise?" Beatrix asked from the counter where she was chopping some vegetables so fast that her hands blurred.

"Of course," Kelly said. "When did you get back, Dimpleton?"

"Oh, just a few hours ago." Dimpleton sat down cross-legged on the couch. He patted the cushion to his left.

Kelly joined him. "And what were you doing when you were away?"

Dimpleton fiddled with his shirt collar. "You know, diplomatic things. If I told you, it would only bore you."

"I doubt that," Kelly said.

Dimpleton raised an eyebrow.

"She thinks you're a spy," Bubbles said. He tried to grab a chunk of carrot off the counter beside his sister.

Beatrix batted his hand away. "Hands off, that's for my soup!"

"Then why can't I eat some now? I'm going to eat the soup later, so what's the difference? It all ends up in my belly either way."

"Is that so? Then would you rather just eat all the raw vegetables, and have no soup?"

Bubbles puffed his cheeks out like he was actually having a hard time making up his mind.

Beatrix sighed. "You're ridiculous." She placed a fistful of carrot chunks into her brother's hands. "Now go over there with the others and get out of my way, or I'll make you cook all our soup from now on."

"But you like cooking."

"Only when you don't pester me."

"Fine then." Bubbles crossed the room and plopped himself down on the couch beside Kelly and Dimpleton. "Carrot?" He extended his arms to offer them some.

"No, thanks," Kelly said. She leaned towards Dimpleton conspiratorially. "So these 'diplomatic things,' that *is* just code for being a spy, isn't it?"

Dimpleton smiled mischievously. "I can neither confirm nor deny that."

Bubbles almost dropped his carrots. "We knew it. That's so exciting."

Dimpleton feigned ignorance with an exaggerated shrug. "I don't know what you're talking about."

"For a spy, you're surprisingly transparent," Kelly said.

"I never said I was a spy," Dimpleton replied. But his eyes were twinkling. "Now, I want to hear all about you, Kelly. How have you been?"

Bubbles tapped Kelly on the knee. "That's called misdirection," he said. "How Dimpleton just changed the subject like that. Smooth. Spies are masters of misdirection."

"No," Beatrix called out, "it's called deflection."

Bubbles shook his head. "I don't think so. See, first there was the original direction the conversation was going in, and then he took it off course. He *mis*-directed it."

"Nope. He deflected it."

"You want to bet?" Bubbles challenged, jumping to his feet.

"I don't need to bet," Beatrix replied. She dumped all the freshly chopped vegetables into a pot on the stove. "I know I'm right. If you don't believe me, that's your problem."

"You know what I think? I think you're scared to bet!"

His sister ignored him.

Kelly couldn't help but chuckle at Bubbles's stubbornness. "Sit down, Bubbles," she said.

He sat down with a huff and chomped on his dwindling stash of carrots.

"Where's Stephanie?" Dimpleton asked.

"I invited her," Beatrix answered, "but she said she had other plans before the party."

"Hmpf," Kelly snorted.

Dimpleton raised an eyebrow.

"Stephanie and Kelly had a fight," Bubbles explained.

"I see." Dimpleton put a hand on Kelly's shoulder. "Don't worry, I'm sure you two will work it out."

"I thought so, but now I'm not so sure. Usually we don't stay mad at each other for very long before it blows over. But today I tried apologizing, and she didn't accept."

"Don't worry," Dimpleton said. "Just give it ti—" abrupt his voice dropped off, and he got a vacant look in his eyes.

"Dimpleton?" Kelly asked, concerned. She shook his s der, but he just stared into space.

After a few seconds he snapped back to attention must go. Venuto needs me." He sprang to his feet.

"What is it?"

"Hopefully, nothing."

Kelly could tell he was trying to be nor couldn't completely disguise the worry in hi out of the quarters without uttering anothe

"What do you think that was all about

"I bet it was some last minute dem da," Bubbles said. "I heard she made her hair six different times today. He

"I heard it was *sixteen* times," B

Bubbles's eyes widened like

While the siblings conti ridiculous demands to Lady

Bubbles's eyes followed Kelly's gaze to the pair. "It looks like Stephanie has a new friend," he said.

"Perhaps more than a friend," Bamblelina chimed in.

Kelly's jaw dropped when she saw what had prompted Bamblelina's comment. Blaine had just put his arm around Stephanie, and they were kissing on the lips!

Luckily, she didn't have to suffer through Stephanie and Blaine's unseemly display of public affection for too long. Flimsly and his entourage of musicians marched out onto the platform. The crowd fell silent and leaned forward in anticipation.

The blaring fanfare of the horns went on twice as long as usual. Flimsly's face turned almost as red as his jacket from using so much breath. By the time he brought his instrument down to his side, beads of sweat glistened across his forehead. He cleared his throat. "Please stand for our queen, her Grace the intelligent and fair Carmina Penadas; and esteemed head advisor, our prince, the brave and honest Venuto Grand."

The audience rose to their feet as Carmina and Venuto entered and took their places. Neither of them was smiling.

"And now, please give a warm welcome to our king's mother, the wise, kind, and magnificent Reynalda Penadas."

The audience clapped as Reynalda glided onto the stage, nose held high up in the air. Kelly stifled a laugh at Reynalda's over-the-top costume. Her golden dress had a huge collar like the collars on Queen Elizabeth the First's dresses in history books. The dress's skirt was a multi-tiered hoopskirt with bright pink tutu-like embellishments. As if those fashion statements weren't enough, Reynalda also wore a wide diamond-lined blue sash around her waist, and her hair was arranged in a towering beehive with six giant blue bows matching the sash pinned down the front, one on top of the other.

Reynalda stood center stage and raised her hands. The crowd's applause died down. "Please, take your seats,"

Reynalda said. "Thank you. Now, usually at this point my son would give a speech in my honor, but as you can see, he is running late," she paused to send a harsh glare at Carmina and Venuto, as if Thomas's absence were their fault. Kelly shared a worried look with Bubbles. Was Thomas in some kind of trouble? "So," Reynalda continued, "the speech will have to take place later when my son deigns to grace us with his presence. In the meantime, please enjoy the feast in the mess hall." With that, Reynalda stormed off the stage.

Carmina and Venuto quickly followed.

The audience just sat there, unsure of what to make of the scene. Flimsly cleared his throat. "No need to be alarmed, folks. Everything is fine. Please don't let the food get cold." He hastily vacated the stage before anyone had a chance to ask him any questions.

"This is not good," Bubbles whispered. Uncharacteristically, he made no move to join the majority of the fairies, who, apparently reassured by Flimly's words, eagerly headed for the mess hall.

"Do you think something's happened to Thomas?" Kelly asked.

"I really hope not," Bubbles said. "But he'd never be late for his mother's party if something very important weren't demanding his immediate attention. And that's what worries me."

"Do you think there could have been an attack by Miasmonians?" Kelly whispered.

Bamblelina interrupted with a tug on Bubbles's arm. "Come on, don't you want to join the feast? Let's go."

"All right, all right. I'm coming."

Kelly was just about to follow after her friends when she felt a prickling on the back of her neck, like she was being watched. Along with the sensation came the thought of an oak tree with deep roots. *Ricketer.* He was contacting her telepathically. She gripped the armrests of her chair and hoped she wouldn't accidentally open her mind all the way again when she accepted the connection.

"Hello?"

"*Hello, Kelly. It is good to see you're getting better at mind-to-mind communication,*" Ricketer's voice replied in her mind.

"*Why are you contacting me?*"

"*I wanted to tell you that at this very moment the warden is sleeping at his post.*"

Kelly looked around nervously even though she knew that none of the nearby fairies could possibly be eavesdropping on her mental conversation. "*You can't seriously expect me to break into the jail bubble right now, can you?*"

"*I'm not going to live forever, you know,*" Ricketer replied. "*I need to give you the stone. And now would be the perfect time. Everyone is preoccupied with the feast, Venuto is so busy he won't notice, and you have those stun pellets with you, don't you? They will work quite well on the guards outside my cell.*"

Kelly's hand hovered over the pocket containing the pearl-like beads. "*How do you know about the stun pellets?*"

"*I see many things.*"

"*Do you have any idea how creepy that is?*"

Ricketer's laughter created a tickling sensation inside Kelly's head. "*I have been told as much on several occasions. But the rumors of my creepiness are much exaggerated. Now, you'd best hurry up then before the warden wakes up.*"

"*I don't know about this. Something is going on with Thomas. Maybe I should stay here and try to find out what is happening.*"

"*Oh, I know all about that. Come here and I'll tell you.*"

She believed him without a doubt. After all, he could tell she had stun pellets in her pocket all the way from his cell. "*I'll be right there.*"

Kelly didn't cross paths with a single fairy on the way to the jail complex. Reynalda's feast did indeed provide the perfect distraction. Also, Ricketer's directions every few minutes to wait in one place for a second or to move down an alternate hallway didn't hurt. Kelly couldn't believe the detail of the old fairy's sensing abilities. Before passing through the archway to the jail, Kelly retrieved the stun pellets from her pocket and held them in her left palm for easy access.

She tiptoed through the archway. Slumped down in his chair, snoring loudly, was the warden. She took a cautious step forward. Then another. And another. He didn't stir.

"Very good so far, Kelly," Ricketer said once she'd passed the warden. "Now, keep on walking until I tell you to stop."

Kelly moved forward, trying to walk softly. As she neared the bend in the hallway right before Ricketer's cell, she heard the guards talking.

"Too bad I couldn't get off duty tonight," one of the guards said. "I really wanted to attend the party."

"Don't worry," the other guard replied. "We're getting a bonus for taking this shift, remember?"

"But now that we're actually here, the ten extra glitterons don't seem worth missing all the fun."

"Stop your whining."

"Ha, sounds like you're in a bad mood too."

"Why did you stop?" Ricketer asked.

"Sorry, I heard the guards' voices."

"Don't worry. Go two more steps, and then toss a couple stun pellets around the corner. Easy as pie."

"For you maybe. You're not the one who actually has to throw them." Kelly inched forward two steps and then stopped.

"Hey, did you hear something?" the most discontented guard asked.

"Nope."

"I'm going to check it out."

Kelly's hand shook.

"Now would be a good time to toss the pellets. Throw them, now!"

Kelly chucked the first pellet around the corner. There was a thud as the first guard fell to the ground.

"What the blistering poppy see—" the second guard's sentence was interrupted by the next stun pellet.

Kelly came around the bend and saw the two guards splayed out on the ground, right in front of the transparent archway to Ricketer's cell. Inside, Ricketer sat cross-legged on his bed, eyes closed.

"Nice work. Now, put one of their hands up against the archway so it unlocks."

Kelly tentatively poked one of the guards in the shoulder with an index finger. When he didn't budge, she put the three remaining stun pellets away and grabbed hold of the guard's arm. She pressed it against the archway and the unlocking chimes pealed loudly.

"Is the warden still sleeping?" she asked Ricketer.

"Like a baby."

Kelly entered the cell.

Ricketer opened his eyes and smiled. "Great job."

"It was—"

"Fun?" he asked, eyes glittering.

"I was going to say it was easier than I expected."

Ricketer gave a sage nod. "Most things we're afraid of usually are."

"How long will the guards be unconscious?" Kelly asked.

"Three minutes or so."

Kelly gasped. "It's already been at least a minute! Hurry up and give me the stone so I can get out of here in time."

"Don't worry. Now that you're right next to me, I can make it so they don't notice you."

"You mean...you'll make me invisible?"

Ricketer laughed. "No, they just won't see you."

"If you're so powerful, why are you still stuck in here, exactly? Couldn't you just break yourself out?"

"Not when I first got here, I couldn't. Over time I've reached a high enough stage that I suppose I could escape if I wanted to. But I like it here."

Kelly's reply was a quizzical look.

"I can see how it would be hard for a young person like you to understand. For me, it's very quiet, I get all my meals delivered to me, and I can meditate as much as I want. It's a peaceful existence. Besides, now the point is moot, since I only have a few weeks left on this Earth at most."

He uttered those last words without a trace of sadness. "Aren't you afraid to die?" she asked.

"No."

"How is that possible?"

He chuckled. "Ah, that's another point difficult for someone your age to understand. My time is coming no matter if I'm afraid or not. So, why be afraid?"

Kelly frowned. He talked about fear like it was a rational choice, not an emotion.

"Well, since I don't have long to live we'd best not waste any more time." Ricketer winked. He held his hand over his tattoo. The 'ink' rose out towards his palm in a swirl of smoke before solidifying into the dark purple stone. The old fairy extended it out to her.

But Kelly's attention was drawn to the archway, where the guards were coming to their senses. One of them leapt to his feet and poked his head into the cell. Kelly held her breath. They were about to find out if Ricketer's concealment spell was working.

"Oldtimer," the guard began, "have you noticed anything strange?"

Ricketer raised an eyebrow in amusement. "You mean

anything stranger than you and your colleague falling asleep on the job?"

"Er...we didn't fall asleep. Something weird happened. We just, passed out. Something must have caused it."

"If you say so, lad. But do you want to know my theory?"

The guard shrugged. "Sure, Oldtimer. Let's hear it."

"My theory is that you and your partner drank too much nectala."

"Balderdash. We don't drink on the job."

Ricketer's eyes narrowed. "You *did* drink on the job, just this once. In honor of Reynalda's birthday."

The guard nodded dumbly. "You're right. We did. Let's just keep this between us, all right? Don't tell the warden."

"Not to worry, lad. Your secret is safe with me."

The guard retook his position outside the cell. The other guard also now stood at his original post, as if nothing had happened.

"Did you just brainwash him into thinking he got drunk on the job?" Kelly asked.

"Tsk. Brainwashing is such a loaded term. Let's just say we don't need to worry about him or his friend asking any more questions. Now, take the memory stone. It's yours now."

Ricketer placed the stone on her outstretched palm. It was much heavier than she'd anticipated, and she brought up her other hand for added support.

"Don't just stare at it, put it in its place." He gestured towards her ankles.

"Can I put it on my stomach instead?"

"Why would you want to put it there?"

"So my mom won't see it if I wear shorts and sandals."

"Suit yourself."

Kelly lifted the front of her shirt a few inches to expose her belly button. She took a deep breath and brought the stone close to her skin. Nothing happened. "It's not working."

"Just give it a minute. It has to adjust to you."

He was right, of course. A few seconds later the stone trembled and dissolved into the swirling mist. As the mist contacted her skin, it tingled. Kelly watched in awe as the abstract bird shape formed on her skin. For some reason it was much more impressive when it was happening to her than when she'd seen the exact same process on both Ricketer and Witherings.

Ricketer nodded his approval. "Just as I predicted. It likes you."

"The stone has feelings?"

"In a manner of speaking. You must take it out often and build your relationship with it, so that one day it will reveal its secrets to you."

Build a relationship with it? Kelly was starting to wonder if Ricketer was losing his mind. "How am I supposed to build a relationship with an inanimate object?"

"You try and connect to it. Try to get it to open up to you. If I knew exactly how to do that, I would have done it myself. But I know you will be able to do it. You have the power. More than the young Venuto, and more than Thomas too. I'm not entirely sure which one of them has more than the other, they are pretty evenly matched I think—"

"That's all very interesting, but, I'd really like to know what is going on with Thomas. You said you know?"

Ricketer's expression grew solemn. "I'm afraid it's not good news. The king is missing. He hasn't been sensible for several hours. Even I can't tell where he is."

A knot formed in Kelly's chest. "Does that mean...is he dead?"

"Not necessarily. But if he's alive then he's either using his fairy senses to conceal himself, or he is being concealed. The latter is more likely, given the fact he hasn't responded to any of his wife's or Venuto's repeated attempts to contact him."

Kelly felt a chill sweep over her. There might be many

fairies out there with nefarious agendas, but as far as fairies who would want to capture Thomas, one name was at the top of the list: Miasmos. Kelly shuddered to think of what Miasmos might be doing to Thomas, if the evil fairy was responsible.

"You'd best be going now," Ricketer said. "Before your friends miss you."

She eyed the guards in the hallway. "It's a good thing I still have some stun pellets left."

"No need for those," Ricketer said. "Use the ceiling."

"What? The warden said the ceiling was non-pervious."

"Not at the moment, it isn't."

"You're incredible," Kelly said. "I hope my powers will be as good as yours when I get to be your age."

"If you work hard, it might only take you thirty years."

"I guess I'll have something to look forward to on my forty-forth birthday, then." She pulled out her underwater breathing mask and put it on.

"One more thing, Kelly."

"What's that?"

"Remember, don't tell anyone you have the memory stone. If you do, you will attract evil forces."

Kelly thought back to Witherings's warning. *If my father found out that someone else, like you, for example, had the stone instead, well, it would be quite easy for him to get his hands on it.* "I don't intend to tell anyone."

Ricketer closed his eyes and retook his meditative posture. *"Goodbye, Kelly."*

"Goodbye." When she entered the water, she realized that she would probably never see the old fairy again. Even though she'd barely gotten to know him, the thought made her sad. She would miss him.

8

SUSPICIONS

Kelly was swimming back to the mess hall when she felt the sensation of somebody trying to contact her mentally. Again this time, along with the feeling of being watched came a faint impression of the source fairy's vibrations: a subtle hint of evergreen needles and honey. *Venuto.* Kelly didn't want to keep the prince waiting, but while she was getting much better at accepting telepathic connections, she didn't dare risk it while swimming underwater. She didn't trust her underwater breathing mask to stay in place that much. Instead she quickly descended to the nearest bubble, a transport bubble not far from the jail complex. All the while the sensation grew, as Venuto tried harder to get her attention.

By the time Kelly set down inside the transport bubble, it felt like Venuto was pounding on the inside of her head with a hammer. She pressed a hand against the podium in the center of the room to root herself to her physical surroundings. Then she accepted the connection.

"Finally," Venuto's exasperated mental voice said. *"Why were you ignoring me?"*

"I'm sorry. I wasn't ignoring you. I just had to find a safe place."

"The water is as safe a place as any."

Her heart fluttered. Of course he would have been able to sense her location. Good thing he hadn't chosen to contact her a few minutes earlier, when she would have still been in the jail bubble with Ricketer. *"It didn't feel as safe to me."*

"Well, never mind that," Venuto replied. *"We need you at the royal quarters at once. Bring the spy ring."*

When Kelly reached the royal quarters, Flimsly quickly ushered her back to Venuto's study, which looked very much like Thomas's except for it wasn't as dusty. Inside, Carmina and Venuto sat behind the wooden desk, examining maps. Milak stood across from them, glowering with his one good eye.

Venuto looked up. "Kelly, we have some disturbing news. Thomas and his bodyguards never came back from their trip to obtain the peacock feathers."

"I had gathered as much," Kelly said. Venuto raised an eyebrow. "I think most everyone else in Glendenland did, too," she added.

"That's why I suggested we cancel the ceremony," Milak said. He sent a pointed *I-told-you-so* look to the prince.

"Yes, you've made that abundantly clear, Milak. But as you know Reynalda insisted she go before the crowd."

"Hmpf," Milak scoffed. "You speak as though she's the one in charge around here."

Venuto sighed. "She's in denial. She's convinced Thomas is just running late. I thought it would be unkind to force the issue."

"Who cares about Reynalda?" Carmina shouted suddenly. "I can't sense my husband!" Tears welled up in her eyes. "I can always sense him. No matter how far away he is."

Venuto and Milak stared at the queen, uncertain of what to do. Kelly stepped forward and patted Carmina on the shoulder.

"Let me see the spy ring, please, Kelly," Venuto said.

Kelly placed the ring in his outstretched palm. He brought

it close to his face and stared at its flat, black stone with intense concentration. After a few moments his face fell. "Nothing."

Carmina tried next. She didn't have any luck either. Her shoulders slumped in defeat as she handed the ring back to Kelly.

"Do you want to try?" Kelly asked Milak.

Milak snorted. His features oozed disdain as he wrinkled his nose down at the ring. "I already knew that ring wouldn't spy him if we couldn't. It's a mere crutch for weaklings." He put special emphasis on the last word, sending a steely glare Kelly's way.

She frowned.

"It was worth a try," Carmina said. "Whatever is blocking us from sensing Thomas wouldn't necessarily influence the ring."

Milak drew his lips into a tight line.

There was a swooshing sound at the archway and Dimpleton entered the room. His expression was serious. "I reached my contact," he began. "The Pixelori claim Thomas and his guards left on schedule with the peacock feathers."

Carmina sniffled. Then her eyes narrowed suspiciously. "Wait, they *claim* he left on schedule? Does that mean you don't believe them?"

Dimpleton nodded. "There was something strange in my contact's words. It felt like he was hiding something. But I can't be sure from such a long distance."

"You will go there at once, then," Carmina said. "Try to get to the bottom of this."

"But use discretion," Venuto added. "If the Pixelori had something to do with it, you need to be very careful."

"Of course." Dimpleton spun around to leave. He gave Kelly a reassuring wink on his way out.

Milak clenched his fists. "I'd bet my bottom glitteron that Pixelatus had something to do with this."

Kelly thought back to the council meeting a few short

months ago when the leader of the Pixelori, Pixelatus, had made an appearance. His multi-colored, kaleidoscopic wings were still clear in her mind. So was his theatrical exit amidst blazing sparks after he and his band selfishly declined to help the Glendenians in their fight against Miasmos. What Milak was implying went well beyond selfishness, however. Why was he so suspicious of Pixelatus? What could the Pixelori have against Thomas?

"Let me go to their realm too," Milak said, a vein in his forehead bulging from his excitement. "I'll get Pixelatus to talk!"

Venuto smiled, either amused or pleased by Milak's determination, Kelly couldn't tell. "We need you here," the fairy prince said.

Milak crossed his arms and scowled, but he didn't argue.

Kelly could understand his impatience. There had to be something more that could be done. "You're all not just going to sit around here and wait for word from Dimpleton, are you?" she asked.

"Of course not," Carmina said. "We're pursuing multiple angles. We've already dispatched search parties to retrace Thomas's route."

"Are you going to tell everyone what is going on?" Kelly asked next.

Venuto sighed. "There is no use denying it. Carmina will make an announcement later, if she is up to it."

Carmina nodded.

"I wish there was something more I could do to help," Kelly said. She cringed to think that Thomas might be lost and alone somewhere, possibly injured. Or worse, he could be in the clutches of Miasmos or his minions.

"That's thoughtful of you, Kelly," Carmina said. "We'll let you know if we think of something."

Milak rolled his good eye. It was clear he didn't think Kelly could be of much use to them. She sent him an icy glare of her own.

"I suppose I should be getting back home, then," Kelly said. "My mom will start to wonder where I am."

As she turned to leave she heard Venuto's voice behind her. "Wait a minute."

"Yes?"

He cocked his head to the side and squinted at her. "Is there something different about you?"

Her hand reflexively went to her stomach, where the fresh mark of the memory stone lay hidden underneath her shirt. "Er —what do you mean?"

He pursed his lips in thought. "I don't know. I can sense a very subtle shift in your vibrations. They seem some-what...denser, or something. It is hard to describe."

Carmina leaned forward. "Ah, now that you mention it, Venuto, I can feel it too."

Kelly tried to appear as nonchalant as possible. "Beats me." She shrugged. "I'm a teenager. Maybe it's hormones."

"Vibrations don't just up and change on their own," Milak said. "Not even in puberty."

"She's a fadaman," Carmina said thoughtfully. "Maybe it's different for them."

"Perhaps," Milak replied, but from the look in his eye it was obvious he didn't believe that explanation for a minute.

THE MIST WAS THICK, *clinging to her skin like the breath of a ghost. She stood in a cloud. All around her it was silent. Empty. Like there was no one else in the world. A loneliness — aching, piercing — spread through her. Yet it was not hers. Then she heard them. The whispers. Faint and far away, like wind whistling through a gap*

between rocks. Someone, or something, was there with her. A presence. It spoke in alien tones, carrying shards of glass on its breath, clanking gently together, raindrops of notes. Not one voice, but many. Not many, but one. She listened. The more she strained to catch the sounds the further away they seemed, just beyond reach. Her right palm tingled. She realized she was holding something in her hand. Something small and round. The memory stone.

Kelly opened her eyes, the unfathomable whispers lingering in her ears for a moment. She glanced at her alarm clock. It was three in the morning. Suddenly, there was knocking on her window. She jumped at the sound and squinted through the darkness. To her surprise, Stephanie and Blaine hovered outside. Stephanie waved.

"What are you two doing here?" Kelly asked as she opened the window.

"We came to talk to you, of course," Blaine replied smugly. He made to fly inside but Kelly put a hand up to stop him. "Not so fast."

He stopped short. "You aren't going to let us in?"

"I haven't decided if I'm going to let *you* in. I want to talk to Stephanie first. Alone."

Blaine looked to Stephanie for her reaction. Stephanie nodded and flew inside. Kelly closed the window. Blaine pressed his face against the glass. Kelly flicked it. He jumped back, startled, and rubbed his nose.

"That wasn't very nice," Stephanie said.

"What are you doing here?"

"Well, I came to apologize, but I might have second thoughts if you don't start being nicer to Blaine."

"Oh."

"What, you aren't happy to see me?" Stephanie asked.

"I'm just surprised. I thought you were still really mad at me."

Stephanie plopped her fairy-sized self down on Kelly's bedside table. "I was, but, when they said Thomas had gone missing, it made me realize life is short, you know?"

Kelly's stomach twisted. She pushed away the thought that Thomas might not be coming back.

"I realized that we shouldn't lose sight of what really matters," Stephanie continued. "You're my best friend. We shouldn't let dumb stuff divide us. Besides, I don't mind if you date Dmitri anymore." She winked, inclining her head to where Blaine waited outside. He motioned impatiently for them to open the window.

Kelly shook her head. "Remind me exactly what you see in him again?"

Stephanie just giggled. "Will you let him in now?"

"Fine." Kelly opened the window.

"It's about time," Blaine said. He raced inside and made himself comfortable next to Stephanie. He noticed Kelly's alarm clock and reached for the big red alarm button.

"Don't touch that," Kelly snapped.

He pulled his hand back. "Burnt butterscotch. Somebody's in a bad mood."

"Do you have any idea what time it is?" Kelly retorted.

"Three in the morning. Can't you read?" He pointed to the alarm clock.

Stephanie laughed, but stopped when she received a sharp look from Kelly. "Sorry. We wanted to know what you know about Thomas."

"I don't know more than anyone else does."

"Did you ask *you-know-who* yet?" Blaine asked, a spark in his eye.

"Who?"

"You know..." He stuck his tongue out and rolled his eyes back in his head, groaning.

"Um, is he having a seizure?" Kelly asked Stephanie.

Blaine perked up. "No, silly, I was impersonating being in a coma. Like *you-know-who*."

"You mean Marcos?"

Blaine frowned. "I was going to say Witherings, but yeah."

"Why couldn't you just say who you meant in the first place?"

He grinned. "It was more fun to make you guess."

She scowled at him.

"So, have you asked him if he knows where Thomas is?" Blaine asked.

"No."

"Why not?"

"I don't know. It didn't occur to me." Now that he'd brought it up, though, she wondered why it hadn't.

"I don't think he'll tell her anything," Stephanie said. "For all we know, he and his father could have kidnapped Thomas together."

Kelly flinched. She didn't want to believe Witherings was responsible.

"She should still ask him," Blaine replied. "He might let key information slip. You said that he let a lot of details drop about the ten curtains and some special stone he has when you met him at the museum."

Kelly's jaw dropped. "You told him all about that?"

Stephanie fixed Kelly with her puppy-dog eyes. "Sorry. Don't be mad, please?"

"Fine, I'm not mad. But you," she jabbed a finger at Blaine, "you'd better keep your mouth shut."

He smirked. "I know how to keep a secret."

"Let's get on with it," Stephanie said. "Do your mental mumbo jumbo to reach Witherings. Or, better yet just call him and put him on speaker so we can hear too. His number is in your phone, isn't it?"

"Call him? At this hour?" Kelly asked.

"Why not?" Blaine said. "Evil people don't sleep."

"That's ridiculous." But she picked up her cell phone and found the number for Witherings. She pressed send.

He answered on the first ring. "Hello, Kelly."

She pressed speaker mode. "Hello, Marcos. I'm calling to ask you if—"

"I had anything to do with your king's disappearance?" he finished her sentence for her. He didn't sound upset. If anything, she thought there was a slight hint of amusement in his voice.

"Yes," Kelly admitted.

"Well, I didn't. I had nothing to do with it."

"How did you know he was missing, then?"

"I have my sources."

"Why should I believe you?"

"I'm offended, Kelly. I thought I'd earned a little trust by now."

Kelly felt an unexpectedly strong stab of guilt. "All right, maybe you have earned a little bit. But your father hasn't. Is he responsible?"

"He didn't mention anything to me. He would have, if he'd been planning something. Besides, I know he couldn't have done it. He's not anywhere near Glendenland."

"But Thomas didn't go missing from Glendenland."

"Oh." Witherings hesitated. "Where did he go missing from, then?"

"New York City."

"With...the Pixelori?"

"Yes."

"I have to go."

"Wait—"

It was no use. He had already hung up. Kelly didn't bother redialing. She didn't think he would pick up this time.

"That was illuminating,' Blaine said.

"How so?" Stephanie asked.

"It sounds to me like he didn't know who was responsible for Thomas's disappearance when Kelly called him, but when she mentioned that Thomas went missing near the Pixelori, that changed."

"So, you think the Pixelori are responsible?" Stephanie asked.

"Maybe," Kelly said. "Either that or Miasmos was in New York too."

Stephanie's eyes widened in understanding. "I see where you're going with this. Witherings said his father wasn't anywhere near Glendenland."

"Right," Blaine said. "Which means if Miasmos is to blame, then Witherings wasn't in the loop."

Kelly nodded. "Exactly. Which is very encouraging. Maybe Miasmos doesn't trust his son anymore. Maybe he knows Marcos is different now."

"Maybe," Stephanie said. "Or maybe that's just what they want you to think."

"Oh, come on, Steph. Why is it so hard for you to believe Marcos could genuinely be a better person now?"

"Are you kidding me? Why are you suddenly on a first name basis with him? I mean, 'Marcos' this and 'Marcos' that? If I didn't know any better I'd think you two were best friends."

"It's not like that."

Stephanie frowned. "What is it like, then?"

Kelly fiddled with the spy ring on her finger. "It's just...he's the only other fadaman I know. I guess I feel like we're connected somehow. It would be really nice if we didn't have to be enemies."

"You know what I think would be really nice?" Blaine asked.

"What?"

"If when it snowed it snowed marshmallows, and when it rained, it rained chocolate syrup."

Stephanie giggled. "That would never happen."

"My point exactly." Blaine smirked at his own cleverness.

Kelly was not amused. "I think it's time you two got going."

9

FOUND OUT

"Kelly, wake up!"

Kelly groaned and rolled over. Her mother yanked the blankets off the bed.

"Mom, what are you doing? It's too early."

"It's not early. You slept through your alarm clock. Hurry up, or we'll be late for your appointment."

Kelly sat up. "You mean I'll be late for school?"

"No, we'll be late for your appointment. With the neurologist. Did you forget?"

"Obviously."

Mindy's eyes narrowed. "Why do I get the impression you aren't taking this seriously?"

"Because I'm not. Seeing a specialist is completely unnecessary."

"Kelly Elizabeth Brennan!"

"What?"

"You passed out twice. Twice! And an ambulance was called. You could have died."

"Stop being so dramatic, Mom."

"I'm not being dramatic." Mindy stormed over to Kelly's closet and pulled out a T-shirt. She threw it at her daughter. "Get dressed."

A second later a pair of sweat pants landed on Kelly's head. "All right. I get the point."

"Good. We leave in five minutes."

THE WAITING room of Dr. Richard Bellefleur's practice was not the typical doctor's waiting room. The backs of all the wooden chairs were unique, as if they'd been hand carved. What looked to be silk-covered pillows, with intricate Chinese-inspired floral designs, graced the seats of each chair. Soft ocean sounds played from hidden speakers. A long glass table stretched across much of the room, on top of which sat several sculptural water features.

"Is this guy a neurologist or a yoga teacher?" Kelly asked.

"I think it's very inviting," Mindy said. They crossed over to the receptionist's window. It was made out of a frosty blue glass. "Neat color," Mindy said. "And look, a tiny meditation gong. That's so much better than one of those cheap desk bells." Mindy picked up the little wooden mallet that hung beside the suspended metal disc and gave it a whack. A discordant high-pitched ringing ensued.

Kelly pressed a hand against the gong to still its vibrations. "I think you were supposed to tap it gently, not bang on it."

"Sorry. Should I try again?" Mindy asked eagerly.

"I don't think so." Kelly took the mallet from her mother and set it back in its position. Mindy's shoulders sank in disappointment.

The frosty blue window slid to the side without a sound. A woman with a braid down to her waist and a flowing patchwork dress stood on the other side. She greeted them with a warm smile. "Welcome." She handed Mindy a clipboard. "Please fill out these forms."

While Mindy filled out the forms with Kelly's insurance information, Kelly amused herself by pushing the sand inside a little sandbox on the edge of the table around with a miniature wooden rake.

About ten minutes later the receptionist led them back to the interior of the practice. Exquisite framed paintings of ocean waves and trees dotted the blue walls. After getting Kelly's height and weight, the receptionist guided them into an examination room. Kelly hopped up onto the exam table, and Mindy took a seat in one of the two hand-carved chairs beside it.

There was a courtesy knock at the door and then Dr. Bellefleur walked in. He was tall and fit, with deep brown eyes and wavy dark hair that came down to his shoulders. He looked young, probably in his mid-thirties like Mindy. Instead of a typical white coat, he wore a dress shirt and crisp dark blue jeans. Kelly was not in the least surprised to see a golden dragon embroidered on his black silk tie. He gave them a broad smile and shook their hands.

"Nice to meet you both," he said. Kelly thought she would have liked to have a doctor like him, if she'd actually needed one, that is. "So, I hear you've been having some fainting episodes?" he continued.

"It only happened a few times," Kelly said. "I'm fine now."

"The fact it happened at all is some cause for concern," Dr. Bellefleur replied. "It's good that you came to see me."

"Could it be seizures?" Mindy asked.

Dr. Bellefleur flipped through Kelly's file. It looked like he already had copies of the reports from the hospital. "I've reviewed the previous tests. If it was a seizure, it was atypical. It was not what we'd typically see with fainting, either. The most recent episode lasted quite a long time. Honestly, I'm a bit stumped as to what it could be. All of your test results have come back normal so far."

"See, Mom? My test results are normal."

"That just means you might have something they've never seen before. Something they don't know how to treat." Mindy's lower lip trembled.

Dr. Bellefleur put a hand on Mindy's forearm. "I'll do my best to get to the bottom of this, Mrs. Brennan."

"It's *Miss*," Mindy replied. "I'm not married."

Dr. Bellefleur smiled. "I see." He turned back to Kelly. "Have you had any headaches? Trouble sleeping?"

"No."

"Hmmm..." he glanced back over the charts. "You aren't on any medications, and your tox screens were negative. And you don't have any relatives with a history of neurological disorders. Oh wait, we don't have a complete history. We just have your mother's side. Is there any history of neurological disorders on your father's side?"

"Um..." Kelly exchanged a look with her mother.

"Unfortunately, we don't know," Mindy said. "Her father never talked about his family."

"Is there any way to track down that information?" Dr. Bellefleur asked.

"I'm afraid not. Her father was killed in an accident before Kelly was born."

"My sympathies. Well, we'll make due with what we have. Kelly, have you been under any extra stress lately?"

"No," Kelly said.

"Don't lie to him, Kelly. He's trying to help you."

Kelly couldn't believe her mother was telling her not to lie; Mindy was the one who had just recited the same old lies about Kelly's father. "Are you kidding me?" Kelly asked.

Mindy fixed an earnest gaze on the doctor. "She was abducted this summer."

"Mom, why are you bringing that up? That has nothing to do with this."

A concerned frown took shape on Dr. Bellefleur's face. "There may be a psychological component. Serious emotional trauma can sometimes manifest physically."

"I don't have serious emotional trauma. It was just a case of mistaken identity. I was detained for a few days by the authorities. Nothing...untoward happened."

Dr. Bellefleur gave her a quizzical look, but he selected not to press the issue. "In any case, I want to get some more blood work and another MRI, just to see if there are any changes since the last one. If everything is normal again, and you still don't exhibit any symptoms, we'll just continue monitoring you every few months."

"Do we go back to the hospital to get the MRI?" Mindy asked.

"No, I have one here."

"Impressive." Mindy grinned.

Kelly thought her mother might have also just batted her eyelashes. *Great, now she's flirting with my doctor,* Kelly thought.

Dr. Bellefleur stood up. "We can go on back. Kelly, it doesn't look like your outfit has any metal buttons or zippers, so you can keep your regular clothes on."

Kelly fumed about the entire situation as she lay on the motorized table that rolled her slowly into the narrow white tube of the MRI machine. It was a good thing she didn't mind closed spaces.

"Try to hold still," Dr. Bellefleur instructed through the headphones he had given her when she had entered the MRI room. He and Mindy watched from an adjacent room, behind a layer of glass.

"You're doing great, honey," Mindy said.

At least I'm getting to miss German class, Kelly thought. If there was one thing worse than an unnecessary MRI, it was sitting through a class with Tommy Thompson.

"We are going to start collecting images now," Dr. Bellefleur said.

The machine began its work with loud buzzing and thumping sounds. Kelly was grateful that the headphones muted the sounds somewhat. After a few seconds, however, the machine's loud operation was no longer her primary concern. She felt a strange tingling feeling around her belly button — where the memory stone was. *Uh-oh.* Dr. Bellefleur had warned against metal buttons and zippers. And there Kelly was, lying in the machine with an ancient metal artifact underneath her skin. She kicked herself mentally for not thinking to remove the stone before entering the machine. The tingling quickly turned into a sensation of heat, then burning. She clenched her jaw and squeezed her eyes shut, trying to ignore it.

The loud noises paused for a moment. "Are you all right in there?" Dr. Bellefleur asked. "We're getting some interference."

"I'm fine," Kelly lied. "But...how much longer is this going to take?"

"About half an hour," came the reply.

The pain intensified into a searing burn. It was like a hot iron was being pressed against her stomach. *Thirty more minutes?* "Um, I don't think I'm going to be able to last that long."

"What's wrong?" Mindy asked.

"My stomach hurts."

"Hold on. We're pulling you out," Dr. Bellefleur said.

As soon as Kelly's stomach was no longer inside the machine's tunnel, the sensation of burning stopped, subsiding into a pulsing ache. Mindy and the doctor rushed in.

"Are you all right?" Mindy asked.

Kelly sat up. "I think so. My stomach just felt really weird."

"Let me take a look," Dr. Bellefleur said.

"That won't be necessary." Kelly stood up quickly. The movement caused her shirt to rub across the sore spot on her stomach. She flinched.

"I beg to differ," Dr. Bellefleur said. "Lie back down and let me take a look."

"No." Kelly tried to move towards the door but Mindy grabbed her elbow. Before she had a chance to react, Mindy lifted up the bottom of Kelly's shirt. Mindy's eyes widened in shock as the tattoo was revealed. The skin all around it was red and inflamed.

"What is the meaning of this?" Mindy shrieked.

"It's just a design. It doesn't have any special meaning."

"You know that's not what I was asking, young lady." Mindy let go of Kelly. "When did you get that? Where did you get it? Who gave it to you? I will give them a piece of my mind—"

"Calm down, Mom. It's just a temporary tattoo."

"Don't insult my intelligence, Kelly."

Up until this moment, Dr. Bellefleur had been standing awkwardly to the side, watching the exchange. Mindy swirled around to face the doctor and channeled her rage towards him. "I thought this machine was supposed to be safe. It burned my daughter!"

"It is safe, Miss Brennan. Tattoos aren't a problem unless they were made over twenty years ago. Older inks had certain dangerous metals, so older tattoos can sometimes react with the magnetic fields in the MRI. Nowadays you don't see that, except for rarely with unprofessional tattoos, like some prison tattoos."

Mindy swirled back to Kelly. "Did you hear that? Metals? Prison tattoos? Did you let some random person off the street give you a tattoo with ink from a pen or something? Was the needle even clean?"

"Of course, Mom, I'm not stupid. If you must know, I did it on myself," Kelly lied.

"Unbelievable. You're so grounded."

"But—"

"I don't want to hear it. You can just tell Dmitri you're sorry about tonight. Maybe he'll find someone else to go to the movies with him."

"You're being so unfair!"

Dr. Bellefleur put a hand on Kelly's shoulder. "I don't mean to interrupt this, er, discussion, but we should really get some ointment on that so it heals properly."

EVEN THOUGH IT was still before lunchtime, Mindy insisted Kelly go home and rest instead of returning to school. Up in her room, Kelly sulked. She had no intention of missing her date, however. She hadn't done anything wrong. *I'll just fly out my window,* she thought with grim satisfaction. At times like this being a fadaman came in quite handy. She needed to call Dmitri though, since he was planning to come pick her up at her house.

Dmitri answered the phone on the first ring. "Hello?"

"Hi, Dmitri, I wanted to talk to you about tonight."

"I know. Your mother called me and told me you were grounded."

Kelly's cheeks grew hot. "She what?"

"She said you got a tattoo."

Kelly groaned. "I can't believe she went behind my back and called you. How embarrassing. I'm going to give her an earful about that."

Dmitri chuckled. "Don't worry. I know how mothers can be. I am intrigued about this tattoo, however. You'll have to show it to me when I see you in school on Monday."

"Well...I was thinking we could still go out tonight."

"Even though you're grounded?" He sounded surprised.

"I don't usually sneak out, but, my mom is completely in the wrong here. What do you say?"

He didn't think about it for very long. "Sure, why not? But would you mind watching a DVD at my house instead of going to the theater? Since I thought you weren't going to make it I told my mom I'd stick around tonight."

"No problem. See you then."

IT DIDN'T TAKE LONG to reach Dmitri's house, especially at the anger-induced speeds Kelly was flying. At dinner she had brought up Mindy's inappropriate phone call to Dmitri, but Mindy had stubbornly refused to admit she had done anything wrong. She claimed she'd been 'protecting' Kelly. From what? Dmitri? It was ridiculous. *I wish I could erase her memory of this summer,* Kelly thought. It was like her mother didn't trust her anymore.

Kelly tried not to think about her mother as she set down a few blocks away from Dmitri's house. She transformed to human form behind a bush and walked the rest of the way. The house was small, with a tall gabled roof. It was painted a dreary gray, but the green shingles and rows of bright red flowers in the window boxes kept it from looking too sad.

Dmitri opened the door just as Kelly was reaching for the doorbell. He must have been watching out the window waiting for her to arrive. "Hi, Kelly, come in."

Kelly followed Dmitri inside. She recognized the room she had spied Dmitri and his brother in with the spy ring.

"This is the living room," Dmitri explained. "That's the kitchen." He pointed off to the right where the connected kitchen was. "And then down that hallway are the other rooms."

After a quick glance at her surroundings, Kelly's eyes fell on the blue stuffed hippo Dmitri was holding. It was about the size of a football, and it had a garish pink bow on its head. It looked new. "Uh, that's not for me, is it?" she asked quizzically.

"Huh?" Dmitri looked down. "Oh, no. I was just cleaning up some of my brother's toys."

"Would you be insulted if I said that was a relief?"

Dmitri laughed. "Not at all. I hope you don't have something against stuffed animals, though," he said. "Because I did get you a present."

"I wasn't expecting a present."

"I know, but I wanted to thank you for helping me with math." Dmitri pulled something from his pocket and handed it to her.

It was a miniature teddy bear, just about three inches tall. It had a tiny T-shirt on it that read *MATH GENIUS*. Kelly didn't usually like stuffed animals, but this one was absolutely adorable.

"Do you like it?" Dmitri asked.

"Yes, it's very cute. Thank you."

Just then they were interrupted by a loud female voice from down the hallway. "Dima? Is that your friend? Bring her back here to meet me."

Dmitri sighed. "That's my mother. She said she wanted to meet you. We'd better get back there before she yells some more and wakes up my little brother."

"Dima? Did you hear me?"

"Yes, Mom. Be quiet, we're coming!"

They went to the end of the hall. Dmitri pushed the door to the last room open. Inside, a woman lay in a bed, hooked up to a home dialysis machine. Dark purple bruises covered much of her arms. Despite her clearly weakened state, when she smiled at Kelly her beautiful green eyes shone with welcoming warmth. "You must be Kelly."

Kelly nodded, trying not to stare at the place where the tubes went into the woman's arms.

"I'm Katerina, Dmitri's mother."

"Nice to meet you," Kelly replied.

Katerina squinted and looked Kelly up and down. "I must say you are even prettier than Dmitri said."

Kelly blushed.

"And much prettier than his last girlfriend," Katerina added.

"Mom!"

"What? Did I say something bad? She *is* prettier. Women like to be told when they are pretty. Isn't that right, Kelly?"

"Sometimes," Kelly said.

Dmitri put a hand on Kelly's elbow and guided her towards the door. "Well, Kelly and I are going to watch a movie now." He seemed very anxious to get Kelly away from his mother. Maybe he was afraid Katerina would say more embarrassing things about his ex.

"All right," Katerina said. "I hope I see you again soon, Kelly. Oh, and Dima?"

Dmitri paused in the doorway. "Yes?"

"Make sure you offer Kelly something to eat."

"I know how to treat a guest, Mom."

"I know. I taught you," she replied with a smug grin.

Dmitri rolled his eyes, but there was a hint of amusement on his face. Once back in the living room, they sat down on the couch. "So, are you hungry?" Dmitri asked.

Kelly chuckled. "No, I already ate. But thanks, that's very polite of you. Your mother would be proud."

Dmitri groaned. "Speaking of which, I guess your mom and my mom are even, as far as embarrassing acts of the day."

"I don't think your mom was so bad."

"She brought up my ex girlfriend. Not exactly a topic for a first date," Dmitri replied. "By the way, that is ancient history," he added.

"Don't worry. You'd better just hope she doesn't pull a stunt like my mom did and call me to spill all the details about your life."

Dmitri shook his head in disbelief. "That was something, wasn't it? Does she always do stuff like that?"

"No. She didn't used to anyway. She's just not been herself after what happened this summer."

Dmitri furrowed his brow. "What happened this summer?"

"I found out I was a..." Kelly clamped a hand over her mouth to shut herself up. She couldn't believe how close she had just come to finishing that sentence with *...a half-fairy, then I got kidnapped on orders of an evil maniac named Miasmos who is trying to take over the world, escaped, went to an underwater fairy kingdom called Glendenland, learned some magic, beat Miasmos's son in a duel, and fought in a battle against the Miasmonian army.*

Dmitri's voice broke her out of her thoughts. "If you don't want to talk about it, I understand."

Kelly brought her hand down from her mouth, embarrassed. *Way to act weird, Kelly,* she thought. "No, it's not that I don't want to talk about it. I'm just not really supposed to. You see the government thought I was someone else, a criminal, and they took me into custody."

Dmitri's jaw dropped. "That's terrible."

The worried look on his face was very sweet, but it also made her feel even guiltier for lying. "It wasn't so bad. It was just a case of mistaken identity. It was resolved quickly, but my mom was really shaken up."

"I see."

Dmitri's brow was still furrowed in thought, and he looked like he might be preparing to ask something else. She didn't want to give him a chance to dwell on the subject. "Let's just forget about that," she said. "What do you want to watch?"

"I don't know. Let's see what there is."

Dmitri had an impressive DVD collection, with movies from all different genres. They decided on a Russian movie with English subtitles. Kelly had never heard Russian spoken that much so she thought it would be interesting to hear it.

Only about fifteen minutes into the movie, Katerina interrupted. "Dima?"

Dmitri paused the movie with the remote. "Sorry, I'll be right back."

He was gone for about five minutes.

"Is she all right?" Kelly asked when he got back.

He shrugged. "Relatively speaking."

Kelly frowned.

"It's not as bad as it looks," he added in response to her concern. "She's only on the machine a few hours each day."

"Do you mind if I ask what she has?"

"It's her kidney. She was born with a kidney disease. She got a transplant as a teenager, back in Russia, and she was fine when she had me and my brother, but a few years after that her new kidney started to fail."

"Can she get another transplant?"

Dmitri shook his head. "They don't think she's a good candidate for a new one now."

"I'm sorry. I can't imagine how hard that must be for you"

He shifted uneasily. "Well, lots of people are worse off than I am."

She reached out and took his hand. "Still, I think you handle it really well."

He interlaced his fingers with hers. "I don't know about that, but I do feel better after talking to you."

Kelly smiled. "I'm glad."

"Should we get back to the movie?" Dmitri asked.

"Sure."

He pressed a button on the remote to unpause the movie. About thirty minutes later Kelly thought she heard a sound from the fireplace — a light rustle. Then a few seconds after that, another one. "Did you hear something?" she asked Dmitri.

"No. What did you hear?"

Just then the source of the sound revealed itself: Bubbles popped out of the fireplace in his invisible-to-humans form, covered in soot. "Never mind," Kelly said. "I think it was just a background sound from the movie."

Dmitri accepted that explanation and returned his attention to the television screen.

Bubbles zoomed across the room and landed on Kelly's knee. "Kelly, Kelly!" He wiggled his shoulders and soot flew off of him onto her lap.

"Bubbles, you're making a mess!"

Bubbles sneezed. Kelly glanced sideways at Dmitri, but luckily he didn't seem to have noticed the disturbance so far. *"What are you doing here?"* she asked her fairy friend mentally. *"Can't you see I'm a little busy?"*

"But I have news, amazing news, it can't wait!"

Kelly's heart skipped a beat. *"Is it about Thomas? Is he back?"*

Bubbles shook his head. *"No. It's Bamblelina. I finally asked her to marry me."* He flew a hyper circle around her and Dmitri, causing a burst of air in their faces as he blew past.

"Did you feel that?" Dmitri asked.

"What?" Kelly asked innocently.

"Like, a draft or something?"

"I didn't feel anything."

"Weird," Dmitri said before turning back to the television.

Kelly sent Bubbles a stern look. *"Will you calm down?"*

"Sorry. I'm just so excited. She said yes!" Bubbles flopped back down on Kelly's lap.

"That's great, Bubbles. But, maybe we'll talk later?"

"Why not now?"

"Because I'm on a date."

Bubbles's eyes widened. *"You're not studying?"*

"Does this look like studying to you?"

He looked from Kelly to Dmitri, then back again. *"I guess not. You don't have any pencils and papers. And you're sitting awfully close. And you're holding hands. And..."* It seemed like he was going to continue listing observations, but then his eyes fell on the TV screen. *"Hey, a movie. Can I stay and watch?"*

"No."

He pouted and crossed his arms. *"Why are you spending time with this human anyway?"*

"Because I like him. Now, go away."

"Fine." He wrinkled his nose in Dmitri's general direction. *"Just don't forget who you are."*

Kelly scowled at his back as he flew away. *Don't forget who I am? What's that supposed to mean?* She would have to take that up with him later.

Bubbles raced through the air back towards the chimney, but inches before he reached it he came to an abrupt stop. Hovering, he lifted his nose in the air and sniffed. *"I think I smell...could it be...borscht? Yes, it is! Oooh!"* He zoomed for the kitchen. A second later there was a loud clatter as several pots and pans tumbled to the ground. *"Oopsy!"*

Dmitri jumped up and ran towards the sounds. "What the...?"

Kelly joined him at the edge of the kitchen. Bubbles had made a real mess. One of the pots that had hit the ground had been full of a reddish soup. Bubbles grinned and licked the insides of the overturned pot.

"Bubbles!"

His shoulders jerked. He surveyed the disarray around him and his face fell. *"I'm sorry. But it smelled so good, I just couldn't* resist. I only had one dinner." He sniffled. "I didn't mean to knock it over. You aren't mad, are you?"

"What do you think?"

His shoulders sank. "You are mad. But don't worry. I'll make it up to you. I'll make you a cake!"

She shot him an icy look.

"Or a cupcake?" he asked hopefully. He sighed. "Or not. All righty, I'll be going now." He flew away and disappeared up the chimney.

Dmitri grabbed some paper towels from the counter, preparing to tackle the mess. At that moment a door in the hallway opened and Dominic, in superhero pajamas, walked out. "Dima, I'm scared." He grabbed his older brother's hand.

"It's all right, Dominic. Some pans just fell over. Go back to bed."

"I want you to read me a story."

"I can't. I have to clean this up. Why don't you ask Mom to read you a story?"

"I like it when you read to me. Please?" Dominic begged. "If I help clean it up will you read me a story?"

"Um..." Dmitri looked torn.

"Why don't I clean it up and you two go read a story?" Kelly offered.

"No, it's not right for you to clean it up," Dmitri said. "Besides, if I read to him it will take at least half an hour."

"It's getting late, anyway. So, I'll just clean up the spill so it doesn't stain, and you can put the pots away later." She grabbed the bunch of paper towels from his hands before he could protest. "You go read to Dominic, and I'll show myself out."

"Are you sure?"

"Yes. I don't mind, really."

He still didn't look convinced.

His little brother tugged on his hand impatiently. "I want Kelly to leave so you can read to me!"

"Dominic, don't be rude."

"It's fine, Dmitri. Don't worry about it."

"I'm really sorry about this, Kelly," Dmitri said.

"It wasn't your fault, trust me," she replied.

"All right. Thanks for your help."

"No problem. See you Monday."

Little Dominic waved. "Bye, Kelly!"

AS KELLY FLEW HOME, she reflected on the evening. Up until Bubbles had showed up, it had been really nice. Except for when Dmitri had asked her about what had happened that summer. She thought he might have sensed she was hiding something. She'd have to be really careful from now on. And she'd have to make it very clear to Bubbles not to crash her dates.

When Kelly got close to her house, she saw a small light flickering on a tree branch in her backyard. *That's weird*, she thought. When she got a little closer she saw that the light was coming from a small lamp, carried by a fairy — and not just any fairy. It was Milak. Standing beside Milak was Venuto. Kelly frowned. She had not been expecting visitors. Especially not those two.

Venuto motioned with his arm. "Kelly, down here."

Kelly set down on the tree branch next to them. Close up she could see that both fairies were wearing stern expressions. That was nothing new from Milak, but it had been some time since she had seen such a sour look on Venuto's face. It made her nervous.

"What brings you two here?" she stammered.

Milak gave Kelly a look that sent a shiver down her spine. "You tell us."

Her hand reflexively went to her belly button. "What's that supposed to mean?"

Venuto's eyes narrowed. "This isn't a time for games, Kelly. Where is it?"

A nervous laugh escaped Kelly's lips. "Where's what?"

"This is a waste of time," Milak said. "We couldn't read Ricketer's mind, but we can read hers. I'll make her tell us." Milak lunged forward. Luckily for Kelly, Venuto put a hand on his shoulder to stop him.

"That's not necessary," the prince said. "Yet," he added with a pointed look to Kelly.

Milak took a step back, but he was still poised to lurch forward at any moment. "We know you have the stone," he snarled. "Hand it over, or else."

"I don't know what you're talking about."

"Ricketer died today," Venuto said. "It was only when I went to see his body that I noticed the difference in his vibrations. The absence of something. Somehow he had the stone with him all along. Remember the change I felt in your vibrations yesterday? Now I understand I was sensing the stone's vibrations. You have it on you right now, in fact."

Kelly was silent. She tried to think of something to say, but she couldn't come up with anything convincing.

Venuto sighed. "I don't know what Ricketer told you, but I'm disappointed that you would trust him more than me. Why would you keep this from us?"

Kelly looked down at her toes. "He said I had a special power to unlock the stone," she confessed. "He said it had to be passed directly to me."

Milak snorted. "A special power? You believed that old nutter?"

"He had more wits about him than you do," Kelly retorted.

Milak took a step forward. "You'd do well to learn to respect your elders."

"Ricketer was your elder," Kelly said. "You called him a nutter. How respectful was that?"

"That's enough," Venuto said. "This bickering is below both of you. The point is, Kelly, we can't let you keep the stone."

"But, Ricketer said—"

"I don't want to hear it," Venuto interrupted. "Give it to me now or I'll be forced to lock you up in the jail bubble."

Kelly's stomach dropped. "You would do that?"

Venuto nodded. "I would. You've already broken the law by accepting it. However, I'm willing to overlook that if you give the stone back now."

Kelly thought about it.

"My offer doesn't last forever," the prince said. "You have about five more seconds to decide." It was clear from his tone that he meant it.

"Some choice," she mumbled. She exposed her tattoo and placed her hand over it. It took a few extra seconds for the mist to form, and it stung like a thousand needle pricks as it forced its way through the scabs that had formed over her burnt skin. Finally, the polished stone sat in her palm, but she didn't want to let it go. She stared down at it. The edges of the stone seemed to waver, getting bigger and bigger. She felt a push on the inside of her mind, an invitation. Before she even thought to accept it, everything dissolved around her.

The mist was cold, like the breath of a ghost. She stood in a cloud. A loneliness — aching, piercing — spread through her. Yet it was not hers. The whispers came again. Faint, far away, like wind whistling through a gap between rocks. Alien tones, carrying shards of glass on their breath, clanking gently together, raindrops of notes. She strained to hear them, but just when she had focused on one, it had already gone. Then, everything went deathly silent, and the loneliness permeating the atmosphere turned into something else — fear, then panic. A shrill, ear splitting shriek cut through Kelly's skull without warning. It was not like any human voice, or like any animal Kelly had ever heard. But there was a presence behind it, something...alive? Kelly pressed her hands against her ears but it did nothing to diminish the harsh, high-pitched grating, like nails on a chalkboard.

With a jolt Kelly was back on the tree branch. She blinked, heart racing. To her great relief she hadn't fallen off. Since the vision had felt like it lasted at least a minute, she thought that surely she would have fallen — but in reality it looked like barely a split second had passed. She was standing in the exact same position she had been before the vision, but her palm was newly empty. Venuto held the stone in his hand, like he had just taken hold of it. "Thank you," he said. He raised it to the lamplight and examined it. Milak squinted at it with what Kelly thought might be trepidation, but she couldn't be sure.

"Don't thank me. I only gave it to you because you made me. The stone is not happy you took it."

Venuto raised an eyebrow. "The stone has feelings?"

She remembered that she had said the exact same thing, with a similar incredulous tone, to Ricketer just a day ago. "In a manner of speaking," she replied.

"Interesting. I'll have to get to know it then." He tucked the stone in his pocket.

"Assuming it will let you," Kelly said.

Venuto frowned. "Kelly, I hope you understand I'm just doing what is best for everyone. Ricketer was not wise. He endangered you by giving you the stone."

He did have a point about that, Kelly admitted, remembering Marcos's warning about the stone. But deep down she knew that Ricketer was wise, contrary to what Venuto thought. In fact, he had been wiser than every fairy she knew put together. So if he thought she was the only one who might be able to unlock the secrets from the memory stone — the secrets that might be their only hope of stopping Miasmos — then she believed it. "Will you at least let me visit the stone in Glendenland?" she asked.

"That's out of the question," Venuto said.

"But..."

"My decision is final." He turned to leave, then paused. "You'd best give me those stun pellets in your pocket, too."

Kelly retrieved the pellets and dropped them into his open hand. "You're making a big mistake," she said. "I hope you realize that before it's too late for all of us." With those words she shot into the air and flew to her window. The fairies didn't try to stop her.

10

REJECTION

I t was hot. Hot and dry, so dry the air scraped the back of her throat as she breathed in, like sand paper. The cracked ground stretched as far as she could see, a dark red like wilted rose petals. Up above, two suns blazed down from a purple sky, which seemed to press down on her, creating a claustrophobic feeling despite the miles of emptiness all around.

She picked a direction and walked. There must be some reason for her to be here: something to find, something to see. She walked and walked, until she was weak with exhaustion, but nothing changed. Flat, the scenery was identical — the suns, they hung at the same place in the sky, unmoving, as if trapped in a moment that lasted forever. Would she be trapped too? Trapped in this place, this ghost of...a memory? As if in reply to her thoughts, a familiar ear-splitting shriek cut through her skull without warning. It didn't speak in any words she could decipher, but it held a discernible intent. It felt accusing, angry. She collapsed to the ground, pressing her hands against her ears but it did nothing to diminish the pain.

Kelly woke up with a headache, and a vague image of a desert with a purple sky. After splashing cold water on her face, her mind felt a little clearer, but she was still groggy as she made her way downstairs.

"Kelly, you look terrible," Mindy said from where she was frying eggs for Sunday breakfast.

"I didn't sleep very well."

Mindy frowned with concern. "Were you in pain from your stomach burn?"

"No, it's healing nicely. See?" Kelly lifted up her shirt to show where the red skin was healing.

Mindy gasped. "The tattoo, it's gone!"

"I told you it was temporary." Kelly put on an exaggerated pout and crossed her arms. "But you didn't believe me."

"Oh no, and you missed your date! I'm so sorry, Kelly. I will make it up to you. In fact, I know just the thing."

"What's that?"

"I thought we could put up the Halloween decorations this afternoon."

"Isn't it a little early for that?" Kelly asked.

"It's almost October. Besides, you love putting them up."

Kelly bit her tongue. The truth was she only pretended to like putting up the decorations for her mother's sake.

The eggs were done, so Mindy transferred them onto two plates, along with some toast. "So, how about it?" she asked her daughter.

Kelly shrugged. "Sure." *It's not like I have anything better to do*, she thought.

They sat down to breakfast. Mindy's eyes brightened. "You should invite Dmitri!"

"To decorate for Halloween? I don't think so."

"I could call him for you," Mindy offered.

"Don't even think about that, Mom."

"Well, hurry up and eat your eggs before they get cold."

Just as Kelly brought the first bite to her mouth, out of nowhere the idea of Marcos Witherings popped into her mind.

She felt a rush of cold throughout her body, like ice on a lake. She dropped her fork.

"Are you all right?" Mindy asked.

"I...think so," she answered through chattering teeth, shivering from the cold.

"Are you sure?"

In a flash the feeling vanished. *How strange*, Kelly thought.

"Kelly?"

"I'm fine." She picked up her fork and took a large bite of eggs to appease her mother.

Kelly excused herself as soon as she had cleared her plate. She stole away to her room and dialed Witherings's number on her cell phone. She hadn't felt the telltale feeling of being watched at breakfast, but she was sure she had sensed something from him, and she wanted an explanation. The phone rang and rang before finally going to voicemail. Next she tried to summon his image in the spy ring, but she got nothing. Finally, she attempted to contact him telepathically, but all she achieved from that was a fresh headache.

She felt a tightness in her chest and realized she was worried. Had Witherings found something out about Thomas? Should she tell Carmina or Venuto? For a moment she considered going to Glendenland, but she was still too bitter about the other night. How could they just take the memory stone away like that? *They want me to trust them, but how can I, if they don't trust me?*

Her phone rang. She jumped. "Marcos?"

"No, it's Dmitri. Who's Marcos?"

"No one."

"It has to be someone," he replied with a teasing tone. "Should I be worried?"

"Are you jealous?" she asked.

"Maybe a little," he admitted.

"Don't be. He's no one you need to be concerned about."

He chuckled. "Good. Listen, I want to make up for Friday night. How about we go to the park? Assuming you can sneak out again."

"No need, I'm not grounded anymore."

"How did you manage that?"

"I removed the tattoo."

"You can do that?"

"With certain kinds," she said.

"Huh. Well, what do you say?"

"I would love to, but, unfortunately I promised my mom I'd help her put up Halloween decorations. You could come if you wanted, but, I wouldn't want to make you suffer through that."

"Actually, I think that would be fun."

"Really?"

"Of course, because you'll be there."

She smiled to herself. "Good answer. Be here at three."

"WHERE SHOULD I PUT THIS ONE?" Dmitri asked. He held up a plastic spider. He stood on the top step of a stepladder beside the porch. The sun hit his hair, and the reflection off his blond locks was so bright it almost hurt to look at him.

"I don't know, maybe there?" Kelly pointed at an expanse of fake spider webs hanging from the ceiling behind him.

"Where exactly?"

"There."

"Why don't you come up here and show me?" He winked.

He extended his free hand to help her up onto the stepladder. She joined him on the top step. It was a little wobbly, and there wasn't much room, but neither of them was complaining. Kelly was glad her mother had just gone inside to make dinner, leaving them alone to finish up with the decorations.

"So, where is the best home for this little guy?" Dmitri asked, turning his attention back to the spider.

"How about there?" Kelly suggested another open spot behind him.

His eyes focused instead on a spot behind Kelly's head. "I think this would be better." He leaned forward and stretched his arm to the spot, bringing his face quite close to hers in the process.

They both stayed still for a moment, like statues, before Kelly put a hand on Dmitri's cheek and leaned even closer. Just as their lips were about to touch — a rush of icy coldness swept over Kelly, just like earlier in the day. She stumbled sideways.

Dmitri grabbed her arm to steady her. "Are you all right?"

"I just got a little dizzy." She rubbed her temples. Her head hurt like brain freeze after drinking an icy drink too fast.

Dmitri frowned. "It isn't like what happened in school, is it?"

"No."

He helped her down from the stepladder. She sat down on the porch. "Should I get your mother?"

"No way. She'll have a big fit. I just need a minute." The feeling had already started to subside.

"Hey, who's that?" Dmitri asked.

Kelly looked up to see a blue sports car had just pulled up in front of the house. Kelly's jaw dropped as none other than Dr. Richard Bellefleur stepped out of the car, looking sharp with his windswept hair, sunglasses, and a flowing Chinese dress shirt over tight blue jeans. He strutted up the path to the porch. He stopped at the base of the steps and flashed Kelly and Dmitri a bright smile.

"Hello, Kelly." He took off his sunglasses and tucked them into his collar. "And you must be Dmitri. I'm Kelly's neurologist. You can call me Rick." He offered a hand to Dmitri. Kelly watched in a daze as Dmitri shook the doctor's hand. *How does Dr. Bellefleur know who Dmitri is?*

"It's good you're here, Rick," Dmitri said. "Kelly just had a dizzy spell."

Dr. Bellefleur, looking concerned, put a hand on Kelly's forehead. "Have you drunk enough water today?" he asked.

She batted his hand away. "Cut it out, I'm perfectly fine. What are you doing here, anyway?"

"Your mother invited me for dinner."

"What? She just met you the day before yesterday."

Dr. Bellefleur's eyes sparkled with amusement. "And your point is?"

The screen door creaked as Mindy came out onto the porch. "Rick, I'm so glad you could make it."

"I wouldn't dream of missing it." The doctor leaned in and kissed her on the cheek, sickeningly suave. "You look lovely today."

Mindy beamed. "Thank you. You don't look so bad yourself."

Kelly groaned. "You've got to be kidding me."

"Don't be rude," Mindy said.

"Rude? Give me a break. You're the one dating my doctor. My doctor! And you only just met him."

"Sometimes when two people meet, they feel a deep connection, like they've known each other for a very long time," Dr. Bellefleur said.

Kelly rolled her eyes. "Please, your lines might work on my mother but they won't work on me."

Dr. Bellefleur raised his eyebrows. He looked like he might laugh.

Mindy's face reddened. "Kelly, don't you think you're being a little immature?"

Before Kelly could reply another blast of ice cold hit her. This time, there was a very faint feeling of being watched along with it. She opened up a part of her mind to accept the connection.

"Kelly?" The voice was weak, strained.

"Marcos? What's wrong?"

"I've been trying to reach you, but, I'm so tired. I can't...I can't concentrate."

Kelly's chest tightened. *"Are you hurt?"* In reply she felt a searing pain across her back. Was it his pain? *"Marcos?"*

"Kelly?" Mindy, hands on her hips, scowled down at her daughter. Dr. Bellefleur and Dmitri looked on, Dr. Bellefleur still amused, and Dmitri shifting from one foot to another nervously.

Kelly ignored them all. *"Marcos?"*

There was a rueful laugh from the other side. "You were right, Kelly. About my father. He tried to kill me. Maybe...he succeeded. I don't feel so good." The connection was getting weaker, his voice was fainter, so that now she could barely hear him. He was in trouble.

"Hold on, Marcos. I'm coming."

"But you don't kno—"

"Yes, I do. I know exactly where you are," she cut him off, surprised at her certainty. She could sense where he was and she knew she could get there.*"Just don't go anywhere."* He didn't answer. *"Marcos?"* Silence. The connection was gone.

Kelly jumped up and ran. Behind her, Mindy called her name, and next she heard footsteps pounding behind her. Just before she reached the sidewalk someone grabbed her elbow. It was Dmitri. She hesitated.

"Where are you going?" he asked.

"I'm sorry, I can't explain right now."

"Does it really bother you that much that your mom is dating your doctor? He seems like a really nice guy."

"It doesn't have anything to do with that."

"What is it, then?"

He gazed into her eyes with an earnestness that cut straight to her soul. She averted her gaze. "I really want to tell you, but I can't."

"What's that supposed to mean?"

She hated to leave Dmitri hanging like this, but she didn't have time to spin a cover story he might believe. "I'm sorry. I have to go." She turned and ran away down the sidewalk. He didn't follow. A glance over her shoulder revealed he was watching her go with an expression that reminded her of an abandoned kitten. She did her best to block him out of her mind. She had to focus on getting to Marcos. When she rounded the corner, she transformed to fairy form and flew as fast as her wings would carry her.

It took barely five minutes to arrive at her destination, but it felt like five hours. The structure she'd sensed Marcos was in was a gutted building that used to be an Italian restaurant with apartments above it. Kelly hovered high above the street, considering the best avenue for approach. There were too many people on the sidewalk for her to fly up to the front door in fairy form. Luckily the building had many windows, which were mostly missing their glass. Plastic sheets had been tacked over them in an attempt to keep out the elements.

Kelly spotted a tear in the plastic that covered a window on the top floor. She crawled through it. Inside, she smelled sawdust. Haphazard piles of wooden planks and stacked drywall littered the room. She paused just inside the window and pushed her awareness outwards, hoping she would sense if there were any Miasmonians nearby. She sensed nothing at all, until she picked up on a cold, silvery presence two levels down. Marcos. She flew to the stairway. Being away from the windows, the stairwell was pitch black. She made a small fireball and sent it ahead for light.

Two levels down, on the landing, Marcos lay crumpled in a fetal position. Kelly directed the fireball to hover over his head. Her stomach dropped when she saw that his right leg was bent at an unnatural angle, his left wing was ripped nearly in half, and a pool of blood stained the floor underneath him.

She rushed to his side. "Marcos. Wake up."

He moaned.

"Marcos!"

He opened his eyes slowly. "Kelly?" His voice cracked.

"Yes, it's me." Her eyes traced the jagged edge of his wing. The wing tear led to a gash across his back. The T-shirt he had been wearing was shredded to bits. His right shoulder blade poked out of his skin. It looked like he'd been attacked by some savage animal. "Your *father* did this to you?"

He grimaced. "Don't look so surprised."

"But...you're his son."

"I'm pretty sure I was just disowned." He struggled to sit up.

"No, don't move. We have to get Margretta here to help you."

His eyes flashed with fear. "No, I can't go to Glendenland. They all want me dead."

"That's not true," she said, but doubt crept swiftly into her mind. "They would help you," she added, trying to convince herself as much as him.

He sank back to the ground. "Even if they helped me, they would just lock me up again after."

She racked her brain for a solution. If he wouldn't let Margretta help, what could they do? Her heart ached to see him like this. She had never seen him look so fragile. "What if...what if you were in human form, do you think regular human doctors could fix you?"

He nodded. "I think so."

"Can you transform yourself?"

He squeezed his eyes shut with effort. Sparks began on his hands and feet, but they quickly fizzled out. He groaned in defeat. "I'm too weak."

She took a deep breath and pressed her hand against his forehead. *I hope I don't regret this*, she thought.

"What are you doing?"

"Remember what you did when you escaped from Glendenland? Do it again. Use some of my energy."

"No, I won't do that."

She pressed her hand harder against his forehead. "Do it."

"No."

"It's the only way. You don't want to die here, do you?"

"I don't know if I can control it in my current state. I might take too much." Fear flickered in his eyes again — this time not fear for himself, but fear that he would hurt her.

In that moment any tiny doubts remaining as to whether he had indeed changed for the better were wiped away. "Do it," Kelly commanded. "I trust you."

He nodded grimly and closed his eyes. Kelly felt a light tingle in her palm, which soon turned into heat. A creeping coldness overtook the rest of her body as her energy flowed into him. She started to feel woozy, but it was working. Sparks appeared on Marcos's fingers and toes and then spread throughout his body. In a few seconds he was in his human form, and Kelly realized she had transformed as well. Also, the energy transfer had stopped; warmth returned slowly to her limbs. She let her hand drop to her side.

"Are you all right?" Marcos asked.

She nodded.

His face relaxed with relief, but then contorted in pain.

"What is it?"

"My back feels different now," he replied.

In human form, the damage to his back looked worse. Kelly assumed the reason was because his wing injuries were now somehow integrated into his wingless human body. The gash stretched from his shoulder all the way across his back and down to the opposite hip. But on a positive note at least now his face didn't look as pale. Maybe the energy she had given him had helped more than just change him into human form.

Kelly pulled out her cell phone and called 911.

"They'll be here soon," she told Marcos when she got off the line with the 911 operator.

"Kelly, I—"

"Maybe you shouldn't try to talk any more."

"I want to tell you what happened, in case...just in case."

"All right, if it makes you feel better. But you're going to be fine."

He fixed his eyes on the ground and spoke softly. "After you called me about the disappearance, I realized my father was in New York when Thomas went missing. When my father got back, I confronted him. He said that he was the one who had captured Thomas, and he hadn't told me because I was going 'soft.' He said that to prove I was still strong, that I had to kill Thomas and take the Key to Embralia from him."

Her heart skipped a beat. "You didn't, did you?"

"No. But...the worst thing is, for a few seconds I tried to make myself do it. I didn't want my father to hate me."

"You didn't do it, though. That's what matters."

He frowned, unconvinced.

"That's when he tried to kill you?" Kelly asked.

"No. He tried to kill me when I helped Thomas escape."

"Thomas is safe, then?"

"I don't know. He got out, but my father chased after him."

The sense of relief Kelly had felt upon hearing Thomas had

escaped evaporated. *Miasmos caught Thomas once, he could catch him again.*

"You were right about my father," Marcos continued. "I just kept hoping he could change. But it's useless. He's insane."

Kelly wished she could think of something comforting to say to that, but she drew a blank. So she just patted Marcos's hand.

After a few moments of silence they heard sirens in the distance. "Maybe we should think of something to tell the paramedics," Kelly suggested.

Marcos smirked. "That's easy. We'll say it was an assassination attempt."

"By the same domestic terrorists who supposedly kidnapped you?"

"Those are the ones." He coughed. "This will be great for my standing in the polls."

KELLY SHIFTED AROUND YET AGAIN, trying to find a comfortable position. The chair beside Marcos's hospital bed was far from comfortable. *At least I'm not as uncomfortable as he's going to be when he wakes up,* she thought. Her eyes went to Marcos's right leg, which was wrapped in a full cast and held in an elevated position by a giant sling hanging down from the ceiling.

She looked at her watch; it was almost eight o'clock. Her mother hadn't tried calling. *She's probably having too much fun with 'Rick,'* Kelly thought with disgust. She slumped down in the chair and closed her eyes. The steady beeping of the Marcos's heart monitor was a reassuring sound.

She felt a tug inside her mind as someone reached out to her telepathically. It was Bubbles. *"Kelly, Kelly, I have news!"*

"What is it?"

"Thomas is back in Glendenland!"

Kelly breathed a sigh of relief. *"That's wonderful. Is he all right?"*

"He's fine," Bubbles replied. *"Well, he has some bruises and a broken arm but he will be better in no time."*

"That's good to hear."

"He said he wants to see you."

Kelly looked over at Marcos. She wanted to be there for him when he woke up. And she didn't want to leave him unconscious and defenseless. There were officers posted outside the door, but they were human. A fairy could fly right past them. *"Bubbles, I can't come to Glendenland until a little later tonight."*

"What do you mean you can't come until later?" Bubbles asked, clearly suspicious.

"I just can't."

"Why? Wait...am I sensing you in the hospital? What happened? Should I come over there?"

"No! I mean...that's not necessary. I just have to take care of something first. Tell Thomas I'll be there as soon as I can."

"But..."

Marcos stirred.

"Please, Bubbles, will you just tell him I'll be there later?"

"Fine. But you'd better tell me what's going on when you get here."

"I promise."

"Good."

Kelly dropped the connection with Bubbles. A few moments later Marcos opened his eyes.

"How are you feeling?" Kelly asked.

"Splendid," he deadpanned.

Kelly grinned. "Well, the doctor said you'll make a full recovery."

"My body might. Not sure about my pride."

"Miasmos is very powerful, you shouldn't be embarrassed he beat you in a fight," Kelly said.

"That's not what I meant."

'What did you mean, then?"

"Never mind."

There was an awkward silence. Kelly decided to change the subject. "I thought you'd want to know, that Thomas is back in Glendenland."

Marcos perked up. "Does he still have the Key to Embralia?"

"I don't know."

Marcos furrowed his brow in thought.

"Can your father sense that you're here?" Kelly asked him.

He shook his head no. "I've been shielding myself."

"Even when you were unconscious?"

He nodded. "Yes. But I will summon some fairies that are loyal to me, just in case."

"You'll summon them?"

"Of course. How else would they know to come here?"

"Couldn't you just ask them to come?"

He snorted. "You don't *ask* your underlings to do things, Kelly, you *command* them to do things."

Kelly frowned.

Marcos pointed to the remote control on the little table beside Kelly's chair. "You should turn on the TV," he said.

"Why?"

"You'll see."

Kelly switched on the TV. She nearly fell out of her chair when she saw the words: *News Flash, Marcos Witherings hospitalized* written across the bottom of the screen. A smartly-dressed female reporter with black hair stood outside the hospital. "I'm Melinda Tari, here to bring you a breaking news report. We've received reports that Marcos Witherings is hospitalized here, possibly as a result of an assassination attempt. An onlooker was able to capture this video on their cell phone."

The view cut to the outside of the building where Kelly had found Marcos. Kelly gasped when she saw the paramedics wheeling Marcos out of the building — and herself walking next to the stretcher. Someone on the street must have taped them.

"This video shows Mr. Witherings being put on the ambulance, accompanied by a mystery girl, rumored to be a high school student working on his campaign." With that the camera zoomed in on a close-up of Kelly's face. "Mr. Witherings is reported to be in stable condition. We'll have more news soon."

Oh no, I hope my mom doesn't see this, Kelly thought.

"Why the long face?" Witherings asked. "This is just according to our plan."

"I don't remember me being on TV being part of the plan." Her cell phone rang. "Great. It's my mother."

"Are you just going to stare at your phone or are you going to answer it?"

Kelly sighed and tapped the screen. "Hello?"

"Kelly Elizabeth Brennan!"

"Ouch, Mom, you don't need to yell."

"I'm sorry, dear. I just saw you on TV. I can't believe it! An assassination attempt? You could have been hurt."

"I'm fine, Mom."

"Why didn't you tell me you were working on Marcos Witherings's campaign?"

"I was going to tell you, but I just started today. Earlier I freaked out because I remembered I was supposed to meet Mr. Witherings this afternoon, and I was late. I'm sorry I ran off like that."

"It's all right, sweetie, I'm just glad you're okay. This is actually so exciting you are working on his campaign. Rick and I are coming to the hospital right now to pick you up, with Dmitri."

"Dmitri's still there?"

"Yes, he was worried about you. He stayed for dinner."

Kelly groaned internally, imagining how awkward dinner must have been for Dmitri without her there.

"So, we'll see you in a few minutes?" Mindy asked.

"Okay." Kelly hung up, rolling her eyes.

Marcos shot her a questioning look.

"She's positively tickled that I'm 'working on your campaign,'" Kelly said.

"How would you like to work on my campaign for real?" he asked.

"Um…"

He raised an eyebrow. "What, you don't want me to win?"

"To be honest, I'm still not sure."

"Fair enough. With our history I don't blame you. But I do hope you will give me a chance to show you I'm worthy of your support."

"Is that you talking, or the politician in you talking?" Kelly asked.

"Both."

KELLY ENTERED the general waiting area to see her mother, Rick, and Dmitri standing by the receiving desk. Mindy saw Kelly and rushed towards her, squeezing her tightly in a large bear hug.

"Mom, you can let go now."

Mindy squeezed tighter.

"Mom!"

Mindy reluctantly let go. Rick walked up and whispered something in Mindy's ear. Mindy gave an exaggerated nod. "We'll be just outside, in the car," she said. "You and Dmitri join us when you're ready."

"All right, Mom. Thanks."

Mindy and Rick left, arm in arm. Kelly wrinkled her nose in disgust.

"So, what's really going on?" Dmitri asked.

"What do you mean?" she asked innocently.

He didn't buy it. "Look, Kelly, I like you. I like you a lot. But I know you're holding something back. I want you to be honest with me. If you don't have trust then you don't have anything." He crossed his arms and waited for her to say something.

What is it with everybody and trust these days? "The truth is..." she began, wanting to tell him everything so much it hurt. But she knew letting him into the fairy world would only expose him to dangers — dangers like Miasmos and his minions. She couldn't bring herself to do it. "The truth is," she continued, "that there are just certain things about me that I can't share with you."

"That's it? That's what you're going to go with?"

"Yes. I hope you can accept that."

He was silent for a long time, staring down at his toes. Finally, he shook his head. "I'm sorry, but I don't think I can."

LATER THAT NIGHT Kelly flew out of her window into the crisp autumn air. On the flight to Glendenland she tried not to think about Dmitri. She kept telling herself she had done the right thing. He was better off this way. They both were. She didn't need more complications in her life right now.

When she arrived at the royal quarters Flimsly showed her back to Thomas's study. Thomas sat behind his desk. He had a black eye, and his right arm was in a sling. He looked very tired. Yet he still managed to grace Kelly with a warm smile. "Kelly, thank you for coming. Please, have a seat."

She sat down across from him. "I'm sorry I couldn't get here any earlier. I hope you didn't stay awake on my account."

"I'm afraid I won't be getting any sleep tonight." His expression darkened. "Or any night soon, for that matter."

"Why not?"

He glanced at the doorway, as if to assure himself Flimsly had left them, and that no one else was nearby. "This is very important," he whispered. "What I tell you now can't go beyond this room. Only my wife, Venuto, Dimpleton, Milak, and myself know." He paused, squinting at her. "What's the matter?" he asked.

"I'm just wondering, if it is such a big secret then why would you tell me?"

"Because of your connection to Marcos Witherings. He's the one person you may tell. He needs to know."

A shiver ran down Kelly's spine. "It's the Key to Embralia, isn't it? Miasmos has it."

Thomas gave an almost imperceptible nod.

"Does he know where Embralia is?"

"No, but it is only a matter of time until he finds the rest of the ten curtains. He's found at least one recently. Venalaz's wand."

"Like the Venalaz from the legend? The one who almost unleashed Embralia's power?"

"Yes. His wand is imbued with his evil even to this day. Anyone who possesses the wand becomes obsessed with the Key to Embralia. Miasmos gave the wand as a gift to Pixelatus about three weeks ago. Needless to say, soon after that the Pixelori entered into a secret alliance with the Miasmonians. They were all too happy to help Miasmos lay his trap for me."

Kelly's pulse quickened. The Pixelori were a large fairy band. They were almost four times larger than the Glendenians, in fact. If they were in league with Miasmos, then Miasmos had a brand new army. She felt a panic rising up inside her. It was hard to breathe. Thomas wavered like a mirage, then all of the sudden she was somewhere else.

The suns beat down on her, relentless. There was nothing except that same dark red ground in all directions, for as far as the eye could see. Wait — there was something on the horizon. She squinted. What was it? A building? A mountain? She felt a sweeping sense of déjà vu, and in the distance, she heard them: the whispers. Faint and far away, like wind whistling through a gap between rocks.

"Kelly?"

She jerked out of the vision and blinked a few times to reassure herself of her surroundings.

"What just happened?" Thomas asked.

"I've been having these, these flashes, ever since Venuto took the memory stone away from me."

"That's not good," the king said.

"Maybe if you gave it back to me, then they would stop," she suggested.

"Nice try, but I'm afraid I can't do that. The fact that the stone has such a hold over you even at a distance is a sign you aren't ready to be its master. You need to stay as far away from it as possible for the time being."

"But Ricketer said I had the power. He tried for years and he couldn't see into the stone. If he's right, and I'm the only one who can communicate with it, how else will we know how to defeat Miasmos if he finds the way to Embralia?"

Thomas massaged his forehead. "Maybe in a few months, when you are better at magic, maybe then, under my supervision, it will be safe for you to be near it for limited times."

"A few months?"

"I'm sorry, that's the best I can do."

"What if it's too late by then?" Kelly asked.

"We'll just have to hope it isn't."

~

BUBBLES WAS WAITING for Kelly in the hallway outside the royal living quarters. "So, time to spill your beans," he said.

"It's spill the beans, Bubbles. Not spill your beans." She started walking down the hall, and Bubbles fell into step beside her.

"Oh, well, whatever it is, spill it. What were you doing at the hospital?"

"Marcos Witherings got attacked by his father and I was helping him."

Bubbles's eyes bulged. "You were helping him?" he screeched. "Whatever possessed you to do that?"

"He reached out to me. I couldn't just leave him to die."

"You should have. This world would be better off without the likes of him."

"Don't say that. I'll have you know, Thomas wouldn't be alive right now if it weren't for Marcos. He helped Thomas escape."

Bubbles's cheeks puffed out and his face turned beet red. He looked like his head might explode. This news was just too shocking for him to absorb.

"Take a deep breath, Bubbles. Calm down."

"How could...how could this be?" he sputtered.

"Marcos has changed. He's a better person now."

Bubbles punched the air. "No, I don't believe it. I won't believe it. He must be pretending. It's part of a devious plan, I know it."

"I wish you wouldn't talk about him like that. He's...my friend."

Bubbles's eyebrows shot to the ceiling. "Your friend?" He put a hand on her shoulder, very serious. "People like Witherings don't have friends, Kelly. They have people they use."

She swatted his hand away. "You're being close-minded."

"You're being too trusting."

"Yeah? Well, if you don't have trust then you don't have anything." She thought of Dmitri and her stomach twisted.

Bubble's eyes brightened. "Oooh, that's a good saying. Is it from one of those, what do humans call them...oh yes, 'greeting cards'?"

He wasn't being sarcastic in the slightest. He waited eagerly for her answer. Kelly just rolled her eyes. "Good night, Bubbles."

11

WHISPERS

Right after Kelly took her seat in German class the next morning, Tommy Thompson plopped himself down in the empty chair beside her. He tossed a spiral notebook onto the desk in front of him.

"I saw you on the news," he said, eyes gleaming. "Can I join the campaign too?"

Kelly gave him an inquisitive look. "You do know we're too young to vote, right?"

He snorted. "That's not stopping you, is it?"

I walked right into that one, Kelly thought. She rolled her eyes.

"Guess what?" Tommy asked.

Kelly sighed. "What?"

"I thought of a new nickname for you." He waited. Clearly, he wanted her to ask him what it was. When she didn't, he frowned. "Don't you want to hear it?"

"If I let you tell me, will you go away?"

He flinched. "There's no need to be mean. Maybe I'll just leave." He picked up his spiral notebook and hugged it to his chest.

She hated that his reaction made her feel guilty. "Fine, Tommy. What is it?"

He sniffled. "You don't care."

"I do care," she lied. "I want to know. Really."

"Really?" His eyes met hers, hopeful.

"Really."

He grinned. "Then I'll tell you. It's Wither-girl! Get it? Because you are a girl and work for Marcos Witherings."

Kelly stifled a laugh. "Wither-girl? Don't you think that's kind of...silly?"

"No way, Kelly. It's cool. Like a superhero. See, I drew you." With pride he opened the spiral notebook and showed her his drawing. Kelly tried as hard as she could to keep a straight face at his artwork, which looked like something Kelly might have drawn in kindergarten. Wither-girl wore a tight pink leotard and a purple cape. Tommy had scrawled a shaky purple *W* on the front of the costume. "Well?" Tommy asked. "Do you like it?"

Kelly held her tongue. She didn't want her true thoughts to slip out. No need to make him cry. "It's interesting," she said finally.

His lower lip trembled. Interesting must not have been the answer he had been hoping for.

"At least Wither-girl is better than Fallgirl," Kelly added.

Tommy grinned, reenergized. "I drew a picture of that too, want to see?"

"Uh..."

Thankfully, before he had a chance to show her his vision of Fallgirl, Kelly's German partner arrived and Tommy went back to his usual seat.

~

IN THE LUNCH line it became clear that Tommy Thompson wasn't the only one who had seen Kelly on TV. Students kept coming up to her and asking for a firsthand account of the assassination attempt. She enjoyed seeing the looks on their faces when she told them she couldn't give any details for the sake of 'national security.' They gazed at her with looks that hovered somewhere between awe and jealousy. The one person who steered clear of her was Dmitri. She scanned the lunch area for him while she waited, trying not to be too obvious. She spotted him at the table where he always used to sit at the beginning of the school year, surrounded by his popular friends. Dmitri's eyes caught hers briefly, but he quickly looked away. *Ouch.*

"Whoa, what's with you and Dmitri?" a familiar voice from behind Kelly asked.

"Stephanie!" Kelly spun around and gave her friend a hug. "Where have you been? I tried calling you last night but you didn't answer."

"Sorry about that. I was with Blaine." Stephanie winked. "So, what's the matter with Dmitri?"

"He doesn't want to see me anymore because he knows I'm keeping secrets."

Stephanie grabbed a lunch tray. "That's rough," she said. "But it's not like you can tell every guy you like what you are."

"I know, but that doesn't make me feel any better."

"I'm sorry, Kelly. Really, I am." She patted Kelly's shoulder. "But maybe it's for the best."

Kelly stole another glance at Dmitri. While his friends laughed around him, he stared down at his plate, somewhere in his own world.

Once Kelly and Stephanie made it through the line, they sat down at a vacant table in the emptiest part of the cafeteria. Despite their relative isolation, Stephanie still looked around to make sure no one was eavesdropping on them. Then she leaned forward with a conspiratorial look in her eye. "Now, I saw the news like everybody else, but it's time you told me what really happened."

While Stephanie started in on her Salisbury steak, Kelly filled her in about the happenings of the day before. When she got to the part about Rick, the doctor, getting involved with Mindy, Stephanie interrupted. "You've got to be kidding," she exclaimed.

"I'm afraid not."

"That's so unprofessional," Stephanie commented with an eye roll.

"Tell me about it."

"What do you think he wants?"

"Besides the obvious?" Kelly asked. "I have no idea. It's not like she has money or anything, and he seems to have plenty."

Stephanie shook her head. "Men are strange." She shrugged. "Go on."

Kelly continued, finishing up with how Bubbles had reacted to the news of Witherings's break from his father. "Can you believe Bubbles is being so close-minded?" Kelly asked.

"Well..." Stephanie pushed her mashed potatoes around with her fork.

"Don't tell me you're on his side."

"Not entirely," Stephanie said with a frown. "It's just, being a 'good guy' is kind of new for Witherings. Are you sure it will last?"

"I'm sure."

"I hope you're right." Stephanie abandoned what was left of her mashed potatoes and tore the lid off of her vanilla pudding. "Oh, I almost forgot. Blaine said I should ask you if you wanted to start Ardagali lessons this afternoon. Even though he'll be there with you when you go to find your dad, he thinks you should learn some of their language too."

"I still haven't agreed to let him come," Kelly reminded her friend.

Stephanie chuckled. "Come on, we both already know you're going to let him come." She paused to lick the pudding lid. "Am I wrong?"

"No, you're right," Kelly admitted.

"Good. Because I already told him to meet us at your place after school."

~

BLAINE LOUNGED COMFORTABLY in Stephanie's lap. His head rested on the back of her left hand. Kelly thought the pair looked very odd when Stephanie wasn't shrunk with fairy dust. It was like Blaine was Stephanie's pet.

"The Ardagali have a rigid social structure," Blaine explained. "You always have to use the proper forms of address with them. Also, they are very superstitious."

"What do you mean, like, 'don't walk under a ladder' superstitious?" Kelly asked.

Blaine nodded. "Pretty much. They have hundreds of superstitions. For example if you wear a black scarf with a red shirt, it's very bad luck. But a red scarf with a black shirt is good luck."

"Why?" Kelly asked.

Blaine shrugged. "How should I know?"

Stephanie giggled. "Tell her about the idioms thing."

Kelly raised an eyebrow. "What idioms?"

Blaine's eyes sparkled. "If you think the superstitions are bad, Kelly, you're going to love this."

Uh-oh, Kelly thought.

"You see, the Ardagali love idioms. That means, even if you happen to recognize all the words they are using, you still might have no clue what they're talking about."

"Can you give an example?" Kelly asked.

"Sure. The most obvious one is that they don't like to say 'yes' or 'no' directly. Those words exist, but it is considered rude to use them."

Kelly frowned. "Then what do you say instead?"

"To say 'yes,' you might say 'blue looks stunning on the queen.' It's a reference to when the first king of the Ardagali was asked if his wife should wear a blue dress."

"That's not so hard to remember," Kelly said.

Blaine shook his head. "It's not that simple. That only means 'yes' in certain kinds of situations."

"Like when?"

"Like, situations about fashion or relationships." He stroked his chin pensively. "It's really hard to explain. You just kind of get a feel for it over time."

Kelly groaned. "I don't have time."

"Try not to worry too much," Blaine said. "I'll be there too, remember?"

"How would the Ardagali say 'no'?" Stephanie asked.

"Well, Buttercup, there are literally thousands of ways. They actually take pride in making the most obscure references possible. Once an Ardagali said 'no' to me with 'a rainstorm in May is a welcome respite.' I still don't know what that refers to, but I know he meant 'no' because a few seconds later he shot a fireball at me."

There was a knock on the door. "Kelly?"

"It's my mother," Kelly said. "Quick, go invisible."

Blaine snapped his fingers and became transparent.

Mindy pushed the door open a few inches. "Girls? Can I come in?"

Kelly nodded.

Mindy entered, cradling a fancy gold-trimmed envelope like it was worth a million dollars. "This was just delivered by private messenger," she said. Her voice trembled with excitement. She sat down on the bed beside Kelly and handed her the envelope.

Stephanie leaned over Kelly's shoulder to see, and Blaine flew up into the air over their heads to get a better look. The beautiful flowing script on the envelope read: *To Kelly Brennan from Marcos Witherings.*

"What are you waiting for? Open it," Mindy said.

"I'm getting to that, Mom."

"Sorry, I just really want to know what it says."

Kelly opened the letter and read it aloud. "You are cordially invited to a gala in your honor at the residence of Mr. Witherings, on the fifteenth of October—"

Mindy interrupted with a high-pitched squeal. "This is so exciting. He's having a party for you because you were so brave when the assassins tried to kill him."

Kelly didn't share her mother's excitement. *He'd better not be expecting me to make a speech,* she thought.

"Is there more?" Mindy asked.

Kelly read on. "Your mother is also invited. Please return the RSVP cards." Kelly handed Mindy's RSVP card to her.

Mindy giggled like a schoolgirl. "It says we can bring a plus one! Rick will be over the moon. He's almost as big a fan of Marcos Witherings as I am."

"I doubt that," Stephanie quipped.

"Mom, do you have to bring Rick?" Kelly asked.

"Why not? Listen, I know it's weird for you because he's your doctor. But don't worry. He says he has a partner in his practice that works with him. So you can just switch doctors. That will solve the problem entirely."

"No, it won't," Kelly said.

Mindy jumped to her feet, nearly bumping into Blaine, who did a quick sideways somersault to get out of her way. "Kelly, I really wish you wouldn't stomp all over my plant like that," she said.

Kelly raised her eyebrows. "Your plant?"

"Yes. My relationship with Rick is a tiny little plant that wants to grow into a flower, but you keep trying to kill it." Mindy's lower lip trembled. She was on the verge of tears.

Kelly didn't know what to say. She *was* trying to kill the 'plant,' after all.

"I'm sure Kelly will warm up to Rick in time, Mrs. Brennan," Stephanie said in her best reassuring voice.

Mindy sniffled. "I want to hear her say that."

Stephanie gave Kelly a look that said: *you'd better tell her what she wants to hear or she'll never leave us alone.*

Kelly sighed. "Fine, Mom. I'm sure I'll warm up to him eventually. Are you happy now?"

Mindy nodded. "Yes, I feel much better."

Stephanie pointed to Kelly's RSVP card. "I'm your plus one, right Kelly?" she asked.

Kelly grinned. "Of course. I wouldn't bring anyone else."

Mindy brought a hand to her chest dramatically. "My goodness, the fifteenth is barely two weeks from now. What am I going to wear?" She ran out of the room. A few seconds later they heard her hangers clanging around in her closet.

"Speaking of which, what are you going to wear?" Stephanie asked Kelly.

"I don't know. Something fancy I guess."

Blaine sat back down on the bed and snapped his fingers to return to his fully visible form. "Are we going to continue our lesson, or should I leave you two alone to be girls?" he said with a smirk.

"Hey, there's no need to be jealous because you weren't invited," Kelly said.

"Or because you don't get to wear pretty dresses like we do," Stephanie teased.

Blaine laughed. "Trust me, I have no desire to wear a dress."

"I'm glad to hear it," Stephanie said. "Because if you did I might just have to dump you."

WHEN BLAINE and Stephanie left that evening, Kelly wasted no time in calling Marcos Witherings. He answered on the first ring.

"Hello, Kelly."

"A gala, Marcos? Seriously?"

"What's the matter?" His voice was laced with amusement. She could imagine the self-satisfied glint he must have had in his eyes. "You don't appreciate parties in your honor?"

"I might, if it weren't such an obvious publicity stunt," she replied.

His chuckle rasped through the speaker. "You are very astute. You really should consider working on my campaign for real."

Kelly was silent.

"Does this mean you aren't going to attend?" Marcos asked. "It's difficult to have a gala without the guest of honor."

"I didn't say that. My mother is too excited about it for me not to come. But I'm not giving a speech. Or talking to reporters."

"Very well. All I ask is that you pose for a few publicity shots."

Kelly groaned. "If you insist."

Marcos laughed. "You really need to learn to enjoy the limelight, Kel."

"Why?"

"Because the way things are going, you're only likely to get more of it." He coughed.

The reality of his recent injuries flashed in her mind. "How are you feeling?" she asked.

"I'm on the mend." She heard a rustle through the speaker as he shifted positions. "My sources tell me that my cousin is also on the path to recovery."

"Your cousin?"

"Yes. Glendenland's king, of course."

"Oh," Kelly said. "I keep forgetting Miasmos is Thomas's uncle. It's hard to believe they're related."

"Well, I'm sure Thomas would just as soon forget the same blood runs through their veins. I know the feeling."

The pain in his voice tugged at Kelly's heart. She could only imagine what it must be like to have someone like Miasmos as a father. If her father were someone like him, she would rather never find him. *And what do I know about my father?* she thought. *Almost nothing.* What if he wasn't a good person? After all, he had abandoned his own daughter, and possibly erased Mindy's memory. She shuddered.

"Have you spoken to Thomas?" Marcos asked.

Kelly's heart sank. "I'm afraid so."

Her tone must have said it all. "Miasmos has it then," Marcos said grimly.

"Yes."

He was silent for a long time. She waited, expecting him to say something about what they should do now — an idea, anything, about how they might stop his father now that he'd acquired the Key to Embralia. But when Marcos finally spoke, all he said was: "Good night."

THE WHISPERS DRONED in the distance, indecipherable yet insistent, urging her to move forward. At least, that's what she thought they were doing. If felt as though she had walked for days, but the object that beckoned on the horizon appeared no closer than before. It was still too indistinct to make out, no more than a purple blob easily

obscured by her fingertip. How was it still so far away? Could it be moving? As soon as she had that thought, some of the whispers erupted with light clanking sounds, like hundreds of toast glasses at a formal occasion. These clanking sounds were imbibed with mirth. It, or they, were…laughing? At her? She stopped in her tracks. "This is funny to you?" she shouted. "Having me walk and walk, getting nowhere?"

Silence. Surprise. Not even the hint of a whisper.

"This place isn't even real," she continued. "You're creating it in my mind. Well, if you want to show me something, then show me. Take me to it!"

Silence. Tension.

"I refuse to go on like this," she yelled. She plopped herself down on the ground.

Potential energy.

She held her breath, hoping she hadn't pushed too hard. She knew how it felt when the stone got mad. She braced herself for the ear-splitting shriek, but it didn't come. Instead, without warning, something small and round fell from the sky — and onto her head. Hard. She cursed, rubbing the impact point. It would bruise for sure, if this were real. She looked around for the object. A small, metallic ball glistened on the ground beside her. It resembled the memory stone, but it was tinted blue, not purple. She'd seen it before. It was the stone Marcos had — the bearer. Kelly picked it up. Her palm tingled under its touch.

As she gazed at the stone, the whispers began again, running over and under each other, bubbling like a brook. Energetic. Excited. They expected her to do something. They wanted her to use the stone for something. But what?

Kelly jerked awake. Her alarm clock read five in the morning. There was only a little over an hour left before she had to get ready for school. She groaned. She felt drained, like she had been up all night doing math equations. She ran her finger over the still-sore skin around her bellybutton. She hated to admit it, but maybe Thomas and Venuto were right about the memory stone. If it was tiring her out so much all the way from Glendenland, what would it be like if she still had it under her skin?

There was a tap on her window. She squinted through the darkness. Bubbles's face was pressed up against the glass. He waved. She got up and opened the window.

Her fairy friend flew inside. "I'm glad you're awake," he said. "I wanted to talk to you, but I didn't want to wake you up. But then I saw that you woke up, so—"

"Just, get to the point, will you, Bubbles?" Kelly massaged her forehead.

He cocked his head to the side and looked her up and down. "What's the matter with you?"

"Nothing, I just have a headache."

"Then I'll be quick." He sat down on her pillow. "Ooh, comfy. Is this new?" He bounced around happily.

"Yes, my mom bought me a new pillow a few weeks ago."

"She has good taste." He nodded approvingly. "Do you think I could get one in fairy size?"

Kelly gave Bubbles a stern look. "You said you'd be quick."

"Oh, right, sorry. I came to tell you that Reynalda's birthday celebration has been rescheduled for this afternoon. Right after your human school ends."

"All right, thanks." She got back into bed and nudged Bubbles off her pillow.

He rolled to the side with a squeal of delight. "I really love your pillow, Kelly. Can I take a nap here when you're at school?"

She closed her eyes. "I'm going back to sleep now."

"Well, can I?"

"Yes, you can take a nap here when I'm at school."

"Kelly, you really are the best. See you at the party!"

She heard the sound of his wings flapping as he flew out

the window. She was too tired to get up and close it. Besides, she could use the fresh air.

~

"WHY ARE YOU FLYING SO SLOWLY?" Stephanie asked, spinning around to glare at Kelly. She hovered in the air, hands on her hips, at least fifteen feet ahead.

"Why are you flying so fast?" Kelly retorted.

"Fast? This is nothing." Stephanie shot off at top speed towards the river.

"Showoff," Kelly muttered under her breath. Stephanie never seemed to get tired out by flying; it was one of the perks of her prosthetic wings. Kelly, on the other hand, did, although she shouldn't have been this tired. They were only halfway to Glendenland. *It must be because I didn't sleep very well last night,* she thought.

"It's about time," Stephanie said when Kelly finally reached the tree by the river. Stephanie was perched on one of its branches. Kelly set down beside her, panting. Stephanie pointed to the lion statue. "We'll just wait for that little kid to walk by, then we can go down."

"Why don't we just go through the river?" Kelly asked.

"And risk smearing these?" Stephanie batted her eyelashes. "I don't think so."

Kelly watched the child who was playing by the statue. He rolled a ball back and forth along the ground. "It doesn't look like he's going to leave anytime soon."

"We're early. We can afford to wait a few minutes. Besides, it will give you a chance to catch your breath."

Kelly was about to reply with a snide remark when a high-pitched scraping sound startled her. She flinched.

"What's wrong?" Stephanie asked.

"Did you hear something?"

"No. What did you hear?"

Kelly listened closely for the sound, but it was gone. She shrugged. "I guess it was nothing." But a second later something pressed on the back of her mind. An invitation. Along with it came the whispers, buzzing with their strange, amorphous tones. She did her best to ignore them.

Stephanie gave her an odd look, somewhere between suspicion and concern. "If it was something, you would tell me, wouldn't you?"

"Of course." Pressure built up behind Kelly's eyes.

Stephanie nudged Kelly with her elbow. "Look, the kid just got called away by his mother. We can go down now." She hopped off the tree branch and flew down to the statue.

Kelly got up to follow. After only a few wing flaps, the whispers grew harsher, closer. Filling up her mind so that they were everything. She couldn't think. Then her view of Stephanie down by the lion statue wavered like a mirage.

Back in the desert, she examined the stone intently. The whispers were faster now, close by, tumbling about her like the raging rapids of a river. Energetic. Impatient. "I don't understand," she said. "What do you want me to do?"

Discordant harmonies. Glasses shattering one after another. Frustration.

"All right, all right. I'll keep trying." She brought the stone closer. Very faint lines, in a spider-web like pattern, were etched into the surface. Maybe they held the answer.

Kelly blinked. She lay flat on her back at the base of the lion statue.

Stephanie leaned over her. "So this is what 'nothing' looks like?" she asked. "I thought you were good at telepathy without passing out."

"I am, well, with fairies anyway."

Stephanie's brow furrowed. "Are you all right? You took quite a tumble."

Kelly moaned. Her head ached, and though the vision was gone the call of the memory stone remained. The raindrops of notes crashed against each other, building to a downpour. She had to get away from them. She scrambled to her feet.

"Where are you going?" Stephanie asked.

"I'm going home to rest."

"What about Reynalda's birthday party?"

Kelly's skull shook under the cacophonous torrent. "If you see Reynalda, give her my regards." She jumped into the air and flew away as fast as her wings could carry her.

KELLY PLACED a teabag in a mug and poured boiling water over it. She leaned against the kitchen counter and dunked the teabag up and down in the water so it would steep faster. *Not like I'm in a hurry,* he thought. It was midnight, and she was afraid to fall asleep. Tea had seemed like a good idea. It had caffeine. Too bad there wasn't any coffee in the house.

The tea didn't smell like anything, but the water was already a dark brown. Kelly removed the teabag. She blew on the tea before taking a sip — then promptly spit it out. *Yuck! What is this stuff?* It tasted like rotten banana peels. Kelly grabbed the tea box and took a closer look at the label. It read: *Tantric Splendor Tea.* Kelly wrinkled her nose. *Well, it's not very splendid.* Her mother had never bought this kind of tea before. Kelly turned the box over to read the ingredients. When she did, she saw a handwritten note. *To Mindy, from Rick. Drink this and think of me.* Kelly dropped the box like it was a hot potato. *Ew!* She ran the faucet in the sink and rinsed her mouth out under the stream of water.

After the rotten aftertaste was gone, she sat down at the table and rested her head on her hands. She yawned. She needed something to keep herself awake. Practice using her fairy senses might keep her mind active. She sat up straight, closed her eyes and took a deep breath as she pushed her awareness outwards and upwards, to where her mother slept upstairs. She sensed Mindy's energy flickering peacefully in her bed. *At least someone in this house can sleep without an ancient artifact bothering her,* Kelly thought.

She let her awareness drift to the rest of the house. Her fairy senses picked up nothing in the other rooms upstairs or in the living room downstairs. She pushed her awareness out onto the front porch. To her surprise, a mass of boisterous energy was heading straight for the door. It was a fairy whose vibrations reminded her of a festive state fair.

She ran to open the front door. "Dimpleton!"

"Hey-o, Kelly." He flashed a wide grin and flew inside. "I was just about to ask you to let me in, but I see your fairy senses have gotten much better. I'm impressed."

"Thank you." She closed the door. She transformed into her fairy form and they sat down on the couch. "What brings you here?" she asked.

"We missed you at the party. I was hoping to see you before I leave for my next assignment in the morning."

"What assignment?"

He winked. "You know I'm not supposed to give any details."

"Oh, right."

Dimpleton raised an eyebrow. "I thought you'd be more curious. I expected you to pry."

"Do you want me to pry?"

"No, I'm just surprised you didn't."

Kelly shrugged. "I didn't need to. There are only a few things it could be."

Dimpleton squinted. "How do you figure?"

"Either your mission is to see what the Pixelori are up to, or it's to try and find out what Miasmos is up to, or it's to try and get to the rest of the ten curtains before Miasmos does."

He laughed. "Not much gets past you, does it?"

She grinned. "Nope. So, which is it?"

He lowered his voice to a whisper. "I can only speak hypothetically, you understand."

Her grin widened. "Of course."

"Thomas already let you in on the secret that the Pixelori have sided with Miasmos," he began.

Kelly nodded.

"That much we know. What we don't know is what percentage of their band is in agreement with that decision. Are they united in force? Or is Pixelatus acting out of line with the rest? We must determine which it is. If they are unified, they may soon declare war upon us."

Kelly's heart skipped a beat.

He patted her knee. "Don't look so scared, we're not there yet."

"We might be soon."

"True," he acknowledged. "But cheer up, Kelly. There's no use getting all twisted up about it."

"How do you do that?"

"Do what?"

"Be so happy all the time."

He laughed. "I suppose it's in my nature."

Kelly yawned.

Dimpleton stood up. "I shouldn't keep you. It's late for you, isn't it?"

"I'm afraid to go to sleep."

He sat back down, concerned. "Why?"

She told him about the memory stone infringing on her dreams.

"You need to put up a mind barrier," he said matter-of-factly once she had finished.

"You make it sound so easy," she said, discouraged.

"Don't worry, it is. Before you go to sleep, just imagine that there is a protective bubble around you, and that nothing can come inside unless you invite it."

Her eyebrows shot to the ceiling. "That's it?"

He chuckled. "Yes. Visualize it as you fall asleep. Trust me, it works like a charm."

Kelly frowned.

"Look, if you could sense me on the porch, your fairy senses are strong enough."

"I don't know about that," Kelly said. "But I'll give it a try."

After Dimpleton left, Kelly lay in bed and closed her eyes. Here goes, she thought. She imagined she was inside a protective cocoon of energy. She visualized it as an impenetrable orb that any incoming whispers would simply bounce off of before dissolving into nothingness. The air became very still and quiet all around her, and she felt a deep sense of calm. That night she slept the best she had in weeks.

12

LAND OF THE TERRIBLE ONES

Kelly pushed her mother's door open. "Are you ready yet? Your boyfriend is going to get impatient." She almost gagged upon using the word boyfriend to describe Rick.

Mindy pressed an eyelash curler up to her right eye. "Don't be silly. He doesn't get impatient."

Kelly snorted. "Really? Let me guess, he walks on water too."

Mindy ignored Kelly's remark. She stared intently into the mirror as she curled the lashes on her other eye. Then she applied a thick coating of mascara. Mindy looked stunning in a knee-length black dress with a plunging neckline. Kelly wore a light lavender dress and minimal make-up. It had taken her all of ten minutes to get ready. Her mother had been primping for over an hour.

The doorbell rang. Kelly heard Rick's footsteps as he crossed the living room below to answer it. "Mom, that's the limo Mr. Witherings sent. Let's go."

"In a minute." Mindy carefully unscrewed the cap off her red lip liner.

Kelly sighed.

Fifteen minutes later they finally made it outside. An elegant stretch limo awaited on the curb.

"Mr. Witherings certainly spares no expense," Mindy commented.

When the driver opened the door for them, Kelly saw that Stephanie was already inside, lounging comfortably on a luxurious leather couch that stretched almost the entire length of the interior. She sipped a sparkling liquid from a slender glass.

Kelly sat down next to her friend. "Is that champagne?" she asked.

"Sparkling apple cider. Here, have some." Stephanie leaned over to the miniature bar anchored to the opposite wall. She filled a fresh glass with cider and handed it to Kelly. Kelly took a sip. It was just right — not too sweet, but not too sour.

"I like your outfit, Rick," Stephanie said once the doctor and Mindy were situated in the limo.

"Why, thank you," he said, puffing his chest out with pride like a peacock.

Kelly wrinkled her nose. Instead of a traditional suit, Rick wore flowing silk pants and an Eastern-inspired shirt that reached past his knees. He looked like he was headed for a martial arts exhibition. His hair was down and curled in neat ringlets. He'd probably used a curling iron. Rick leaned over and whispered something in Mindy's ear. She giggled.

Kelly handed her glass back to Stephanie.

"You don't like it?"

"Suddenly I feel sick to my stomach," she replied with a sideways glance at her mother and Rick.

Stephanie nodded in understanding. "I see."

A half-an-hour drive brought them to the residence of Marcos Witherings. A stately circular driveway looped before a majestic brick dwelling. As they came to a stop, Mindy pressed her hands against the limo's window and peered out.

"It's beautiful. I had no idea Mr. Witherings lived in a mansion."

"He is one of the richest men in the United States," Rick said. "I'm surprised it isn't bigger."

"Maybe he owns more than one," Stephanie suggested.

Kelly found it hard to admire the house; she was too distracted by the fact that a crowd of photographers waited like vultures behind the red velvet ropes that lined the path to the front door. *Why is Marcos so addicted to publicity?* She didn't understand it. The feeling she got from being the center of attention was far from pleasant. She wiped her palms on her dress. The driver came around to the passenger door. He opened it and offered a gloved hand to help the guests out. *No use delaying the inevitable,* Kelly thought. She accepted the driver's hand and stepped out.

The photographers erupted with activity. Flashbulbs went off a mile a minute, so bright that Kelly feared her entire vision would be overtaken with afterimages. People called her name, but she didn't even know where to look amidst the sea of flickers.

"This must be what the celebrities feel like," Stephanie said through a wide smile.

Kelly glanced at her mother and Rick. They seemed to be enjoying the attention just as much as Stephanie. Mindy gave the perfect pageant wave, and Rick strutted along like he was God's gift to humanity. The three of them paused so many times to pose for the cameras that they'd barely moved forward at all. Losing patience, Kelly strode ahead. She ignored the frantic shouts of: "Kelly, over here!" and "Smile for us, Kelly!"

In front of the door a muscular man in a suit, with a curly wire ear bud, stood beside a podium. He swiftly unhooked the rope blocking the door, then moved on to the door itself. Kelly breathed a hefty sigh of relief as she stepped over the threshold and into a spacious anteroom.

The anteroom sported plush carpets in dark blue and walls in a calming shade of cream. A gorgeous blonde woman in a gray pantsuit waited just inside the door. She extended a hand for Kelly to shake. "Hello, Kelly, I'm Candice, one of Mr. Witherings's assistants. He requested I greet you and show you to the ballroom."

"Nice to meet you," Kelly said.

"Likewise. Would you like to go now, or would you prefer to wait for the rest of your entourage?"

My entourage? That was an odd way to refer to her companions. "Um, we can wait for them."

When Stephanie, Mindy, and Rick finally made it inside, Candice led them all down a series of long hallways. Classical landscapes and portraits of old men in suits lined the walls at regular intervals. The last hallway ended in two massive wooden doors. As they approached, the doors swung open without a sound to reveal to a beautiful ballroom. An impressive chandelier hung from the domed ceiling, casting sparkling patterns of light onto the polished marble floor. Two sets of stairs curved along the far walls up to a narrow balcony, from which one could survey the crowd. A fair amount of people milled around the hors d'oeuvres tables that dotted the sides of the room.

Stephanie nudged Kelly. "Look, it's you."

Kelly's eyes followed the direction of Stephanie's finger. Standing almost dead center in the ballroom was a life-sized cardboard cutout of Kelly. She recognized the photo from last year's school yearbook. A cardboard cutout of Marcos sporting an arrogant smirk had been placed next to hers.

Kelly groaned. "That's ridiculous."

"I think it's cool," Stephanie said. "I've always wanted a life-sized cardboard cutout of myself."

"Why?"

Stephanie shrugged. "No particular reason."

"I see the guest of honor has arrived," a familiar voice said.

Kelly turned around. Marcos was a few yards away, and quickly closing the distance. He somehow moved with both grace and speed in spite of the fact that he was on crutches. He also managed to look quite fashionable; his crutches were jet black, just like his suit, and a dark fabric had been pulled over the visible parts of his cast.

"You must be Mindy," Marcos said. He took Mindy's hand and kissed it. "You're even more beautiful than your daughter said you were."

Kelly rolled her eyes.

Marcos's compliment made Mindy blush with pleasure. For a split second jealousy flashed on Rick's face, but he recovered his composure by the time Marcos shook his hand.

"This architecture is amazing," Rick said. "I particularly appreciate the crown molding on the ceiling."

Marcos smiled graciously. "You have a good eye. Would you like a full tour?"

"That would be splendid," Rick replied.

Marcos put a hand in the air and snapped his fingers. Before Kelly could blink Candice was by his side. "Candice, our guests Mindy, Rick, and Stephanie would like a tour."

"Of course, Mr. Witherings."

"What about Kelly?" Stephanie asked. She glared at Marcos suspiciously.

"I would like to borrow her for a few minutes, if I may."

Candice extended an arm. "Right this way."

Stephanie scowled, but followed Candice after receiving a reassuring look from Kelly.

Kelly turned to Marcos. "What do you want to borrow me for?"

"To go over your speech, of course."

"What? I told you I wasn't giving a speech!"

His eyes sparkled. "Relax, I'm only kidding. But the look on your face was priceless."

"That was so not funny," Kelly said.

"I beg to differ." He nodded cordially to an older gentleman who walked by. "Let's go up to the balcony, it's more quiet up there," he suggested.

Kelly's eyes went from the stairs to his crutches, and back again.

He chuckled. "Don't worry, there's an elevator." He led her over to the sidewall, where an inconspicuous door, painted the same white as the wall, concealed a sleek elevator.

"Nice," Kelly said when they stepped inside.

Once up on the balcony they leaned against the railing and looked down on the crowd.

"Do you like your party?" Marcos asked.

Before she could answer she felt a pull on the inside of her mind, along with the faint sound of glasses clanking together. The whispers. She closed her eyes and imagined the barrier like Dimpleton had shown her. They faded away.

When she opened her eyes Marcos gave her an inquisitive look.

"Sorry," she said. "It's the memory stone." She went on to explain how it kept trying to connect with her, despite their physical separation.

"Most fascinating," Marcos said. "You should try accepting sometime. It could be trying to tell you something important."

"I know, but it can be very overwhelming so my friend Dimpleton showed me how to block it." She remembered how Marcos's stone had figured prominently in her last visions. "Does your stone try to communicate with you?" she asked.

"No. I don't think it contains any information to be accessed."

"Have you figured out what it's for then?"

He shook his head no.

"I think it might have something to do with the lines on it."

He raised an eyebrow. "What lines?"

"Look closer, maybe they will show up. They did in my vision."

"I will do that," he said. An older woman standing by the cardboard cutouts below waved up at them. Marcos nodded politely in acknowledgement.

"Who's that?" Kelly asked.

"She's a policy advisor. Her son just volunteered for the charity house-building project for youths I'm running this Thanksgiving."

"I thought politicians were supposed to spend time with their families on the holidays."

He snorted. "With my family? My mother died years ago, and as you know I'm a bachelor. So my PR department came up with this idea as a substitute. Charity always looks good."

Kelly frowned. "So you don't really want to help people. It's just for show."

"I didn't say that. It's just two birds with one stone, so to speak. You should come."

"I can't. That's when I'm going to the Ardagali to try and find my father."

"Oh yes, I'd almost forgotten you intended to venture to the Land of the Terrible Ones."

"I still need something to tell my mother that she will believe, though. Is there any way I could pretend to go on your charity trip?" Kelly asked.

He brought an index finger to his chin, considering it. After a moment he nodded. "Very well. None of the attendees know you, or intersect with your life, so it shouldn't be a problem. It will be a good cover story. We can even digitally insert you into some of the photos to show your mother. She will love it."

"Thank you, that will be a huge help," Kelly said.

"That's what friends do, isn't it? They help each other."

She smiled. "Yes." She thought back to the first time she and Marcos had met. He had kidnapped her, tried to force her to join him and his father, and then gleefully zapped her with electricity bolts. If anyone had told her then that a few months later she would consider Marcos a friend, she would have thought they were crazy.

Marcos must have been having similar thoughts. "It's funny how things work out sometimes."

She nodded in agreement. They looked down on the party in silence for a few moments. Below, people posed next to the cardboard cutouts and took pictures. *That's silly*, Kelly thought. If they wanted pictures, why didn't they just come up to the balcony for pictures with the real thing?

"Kel, about your father, you may not believe me, but I'm glad you are going to look for him. I know what it's like not knowing who your father is."

"You do? I thought Miasmos raised you."

At that he laughed so hard that it turned into a maniacal-sounding cackle, probably a trait he had picked up over the years from Miasmos. *He needs to work on his non-evil laugh,* she thought. But she kept that observation to herself. "He didn't raise me," Marcos said, once he'd stopped cackling. "He doesn't have it in him to deal with babies. I didn't know about him until I was fourteen, when my fairy side manifested itself. Then he came to find me."

Her chest felt hollow. *Why didn't mine come to find me?*

A pained expression took shape on Marcos's face. "I just hope that when you find your father, you have better luck than I had with mine."

"Somehow I'm both touched and depressed by that sentiment," she replied.

He adjusted his tie. "I do have a way with words."

"Marcos, can I ask you something?"

"Of course."

"Why are you still running for president? Wasn't that part of your father's master plan?"

"That's simple. As president I'll have more resources at my disposal. And most importantly, I'll be in charge of the secret fairy program."

Her jaw dropped. "The government knows about fairies?"

He chuckled at her surprise. "Oh yes. But it requires the highest clearance level. Only a handful of military and scientists are involved. They are trying to figure out how magic works. Needless to say, they haven't gotten very far."

"How do you know about this?"

"I have my sources," he said with a sly grin. "Oh, look, your friends are done with their tour. Shall we go mingle?"

When they stepped out of the elevator, Mindy and company were waiting for them. "How was the tour?" Marcos asked.

"It was great," Mindy said. "Your house is beautiful."

"Thank you."

"What were you two talking about?" Mindy asked.

"Mr. Witherings was telling me about the charity trip he's running over Thanksgiving," Kelly said.

"That sounds fabulous. Tell me more, Mr. Witherings."

"My pleasure. Shall we have a seat over there?" He winked at Kelly over his shoulder as he and Mindy approached a row of chairs on the far wall. Rick followed a few steps behind them, like he was afraid to get left behind. Kelly watched with smug satisfaction. For all of his posturing, Rick seemed very insecure. Or maybe he was just intimidated. Marcos was clearly a more accomplished man than he was.

Stephanie grabbed Kelly's elbow. "Come on, you have to see the hors d'oeuvres! They have brie tartlets that are just to die for."

KELLY STUFFED her hands in the pockets of her sweatshirt. It was chilly, and the leaves had turned on nearly all of the trees. Dead ones crunched underfoot as she walked down the street. Leftover Halloween decorations peeked out of a trash bin in front of a row of houses. She felt a tug in her heart when she remembered Dmitri helping her decorate. Since that day he'd pretty much ignored her, except for sending her hurt looks from the corner of his eye every so often when he thought she wasn't looking. She'd wanted to talk to him again, but she didn't know what she could say. As much as she wanted to tell him everything, she knew it wasn't wise. She worried enough about Stephanie being in danger because she knew about fairies. It was safer for Dmitri to stay away from her.

Her phone buzzed in her pocket. "Hello?"

"Kelly, where are you? You were supposed to meet us for your last Ardagali lesson."

"Sorry, Stephanie. I completely forgot. I went for a walk."

"Well, your mom let me in. So just get back here soon."

"I'm on my way."

A few minutes later Kelly stepped in through the front door to find Mindy waiting for her on the couch, hands crossed in her lap, and a serious expression on her face. "Kelly, do you have a minute?"

"Not really. Stephanie is waiting for me upstairs."

"Please, just a minute."

"All right." Kelly sat down beside her mother. "What is it?"

Mindy took a deep breath. "We need to talk about Rick."

Kelly groaned.

"I really like him, Kelly, and he likes me. I want you to accept him. He knows you don't like him."

"You can't force someone to like someone else."

Mindy grimaced. "This attitude from you has gone on long enough. Doesn't my happiness mean anything to you?"

Kelly sulked. "That's not fair."

Mindy rested a hand on Kelly's knee. "I want you to know that even though I care for Rick deeply, I still care for you. I love you. Nothing will change that."

Kelly wondered if her mother had gotten this script from a self-help book on parenting. "Trust me, Mom, it isn't about that."

"What is it about, then?"

Kelly crossed her arms. "I don't know. He just gets on my nerves."

"You need to give him a chance. A real chance."

"Are we done now?" Kelly stood up.

"Is this about your father?" Mindy asked suddenly.

"Don't be ridiculous." Kelly stormed up the stairs, leaving a dejected Mindy behind.

When Kelly entered her room, she was greeted with the sight of Blaine and Stephanie sitting cross-legged like statues on the bed. The blissful looks on their faces could only mean one thing — FSP.

"Guys!"

They didn't move. Their eyes remained closed and their expressions serene. Kelly swatted Stephanie on the back of the head. Her friend's eyes jerked open. "Ow! What was that for?"

"For doing FSP in my house." Kelly flicked Blaine in the stomach.

He sprang into the air, eyes wide. He reached for his wand, but stopped himself when he realized it was only Kelly. He waved. She glared at him.

"I'm sorry, Kelly," Stephanie said. "But we were bored and you weren't here yet." Her eyes brightened. "And guess what? I saw myself in that blue ball again. We were racing over the ocean, and—"

"I don't want to hear about your vision," Kelly interrupted.

Blaine settled back down on the bed beside Stephanie.

"You're missing out, Kelly. Are you sure you don't want some?" He pulled a small black pouch from his shoulder bag.

"Put that away. I won't touch that stuff. You shouldn't either, but if you insist, do it on your own time, far away from me. I shouldn't have to tell you never to do it in my room!"

"You're right. We're sorry," Stephanie said. "We won't do it again, we promise."

"You'd better not, because then I'd get really mad."

"I thought you were really mad now," Blaine said.

Her eyes narrowed. "This is nothing. You haven't seen a fadaman get angry."

Blaine shifted uncomfortably under her steely gaze. "Er...how about we get started on the lesson?" he asked.

"Let's." Kelly smiled inside at the fact Blaine had been scared by her angry fadaman line. "You were going to quiz me on my Ardagali?" she asked.

"Right." Blaine pulled a bunch of crinkled papers from his shoulder bag. "What about 'take me to your leader,'" he said. It was one of the stock phrases Kelly had memorized.

"Turag...iet ot di frost usiessa," Kelly recited.

Blaine nodded. "Good. How about, 'I am a friend.'"

"Ié ken wu amanost."

"I have one," Stephanie said. "I apologize if I have inadvertently offended you or your family."

"Ié...shonale iliho ié vli...lastotigl niplanint usit olo di faminda usiessa."

"That's a mouthful," Stephanie said.

Kelly nodded. "No kidding."

"I am Darindian's daughter," Stephanie said next.

"Ié ken wu tetorana peni Darindian."

"Let's try one more," Blaine said. He ruffled through the papers. "Ah, this is one of my favorites. 'Please do not tie me to a tree and leave me to die.'"

"Seriously?" Kelly asked.

"Trust me, it's a very useful phrase."

Kelly shot him an incredulous look.

"Well?" he prodded.

"What's the word for tree?" Kelly asked.

"Aba," Stephanie said.

"Right. Okay. So it would be: beten ni bindút iet ot wu aba unt luret iet stobanig."

"Nice." Blaine tucked the papers back into his shoulder bag. "I think you're ready."

Butterflies fluttered about in Kelly's stomach. "I don't feel ready."

KELLY SAT ON HER BED, her backpack in front of her. She'd gone over her packing list at least ten times, but one final time couldn't hurt. Cinnamon sticks. Check. (Blaine said the Ardagali loved cinnamon). Rowenian dagger, shrunk to fairy size to avoid any issues with airport security. Check. Clothes, her Ardagali vocabulary lists. Check. Satisfied, she closed her backpack.

The last thing she needed was a picture of her mother to show her father. She picked up the framed picture from her desk. It showed Mindy and her posing in front of the Washington Monument. She flipped it over and pulled it out of the frame, then tucked it into her back pocket.

There was a knock on her door. "Kelly, we need to leave for the airport now or we'll be late. Mr. Witherings said your group is meeting at one o'clock sharp!"

"I know, Mom. I'll be right there." Of course she wasn't meeting up with any group at the airport, but she did need to get to the airport by one if she wanted to make her two thirty flight.

She grabbed her backpack and headed for the door, but

stopped short when she realized she was still wearing her fairy sense necklace. Considering she'd followed Thomas's advice and carefully avoided mentioning anything about the trip to Bubbles, wearing the necklace while heading into Ardagali territory would be a bad idea. She unclasped the necklace and tucked it inside her sock drawer. As she placed her hands on the outside of the drawer to close it, she noticed the *MATH GENIUS* bear's face poking out from a pair of socks, where she'd buried it so she would't have to look at it. But now, instead of making her feel sad and lonely, the little face was comforting. She picked it up and placed it in her front pocket.

"Kelly, are you coming?"

"Yes, Mom!" She hurried downstairs.

"Would you like something to drink?" the flight attendant asked.

"Pineapple juice, please," Kelly said.

Blaine, who sat on the edge of the seat in front of her, wrinkled his nose. "Pineapple juice is gross."

"Then be grateful you're not the one to drink it," Milak snapped. The two fairies had been trading jibes the entire flight. Milak scowled from his perch on the edge of the seat in front of Kelly's neighbor, a portly businessman who looked to be in his sixties, and who had been playing Word Freeze on his smart phone ever since the pilot okayed the use of electronic devices. He was so absorbed in his game he'd actually ignored the flight attendant when she'd asked him if he'd wanted anything.

The flight attendant placed Kelly's pineapple juice in front of her with a smile, then moved along to the next row.

Blaine shot Milak a dark look. "You know what? You need to take that stick out of your—"

"Shhh...quiet," Milak hissed.

Blaine was too startled by Milak's sudden alertness to finish his insult. "What is it?" he whispered.

Milak didn't answer. He pulled his battle wand out and flew up to the overhead compartment. He hovered there, listening. Kelly focused her attention on the compartment, but she didn't sense anything. Milak took aim and hit the latch with a blast of air. The compartment popped open — and Bubbles and Beatrix tumbled out — colliding with Milak mid-air. They all fell to the ground in a clump. Luckily, Bubbles and Beatrix were in their invisible-to-humans forms like Milak. Otherwise things on the plane would have gotten very interesting. But since no one could see the fairies, all that happened when the bin popped open was that a passenger from across the aisle stood up and calmly closed it, then went back to reading a romance novel.

Meanwhile, Beatrix and Bubbles rose back up to Kelly's eye level and dusted themselves off. Milak searched the floor for his wand, which had been knocked from his hand in the commotion.

"Ooh, pineapple juice," Bubbles exclaimed. He planted himself on Kelly's tray and slurped at the contents of her glass. Kelly stared at him, not believing her eyes.

Beatrix flew up to the window. She uttered a string of lighting fast speech, which to Kelly's human form ears came out as gibberish. Kelly sent Bubbles an inquisitive look. He paused from slurping the pineapple juice. "She said the view is nice."

Milak, having found his wand, flew up to the others. "You two, explain yourselves," he roared.

Beatrix's shoulders jerked in fright, but she quickly recovered. She raised her nose up in the air. "We're not..." she crunched up her face with the effort to speak slowly enough for

Kelly to understand, "We're not going to let Kelly go to the Land of the Terrible Ones alone."

Milak jabbed his wand in her face. "Does it look like she's alone?"

"Yeah, we're here,' Blaine chimed in.

Milak silenced him with a sharp look.

"How did you even know about my trip?" Kelly whispered, bringing a hand to her mouth to conceal her words from her human neighbor. She needn't have bothered, because he was still as absorbed as ever with his word game.

Bubbles waved a dismissive hand. "I knew you were up to something weeks ago. I'm very hurt you didn't invite us."

Beatrix nodded. "Yes, that was rude."

"I wanted to tell you, but Thomas said I had to keep the group small, to avoid upsetting the Ardagali more than necessary," Kelly explained.

"Quite right," Milak said. "That's why you two aren't coming with us."

"Who are you to order us around?" Bubbles demanded. He flew up to face Milak. As he bolted through the air, his wings brushed the nose of Kelly's neighbor, who absent-mindedly scratched the impact point.

"In case you've forgotten," Milak said, "you are still a member of the Glendenian Armed Forces, and I am your superior. So if I give you an order you will obey."

Bubbles waved his fists in the air. "You can't order me around when we're not on an official military operation, and you know it!"

"My brother is right. We're coming," Beatrix said. "You can't make us leave."

Milak pointed his wand at the siblings. "You're mistaken about that," he growled.

Bubbles and Beatrix whipped out their wands. Blaine leaned forward eagerly, like a kid watching a playground fight.

"Stop this!" Kelly said.

Her neighbor dropped his smartphone, startled. "Did you say something?"

"Sorry. I wasn't talking to you."

"Hmpf." He didn't even bother to ask whom she had been talking to. He picked up his phone and resumed his game.

"I won't have you guys fighting," Kelly whispered. Too bad she couldn't make multiple telepathic connections at once. "It's my decision to make. Blaine, since you know the most about the Ardagali, I will defer to your expertise. Do you think it is too many if Beatrix and Bubbles come with us?"

He thought about it for a moment. "I don't think it makes a difference. The Ardagali are likely to attack whether we are one or ten. Milak can attest to that."

Milak grunted and adjusted his eye patch.

"It's decided then," Kelly said. "They come with us."

Milak scowled. "Fine, but I warned you. When I say I told you so, I hope it isn't to your corpse." He flew off to the front of the plane.

Bubbles shook his head. "Sore loser," he muttered. Beatrix and Blaine laughed. None of them seemed to take Milak's last comment seriously. But it left Kelly with a tight knot in the pit of her stomach.

"I'M HUNGRY," Bubbles complained.

"Then you should have brought supplies," Milak said.

"I thought I could pick late berries or something."

"Too dangerous."

"What do you mean? Those flowers over there are edible," Bubbles said. He prepared to dive for them.

Milak blocked him. "They could be poisoned. The Ardagali

are known to smear undetectable toxins on plants this close to their territory."

Bubbles pouted.

Kelly pulled an energy bar from her backpack and handed it to him. He accepted it gratefully.

They had been flying through the wilderness for over six hours, after a long bus ride from the airport. The forest really was incredible. Tall pine trees gave a captivating scent to the freshest air Kelly had ever breathed in her life. Squirrels chased each other up and down the trees, and every so often Kelly spotted deer peacefully foraging in the underbrush.

Bubbles rubbed his stomach and handed Kelly back the wrapper to the energy bar. "Thanks Kelly, that was yummy."

She stuffed the wrapper into her backpack absent-mindedly. Something felt strange — a vague uneasiness settled into the back of her mind. It took her several minutes to realize what was causing it. There were no more sounds in the forest. It had gone dead silent. She looked around carefully but could see no more squirrels, no birds, no hints of any living creatures besides the five of them.

"Why is it so quiet" she asked Milak, lowering her voice to a hushed whisper.

"We are approaching the mind barrier."

"What's that?"

"It's supposed to warn you to go away," Blaine said, flying up to her side. "Sort of like an invisible fence. Fairies can feel it, and so can humans, but not in the same way. It makes humans feel very scared and paranoid. They tend to turn back."

"Yes, and those who don't turn back, tend to never be found," Milak said darkly. "Once we pass the barrier, we must be extra careful. The traps are set."

"What traps?" Beatrix asked from above them.

"Sticky tree branches, spiderweb-like webs," Milak answered. "It's best not to touch anything."

"Don't forget the sand holes," Blaine said.

Milak frowned. "I've never heard of those."

"They're hidden along the ground."

"Then we should stay airborne as much as possible," Milak instructed.

About fifteen minutes later they flew through the invisible mental barrier. It was cold, like fog, and left a clammy feeling on the skin, along with an intense burst of fear. It reminded Kelly of the wisps of emotional suffering Miasmos enjoyed shooting at his enemies. She shivered. When they were a mile or so past the barrier, the regular sounds of the forest returned. But they gave Kelly little comfort. The initial burst of fear from the barrier lingered, perhaps fed by her own anxieties.

Every so often Milak would stop them and close his eyes, sensing their surroundings for trouble. The third time he did so, he remained still for a very long time. When he opened his eyes he threw his hands up in frustration and cursed.

"What's wrong?" Kelly asked.

"My fairy senses are completely blocked. We're going in blind. I don't like it."

Kelly gazed into her spy ring.

"That bauble of yours won't get us anywhere," Milak said.

The black stone had revealed nothing so far. Kelly was about to give up when a cloudy image formed in the ring. Misty and faint at first, it gradually grew clearer. In spite of himself, Milak leaned closer with interest.

The image showed a white female fairy, no older than Kelly, with pale purple wings dusted with silver. She wore her black hair in tight braids. Her outfit could be described as fairy-camouflage — a jacket splotched with different shades of browns, maroons, and deep greens to blend in with the forest, and pants to match. The fairy's eyes were closed tight in concentration as her fingers danced intricate acrobatics over the strings of a banjo-like instrument.

"Unbelievable," Milak said. "They're deploying the wasps for just five of us."

"The wasps? It can't be," Blaine said. He grabbed Kelly's wrist and brought his face so close to the ring that his nose touched her hand. When he saw the girl's image, he jumped back with terror in his eyes.

"Wasps?" Kelly asked. "Would someone care to fill me in?"

"Trained attack wasps," Milak said. "That girl is controlling them." He squinted through the trees and drew his wand. "We don't have much time. You'd better see if you can find her and stop her."

"Me?" Kelly asked. "But your fairy senses are much—"

Milak made a fist in the air for silence. He cupped a hand behind his ear, straining to hear a sound in the distance. Kelly heard it too. A low drone, getting closer. The buzz of hundreds of wings cutting through the air. Beatrix and Bubbles drew their wands and positioned themselves beside Milak. Blaine hung back, uncertain, as did Kelly.

"Well, don't just hover there!" Milak said. "Go find her, Kelly. I never thought I'd say this, but you have a better chance with that ring of yours than I do. Besides, you're a fadaman so they will have trouble sensing you."

"What are you going to do?"

"We're going to try and hold them off long enough for you to stop the conductor." He checked that his eye patch was secured tightly. "Oh, and I'll go ahead and say 'I told you so' now, in case I don't get a chance later."

"Here they come!" Bubbles yelled. He rushed forward and shot a string of sparks at the first pair of wasps. The wasps were at least the size of his forearm, and their stingers looked as long as his hand. He did a backwards somersault and shot three fireballs in quick succession at the closest one. It burst into a ball of flame and plummeted to the ground. The other wasp met the same fate. As soon as those wasps were down, another pair came from the trees to replace it. Then another. Beatrix, Milak, and Blaine joined Bubbles, ducking, dodging and combating the wasps with air, water, and fire.

Kelly hesitated. *I can't just leave them.* But the wasps kept coming. Soon there might be too many to fight off. Their best chance was for her to stop the girl. Kelly dashed through the trees. She flew a few meters to the right and then raced in the direction the wasps had come from. To her surprise, none pursued her. She heard them, to her left, still moving towards the others. Her heart pounded in her chest as she pushed herself to fly faster. But she didn't know exactly where the girl was. She could only see what the girl was doing. She needed more information. She slowed down and took a few deep breaths to calm herself enough to concentrate, then looked into the spy ring. The view was still limited to the girl and her instrument. Maybe she could get it to zoom out like a camera, if she willed it to happen strong enough. She sent her intent into the ring. *Zoom out. Expand. Long view.* Nothing worked. The buzzes to her left grew louder and louder as more wasps joined the horde. *There must be hundreds of them.* She tried again. The girl's image remained unchanged, except for now her fingers were moving even faster in their mad frenzy over the strings.

Kelly thought of touch screens and how she could scroll around them with her fingers. Kelly shrugged. *It's worth a shot.* She placed the fingertip of her pinkie up to the surface of the ring's stone. Then she dragged her finger to the left. She nearly shouted from excitement when the image shifted over a tiny bit, enough so that she could see the girl was leaning against a rock. She moved her finger again. The girl sat in a large clearing, beside a formation of boulders.

Kelly flew upwards. She kept going until she was well above the trees, high enough so that she could see the forest below. Looking down, she quickly spotted a void in the trees. The clearing. She dove towards it.

The girl was alone. Kelly set down on the ground at the far edge of the clearing. The fairy didn't move. From this distance Kelly could finally hear the sounds of the instrument. The melody wasn't a melody in the traditional sense. It was more like multilayered buzzing sounds, almost like the sounds produced by the wasps themselves. Kelly tiptoed up behind the fairy. She kept looking around as she moved forward, but sensed nothing and saw no movement from the trees. Still, she felt exposed.

When Kelly stood only a step from the fairy's back, she spoke. "You, stop it!"

The fairy didn't even flinch. She kept playing her wasp-controlling theme.

Kelly poked the fairy in the back with a finger. "Stop, or I'll shoot you." After she spoke she realized she'd addressed the fairy in English. But seeing as the girl still hadn't moved, maybe it didn't matter. She seemed to be so deeply absorbed in her trance that she was dead to the world.

Kelly circled around to stand in front of the fairy. She reached forward with the intent to grab the instrument. This action proved the girl was not as deeply absorbed in her trance as she looked. Eyes still closed and maintaining the melody with one hand, the fairy raised the other and pointed a finger directly at Kelly. Then she unleashed an electricity bolt. The air sizzled and Kelly jumped to the side, narrowly avoiding impact. She retaliated with a stream of water to coat the instrument. She followed up with a quick blast of cold air.

The girl finally opened her eyes, which were a brilliant green. When the strings on her instrument froze over, she dropped it in surprise. As she dove to pick it up Kelly knocked her flat on her back with another burst of cold air. The girl lay on the ground, shivering. Kelly kicked the instrument out of the girl's reach.

"Usá ni movag," Kelly said, hoping it meant 'don't move' like she thought it did.

The fairy laughed. At first Kelly thought the girl was laughing at her lack of Ardagali language skills, but then the pressure of a wand against her back proved otherwise. Kelly's heart skipped a beat.

"*Usié* ni movag," a male voice behind her said, with emphasis on the first word which Kelly had confused with another.

Kelly ran through her options. Could she duck before he managed to get a shot off from his wand? Would her fadaman shield protect her if he did shoot her? Should she attempt to reason with him or try to disarm him? Before she could put any plan into action, about a dozen camouflaged fairies emerged from the trees. They formed a circle around them, standing shoulder to shoulder with wands drawn. Their hostile expressions made Kelly think they were just waiting for the smallest excuse to attack. And judging by the fact that the few fairies in the group who hadn't concealed their wings under camouflaged wing coverings all had stunning blue, purple, and silver wings, they almost certainly had enough combined strength to overpower her with ease. *This situation is less than ideal,* she thought.

The girl, having recovered from Kelly's cold air blast, stood up. Her face reddened with anger as she berated Kelly in a string of rapid Ardagali.

Kelly just stared at her.

The girl yelled some more, then stopped, glaring at Kelly with a look that was both accusing and questioning. She expected Kelly to provide some answer. In halting Ardagali, Kelly told her she hadn't understood a word the fairy had just said.

"You...break connection wrong. You...kill...wasps!" the girl shouted in English.

Kelly's stomach dropped. *Uh-oh.* She had no idea that stopping the instrument would have killed all the wasps. *Now they have another reason to hate me.*

The girl reached into her jacket and pulled out a dagger. She waved it threateningly in the air whilst shouting some more in Ardagali. Kelly felt the pressure of the wand against her back disappear as the male fairy stepped out to position himself between Kelly and the angry fairy. He looked to be about the same age as the girl fairy, and his purple wings were identical to hers. His hair was black too. Kelly wondered if the two fairies were related to each other. Then she wondered if they could be related to her. After all, she had purple wings too, with silver lines running through them.

The male fairy addressed the girl as Proxy, then murmured something to her in low tones. She protested, again too fast for Kelly to understand, but Kelly did catch the girl calling her companion Xander several times, which Blaine had once mentioned was a very common Ardagali name. *At least I understand their names,* Kelly thought sarcastically, discouraged that she didn't understand any more. Xander made some additional comments, and when he finished, Proxy put her dagger away but sent Kelly a look that could curdle blood.

Xander turned to Kelly without a word. He grabbed her arm and pulled her along after him as he headed for the trees. Proxy followed close behind. The other fairies parted to let them through, then followed along in single file. They were headed back in the direction Kelly and her friends had first encountered the wasps. After just a minute of walking, they had to tread very carefully to avoid the dead wasps scattered on the ground. Kelly wondered why they didn't simply fly to avoid the potential of stepping on stingers, but, even if she had been confident of how to ask that in Ardagali, she thought it best to stay quiet for the time being. Tears flowed freely down Proxy's cheeks as she looked upon the bodies of her beloved pets.

Up ahead, Kelly saw another tight circle of Ardagali fairies. They must be surrounding her friends. Her pulse quickened. Had she stopped the wasps in time? They reached the fairies and Xander tapped one of them on the shoulder. In response the fairy stepped back to make an opening in the circle and Xander pushed Kelly inside. Beatrix lay on the ground with a puncture wound in her calf, conscious, but very tired. Milak examined the wound calmly while Bubbles and Blaine argued, seemingly oblivious to the Ardagali who stood guard over them with wands drawn. They hadn't even noticed Kelly's arrival.

"It's your fault she got stung!" Bubbles shouted at Blaine.

"My fault? It's her fault for being too slow."

"Well, if you hadn't been flying backwards like a coward and gotten in her way, she wouldn't have gotten stung!"

"Um, maybe you guys should save the fighting for later?" Kelly suggested.

They jumped, startled, then fell silent and stared at their toes.

Proxy and Xander stepped towards them. "You...trespass. Must pay!" Proxy said.

"Beten ni bindút iet ot wu aba unt luret iet stobanig," Blaine exclaimed.

Seriously? The tree line? "Don't give them any ideas," Kelly whispered.

Xander's eyes glinted with amusement. He said something in Proxy's ear. She pursed her lips in thought.

Bubbles nudged Kelly. "Maybe you should tell them who you are. And ask to see who's in charge."

"Good thinking." Kelly cleared her throat. "Turag...iet ot di frost usiessa," she said. The fairies looked at her curiously. "Ié ken wu tetorana peni Darindian," she added.

At the mention of Darindian, the Ardagali fairies gathered in a tight huddle. They talked fast, voices raised with strong emotions. They were arguing. Proxy kept gesturing emphatically at the piles of dead wasps on the ground. Kelly only caught a few words here and there: they sounded like *enemies* and *lies*. She turned to Blaine. "What are they saying?"

"They are debating whether or not to kill us all now."

"Tell them that would be a mistake," Kelly said.

"Is that supposed to scare them?" he asked.

"Yes. Darindian is supposedly a prince, right? It they are smart, they won't want to risk him getting angry at them for killing his daughter, will they?"

Blaine nodded. "Good point." He turned to the Ardagali. He launched into a monologue that lasted nearly thirty seconds. The fairies let him speak. As he went on, they gave each other nervous looks. It was working.

When he fell silent, the Ardagali fairies whispered amongst themselves for several minutes. Finally, Proxy pulled five strips of cloth from her shoulder bag and came towards them.

FLYING BLINDFOLDED WAS MORE DISORIENTING than Kelly had expected. It made her seasick. She tried to sense her surroundings as they flew, but they moved too fast for her to get much detail. After nearly an hour of flying, she thought she sensed fairies below, like one might find in a fairy city. Once in a while she thought she heard muffled sounds of fairy children laughing beneath them. Nearly an hour after she first sensed activity below, the air suddenly got cooler, then quieter. They had entered a massive structure. A cave? A fairy building? She couldn't tell.

Hands on her shoulders guided her downwards until her feet contacted a solid surface. They walked on from there, down twisting corridors and long staircases. She tried to memorize their path but soon lost track. Her ears gave little information. All she heard was their footsteps echoing back to them and occasional hushed whispers between their Ardagali captors.

Finally, they stopped. A rough hand pulled Kelly's blindfold off. She blinked against the sudden brightness. They had been led to a room much like the audience hall in Glendenland. A set of wide stairs ended in a platform with four ornate thrones, two of which were occupied.

"That has to be the king," Blaine whispered to Kelly. "Your uncle."

He was referring to the male fairy seated in one of the two occupied thrones. Her uncle was tall, with high cheekbones and a strong jaw. His hair was dark brown, and cropped very short. He had bright blue wings the likes of which she had only seen once before — on Miasmos. The similarity did not inspire warm and fuzzy feelings. Beside the king sat an elegant female fairy with silver wings. Kelly assumed she was the queen. Both royal fairies wore crowns that appeared to have been carved from solid pieces of green jade.

"If that's my uncle, where's my father?" she whispered back to Blaine.

He shrugged. "Beats me."

Fairies dressed in flowing robes stood along the stairs. They didn't look like bodyguards, more like a royal court, Kelly thought. The way they whispered and giggled amongst themselves gave them away.

Xander and Proxy ran up the stairs and bowed before the male fairy. Then they spoke in low tones. Many of the fairies on the stairs leaned forward with bated breath, trying to hear what the three were speaking about. Kelly took the time to check on her friends. Beatrix stood on bone foot, leaning against her brother for support. Milak scowled, as usual, and scanned the area like a hawk — sizing up the odds against them, no doubt. Or looking for an escape route.

The king waved his hand and Xander and Proxy stood up.

They positioned themselves behind the king's throne, one on either side.

"See where they're standing?" Blaine whispered. "That means they're the kings children."

Great, Kelly thought. *The first thing I did was get on my cousins' bad side.*

The king stood up. "Parig," he commanded. His eyes were on Kelly.

Parig...parig...hmm...oh right, that means speak. He wanted her to say something. "Ié ken wu—"

"I know who you are," the king interrupted in English. "I sensed it immediately. My younger brother has some explaining to do," he added in a tone that sent shivers down Kelly's spine.

She hoped that for her father's sake, there was no penalty for having a fadaman for a daughter. She hadn't thought about how she might be putting him in danger by coming here. "If you know who I am, then why are you treating us like enemies?"

The king laughed. "Just because you are Darindian's daughter, doesn't make you Ardagali," he said. "Not when your mother is a human." He squinted with disdain.

Proxy tapped her father on the shoulder. She whined to him in Ardagali. Kelly took it that she didn't understand enough English to follow the conversation, and she was getting impatient.

"Hoá k'nee net anarena," the king finally snapped with impatience.

Bubbles looked to Kelly for a translation.

"He said I'm not a fairy," she explained telepathically.

Proxy asked him what he meant by that.

"Hoá k'nee wu fadaman," the king explained.

The onlookers gasped at the revelation that Kelly was a

fadaman. The room buzzed with excited whispers until the king silenced them with a wave of his hand.

"You must prove that you are one of us," he directed to Kelly.

"How?" Kelly asked.

He smirked. "The gauntlet."

Blaine went white as a ghost. The gauntlet must be something bad. Something very bad.

The queen frowned. "Brendann, should not Darindian decide?" she asked in heavily accented English. "We should wait until he returns tonight."

King Brendann made a curt reply in Ardagali that Kelly didn't catch. But the sour pout his wife gave in response probably meant he'd told her in so many words to shut up. Then he switched back to English. "Only a true Ardagali can pass the test. If she is one of us, she should have nothing to worry about."

"She worry," Proxy said. "She last...two second in gauntlet." Kelly's cousin appeared to take glee in that prospect. Looking at King Brendann, Kelly thought she detected a hint of a smile on his face as well. She couldn't decipher Xander's expression. The only one who looked the tiniest bit concerned was the queen, and Kelly couldn't be sure it was because she didn't want Kelly to be hurt, or she just didn't want Darindian to be angry that they made a decision behind his back. Her stomach twisted. *They know I'm family and they still want me dead? What kind of people are they?*

"You may pick one companion to accompany you in the trial, but not him." Brendann pointed to Milak. "He's been to our realm before, so he is disqualified."

Kelly's first instinct was to choose Bubbles, but she didn't want to make him leave Beatrix, who clung to him so tightly her knuckles had turned white. Besides, despite his flaws,

Blaine knew the most about the Ardagali. His knowledge might prove useful in the test. "I choose Blaine."

Blaine gulped.

"Very well. Let me emphasize it is not only your fate, but also that of your friends on the line. If you fail, they won't leave here alive."

Like there wasn't already enough pressure, Kelly thought.

"Do you understand?" Brendann asked.

"Does it matter?" she spat angrily.

He pursed his lips. "A rainstorm in May is a welcome respite."

13

GAUNTLET

Blindfolds back in place, Kelly and Blaine were led on another long procession down winding hallways. The entire court came along, chattering amongst themselves and laughing like they were in a festival parade. *This is all a game to them,* Kelly thought. The high-pitched giggles and jubilant shouts made her want to punch them all in the face. *I'll show them. I'll beat this gauntlet thing and then I'll give them a piece of my mind.* But then she remembered the look on Blaine's face when King Brendann had first mentioned the gauntlet. With that her confidence deflated like a popped balloon.

Beatrix, Bubbles, and Milak had been left behind in the audience hall, guarded by a dozen Ardagali. Kelly hoped Milak would behave himself. As they went deeper into the massive structure, the air grew progressively cooler and damper. By the time they finally came to a stop, Kelly shivered all over.

A clumsy hand unceremoniously yanked Kelly's blindfold off. She reflexively smoothed down her hair while taking in her surroundings — an unadorned domed room with smooth stone walls.

"Your wings will be bound with spider's silk," Brendann said. "Attempt to remove it at your own peril. A true Ardagali need not fly to conquer the gauntlet." He gave a clipped nod to his daughter.

Proxy stepped out of the crowd of gawking onlookers. She held a modern-looking spray can. She walked up behind Blaine and took aim at his wings. When she pressed the can's trigger, a stringy white substance shot from it. This 'spider's silk' reminded Kelly of silly string. She felt a tug in her chest as memories of childhood parties surfaced. What would Mindy think if Kelly never made it home? With difficulty, she pushed such thoughts from her mind. Proxy continued to spray the stringy substance along the edges of Blaine's folded wings. When she finished, the silk took on a life of its own. It spread out, directed by an invisible force, and formed a tight cocoon around Blaine's wings.

Proxy moved on to Kelly. The spider's silk struck fast, taking Kelly by surprise. It was shockingly cold — like liquid ice moving across her back, penetrating to her bones. Once the silk solidified, the cold's intensity waned, leaving behind the feeling of a cold pack pressed against bruised skin. She wiggled her shoulders, getting accustomed to the added weight of the silk bindings.

Brendann walked up to the rock wall. He placed a hand upon it and whispered something. As he stood motionless, his wings, majestically unfurled, took on a blue glow. Kelly's pulse quickened. *Miasmos's wings glow just like that,* he thought. She told herself that Brendann was not Miasmos. *But is he any better?* He wasn't making the best impression so far. The king took a step back and clapped his hands. In response, an intricate border of glowing shapes, in the outline of a door, gradually formed on the wall. When the border became so bright it almost hurt to look at, Brendann waved his right arm. The rock inside the border dissolved into nothingness. Beyond it, an ominous blackness lay in wait. Brendann stepped to the side and gave a clipped nod.

A rough shove from Proxy propelled Kelly over the threshold into the darkness. Blaine received a similar push from Xander.

"May the ancestors guide your steps," Proxy said behind them.

Kelly spun around, but before she could utter a reply, the rock in the doorway had reappeared. She and Blaine were alone. Kelly couldn't see a thing. She blinked, waiting for her eyes to adjust. "Did Proxy just say something nice?" she asked. "Or was that a formality?"

Somewhere to her left, Blaine snorted. "Neither. Quite a bit got lost in that translation. She recited a line from a funeral prayer. Said to your enemy, it basically means, 'see you in hell.'"

"Great," Kelly said.

"Don't let it get to you. She's a roach's turd. And your uncle's a slimy tadpole."

She sighed. "It would seem so." She waved her hand in front of her face. She couldn't see it. "I guess we should get some light in here," she said. She was about to form a fireball to illuminate their surroundings when Blaine clumsily bumped into her from the side.

"No, wait. I don't think we're supposed to use magic."

"What? Why do you think that?"

"There's a children's song. About the gauntlet. It has a line that goes..." he paused, humming to himself. "Right, it goes: in the gauntlet do not call on your surroundings for earth, air, water, or fire, for it leads to ruin."

"Those are really awkward lyrics for a song," Kelly commented.

"It sounds much better in Ardagali."

"Oh. Well, what do we do if we can't use magic? We can't just stumble on like we're blind, can we?" Before she completed her question, the answer revealed itself. Tiny flecks of silver appeared in the walls, one after another, growing brighter.

"Devious," Blaine said. "It waited just long enough to try and trick us into lighting it up on our own."

Flecks continued to appear in quick succession. After about thirty seconds, a tunnel of glistening walls stretched before them. "It's beautiful," Kelly murmured.

Blaine elbowed her in the side. "We don't have time for gawking. This is serious business."

"You're starting to sound like Milak."

He frowned. "Sorry. I'm just on edge, and you should be too. Even born and bred Ardagali have failed the gauntlet before," he whispered. "No one is safe."

Born and bred Ardagali can fail? Kelly's stomach twisted. "Then we'd better be on our toes. Come on."

They walked down the tunnel, scanning the path ahead for danger. An eerie silence hung about, clinging to every crevice. Kelly felt an odd familiarity in the air, like something else was there with them — a presence of some sort — not exactly alive, but...conscious. Then they began — hints of sound, from nowhere and everywhere, from far away and near, so much alike yet unlike the whispers of the memory stone. These were not hard; they were soft, like distant ocean waves, the sounds in a seashell brought to one's ear. The gauntlet was *whispering*. She stopped in her tracks. "Do you hear that?"

"Hear what?" Blaine asked.

"You don't hear anything at all? Like wind, or water?"

Blaine shook his head. "It's probably just the sound of your own blood rushing through your ears."

It's definitely not that, Kelly thought, but she said nothing. Maybe she could hear the sounds because her father was Ardagali.

"Look, there's a fork up there," Blaine said.

Up ahead, the tunnel came to an end, leading into a perpendicular tunnel. They had to make a choice: left or right.

"Does that children's song of yours say which way to go?" Kelly asked.

"I don't think so." Blaine's eyebrows drew together. "Honestly, I only remember a few lines."

They stopped just before the opening to the tunnel, thinking. Kelly closed her eyes and listened for the gauntlet's whispers. They were stronger to the right, beckoning. She wanted to go to them. But could they be trusted? Or was their call a siren's song, designed to lure them into a trap? She opened her eyes. "I think we should go right."

"I think we should go left. The air smells fresher. We can always turn around if—"

"No, something bad will happen if we choose the wrong one," Kelly said.

"Then let's hope I'm right." Blaine moved forward — to the left.

"No!" Kelly tried to pull him back, but it was too late. Behind her, a hidden panel of rock slid down from the ceiling, blocking their route back. At the same time, a distant rumble began. It came from down the left tunnel.

"Looks like I was wrong," Blaine said. He brought a hand to his mouth like he was about to be sick.

"Remember that next time," Kelly said. "If there is a next time."

"Come on, don't be like that. It was fifty-fifty. Your guess was as good as mine."

"Mine wasn't a guess."

He gave her a curious look, but there was no time for further discussion. The ground shook. Something was coming from down the left tunnel. Something big and heavy. Kelly and Blaine ran as fast as they could down the right tunnel. The distant rumbles grew closer, and louder. Their pursuer was gaining on them. Kelly chanced a look over her shoulder and saw it. *Great, a large round boulder,* she thought. *Now all we need are whips and fedora hats.*

"Look, we can hide here," Blaine said. He ducked to the left, into a narrow nook in the wall.

She grabbed his elbow and pulled him out. "No, if we do that, then the boulder will block us from going forward. Being trapped forever is the same as being squished."

"Speak for yourself," he muttered. But he joined her as they ran further down the tunnel. They managed to stay ahead of the boulder, which seemed to have stopped accelerating. Instead, it hurtled along at a steady speed, just slow enough for Kelly to think they might have a chance of outrunning it.

The tunnel curved up ahead, and when they rounded the bend Kelly's hopes evaporated. The tunnel ended in an abrupt dead end, only about a hundred paces from their position.

"Now would be a good time, for some Ardagali knowledge," Kelly panted.

"Uh…" Blaine stuttered.

"Think! Does that gauntlet song mention boulders?"

Blaine didn't answer. In seconds they reached the dead end. They spun around and pressed their backs against it. Kelly watched the bend with dread. Any second now and the boulder would round the corner.

"Blaine, think!"

"I don't know…"

The boulder reached the bend, rattling against the walls. Flecks of silver bounced off the inside of the tunnel like sparks off a power saw. They had fifteen seconds, maybe less, before they were squashed like tomatoes.

"Blaine!"

His mouth dropped open, but no sounds came out. He gazed dumbly at the boulder, frozen with terror.

Panic rushed up inside her. She raised her hand. Maybe she

could stop the boulder with a blast of air, or water. It was heavy, but she had to try — magic ban or no.

Blaine sprang into action. "No, Kelly, don't. I've got it." He jumped in front of her, and with his hands on his hips, he shouted one word: "Ardagali!"

It was like his voice slammed on the boulder's brakes. A deafening screech erupted as the behemoth slowed — but it was still coming. Kelly pressed herself up tighter against the wall, but Blaine stood ahead, suddenly confident. Either that, or he'd rather die first to get it over with. Flecks of silver from the wall flew at them like tiny projectiles, stinging as they impacted Kelly's cheeks. The boulder kept coming, but slower and slower. Kelly held her breath. The screeching reached a fever pitch and then — the boulder stopped. Mere inches from Blaine's nose.

Kelly's knees wobbled. "Where did you pull that from?"

Blaine laughed hysterically. "When my life was flashing before my eyes, I remembered something one of my Ardagali friends used to say when we were kids." He laughed some more.

"And that was?"

He stopped laughing long enough to sputter an answer. "It was: 'A rolling giant always stops for Ardagali.' He used to say it about my Aunt Reynalda. She had a soft spot for him. He always managed to get what he wanted from her. He could even change her mind, unlike anyone else. You know how she is."

Kelly chuckled in spite of herself, remembering how strong-willed Thomas's mother could be. She also laughed at the ridiculous simplicity of the password. Blaine joined in, and they were both overcome by a fit of hysterics.

Kelly snapped out of her laughing fit when the wall she leaned against suddenly moved. She jumped away with a start. The wall slid up to reveal a medium-sized room. They peeked inside. Perfectly square and perfectly empty, the room made

Kelly nervous. It was dim. Only the ceiling held silver specks of illumination. On the far wall a rectangular outline awaited — a door. They would have to get to it, then open it, Kelly assumed. No doubt the endeavor would be harder than it looked.

"Shall we?" Blaine asked. He lifted a foot to step forward.

She pulled him back. "Haven't you learned anything? If you hadn't just walked into the wrong tunnel a few minutes ago, we could have avoided that boulder entirely."

"You don't know that," he said. "Besides, there's only one way to go here. Forward. There's no wrong choice."

"I can't believe you can say something like that," Kelly said. "Haven't you ever seen an action movie before?"

"I'm a fairy," Blaine said.

"Is that a no?"

"Yes."

"You could have just said so."

He winked. "Just trying to add a little Ardagali personality to the situation."

She rolled her eyes. "Well, we can't just walk in there. This is a classic shrinking room scenario."

"Huh?"

"The moment we set foot in that room, the walls are going to close in on us."

His eyebrows came together. "You think?"

"After the boulder, I'd bet my bottom dollar on it. Either that, or the room will fill up with sand."

Blaine rubbed his throat, as if feeling grains of sand inside. "What do we do then?"

"There must be some routine to follow, or some password like with the boulder," Kelly said. "Something only a true Ardagali would know."

Blaine stroked his chin in thought. Meanwhile, the gauntlet's whispers again rushed to Kelly's ears. They called from beyond the door. Insistent, persuasive. Distracting. Kelly considered putting up a barrier to silence them, like Dimpleton had shown her. She decided against it. They might prove useful. "Any ideas?" she asked.

Blaine shook his head. "No. I keep trying to remember more of the gauntlet song, but I can't."

"Does it mention anything about a square room? Or a square door?"

He hummed the song again under his breath, but soon stopped, frustrated. "I don't remember."

"How about anything about a path, or steps, or small spaces?"

His eyes widened in excitement. "There was something... something about footprints!"

"Go on."

His face fell. "I'm not sure how it goes, or what it means."

"Just try."

He closed his eyes, trying to remember. "All right, it goes: footprints in the light, or light in the footprints. No, it's: footprints in the light show you to the door."

Kelly stared at the room's floor. Nothing. *Footprints in the light.* Light. The room was dark. "What if we lit up the room with fireballs?" she asked.

"We can't. No fire element, remember?"

"Oh, right." She kicked herself mentally for having forgotten. She scanned the few feet of tunnel behind them, and the boulder itself, looking for anything they could use. Her eyes fell on floor around the boulder. She grinned. "Maybe we don't need fire."

Shards of luminescent silver coated the ground around the boulder, the remnants of the silver flecks that had been knocked from the walls. Some chunks had been ground so fine they resembled glowing fairy dust. Kelly stretch out the bottom of her shirt to form a makeshift sack. She scooped a handful of the sandy powder into it. Then another handful, and another.

Blaine did the same. "Are you sure about this?" he asked her.

They stood, shirts stuffed with powder, just before the opening. "No," Kelly said. She tried to toss some powder into the room without entering the room herself. But it bounced back like it had hit an invisible barrier. Her heart sank. "It looks like we have to step through to find out if this is going to work."

"Figures," Blaine said.

"On three?"

He nodded.

"One, two, three."

They stepped inside. Instantly the stone panel fell back down behind them to block their escape. The ceiling made an ominous pop. The pop was followed by what sounded like mechanical gears, and a moving chain, behind the right wall. The ceiling inched downwards.

"You were right," Blaine said. "I will have to watch one of those action movies some time, if we get out of here."

"We'd better hurry," Kelly said, raising her voice to compensate for the grating of the hidden gears, which grew louder by the second as the ceiling descended. She sprinkled some of the powder on the ground in front of them.

"What exactly do you expect to happen?" Blaine shouted.

The ceiling had already come down nearly halfway, and Blaine, being a few inches taller than Kelly, was already bent over.

"That." Kelly pointed. In the sprinkling of dust, one section glimmered more than the rest, in the shape of a footprint. Kelly stepped into it. With that, the ceiling paused in its descent, as if uncertain. A second later it started back down. "You need to be in the footprints too," Kelly said. She quickly sprinkled more dust ahead of her, and more footprints appeared. She stepped forward into them, and Blaine quickly stepped into the ones behind her. The ceiling paused again. This time it didn't move any more.

Blaine laughed. "You're a genius."

"Not quite. It was you remembering that children's song," she said. "It's safe to say I'd be dead by now without you."

"Thanks. But we're not finished yet."

Careful sprinkling and stepping brought them all the way to the door. It slid open on its own as soon as Kelly stepped into the last footprint. Through it was complete darkness. "Guess we just have to go for it this time." She took a deep breath and walked through the doorway. Blaine followed. The door to the shrinking room slid shut behind them, leaving them just as blind as they had been when they first entered the gauntlet. Kelly cautiously felt the walls with her hands, looking for buttons or triggers.

"I found something," Blaine said. There was a click from the same location as his voice, like he'd pulled a lever.

With a soft swoosh, a round portion of the ceiling dissolved into nothingness, like the stone door at the entrance to the gauntlet. Light shone down from the opening. "Looks like we go up," Kelly said.

Blaine knelt down on, bracing an arm against the wall. "Get on my shoulders."

Kelly placed her feet on his shoulders, carefully avoiding the sticky spider webs on his wings. He stood up slowly, until Kelly could peek her head out of the hole. She saw a long, rectangular hallway, with vertical metal stripes at regular intervals along either side. "Looks clear," she reported.

She grabbed hold of the ledge and pulled herself up. She turned to offer Blaine a hand, but he'd already jumped up and grabbed the ledge himself, and climbed out with apparent ease. He grinned, very pleased with himself.

"Showoff," she teased.

He peered down the hallway. "So, what do you think this challenge is?"

"I don't know. I just hope it isn't snakes." Kelly shivered. The gauntlet's whispers were back, urging her to get to the end of the hallway as fast as possible. She knew better. "Look around for a rock, or a pebble, something we can toss down the hallway."

"Why?"

"Just look. Don't go past that line, though." She pointed to the first of the vertical metal stripes.

"Why not?"

"Just a hunch."

They searched the floor for stray rocks but found nothing they could use. So Kelly reached to pull off one of her shoes.

"You can't use a shoe," Blaine said.

She hesitated. "Why not?"

"You might need it. What if the ground is sharp, or something."

"What then? I'm open to suggestions. Do you have anything we could use?"

"No, the Ardagali took everything. How about you?"

They'd taken everything from her too. *No, not everything*, she thought. Just her backpack and anything they thought could be used as a weapon. They had left her with one thing. She reached into her pocket and pulled it out. The *MATH GENIUS* bear. Resting in her palm, it looked up at her, its face innocent and serene.

"What are you waiting for?" Blaine asked.

"It has sentimental value," she snapped. "I think I'd rather give up my shoe."

"Nonsense." In a flash, Blaine snatched the bear from her grasp. He threw it.

"Hey!"

She watched as the bear traveled in a long arc, as if in slow motion, past the first of the vertical stripes. The response was instantaneous. The stripes were really panels, and they slid upwards in unison to reveal recesses in the walls. A blast of orange flame burst forth from the first one and engulfed the bear. It blazed brightly for an instant, suspended in midair, before its charred remains plummeted to the ground. Kelly gazed at the pile of ash that once was her gift from Dmitri. She felt hollow.

"Sorry, Kelly, but it had to be done."

She took the time to send him a stony glare before turning her attention back to their predicament. Fire was the least of their worries — the other panels held their own dangers. The second one sported a gigantic blade, which swung back and forth like a pendulum. Behind it, was more fire, then a row of razor sharp spikes that shot out from the walls, then disappeared again in quick succession. Beyond that lay more flames and blades that resembled gigantic scissors. They opened and closed with incredible speed, and ominous slicing sounds.

"Anything in that gauntlet song about this?" Kelly asked.

Blaine shook his head no.

Kelly concentrated on the obstacles in their path. "There has to be a pattern." The problem was, she couldn't see to the end of the hallway. And they only had one chance to get it right. "Look, first that big blade swings back and forth one, two, three times, then it pauses. When it pauses, that's when there's a burst of flame right in front of it, like the one that got my bear. So, we'll have to move up after the burst of flame, wait for the third swing, and then step through immediately to avoid the fire."

Blaine's face twisted with worry.

"Then we'll be in another open space, and the spikes, those come out five times, then they pause, and in that pause there is fire in the space before them. So we'd have to move forward right at five, or be burnt. Then those scissor things, they're on a cycle of two. But, that's as far as I can see. Maybe they are the first numbers in a sequence. Do those numbers mean anything to you?"

"Three, five, two. Three, five, two," Blaine repeated. "I'm not getting anything."

"Just, take your time."

He pounded a fist into the wall. "I can't do it!" he screeched, frustration overpowering him. He punched the wall again. When he pulled back blood coated his knuckles.

Kelly put a hand on his shoulder. "Yes you can. Just sit down and take a deep breath. You have to calm down."

He wiped the back of his hand on his shirt. "All right.' He sat down.

"Now, close your eyes and imagine you're in a safe place," Kelly instructed. "Like a field of beautiful flowers, with sunlight on your face, and little children laughing in the distance—"

"Kelly, be quiet."

"What? Were the little children laughing too much?"

He opened his eyes. "No. It worked. I know what the numbers mean." He stood up, confident again, having conquered his emotions for the moment. "It's from the story of the first Ardagali king's birth. It beings: in the third month of the fifth year of the second era, the first one came into the world on the sixth day, after sunrise, at the second hour."

"So that's three, five, two, one, six, and two." She frowned. "The hallway is long, there are way more than six steps."

"There's more to the story: fourteen sages stood by his side, bringing the blessings of the twelve stars and the three stones of the ancient ones."

Fourteen, twelve, and three. That made eight. She eyed the hallway. Maybe eight would get them to the end. *I hope this is worth it.* Images of Mindy, Stephanie, and Dmitri flooded her mind. Was finding her father worth dying over? Was it worth never seeing anyone she cared about again? *There's no going back now.*

Blaine took hold of her left hand. "We'll count together. Go exactly when I go."

Kelly nodded.

They waited for the next blast of fire, then stepped into position. The smell of burnt carbon tickled Kelly's nostrils. She tried not to dwell on the burnt bear at her feet.

"One, two, three."

The blade was so heavy it created a strong gust of wind in their faces as it swung past. They stepped forward as soon as the blade went by for the third time, just as the blast of fire overtook their last location. Hot air on Kelly's back drove home how narrowly they had escaped the flames. They counted to five, then stepped past the spikes. Blaine's hand trembled, like hers. Her heart stopped each time they moved forward. Just one tiny misstep would be the end. Or just one wrong number. *Please let Blaine's memory be correct,* she repeated mentally, like a mantra. If he was wrong, they would be cut in half, burnt to a crisp, or impaled by spikes. At least there were worse ways to go. But not many she could think of at the moment.

They were almost there. Just two more numbers: twelve and three.

"Twelve."

As they stepped forward, Kelly nearly had a heart attack. If they only had one more number left, 'three,' then why were there more crisscrossing lines of blades beyond the spikes directly in front of them. "Uh, Blaine?"

"I see it. Just, go forward on three."

"But—"

"There's nothing else we can do."

On three, they stepped forward. In front of them was another swinging pendulum blade. "Did you see how many times this one repeated?" Kelly asked.

"No. We'll just have to run for it. Wait for a pause."

But the pause came just at that moment — before either of them had a chance to react. *Uh-oh.* Kelly squeezed her eyes shut, expecting a blast of flame at any moment. There was none. The pendulum blade resumed it's swinging.

Blaine laughed. "We're not dead! It's just a new set of numbers."

Kelly let out the breath she'd been holding. "Whoever designed this thing had a cruel sense of humor."

They watched the next layers ahead of them. It was six, one, and one. Blaine decided this sequence referred to the number of children the first three Ardagali kings had.

"How many kings have there been?" Kelly asked.

"Dozens."

"And you know how many kids they all had?"

"No. Just the first fifteen."

Fortunately, Blaine only had to call on his knowledge of the first twelve kings. When they stepped past the final row of spikes, Kelly threw her arms around Blaine, jubilant. "You were amazing! How you remembered all those numbers is beyond me."

"It was a stroke of luck. Let's hope it lasts." He looked around apprehensively.

Kelly followed suit. They stood on the edge of a vast cavern. The ceiling towered above them. It was at least ten times Kelly's height. About thirty paces in front of them, a wide chasm split the floor in two. It stretched the entire width of the cavern. On the far wall, a glowing outline of intricate patterns formed the shape of a door. The whispering sounds urged her to go forward again. But how could she cross the gap? "This is why they bound our wings," Kelly said.

They tiptoed to the edge of the crevasse and looked down. It was too deep to see the bottom. In breadth, it was at least four times Kelly's body length. Way too far to jump.

"How are we supposed to get over there without flying?" she wondered aloud. As soon as she spoke those words, the gauntlet's whispers crescendoed to a raging roar. Like a stormy sea crashing against cliffs, they lashed at the border of her mind, inviting, no, demanding she open up to them. "Can you feel that?" she asked Blaine.

"The dread in my heart?"

"No. A telepathic invitation."

"From whom?"

"This...place. I'm going to connect to it."

His eyes widened. "It could be dangerous."

"What here isn't?"

"Good point."

She sat down on the ground to avoid any risks of falling. Then, she accepted the connection.

Gray sand met a purple sky. Kelly stood on the shore. The sand, warm and fine, tickled between her bare toes. Blue water lapped the shore calmly, kissing her ankles. The air carried a hint of salt, and the captivating perfume of tropical fruits. Kelly felt a presence behind her. She spun around.

A beautiful woman in a flowing black robe stood at arm's length. Her glistening silver hair floated gracefully in the gentle wind. The woman's eyes were silver too, and glowed like the flecks in the walls of the gauntlet. She stared at Kelly, eyes vacant, unnerving.

"Are you true?" the woman asked. Her voice, monotone, almost robotic, and devoid of feeling, sent a shiver down Kelly's spine.

She knew the woman had spoken Ardagali, but somehow she had understood as easily as if it had been English. "I think so," she replied, unsure of which language she had spoken.

"Then stop wasting time. Walk to the door. If you are true the air will support you."

"But, how do I—"

The woman's eye's flashed. "Impertinence." A sharp pain struck Kelly behind her eyes. Her ears rang. She fell down.

Kelly blinked. She found herself on the ground in a fetal position. Blaine shook her shoulders, a panicked look on his face.

She groaned. "Stop shaking me."

He sat back. "You were writhing around, screaming like a madwoman. I thought we were done for."

"We might be." Kelly sat up gingerly, her head still spinning. "We're supposed to just walk to the door. If we're 'true' it will work."

"Walk on thin air?" His eyebrows shot to the ceiling. Then he nodded in understanding. "'Believe and you will not fall.' It's a line from the song. Do you believe, Kelly?"

"I don't know."

He leaned forward, earnest. "You can't have any doubt. You have to know you'll make it across. Absolutely. Like how you don't doubt your name is Kelly and that you are a fadaman."

Kelly's chest tightened. "I don't think I can do that."

"But you *are* Ardagali, Kelly."

"And you said born and bred Ardagali have failed."

He sighed. "If only our wings weren't bound. That's the only other way."

An inkling of an idea formed in Kelly's mind. She looked up at the ceiling. In human measurements, it might only be ten feet high. The chasm, perhaps five feet across. Five feet was a stretch, but it might just be doable. She stood up. "Flying may not be the only way."

"What are you talking about?"

"I'm a fadaman. I can transform."

He gasped. "No, that's magic."

"Yes, and no. You said we can't call on the elements from our surroundings. When I transform, it's all internal. I don't take anything from outside."

He didn't look convinced.

"Listen, you said I couldn't have any doubt or I'll fall. I have doubt. I don't believe I can just walk across. If I transform, I can jump across. Are you with me?"

He hesitated a moment, then nodded.

"Good." She transformed, half expecting to be struck down by a bolt of lighting as soon as the process was complete.

"That never gets old," Blaine said admiringly.

She knelt down and stretched an arm out to him. He crawled up and sat on her shoulder. She walked back to the wall to make space for a running jump. The gauntlet realized what she was planning. The whispers crescendoed to fever pitch, and the stabbing pain returned. She stumbled.

"What is it?"

"I think we made it mad." She quickly threw up her mental barrier and the pain subsided. Thwarted, the gauntlet took a different approach. The ground shook. A crack formed in the ceiling and moved from one side to the next. Rocks started to fall from above. Worse, the chasm began to widen. *It's now or never.* Kelly ran for it and jumped. She looked down at the abyss as she soared across the chasm. Something white and billowy fell down. She realized it was the spider silk from her wings. Transforming to human form must have dislodged it.

Her feet hit something. She'd touched down just an inch over the edge. She tumbled forward awkwardly and landed in a heap on the ground.

Blaine rolled off of her. "You'd better change back now, and quick!"

Kelly hurriedly transformed back to fairy form. Together they ran for the door, dodging large chunks of rock that fell from the sky, barely keeping their balance as the ground rocked beneath them. They reached the door and pushed on it. Thankfully, the rock inside the border dissolved in an instant. They ran through as the cavern behind them caved in.

Kelly's jaw dropped. They were back in the same room where their wings had been bound with spider silk. *How is that possible?* she wondered. *Maybe this room just looks exactly the same.* But everyone was still there. The king and queen, their children, and the rest of the court greeted them with stunned silence. The expression of shock combined with disbelief on Brendann's face made Kelly smile on the inside.

Proxy was the first to break the silence. "Look, her wings unbound. She cheat!"

Murmurs of agreement sprang up from the crowd.

Blaine's eyebrows drew together with worry.

Kelly bristled. "I did not cheat. Your father said to remove the spider's silk at my own risk. He never said it wasn't permitted."

Proxy sported a murderous look. "Tell girl she's wrong, Father."

Kelly broke in. "No, you tell her *she's* wrong, Uncle. I passed the gauntlet, fair and square. Honor your side. That is, if you have any honor."

Just a few members of the crowd grumbled indignantly at her insinuation. She guessed the others might not have understood enough English to grasp it. All eyes were on the king. Brendann drew his lips into a tight line, as he clenched and unclenched his fists. Finally, he twirled around and stormed off in a huff. Proxy and the queen ran after him.

"Does that mean he agreed?" Kelly whispered to Blaine.

He nodded with an audible sigh of relief.

The members of court, now looking bored, dispersed, barely giving Kelly and Blaine another glance. Everyone except Xander, that is. He stayed behind. Once the others had gone, he ran up to Kelly and gave her a warm hug.

She was too surprised to do anything but stand there.

He stepped back, resting his hands on her shoulders. He smiled widely. "Cousin, well met!" It was like a switch had been flipped. Suddenly instead of hating her, he was her new best friend. She must have looked as confused as she felt. Xander laughed. "You passed the gauntlet, which means you are family. This is a most joyous occasion."

"Why don't your sister and father share your sentiments?" she asked.

"Give them some time. My sister loved her wasps, so their loss hit her very hard. But you can't be blamed. You didn't know what the outcome of your actions would be, and you were just trying to protect your friends."

"Will my friends be released now that I've passed?"

"Of course. They should be here any minute, in fact."

Thank goodness, she thought. "How is it that you speak English so much better than your sister?" she asked Xander.

"I like to practice with your father. He's fluent."

Kelly's heart skipped a beat. *My father.* She was bursting with questions to ask about him. So many flooded her mind that she couldn't think of which to ask first.

Xander turned to Blaine. "Let me get that spider's silk off your wings." He pulled a pouch from his pocket and sprinkled a light blue powder onto the cocoon. It dried and cracked, then fell to the ground.

"Thanks," Blaine said.

"Kelly!"

Kelly turned to see Bubbles bounding towards her, followed by Beatrix, who ran quite fast in spite of her newly bandaged leg. Milak followed up in the rear, his trademark scowl in place. He eyed Xander with a mixture of suspicion and wariness.

Bubbles threw his arms around Kelly. "I'm so glad you made it."

Beatrix jumped up and down, clapping. "They did fabulous, don't you think, Milak?"

Milak grunted. "They could have done worse." He crossed his arms and walked off.

Blaine made a face at Milak's back. "He's such a bore." He poked Kelly's arm. "Hey, why are you smiling like an idiot?"

"I'm smiling because Milak just gave us a compliment."

"Could have fooled me," Blaine said.

"It wasn't what he said. It's how he said it," Kelly explained. There had been a spark in Milak's eye, something — dare she think it — something like respect. She never thought she get that from him. It felt good.

Xander offered her his arm. "Would you like a tour of the city?"

"That would be lovely."

14

DARINDIAN

Torches of silver flame lit the stone hallways. Xander led them on a twisting path. "All of this is part of the palace. It was carved from one solid rock. Impressive, no?"

Kelly nodded politely. In truth, she found the act of retracing the route she'd taken blindfolded a few hours before to be downright creepy. The tunnels reminded her of a medieval castle at best, of the subterranean Miasmonian lair at worst.

"We are almost to the entrance," Xander said.

They turned a corner and saw sunlight at the end of a long hallway. Beatrix shot ahead of them, clearly eager for the sun.

"Your sister doesn't like enclosed spaces?" Xander asked Bubbles.

Bubbles nodded. "Not enough room for her to zip around in."

When they reached the opening they flew outside. The first thing Kelly saw was a packed dirt clearing encircling the palace. The palace itself was a huge, smooth rock, with no windows she could see. It had to be at least three times as big as Kelly's house back home.

In the clearing, Ardagali children chased each other about. They played an energetic game with polished sticks and acorns. Beatrix had already made friends, and some of the Ardagali children gestured wildly in an attempt to communicate the rules of the game to her. There was much laughter on both sides.

A line of trees encircled the clearing. Hanging from their branches were dozens of wasps' nests, each at least two feet long. A faint buzzing filled the air as small groups of wasps flew around their nests. "I thought all the wasps were dead," Kelly said.

Xander laughed. "We didn't send all of them just for you five."

"How many did you send?" Blaine asked.

"About a sixth."

Blaine frowned, and Bubbles gulped. No doubt they were both mentally imagining the quantity of wasps that remained.

"Don't worry," Xander said. "They are actually quite docile, unless commanded to attack."

Kelly found Xander's words far from comforting. She half expected the wasps to dive down at her, either on their own quest for revenge or commanded by Proxy. She held her breath as she followed Xander past the nest-bearing trees and into the woods. "Where's Milak?" she asked.

"I believe he flew to the border so he could report back to his king," Xander said. "Our mind barrier blocks long distance mental communications unless you have one of these." He reached under the collar of his shirt to reveal a necklace with a small, milky stone. "We should get you one, cousin. If you are staying, that is." He gave her a hopeful look.

"Actually, I can only stay a few days. I have school."

He frowned.

"We'll come back to visit, though," Kelly added.

His eyes brightened.

"As long as you don't set your wasps on us again," Blaine said.

"We wouldn't. You and Kelly passed the gauntlet, so you are now welcome here."

"What about me?" Bubbles asked.

"You, Milak, and your sister are welcome only if you are accompanied by Kelly or Blaine."

Bubbles pouted. "That doesn't seem fair."

Xander shrugged. "Those are our ways. Ah, look, here are some residences." Xander pointed to a cluster of trees ahead of them. They flew closer.

When they reached the trees, Kelly saw that they contained cleverly camouflaged tree houses, or perhaps they were more accurately described as tree 'nests.' Fairies bustled in and out of the rounded structures, which consisted of twigs and evergreen needles. For the most part, the fairies ignored the visitors. Kelly found this disinterest a bit odd, considering the commotion their arrival had caused in the royal court. A few fairies gave respectful nods to Xander, but they hardly gave a second glance to Kelly, Bubbles, or Blaine.

"Why are they ignoring us?" Kelly asked her cousin.

"They know you aren't a threat because you're with me."

"Aren't they curious when strangers visit?"

"For the most part we Ardagali keep to ourselves," Xander explained. "Don't be insulted, it's just how we are."

"Are all the Ardagali houses like these?" Bubbles asked.

"Most are, yes. Although some fairies prefer to live in hollowed-out trees." Xander's shoulders jerked like he'd been startled by something. "If you'll excuse me for a moment." He got a vacant look in his eye. Someone was talking to him telepathically. After a few minutes, his eyes focused on his surroundings again. He grinned. "Dinner is ready."

Bubbles clapped. "Wonderful! I'm famished."

Kelly realized she was very hungry too.

AN AWKWARD SILENCE hung thickly in the room. A scrumptious dinner of berries, squashes, and flaky pastries filled with a white substance much like cream cheese lay before them, but few were partaking in the feast. At the head of the long stone table, Brendann sat with arms crossed, yet to have touched his food. His queen, who Kelly now knew was named Adair, picked at her food daintily, casting nervous looks at her husband every now and again. Proxy stared at Kelly with an unwavering hostility. She gnawed ferociously on a pastry, taking out her anger on it. Beatrix and Xander exchanged shy looks with each other, while Milak sniffed everything on his plate suspiciously before taking tiny bites. Then he would wait several minutes, before taking a few more tiny bites. Bubbles, on the other hand, was already on his third plate of food, quite content.

Although the food was wonderful, Kelly found it difficult to enjoy with the tension that permeated the air. She wondered why they had even been invited to eat dinner with the royal family, if her uncle and Proxy still hated her. *Why do they hate me?* They were acting like little children. *This has gone on long enough.* She put down her eating utensil, which was a metal spork, and cleared her throat. "I don't understand why you don't like me. What happened with the wasps was an accident. And I'm sorry for that. Are you going to hold it against me forever?"

Proxy's glare intensified.

Kelly felt waves of frustration building up inside. She jabbed a finger in the king's direction. "And you, my own uncle, you act like you want me to die. You were disappointed to see me pass the gauntlet, weren't you?"

He brought a pensive hand up to his chin, considering his reply. She waited. "A stone cast in water creates ripples," he said after a moment.

Proxy smiled at his answer, so Kelly assumed he'd meant yes — he had indeed wanted her to perish in the gauntlet.

"How do you think that makes me feel?" she asked. "I'm your niece. We're family. Doesn't that mean anything to you?"

He raised an eyebrow, amused. "Silver looks cold under moonlit clouds."

She rolled her eyes. Another nonsensical Ardagali reply. Proxy's expression didn't give any clues this time, so she gave Blaine an inquisitive look. He returned it with a clueless shrug.

Kelly looked back to Brendann. "You clearly have a great eloquence with words, Uncle, but I'd prefer it if you would be direct with me."

He smirked. "As you wish. No matter what the gauntlet said, you are half human, and humans are a poison. They have a corruptive influence."

"But you don't even know me."

"All humans are alike," the king replied.

Bubbles slammed a fist against the table. "You're a real piece of work, Mister, you know that?"

Brendann squinted at Bubbles, seeming more perplexed than angered by the sudden outburst.

"Thanks, Bubbles, but let me handle this," Kelly said.

Bubbles glared at the king but said no more. King Brendann stared back. Finally, Brendann broke the eye contact, at which point Bubbles grinned triumphantly.

"The day's events have fatigued me," Brendann said. "I will retire." The king stood up. "Xander, show the fadaman to her father's quarters after the meal. He can deal with her when he returns. The others, they can stay with you, since you apparently like them so much."

"Very well, Father," Xander said.

The king exited the room. Proxy jumped up and followed her father out.

"What a bully," Bubbles muttered.

Milak grunted in agreement.

Xander blushed and stared down at his plate. He didn't defend his father.

With a nervous smile the queen gestured to a pastry-laden plate. "Would you like another, Kelly?"

"No, thank you. I've lost my appetite."

AFTER KELLY SAID goodnight to her friends outside of Xander's quarters, her cousin led her further down the hall. He stopped outside of an archway covered by a dark purple tapestry. "Here we are," he said. "You can wait inside for your father."

"Thank you." She moved towards the tapestry, but Xander put a hand on her forearm.

"Are you all right?" he asked.

"I'm fine."

"You look upset to me."

Kelly sighed. "It's just, this isn't exactly the welcome I was expecting. Don't get me wrong, I didn't expect a party, but, I didn't think my own family would hate me."

"I don't hate you."

"I know. But your father and sister do. Maybe your mother too, I can't tell."

"I don't think she hates you, but she doesn't like to openly disagree with my father."

"How come you're so open-minded?" she asked.

He shrugged. "Maybe it's because of your father. He doesn't

hate humans, obviously. And to be honest I spend more time with him than I do with my own father."

Kelly felt a twinge of jealousy. "What's my father like?"

Xander yawned. "You'll find out yourself soon," he said. "You know where I am, six doors down. Come get me if you need anything."

Once Xander had gone, Kelly pushed aside the tapestry and stepped inside. She found herself in a large, circular living area, with three tapestried arches on the far wall leading to interior rooms. The front room was dimly lit by tall, thin metal lamps with rounded glass tops. They glowed with a warm orange light. A dark purple carpet stretched along the ground. The walls were bare of any decorations, but a few painted stone vases filled with dried flowers dotted the edges of the room. The only pieces of furniture were a slender sofa in the middle of the space and a small table on the right sidewall with two chairs. Shelves had been carved directly into the wall beside the table, and a few jars, pots, and dishes rested on them. Further to the right was one long, wide shelf with open space above it, like a counter. It had what looked to be a sink, and maybe an electric hot plate too. It was a mini-kitchen, probably just for making snacks. Being a member of the royal family, Darindian likely had his other meals cooked for him by the same fairies who'd prepared the evening's royal dinner.

Kelly was curious what lay behind the other tapestries, but she didn't want to snoop around. So instead she took a seat on the sofa and waited.

~

SHE RACED VERY FAST *over the mountains. As she flew, the sunlight came and went, fast like a blinking strobe light as her fairy senses took her mind into the future. She reached a big city. There was water. The Statue of Liberty loomed beside her. In a sudden nose* dive, she flew down into a building and hovered over a young businesswoman. The woman held a paper in her hand. She folded it and put it in an envelope. As the woman leaned forward to lick the envelope, Kelly's view shifted and she was no longer watching the woman; she was looking out through the young woman's eyes. She tasted the glue from the envelope as if she herself had licked it. The muffled sound of a phone ringing in the next office came through the wall.

Almost immediately after the phone rang there was an odd sound — low and rumbling, like far-off thunder. The woman got up and walked to the window. Her high heels pinched her feet. Outside the window, a wall of water headed straight towards her. It crashed around the buildings in the distance as it made its way closer and closer. Cars and buses were tossed around like toys. A strangled scream escaped the woman's mouth, but she seemed frozen in place. Instead of trying to escape the impending deluge, she just stood there, staring at the water. A panic rose up within Kelly. The rumble was now a rushing roar, so loud it overpowered the woman's screams. It was odd to feel like she was screaming at the top of her lungs, but to hear no voice.

The water was there. It smacked into the window, and for a second it seemed as if the glass would hold. Time stood still for a moment, and then the glass shattered. The frigid water hit with immense force, but somehow Kelly, or rather, the woman in her vision, was not unconscious. Shards of broken glass dragged over her skin, and little clouds of the woman's blood floated into the water. She struggled to move to the window, but she couldn't. The water had pinned her back to the wall. It churned with such strength that it rushed its way into her nose and mouth with unstoppable force.

She heard a voice, distorted through the water. She couldn't make out its message.

Kelly jolted awake, coughing uncontrollably, limbs flailing about as if she was still fighting against the water.

"Calm down, it's all right."

Kelly nearly had a heart attack. A male fairy with stunning green eyes knelt beside her, concern clouding his features. He had black hair like hers, and wings much like hers too — purple with bands of silver running through them. Kelly was very glad they weren't the same glowing blue as Miasmos's and Brendann's. The fairy wore black from head to toe, and curiously, he wore a glove on his right hand, but not on his left.

He reached out tentatively to push a strand of Kelly's disheveled hair back behind her ear. "That was some nightmare," he commented. "But you're safe now," he added gently.

She opened her mouth — but nothing came out. Her throat felt raw and dry — from screaming in her sleep. She blushed. "Are you...Darindian?"

He nodded. "That's me."

There was an awkward silence during which they both tried to figure out what to say next. "I never thought..." Darindian ventured, "I mean, how did you..." His eyebrows scrunched together as he struggled to put his feelings into words. Kelly didn't think she could do much better at the moment.

A shrill sound interrupted them. On the hotplate, a teakettle blared to indicate that its contents were ready. Darindian rushed across the room and quickly lifted the kettle off the hotplate. Steam floated from its spout as its shriek diminished to a stuttering whimper. Kelly stared at Darindian as he opened a jar, took some dried leaves from it, and put them into the kettle.

He looked over his shoulder. "Would you like some tea?" Without waiting for her answer he took two cups down from a shelf and placed them on the table. "Do you take cinnamon?" he asked.

"Um, sure."

He reached into another jar and pulled out a brownish red cube, dropped it into one of the cups, then poured the tea. He took a seat at the table and gestured for her to join him.

She sat down across from him.

He took a sip from his cup. "Try yours," he suggested. "The leaves come from my own garden." He watched her expectantly, clearly eager for her opinion of his tea, leaning forward with bated breath — like a lot was riding on it. "It tastes better when it's hot, you know."

Kelly realized she'd been staring. "Oh, right." She lifted her tea with her right hand. The liquid sloshed about, close to the rim, due to the trembling of her hand. She brought her other hand up for added support, at which Darindian's eyes narrowed.

"That ring, where did you get it?" His tone cut sharply through the air as he glared at the ring with a mixture of wariness and...could it be fear?

Her teacup shook even more, though she now gripped it tightly with both hands. She put it back down on the table without taking a sip. "The ring was a gift."

"You don't say," he said. She wasn't sure he believed her. His eyes glinted like penetrating lasers. He raised his gloved hand and wiggled his fingers. "Do you know why I wear this glove?"

She frowned, perplexed. This was not the direction she'd imagined this conversation would take. "Was that a rhetorical question?"

He silently reached up with his left hand and slowly pulled off his glove. Kelly couldn't contain a horrified gasp at what emerged from beneath it. His right hand was robotic — like something from a science fiction movie. He clenched and unclenched the metal fingers, which produced faint clicking and whirring sounds, like gears turning. He rested his arm on the table. "I lost my hand because of that ring on your finger. Harald Penadas wanted it, but I wouldn't give it to him."

Harald Penadas — that was the name Miasmos had been born with. Kelly's jaw dropped.

"Imagine my surprise at seeing you with it," Darindian

continued. "I doubt Harald would have given it to just anyone." His tone was sharp with icy suspicion.

"Are you accusing me of something?"

He placed the glove back over his robotic appendage. "Are you in league with him?"

"Of course not."

"Then who gave it to you?"

"His son Marcos gave it to me."

At her reply his shoulders sank like all of his energy had been drained from him. "You're in league with Harald's son, then? I'd never expect my..." his voice trailed off. "I'd never expect you to be involved with such riff raff."

For some reason, Kelly found his reaction oddly comical. He didn't know the first thing about her. How would he know what to expect? "Relax. He's not like Miasmos, not anymore. He had a change of heart after I put him in a coma."

Darindian's eyebrows shot to the ceiling. "You put him in a coma?"

She nodded.

He sat up straighter. "Impressive. You will have to tell me about that," he said. "But first, about the ring, you shouldn't wear it. It's dangerous. Harald might want it back."

"He won't want it back. He already got what he wanted from it."

"How do you mean?"

"He cleansed it of its vibrations so he could get closer to finding Embralia. The ring was one of the ten curtains, the objects concealing Embralia's location."

He nodded in understanding. "Ah yes, when Harald stole the ring from me he was going on and on about it being a curtain, as I recall. I didn't know what he was talking about at the time. Now it makes sense."

It was strange how Darindian kept using the name Harald instead of Miasmos. He must have known the evil fairy a long time ago, before he'd taken his new name. Did that mean Darindian had been to Glendenland? Is that how he'd met her mother? "How do you know Miasmos?" she asked.

He stared into his teacup. "He was different once." Kelly sensed a note of regret in his voice. "We used to be friends. We're second cousins, in fact."

Kelly's eyes widened. "That means I'm related to him?"

He chuckled at her reaction. "Yes, I'm afraid you're his second cousin, once removed."

She shuddered. "Not removed enough."

"A common sentiment among his relations." He laughed. Then he grew serious. "Speaking of relations..." He paused to clear his throat. "I suppose we should address the elephant in the room."

That was an interesting way to put it.

"How did you find me?" he asked.

She frowned. "When you ask it like that it almost sounds like you didn't want to be found."

He brought his gloved hand to his cheek like she'd slapped him. "You don't mince words," he said once he'd recovered. "I like that. But you misunderstand. I'm surprised, that's all. I had no idea about you until today."

Kelly raised an incredulous eyebrow. He never even suspected he might have a daughter? Couldn't he have sensed it?

He tapped his robotic fingers on the table as he gazed pensively into his teacup. "You must have been so tiny," he murmured, "that neither of us sensed you existed."

Neither of *us*? Who did he mean?

He took a sip of tea. "And then later," he continued, "I never would have picked up on anything, unless I'd been looking, which I had no reason to because the possibility never entered my mind." He looked up at her. "Did you sense me?"

She shook her head no. "Miasmos told Marcos about you, and Marcos told me."

"Of course! Anyone who knows me would sense the relation when they met you. If they have strong enough fairy senses, that is."

That explained why he'd never come looking for her, and how Miasmos had known of their relation to each other. But it didn't explain much else. Kelly pulled the picture of her and her mother from her back pocket and placed it on the table. Darindian picked it up. His expression softened as he looked down at it. "Mindy. Just as beautiful as I remember." He traced a finger along the photograph.

So he had cared for her mother, which was comforting. But how did Mindy of all people get involved romantically with a fairy? "How did you meet?"

He gazed at the picture as he began his account. "There is a waterfall, not far from here. It's very beautiful. Secluded, quiet. I often used to go there to think. One day, when I arrived, I found a human sitting at the water's edge. Your mother." He looked up to gauge her reaction.

Kelly leaned forward, listening with interest. Since when was Mindy a nature enthusiast? They'd never even been camping.

"I was surprised," Darindian continued, "because she was a human, and the waterfall is well within the mind barrier. She should have never come through the barrier, nor been able to make it to the waterfall without falling into any of our traps." He paused, pensive, as if pondering how Mindy might have accomplished said feat. How *had* she?

"Go on," Kelly prodded.

"So, I saw her there, which was amazing in itself. Then an even more amazing thing happened." His eyes sparkled at the memory. "She turned around, and she *saw* me, even though she was a human, and I was in my invisible form."

"How is that possible?" Kelly asked. Mindy had never seen any of her fairy friends before, not even Bubbles, who made a habit of flying all around her when she cooked. He even snuck scraps off the counter from right under her nose.

"I have no idea how it's possible," Darindian said. "But it happened. She wasn't afraid, rather curious. We had a deep connection immediately. I hid her in a cave behind the waterfall and visited her every day. I knew that my brother wouldn't approve, but it felt so right." He smiled at the memory. "We were in love."

Kelly struggled with the cognitive dissonance his account produced. It didn't make sense. Mindy had been in the wilderness, halfway across the continent. Why? Then she had seen Darindian in his invisible form? And they had fallen in love? What could they have possibly had in common? It all raised more questions than answers. "So why can't she remember anything?"

His reminiscing smile disappeared in a flash. "My brother found out. He gave me a choice. Either be exiled, or let him erase your mother's memory and send her away."

Brendann. Kelly clenched her fists. Her anger towards her uncle rapidly multiplied. At this rate the Ardagali king might soon surpass Miasmos as the fairy she detested most in the world.

"I was weak," Darindian said. "I didn't want to give up my status, my friends, my life here. So I let him erase her memory. I wanted him to erase mine too, but he said I needed to remember my indiscretion. He did, however, cast a spell on me so that I couldn't sense her vibrations anymore."

"So you could never find her," Kelly murmured.

He nodded. "Exactly. Later, I felt terrible. I knew I'd made a mistake. But Brendann refused to undo the spell. He said it was best for me. Over time I convinced myself he was right."

"Do you feel that way now?"

He bristled. "What a question. Of course not. This changes everything. If I had known, I'd like to think I would have run away with your mother. It's impossible to know for sure, of course, but I don't think I would have abandoned you."

I would have run away with your mother. Kelly imagined what her life might have been like if he had. She would have known about fairies from the beginning. The revelation she was a fadaman would not have turned her life upside down. She would have been prepared. Most importantly, she would have known her father — she would not have lived the first fourteen years of her life thinking he was dead, and after that wondering where he might be, and why he'd never come to find her. His absence had loomed over her for as long as she could remember; some of her earliest memories were of being jealous of other children at birthday parties, seeing them laugh and spend time with their fathers.

And now she had found him. But even with him sitting across from her, the absence didn't feel any less. If possible, it felt even worse. This fairy, her father — was a stranger. She didn't feel a connection. He didn't *feel* like her father. Would he ever? Her fists clenched again as she thought of how Darindian had repented, but Brendann had refused to undo the spell. Brendann had robbed them, and they could never get the lost time back. But what about the future? It suddenly dawned on her that now that Darindian knew where Mindy was — there was nothing stopping their reunion.

"You could come back now," she said. "Return my mother's memory and you could be together."

He shook his head sadly and placed the picture back down on the table. "I'm afraid it's too late for that. She would never forgive me, even if Brendann would give us the antidote."

"You don't know that."

He fidgeted, adjusting his glove. "That's not the only reason I can't go back with her."

"I don't understand."

"I have other...commitments."

"Could you possibly be any vaguer?"

He sighed. "I'm married."

Kelly blinked, stunned. "What? No one said anything about you being married." She found it hard to believe Brendann hadn't rubbed that detail in her face earlier.

"That's because nobody here knows yet," Darindian explained. "She's not a member of this band. Actually she's from one of our historically sworn enemies. It's one of those never-ending feud situations, where neither side even remembers why they don't like the other one anymore. She and I are trying to find a good time to break the news without starting a war."

"What's her name?" Kelly asked.

"Fiona."

"Do you love her?"

He nodded.

"Like you loved my mother?"

He poured himself more tea, gathering his thoughts. "What your mother and I had, that was young love. In all honestly, I don't know if it would have lasted." He gave her one of those 'responsible adult' looks that verged on pity. "I'm sorry if that's not what you want to hear."

It wasn't what she wanted to hear, obviously. But she supposed it wasn't so strange he had found love again. After all, Mindy had found Rick. At that thought Kelly nearly threw up a little in her mouth.

"Are you all right?" Darindian asked.

"Yes, I'm fine." She finally took a sip of her tea. It tasted like apple cider. "It's good," she said.

He smiled. "I'm glad you like it."

"Will your wife be upset that you have a daughter?" she

asked, hoping her voice didn't betray the twinge of hope she felt at the possibility.

He shrugged. "I shouldn't think so. She'll be excited to meet you. Just like I'm glad you came to see me." He paused, gazing at her uncertainly. "I wasn't around for you before, because I didn't know about you. But I'd like to be here for you now. That is, if you want me to be."

"Of course I want you to be. Why wouldn't I?"

He let out the breath he'd been holding. "I'm glad you feel that way."

There was a rustle at the front tapestry. A young fairy boy popped his head in. "Prince Darindian, the king requests your presence. He says to stop ignoring his mental summons."

Darindian rolled his eyes. "Brendann, impatient as always," he muttered. "Tell him I'll be just a few moments, Petro."

The messenger fairy nodded and ran back down the hall.

"I suppose I should go speak with him," Darindian said. "Though sometimes I wonder why I even try."

"Did you know he sent me through the gauntlet? He wanted me to die before you got back."

Darindian grimaced. "Yes, I'm going to give him words about that. Among other things." He stood up. "I wish I could say that deep down my brother is not so bad, and that he'll warm up to you. But, I'm afraid he's set in his ways. He's always hated humans. And he's not about to change his mind."

"At least you're honest," Kelly said. "Xander keeps telling me to give him time."

He chuckled. "Xander has an almost stubborn faith in others. It's a good quality, an innocence most of us lost long ago." His voice trailed off and he got a faraway look in his eyes. Kelly wondered what he was thinking about — when he'd lost his innocence? After a few seconds he snapped out of it. "I'll probably be a while. Don't wait up."

WHEN KELLY WOKE up it was past ten in the morning. She wondered why no one had woken her up. "Darindian?"

He wasn't in the front room. She was about to go see if he was in one of the back rooms when she noticed the picture of her and her mother was not on the table, but on the sofa cushion next to her, face down. Something had been scribbled on the back: *I have to go away for a while. I'm sorry.*

He had to go away now? Right after she'd found him? Where? And why had he left the picture? She clutched the picture and dashed out into the hallway — and almost bumped right into Brendann. He didn't look surprised to see her. Perhaps he'd even been waiting for her to come out.

"Where's my father?" she demanded.

The corners of Brendann's mouth lifted into a self-satisfied smirk. "He's left."

"Where did he go?"

"Somewhere other than here."

Her eyes narrowed. "Did you do something to make him leave?"

He snorted. "An empty jar sings in the night."

"Stop it with your stupid non sequiturs!" she yelled, surprised that such a big SAT word had just popped out of her mouth.

"Watch your tone, fadaman," Brendann snapped. "He's gone, and he won't be back for some time. You may as well follow suit. I don't want you around here." He waved a dismissive hand, then looked down his nose at her as he brushed past and strutted off down the hall. Kelly knew it would be pointless to try and get more information from him. She ran to Xander's room. He stepped out from behind the entrance tapestry just as she arrived.

"There you are," he said with a smile. "I sent your friends to breakfast already. Bubbles was hungry."

"What did your father do?" she asked sharply.

He frowned, taken aback. "What do you mean?"

"Darindian's gone."

"Oh, don't scare me like that." He brought a hand to his chest. "I thought it was something serious for a moment there."

"This is serious. My father is gone."

He put a hand on her shoulder. "No, don't worry, Darindian often goes off on a moment's notice. For urgent business. He hardly ever says goodbye. He just leaves notes." His eyes fell on the picture in her hand, and the writing on the back. "Like that one, see? There's nothing to worry about. He's fine."

She read the note again, uncertain. After all, Darindian was an Ardagali prince. He must have important duties to attend to. Maybe it was unfair to expect him to drop everything just because she was there. Even so, she still wished he'd woken her up to say goodbye.

"Don't be gloomy," Xander said with a reassuring grin. "You should just stay and wait until he gets back. There are lots of fun things to do here. And you've only seen a tiny fraction of our realm."

"Your father wants me to leave."

His face fell. "That's unfortunate. I will talk to him, so that next time you visit he'll let you stay longer."

"I doubt you'll succeed with that," Kelly said.

He sighed. "Well, shall we go collect your companions then?"

"I suppose so." They started down the hall. "Wait, do you have something to write with?" she asked.

"Just a moment." Xander turned back and disappeared inside his room. He returned with a twig, which on closer inspection turned out to be a species of pencil.

She took the pencil and wrote her address on the back of

the picture. "Give this to my father when he gets back, please." She extended it to Xander.

"I will." He took it.

"Give it to him, and only him," she instructed. "I'm sure Brendann would burn it the first chance he got."

He nodded seriously. "You can trust me. I will give it straight to Darindian. No one else."

"Thank you."

15

PRECIPICE

The path through the forest felt different this time — familiar, peaceful. There were no signs of the dead wasps anywhere. Perhaps the Ardagali had cleared them. Kelly's stomach twisted as she remembered the look on Proxy's face when the wasps had died. She hoped her cousin would forgive her someday. At least she had an understandable reason for disliking Kelly. Brendann, on the other hand, was just hateful, spiteful, and close-minded.

"You could have at least let us stay for the tree sap cakes," Bubbles complained. He was still sour that Kelly had torn him away from his breakfast before the final dish arrived. "They're supposed to be an Ardagali delicacy," he whined. "You can't get them *anywhere* else." He stopped and hovered mid-air, hands on his hips.

Kelly kept flying. "Next time we visit you can try them."

"But I want them now."

"Stop acting like a child," Milak bellowed from where he flew above them. "You're a grown man!"

"Don't tell me what to do," Bubbles retorted. But his face

flushed red with embarrassment and he raced to catch up with Kelly.

Beatrix, despite whatever pain she must have felt from her injured leg, was flying at least twenty paces ahead, full of abundant energy, as usual. Suddenly she came to a stop midair. "We're here," she announced.

Kelly looked around. All she saw was more trees. "We're where exactly?"

Milak snorted. "The mind barrier, obviously."

"Oh." Now that they'd mentioned it, Kelly could sense the invisible wall of energy before them. The air felt slightly more — electric. She took a deep breath before flying through the barrier, remembering the feeling it had produced last time. To her surprise, this time she barely felt anything, only the slightest tingle along her skin.

On the other side, Beatrix shuddered. "Don't like that barrier. It's icky." She shook her limbs out in the air, flopping about like a rag doll. Kelly wondered why she hadn't felt anything as intense as Beatrix apparently had — maybe it was because she had gone through the gauntlet and Beatrix had not. Could the barrier tell she was an Ardagali now? She glanced over at Blaine, who looked similarly unaffected by having just passed through the barrier.

Beatrix finished shaking herself out and shot off ahead of them like a speeding bullet. Bubbles, Blaine, and Milak started forward as well, but Kelly hung back. She felt an icy pressure inside her mind, like she was being watched. *Marcos.* He was trying to contact her. She frowned. From all the way in Denver at his charity project? That was far away. She was surprised she could even pick up on his signal. She accepted the connection.

"Kelly! I've been trying to reach you for hours." Marcos's mental voice carried strain and frustration.

"Sorry, the Ardagali have a mental barrier around their territory. That's probably why."

"Did you find your father?"

"Yes."

"And?"

Kelly tried to formulate a quick summary, but she had a hard time trying to condense her feelings about her father into a few sentences. While she was thinking, Bubbles flew back to her position and stared at her suspiciously. "Who are you talking to?" he asked.

"Kelly? Are you still there?"

"Who is it?" Bubbles pestered. "Who? Tell me. Who?"

"Be quiet Bubbles. It's hard to have two conversations at once." She sent him a stern look. *"I'm still here, Marcos, but I can't really talk right now. Did you just want to know about my father or is there something else?"*

Bubbles's eyes narrowed. "I know. It's Witherings!" he shouted. "Am I right? Or am I right?"

"I need you to come to Denver." Kelly barely heard Marcos over Bubbles's repeated questions.

"Bubbles, stop it!"

He turned his nose up in the air with a huff. "Fine then, be that way." He flew to join his sister, who was so far ahead by now that she was almost out of sight.

"Kelly?"

"Sorry. Why do you want me to come to Colorado?"

"My father has found all but one of the ten curtains. I need you to try and connect to the memory stone — we have to find Embralia before he does."

Kelly's heart pounded in her ears. Miasmos already had the Key to Embralia in his possession. Now all he needed was to recover one more shielding object and he would be able to find the ancient ruins — and unlock the power hidden within them to become the mightiest of all fairies on earth. And it fell on her to stop him. *"But I don't even know what to do when I connect with the memory stone. Besides, it's all the way in Glendenland."*

"Don't worry about that, I have a plan. I'll send one of my heli-copters to get you."

"You have more than one?"

"Of course."

But Denver was over five hundred miles away. *"Isn't that too far for a helicopter?"*

"It can stop to refuel on the way."

When she caught up with the others they wanted an update. She knew Milak would not approve of her trying to connect with the memory stone, because Thomas and Venuto had still forbidden it. So she lied. "Since there's still a few days of fall break left, Marcos is sending a helicopter to bring me to his charity project. That's where my mom thinks I am anyway, so it's good for my cover story."

"We'll come with you," Bubbles said.

"No way," Beatrix said, trembling. "I will *not* get into one of those helicontraptors!"

"But you flew in the plane," Bubbles pointed out.

"That was when Kelly was in mortal danger by going to see the Ardagali without us."

Milak snorted at that comment. Clearly, he was of the opinion that adding Bubbles and Beatrix to their group hadn't contributed much in the way of protection.

"Let's just take a ride on a truck back home," Beatrix said. She fixed a puppy-dog look on her brother.

He sighed. "All right. If you insist. Besides, I love the food at truck stops!"

"Do you want to come with us?" Beatrix asked Blaine.

"I'll go with Kelly, if she'll let me."

Kelly nodded. She turned to Milak, racking her brain for a polite way to tell him she didn't want him along. Luckily, he didn't feel like accompanying her.

"My duty is done," he said. "I accompanied you to the Ardagali, as Thomas requested. Now I should return to Glendenland."

She tried not to smile too widely. "Thank you Milak, for everything."

"Hmpf." He scratched his nose, like that small amount of praise made him uncomfortable. "Just doing my job."

~

KELLY STARED out the helicopter window in awe, marveling at the expanse of nature below. Blaine, in invisible-to-humans form, gazed upon the scenery with a similar captivation. They flew over stunning rock formations and forests, and in the distance towering mountains glistened with blazing white snow.

"Your first time in a helicopter?" asked the pilot, who was a petite woman in her early forties.

Kelly nodded.

The pilot chuckled. "I thought so."

The flight took a little over four hours, with a stop for refueling. It was relaxing for the most part, until the landing in Denver. The pilot guided the helicopter downwards to a cluster of tall buildings with incredible speed. Kelly's heart palpitated with nervousness as they passed through a narrow opening between two glass building faces.

Blaine laughed. "This is spectacular!"

Kelly didn't answer. She was too busy trying not to throw up. Less than a minute later the pilot brought the helicopter to an expert landing on a flat rooftop. Kelly removed the noise-canceling headphones the pilot had given her and covered her ears with her hands. The motor was deafeningly loud.

When the pilot gave her the signal, Kelly stepped out of the helicopter and Blaine flew out beside her. They headed towards a raised cube section of the roof that contained a red door.

When they were clear of the helicopter, the pilot guided it into the air behind them and flew away.

The red door opened — and Stephanie walked out. *What's she doing here?* Kelly thought. *She still doesn't trust Marcos.*

"Stephanie!" Blaine snapped his fingers to become visible and raced to his girlfriend.

Stephanie's eyes lit up when she saw him. He jumped into her arms and she cradled him like a baby. Kelly stifled a laugh. They looked ridiculous.

"You have to tell me everything," Stephanie said when Kelly reached her. "I'm dying with suspense."

"I will, once we get inside. But what are you doing here?"

"My parents wanted me to help them renovate our kitchen. So at the last minute I asked Witherings if I could come here instead."

"But here you're building houses right?" Kelly asked. "How is that so different from renovating a kitchen?"

Stephanie laughed. "You haven't seen my parents do home improvement. It's a nightmare."

"Does this mean you like Marcos now?" Kelly asked hopefully.

"I wouldn't say that. But here I can keep an eye on him."

Stephanie led them down a stairway and out to an interior floor that resembled a typical corporate office suite. At the end of a long hall, two polished wooden doors led to a spacious office-living area. Inside, a grand piano stood beside a pair of white leather sofas, a glass coffee table, a kitchenette, and of course a stately desk, behind which Marcos Witherings sat.

Marcos looked up from a stack of papers. He smiled, but his eyes were weary. "Kelly, I'm glad you're here."

"Glad to be here." She took in the fancy surroundings. "I thought I'd find you in a hard hat at a construction site, covered in dust."

He laughed. "That was earlier. We're done for the day." He stood up and came around to stand beside them.

Blaine waved. "I'm Blaine. You might recall we met before, in the jail bubble."

Marcos nodded. "Ah yes. I do apologize for rendering you unconscious."

"Under the circumstances, I would have done the same," Blaine said.

Marcos motioned for them to sit down. "Would you like something to drink? Or eat? I have some sushi in the fridge."

Kelly's stomach rumbled. "That would be wonderful."

As they nibbled on little rolls of rice, fish, and vegetables encased in seaweed, Kelly and Blaine recounted their trip. Blaine told the story of the gauntlet with impressive theatrical flair. Stephanie, enthralled by the tale, periodically interrupted to exclaim: "Blaine, you're amazing!"

"Hey, I'm amazing too," Kelly joked.

Marcos was very intrigued to learn about the history between Miasmos and Darindian. He told Kelly that Miasmos had only mentioned Darindian in passing, and he had never given specifics about how he had obtained the spy ring. When Kelly revealed that Darindian and Miasmos were second cousins, Marcos's eyes lit up.

"Do you know what that means?" he asked. "It means you and I are second cousins." He beamed, looking quite pleased.

Kelly shared his sentiment.

"And you are also related to Thomas," Marcos added.

"If you guys are all related, how come nobody sensed it before?" Stephanie asked.

Marcos thoughtfully smeared some wasabi paste over a piece of sushi. "The more distant the relationship, the harder it is to sense," he explained. "If we'd been consciously looking for it, we may have been able to sense a second cousin relationship, perhaps. But such a relationship doesn't just jump out at you

like a closer relationship would. The vibrations of close relations really hit you strongly. You must know from when you
met your father, right Kelly?"

I didn't feel anything. Her cheeks grew hot. "I wasn't actually
paying much attention to vibrations at the time."

"That's understandable."

"But he sensed I was his daughter," she said. "And so did my
uncle."

"That sorry excuse for a fairy," Blaine mumbled at the
mention of Brendann.

Marcos nodded gravely. "Yes, I have not heard good things
about the Ardagali king."

After their meal, Marcos said he wanted to go over some
'campaign details' with Kelly alone. To Kelly's surprise,
Stephanie didn't protest — she was more than happy to spend
some alone time with Blaine.

Once Stephanie and Blaine left them, Marcos let his guard
down, and the full extent of his worry showed on his face. "He's
very close to the last curtain, Kelly. I can feel it. We must act
now. If the memory stone will tell you where Embralia is, we
can get there first."

"You said that you had a plan?"

"Yes." He pointed to the spy ring. "That will help you
connect to it from afar."

She twisted the ring back and forth around her finger,
thinking of its history. Part of her felt weird for still wearing it,
considering how it had been on her father's hand when he'd
lost it. The other part of her felt closer to her father when she
wore it — it was a connection they shared.

"Spy the stone first," Marcos instructed. "Then, send out a
telepathic invitation to it through the ring."

It sounded like a long shot to Kelly, but there was nothing to
be lost by making an attempt. She concentrated on the polished

black stone of the ring. After a few minutes, a misty vision of the memory stone emerged on its surface. It rested all alone on a shelf in the center of small, empty room — a secure location in Glendenland. "I see it," she said.

"Good. Can you connect to it?"

Kelly focused on the stone's image, trying to hear its whispers. She got nothing at first, but then she heard a faint whistle, like wind in the distance. Her surroundings wavered like a mirage until they dissolved into something else.

She'd finally reached it — the purple mountain. It loomed overhead, so tall that she could not see the top. She stood only a few paces from its base, and she could see that it was not of stone, nor dirt, nor any other material she could identify. It was gel-like, a gigantic glob resembling toothpaste, undulating, with ever-changing shades of blue and violet flashing across its surface. The whispers sang their song all around her now, enveloping her, so close she felt like she could reach out and grasp them. Yet, still they had no form. Were they coming from within the mountain? A ripple of mirth coursed through the whispers. The mountain hummed underneath them, or from within them all, Kelly couldn't tell.

"Where is Embralia?" she asked.

The whispers grew quiet. Puzzled.

"Please? Will you show me Embralia?"

Discordant chatter. Frustration.

Maybe she wasn't asking correctly. "Can you show me a memory?"

The whispers burst with excitement, running over each other, tumbling here and there with twinkling echoes. Directly in front of her, a glowing handprint emerged on the mountain's surface. The whispers crescendoed, jubilant, spurring her to reach out to them.

She lifted her hand and pressed it against the glowing handprint. An electric jolt ran up her arm and then — she was floating in the air over a field of ice. It stretched as far as she could see. No, she wasn't in the air. Was she under water? It couldn't be, because she breathed, or at least this mental projection of herself felt like she was breathing. Still, there was a resistance unlike air as she waved her hands in front of her face. It felt as though she was swimming, or suspended in a kind of transparent liquid substance — not quite as hard to move through as water, but not as light as air.

She heard nothing. No whispers, no ambient noise. Nothing. It was the most complete silence she had ever experienced. Then, a flicker of light drew her attention, about six paces to her left. Small and blue, it flashed and was gone in an instant. A second later it blinked again. Then again. Like a tiny blue firefly, stuck in place. When the light flashed it made a sound, like a musical, metallic raindrop.

Kelly was about to swim to it when another one appeared, this time off to her right. A second later one blinked into existence in front of her. Then they began to pop into being one after another. Their sounds, which initially produced a delicate sprinkling of notes, rose to a downpour. In less than a minute there were dozens, then hundreds of lights. Then there were thousands — stretching farther and farther away, only inches apart from each other. They were breathtaking.

But what were they? It dawned on her — could they be the memories? The closest one was less than an arm's reach away. She lifted a finger, slowly bringing it closer to the light. Trepidatious butterflies danced in her stomach. When her finger was a mere millimeter from the spark, she felt a warmth in her fingertip. Just as she was about to make contact — the spark darted away. Like it didn't want to be caught.

The spark's movement agitated the others. They all dislodged themselves from their invisible anchor points in a flurry. They were like a school of millions of tiny little fish. They raced about, like a tornado, moving in groups with impossible speed, so that they blurred together in streaks. When Kelly tried to catch one, they would disperse, leaving the area she had grasped entirely vacant in an instant. It was impossible.

The vision ended abruptly, and Kelly was back in Marcos's office. She found herself lying on the couch, with a silk pillow under her head. There was a light blanket over her. She started to sit up, but the movement brought a dizzying pain behind her eyes.

"Don't try to get up right away," Marcos said. He knelt beside her, eyebrows wrinkled with concern.

Slowly and gingerly she settled back down on the pillow. She felt something warm and sticky above her upper lip. She raised a finger to touch it — and found a red smear on her hand. Blood. *What in the...?*

Marcos handed her a warm washcloth to wipe her face. "I thought you were fine, but then, blood started coming from your nose. "His voice shook. "So I woke you up. How do you feel?"

"My head hurts."

"I should never have asked you to attempt that. It was too dangerous." His shoulders slumped. He looked like he might be sick.

She rested a hand on his forearm. "No. It was my decision. And we need to know."

A tentative hope crept into his voice. "Did you discover anything?"

"No."

He frowned. "But you were connected to it for over five hours."

Five hours? It had only felt like a few minutes. "It can't be."

"I'm afraid it was." He took the washcloth back and got up to drop it in the sink. "It was too much of a strain. I won't ask you to do it again."

"If what you said about Miasmos is true, we don't have a choice. I have to try again."

He massaged his forehead. "Just promise me you won't try it alone. If I hadn't been here to wake you up..." his voice trailed off.

"I promise."

16

POWER OF THE GODS

The vacation, if it could be called that, ended too soon. Kelly found it hard to concentrate in German class. The intricacies of the subjunctive mood, the topic of the day's lecture, just didn't hold as much interest as it normally would. Her mind drifted to the Ardagali, the gauntlet, her father, and to the memory stone's enigmatic puzzles. For once she actually considered the possibility of leaving 'humanland' and going to live with the fairies full-time. But she only seriously considered it for a few moments. As a fadaman she knew she belonged in both worlds. Like Marcos, she could accomplish important things in both roles.

Besides, she could never leave Mindy or the other people she cared about. The image of Dmitri's gift bursting into flames flashed in her mind. A deep sense of loss gripped her. She felt a bit silly for letting the loss of a miniature teddy bear affect her so much. Then again, maybe it wasn't the loss of the bear itself that disturbed her so, but rather the loss of what the bear represented.

At last the bell rang. Tommy Thompson looked over his shoulder and waved to try to get her attention. Kelly pretended not to notice. She didn't want to be mean, but she just didn't have the energy to humor him today. She made a beeline for the door, hoping he'd give up. But out in the hallway, she heard his voice behind her. "Kelly, wait up."

She kept walking.

"Kelly!"

She stopped and turned around. "What is it, Tommy?"

"Sheesh." He crossed his arms. "I don't even get a 'hi, how was your break'?"

She rolled her eyes. "Hi, Tommy, how was your break?"

He grinned. "It was great. I visited my sister in New York City. She's in college there. But how was your break? I wanted to ask you what happened." His eyes sparkled with conspiratorial interest.

Huh? He couldn't possibly know anything about what she had been up to. "What do you mean?"

"There's something different about you."

She shrugged, trying to be nonchalant. "No there's not."

"There is."

"Maybe I gained some new muscles from building houses."

He shook his head. "Na-uh. I think it's more than that. But it's okay if you want to be mysterious. I like mystery." He spun around and pranced his way down the hall.

Kelly watched him go, perplexed. There was something odd about him, that was nothing new. But this sudden talent of keen observation threw her off balance. Maybe he'd just gotten lucky. After all, she *did* feel different. She hadn't thought it showed, though. Would Dmitri notice? Her heart skipped a beat. Would he even give her a second glance? Ever since that day weeks ago, he'd been doing his best to ignore her. She'd hoped he would get over it eventually, but as the days had worn on it had seemed less and less likely. So she expected him to still be mad at her when algebra rolled around.

Unfortunately, she didn't get a chance to find out. Dmitri

was absent. Where was he? At first, she resisted the urge to use the spy ring to find him, but when Mr. Patterson droned on and on for the hundredth time in his boring manner about the quadratic formula, it was either that or fall asleep. She stole a glance at her hand, which rested in her lap. An image of Dmitri's mother's room came into the ring. She barely recognized the woman in the bed as Katerina. Her face was swollen and puffy. She was getting sicker. Beside the bed, Dmitri helped to adjust his mother's pillows. Her heart went out to him.

"Whatcha doing?" a voice behind her ear asked.

Kelly jumped.

A ghost-like Bubbles giggled. "You didn't even sense me. What's wrong with you?"

She established a mental connection. *"I was paying attention to something else."*

"That boy?"

She covered her hand. *"What are you doing here?"*

He flew around and plopped himself on top of her textbook. *"I wanted to give you the news."* He paused dramatically. *"I'm married!"*

That was sudden. *"What about the ceremony?"*

"We eloped. Bamblelina said she missed me so much when I was gone, that she didn't want to wait anymore to be my wife." He puffed his chest out with pride. *"I have to go meet her now. We're leaving for our honeymoon."*

"Where are you going?"

"We're going on a human cruise." He sprang back into the air. *"So, see you later! Tell Stephanie, won't you?"*

Kelly nodded. Although Stephanie was right beside them, doodling on her paper, she had no idea Bubbles was there in his invisible-to-humans form. *"She'll be disappointed you didn't tell her yourself, though."*

Bubbles shrugged. *"My wife will be more disappointed if I don't meet her on time."*

"EARTH TO KELLY, SPACE CADET," Stephanie teased, poking Kelly in the arm.

Kelly realized she'd been staring vacantly at nothing. "Sorry."

That afternoon, Stephanie and Kelly rode on the metro together towards Kelly's house. Mindy had invited Rick over for dinner, and Kelly did not want to endure that man's presence alone.

Stephanie pulled some lip balm from her backpack and smeared it on. "What's on your mind?"

Kelly sighed. "I was thinking about Dmitri."

Stephanie nodded knowingly. "You should just forget about him. He's been ignoring you anyway."

"That's just because I won't tell him the truth about me."

Stephanie extended her lip balm out to Kelly.

"No, thanks."

Stephanie put the lip balm away, eyebrows drawn together thoughtfully. "Well, if you really want Dmitri back, you could tell him part of the truth. But not the whole truth."

"What do you mean?"

"You could say you have ESP, you know, extra sensory perception. You could just keep the part about being a fadaman a secret, for now."

Interesting. She lifted the spy ring and thought of Dmitri. Now Katerina was in a hospital bed. Dmitri sat in a chair beside her, talking to a nurse who took notes on a clip board.

Stephanie peered over her shoulder. "You know, if you switch lines at this stop, it'll take you right to the hospital."

Kelly let her hand drop. "What? Go see him now? I couldn't."

"Why not? With his mom in the hospital, who knows when

he'll be in school again?" The train slowed. "Well?" Stephanie asked. "This is the stop."

Kelly took a deep breath. "All right."

"Do you want me to come?"

Kelly shook her head. "No. I need to do this alone." The train came to a full stop and Kelly stood up. "Tell my mom I'll be home later."

~

ABOUT HALF AN HOUR later Kelly got off the train at the hospital stop. She paused on the sidewalk outside the entrance. Cars drove by along the street at a steady pace. The hospital was huge. Where was Dmitri exactly? She leaned against the wall to get out of the way of passersby. She closed her eyes and pushed her fairy senses backwards into the building, slowly expanding up through the floors, attempting to locate Dmitri's vibrations. She sensed lots of unfamiliar people moving about inside, but she didn't hit upon Dmitri.

After ten minutes she thought she sensed a woman who might be Katerina, but she was all alone in her room. Kelly opened her eyes. Maybe Dmitri wasn't inside at all. Perhaps he'd gone out for some air. There was a small park nearby. She closed her eyes again and let her fairy senses travel up the street and into the park, feeling a sense of satisfaction that she could extend them so far with such a level of detail.

In the park, she sensed some children playing, and a few people walking here and there. Then she sensed Dmitri. He was there! She opened her eyes and walked briskly towards his location. When she crossed the street to the park, she spotted him sitting on a bench, staring down at his knees. She walked all the way up to his bench, but he didn't notice. She cleared her throat. "Dmitri?"

His shoulders jerked and he looked up with surprise. "Kelly? What are you doing here?"

She sat down beside him. "I came to see you. I was worried because you weren't in school."

"Oh."

Oh? That's all he has to say? He hadn't even asked how she'd known where to find him. "Your mother's at the hospital?" she asked.

He nodded. "She might not have that much longer. Maybe a few months..." his voice trailed off.

"I'm sorry." She rested a hand on his shoulder.

He shrugged it away. "I don't want your pity."

His words stung. "It's not pity, it's concern. They are two very different things."

He clenched his teeth and stared straight ahead.

"Is this how it's going to be?" she asked. "Can't we even talk anymore?"

He turned to give her an accusatory glare. "Until I can trust what you say, we don't have anything to talk about."

Why did he have to be so stubborn? And why did she have to like that about him? She sighed. "Fine then. I'll tell you."

He waited.

"I can sense things."

His expression softened — slightly. "Like a psychic?"

"Kind of."

He thought about it.

"That's why I had to leave that day," Kelly added. "And that's how I knew you were here now."

"Why didn't you just tell me before?"

"I didn't want you to think I was weird."

"But I like weird." He winked.

She laughed. "Well, it wasn't just that. It's dangerous."

He frowned. "Dangerous? How?"

"If the wrong people knew what I could do, then, there could be problems."

"Oh. I guess that makes sense."

"So you believe me?"

"Yes," he said simply.

She fixed him with a quizzical look.

He chuckled. "Don't look so shocked. I believe in the paranormal. My grandmother could see ghosts."

She felt lighter, like a great weight had been lifted off her shoulders, even though she had only told him a half-truth. "I'm sorry I didn't tell you sooner. But the only other person who knows is Stephanie. My mother doesn't even know."

"You can trust me, Kelly. I won't tell anyone."

They sat in silence for a few moments. "Where's your little brother?" Kelly asked.

"He's spending a few days at a neighbor's house."

Kelly felt a sudden gust of icy wind, and the branches of a nearby tree rattled. But it was in between two other trees that didn't move at all. *That's odd,* Kelly thought.

Then something even odder happened. Marcos and Stephanie ran out from behind the tree and headed towards them. Kelly's jaw dropped. What were they doing together? Stephanie had to have already reached Kelly's house, so how did she get from there to here so fast? And why were they here? That was the one question she knew the answer to immediately. It could only be one thing. Miasmos had found the last curtain. Shivers ran up and down her spine.

As Marcos and Stephanie got closer, Dmitri's eyes widened like saucers. "Is that who I think it is?"

"Um...yes. Sorry, I have to go."

She jumped up and hurried to meet Marcos and Stephanie. She met them halfway across the grass. From his position on the bench, Dmitri watched them dumbfounded.

"The last curtain dropped! I know where Embralia is,"

Marcos panted. "My father is going there now! We have to stop him."

"How?" Kelly asked.

"Over here."

She followed Stephanie and Marcos back to the tree, and they ducked behind it. They were hidden from Dmitri's view, but their position was far from concealed — anyone walking along the other edge of the park would have been able to see them. Luckily, that part of the park didn't look very busy.

Marcos retrieved his stone from his pocket. "I figured out what it's for," he said.

Kelly watched with interest as he held the stone in his palm and stared at it intently. As he did so, the lines from Kelly's vision appeared on its surface — at first faint, then brighter and brighter. Marcos delicately traced an index finger along a twisting path through the lines. When he pulled his finger back, the stone lifted up in the air and hovered over his palm. It began to spin faster and faster, taking on a bright blue glow. It made a whirring sound as it blurred from rotating so quickly. Then there was a bright flash.

Kelly blinked. When her vision cleared she realized they stood in the same position, but they were now inside a blue orb of pulsating energy. Kelly looked out — she could see their surroundings through the energy. "Can people see us?"

Marcos shook his head. "They might see a little mirage-type blur, but they shouldn't see us."

"Isn't it cool?" Stephanie said. "I nearly fainted when he showed me at your house. I broke a mug."

"That could have been avoided entirely if you hadn't been hiding yourself, Kelly," Marcos said.

Hiding myself? What's he talking about? Then it dawned on her. That morning, like many mornings, she'd awoken to the sound of the memory stone's whispers pestering her for attention all the way from Glendenland. So she'd strengthened her mental barrier against them, which must have also concealed her from Marcos's fairy senses.

"I made him promise to bring me," Stephanie gloated. "Or else I wouldn't tell him where you were." She laughed.

"You shouldn't be so proud of extorting people," Marcos commented with a scowl.

Stephanie rolled her eyes. "Mindy thinks we're helping him with the campaign. I told her not to wait up."

"And she was all right with that?"

"Yep. Once Marcos gave his word he'd watch over us."

"Considering what we're planning, that might be a hard promise to keep," Kelly said.

Marcos smiled ruefully. "Well, if none of us make it back, it won't matter, will it? Speaking of which, we've wasted enough time already."

He made intricate hand motions in the air, sort of like a puppeteer. The orb hummed in response. It lifted them about a foot into the air. The pulsating energy didn't look solid, but it carried them upward. *This is why it's called the bearer,* Kelly thought. Maybe it was some kind of force field? She reached for one of the walls, but her hand encountered resistance a few inches inward from the wall itself — it felt like the repulsion created when trying to push two magnets with the same polarity together. Marcos steered the orb to the left, out from under the tree and into the open grass. They hovered in place for a few seconds, and then there was a bump as they shot up into the air. They had to be going over five hundred miles an hour, but there were no inertial changes. It was way better than the helicopter. A faint scent like ozone hung in the air.

"Something tells me 'psychic' doesn't quite cover every-thing," a voice said from beside Kelly. She nearly jumped out of her skin. It was Dmitri?!

"Where did you come from?" Marcos asked calmly, still concentrating on steering the orb.

"I saw you guys just disappear," Dmitri said. "And then the air kind of...rippled. So I ran and jumped into the ripple." He said it as if it were the most normal thing to have done. Could he be in shock? Kelly had read somewhere that people in shock sometimes didn't show emotions.

"That was thoughtless," Marcos told Dmitri. "You could have been vaporized."

"Well, I wasn't." Dmitri looked around. "This is so cool."

"I'm putting you down," Marcos said.

"No!" Stephanie put a hand on Marcos's elbow to stop him from directing the orb downwards. "We don't have time. You said yourself we might not get there in time as it is."

He hesitated.

"Let me come," Dmitri said. "Whenever you get where you're going, I promise I'll wait in the 'car,' or whatever you call this thing. I swear."

Marcos nodded. "All right. But you do exactly as I say, understood?"

"Of course." He grabbed Kelly's arm excitedly. "So, are you going to tell me what's going on?"

"She's half-fairy," Stephanie cut in.

"Stephanie!"

"What? He's already in the super secret energy ship."

Stephanie had a point there.

Dmitri's eyes filled with a child-like wonder. "A half-fairy? Tell me more."

As they left the city behind and raced over the open ocean, Kelly told Dmitri everything.

"We're almost there," Marcos announced.

Kelly, Stephanie, and Dmitri looked down through the floor in the orb. It was night in this part of the world, but the darkness was tempered by the silver light of the moon. They approached a tall cliff on the edge of the ocean. Inward from the edge, the slope stretched upward to form a mountain. Kelly could just make out a cluster of low circular walls about three fourths of the way up to the mountain's peak. *Were they some sort of ruins?* Two concentric stone walls capped the mountain, giving the illusion it was wearing a pair of crowns.

Marcos set the orb down just outside a narrow opening in the outer of the two concentric walls. It was only three feet high, but a scattering of loose stones along its side suggested it had once been taller. Marcos made a fist in the air and then quickly opened his hand flat. There was a flash and the orb fell away around them, leaving the unassuming bearer stone resting in Marcos's palm.

They were too far up to hear the ocean below, and Kelly found it eerily quiet. "Where are we?" she whispered.

"In Galicia, Spain," Marcos said. "Historians think this is an old Celtic settlement. But actually it was a fairy city. See how close together the houses were?"

Kelly squinted at the ancient ruins on the mountain below them. The structures had only been about five feet in diameter — small dwellings for humans, but quite spacious for fairies. Barely one foot of open space separated each structure from its neighbors. It would indeed have been a very tight squeeze for humans to navigate.

Marcos turned to Stephanie and Dmitri. "You two stay here. No heroics, I mean it." His eyes narrowed on Dmitri. "Got it?"

Dmitri nodded.

Marcos handed Stephanie the bearer stone. "Watch this for me. Use it if we don't come back."

"I'm heartened by your confidence," Stephanie deadpanned.

Stephanie and Dmitri knelt down behind the outer wall while Kelly and Marcos climbed over it. They tip-toed up to the inner wall, changed into their fairy forms and flew up to the top. Inside this wall was the summit of the mountain, which turned out to be an unimpressive grassy circle, with a slight dip in the middle like a hole had once been dug there.

"Is Miasmos here?" Kelly whispered.

"I don't think so."

"How do you know?"

He looked around nervously. "I'm guessing?"

"You don't sense him?"

He shook his head no.

Great, Kelly thought. "What do we do then?"

"We wait for him, and when he arrives we surprise him before he has a chance to react."

A chilling cackle cut through the air. "You're a little late for that, sonny boy." Across the grass, a fairy form flew over the opposite wall. Miasmos. The evil fairy flew forward and hovered in the center of the space. "Took you long enough, Marcos. I've been here for hours, waiting for you. I knew you'd come. I didn't want you to miss the show." Miasmos's wings glowed as he pulled a round stone from his pocket — the Key to Embralia.

Marcos drew his wand. "Father, don't do this."

"Or what?"

"I'll fight you." Marcos took aim.

Miasmos raised an eyebrow. "That's it? No sob story first about how I shouldn't hurt poor, 'innocent' humans?"

Marcos gripped his wand tighter. "We're beyond that now. I know there's no reasoning with you. You've descended so far into darkness you've lost yourself."

Miasmos smirked. "That last line was quite poetic. By all means, continue."

"Why should I?" Marcos asked, his voice rising in pitch. "When I look into your eyes I don't even recognize you. I just see pure evil. Nothing more."

"Nothing more?" Miasmos shook his head and sighed. "This is why you disappoint me, Marcos. You lack imagination. Your mind is too small to appreciate my vision for the future. But soon you won't have to imagine it, because it will be here." He extended his arm so that the Key to Embralia caught the moonlight. "All I have to do is use this."

Marcos took a step forward. "We can't let you do that."

Miasmos's eyes flashed orange. "If I recall correctly, you're no match for me."

"I'm stronger than you think!" Marcos rushed at Miasmos with sparks blazing from his wand. The sparks bounced harmlessly off his father's invisible shield.

Miasmos's deranged laughter filled the air again. "You were saying?"

Before Kelly had a chance to join the fight, with a flick of his wrist Miasmos blew a powerful gust of wind at his son. It knocked Marcos off his feet and sent him flying through the air. He smacked against the wall, unconscious.

"Marcos!" Kelly flew down to his side. She shook his shoulders but he didn't wake up. He was out cold. She glared at Miasmos. "You're despicable," she yelled.

Miasmos grinned. "Why, thank you." Without further ado he dropped the Key to Embralia onto the ground. In an instant the earth directly beneath the stone crumbled inward, and the stone fell from view into a new, perfectly round hole.

A second later, an intense beam of white light rose from the opening and focused on Miasmos like a spotlight. Kelly watched in horror as the evil fairy's eyes blazed with an unnatural gleam. Miasmos raised his arms skyward. "It's mine, mine! All mine, the power of the gods!" He ranted something about world domination before chanting in gibberish as the power from the mountain flowed into him.

The ground shook, and the hole widened into a crack that inched towards the wall.

"Kelly, come back," Stephanie shouted from her position. "It's an earthquake!"

Kelly tried to revive Marcos again. He moaned, still unconscious. She slapped him across the face. He sat up with a jolt. "What happened?" He looked around. "Crap."

Kelly tugged on his arm. "We have to get out of here."

He shook her away and fumbled for his wand, which had been knocked from his hand by Miasmos's attack. "We can't leave. I have to stop him."

"He's too powerful," Kelly said. *And he's getting more powerful by the second.*

The ground shuddered, almost knocking Kelly off her feet. She sprang up to hover in the air for stability. Her toes had scarcely left the ground when there was a rumble like thunder from deep within the earth — and a bolt of lightning shot from the crack. It pulverized a section of the wall beside Miasmos. The evil fairy didn't even flinch.

Ignoring the danger, Marcos still felt around for his wand on all fours.

"Marcos!" Kelly shouted to try and get his attention over the rumbling sounds. "It's unstable!" He didn't respond.

Just when she thought the situation couldn't get any worse, there was an ominous pop from the expanding fissure. The pop was followed by a hiss, and glowing smoke rose up around the column of energy that shone on Miasmos. The smoke smelt like sulphur, and it brought a blast of hot air with it. *This can't be good,* Kelly thought. She stared at the ground in trepidation. After a moment a tiny bit of orange liquid bubbled up from the crack and spilled out. It trickled towards them, burning the grass in its wake. The lava stream was soon joined by another that ran parallel to it. Then another. More lava bubbled up steadily from the ground, at a rate like water from a small park fountain. But it might not be long before that fountain became a geyser.

Marcos still stubbornly refused to give up the search for his wand. Kelly didn't know why he didn't just attack Miasmos without it. But she was glad he didn't, because Miasmos was ignoring them for now — giving them a chance to escape. Another lightning bolt surged through the air and vaporized a wide patch of grass. It only missed Marcos by inches. Kelly flew over to him and kicked him in the stomach.

"Ow! Why are you attacking me, have you gone mad?"

"No. You're the crazy one! Don't just throw your life away. That's what Miasmos wants."

Marcos paused and gazed at his father. Miasmos was still in a trance, muttering nonsense as he absorbed the mountain's power.

"We can't beat him now," Kelly continued. "You have to know that. But we can live to try again later."

Those words finally got through to Marcos. He flew into the air and they zoomed back towards Stephanie and Dmitri, who jumped up and down, waving furiously for them to hurry up. Kelly heard another rumble behind her, and a sizzling in the air.

Her friends' eyes grew wide. "Watch out!" Dmitri yelled.

Kelly looked over her shoulder and saw a blazing bolt arcing from the ground towards her. She knew she should move out of the way, but she froze. At the last second Marcos plowed into her from the side and they tumbled to the ground. Lying on her back with Marcos beside her, Kelly watched the bolt whiz by overhead — straight for Stephanie and Dmitri. Neither of the two was quick enough to get out of the way in time. The bolt made a direct hit, and they both fell out of view behind the wall.

"No!" Kelly rolled over and tried to fly -- but a stabbing pain struck between her shoulders when she flapped her wings. She must have injured them when she'd hit the ground, though she hadn't felt anything at the moment of impact. "My wings are broken," she shouted, panic rising within her because her friends needed her help.

Marcos leaned over and ran his fingers along the bones in her wings. She winced from the pressure. "They're not broken," he said. "It's just a sprain. But you can't fly for a few days."

She quickly changed to human form. Her shoulders ached but it was nothing compared to being struck by lightning. Her heart raced with dread as she imagined her friends possibly disfigured and burnt to a crisp. The ground's quaking intensified. Kelly couldn't get to her feet. She had to crawl to where Dmitri and Stephanie had gone down.

When she reached them, they lay in a crumpled heap. At the sight of them her dread was replaced by perplexity. Both Stephanie's and Dmitri's chests rose up and down evenly, surprisingly calm. And there were no outward signs of damage: their skin was pristine, their clothes were uncharred, and they looked like they were simply sleeping peacefully. "How come they aren't burnt?" Kelly asked in shock.

"It wasn't exactly electricity that hit them," Marcos said cryptically. He stood beside her, also back in human form. She'd have to ask him what he meant by that later.

Marcos reached down and pried the bearer stone from Stephanie's fist. He traced the path on the stone's surface. Its bright flash erupted as it encircled the four of them. Kelly felt safer inside its protective blue bubble. In seconds they were airborne. Kelly looked down to see Miasmos was still frozen in place on the mountaintop, arms raised skyward as the light kept going into him. Lava splashed all around him but he just laughed, protected by his shield.

They were perhaps a football field's length over the ocean when an earsplitting clap reverberated in the air. The shockwave nearly knocked them out of the sky. Behind them, a full volcanic eruption lit up the night. Fluorescent lava shot so far into the air it would have reached the top of a skyscraper.

Then the entire mountain split down the middle from the strain. Kelly gasped as it teetered, rocking back and forth like a gigantic toy block before it crumbled into the sea.

"It could have been worse," Marcos said, taking note of her stunned expression.

"How?"

"It could have been a modern human city instead of abandoned ruins."

Kelly hadn't thought of that. He was right. Thousands of people would surely have died had that been the case.

Marcos made a few more hand motions to set their course, then let his hands drop to his sides. He sank to the floor, deflated, and put his head in his hands. "I thought since we're both fadamen, we'd have a chance. But we failed."

"I guess we were foolish to think we could beat him," Kelly said, thinking back to the first time she'd fought the evil fairy. "Thomas, Venuto and I couldn't beat him with our combined strength. Only when Glenden helped us could we even get past his shield."

Marcos didn't answer. Kelly turned her attention to her unconscious friends. She felt Stephanie's and Dmitri's foreheads. Their temperatures were normal. "Are they going to be all right?"

Marcos nodded. "They're just stunned. They should wake up soon."

His words didn't provide much relief, but he sounded like he knew what he was talking about. Kelly's thoughts drifted to the future. "How powerful is Miasmos now?" she asked.

"I don't know for sure. Nobody does. But, he believed that the mountain's power would give him control of the elements on a grand scale. So, he'd be able to control the wind and the water, make hurricanes, tornados, blizzards, and so on."

Kelly bit her lower lip. *The power of the gods...*

"If that's true, and he sticks to the plan he shared with me before," Marcos continued, "he won't strike right away, not directly. He wants to create chaos through 'natural' disasters. He wants to wear everybody down to the point of desperation so that he can sweep in and be the savior."

"That's diabolical," Kelly said.

"Of course it is. It's my father we're talking about." He clenched his fists. "And I don't know if we can stop him."

She rested a hand on his shoulder. "We'll find a way. We have to."

~

Soon after the orb had crossed back into daylight, Stephanie stirred. "What happened?" she asked, propping herself up on her elbows.

"You got knocked out," Kelly said. "How do you feel?"

Stephanie clutched her stomach. "Like I'm going to be sick."

"Hold on, if you can," Marcos said. "I don't know what happens if someone throws up inside this thing."

"I'll try, but I don't know how long I can wait."

Kelly searched the ocean below. She spotted a grouping of tiny desert islands. They'd only passed a few such groupings the entire way, so Stephanie had woken up at the perfect time. "Land over there," Kelly said.

Marcos nodded. He guided the orb downwards. It was all good until they reached the ground, where the orb skidded wildly along the sand, bouncing as Marcos tried to slow it down.

"This...is not...helping," Stephanie gasped.

"Sorry. It's the first time I've landed on a beach." Marcos made a swift hand motion and they jerked to a stop beside a row of palm trees.

Marcos clenched his fist and then opened it. The orb

flashed and transformed back into the bearer stone. Marcos tucked it into his pocket.

Stephanie rolled over and threw up on the sand.

Kelly patted her friend's back. "Are you all right?"

"I think so."

"Good. I never would have forgiven myself if..." Kelly couldn't bring herself to complete the sentence.

Dmitri groaned and sat up, dazed. "Where are we?"

"A desert island," Kelly said.

He brought a hand up to shield his eyes from the sun and squinted at the horizon. "I hope we're not stranded. I need to get back to my mother."

"Don't worry, we're not," Kelly said.

Stephanie staggered to her feet and looked around. Her face took on a peculiar expression. "I've seen this place before," she murmured.

"What do you mean?" Kelly asked.

Stephanie raised her right arm and pointed at the nearest tree. "That palm tree, it...I think I..." She fell silent and squinted at the tree, concentrating. The air around them charged with static electricity. A second later, a blue lighting bolt shot from Stephanie's finger and hit the tree. Its wide, green fronds burst into flame.

Kelly was speechless. Dmitri stared open-mouthed at Stephanie, looking just as shocked.

For his part, Marcos seemed tickled. He laughed. "Incredible! Can you do it again?"

Stephanie energetically blasted the tree once more.

"Bravo!" Marcos exclaimed. "Oh look, let's go try it on that tree over there."

Stephanie and Marcos ran for the next tree like two children excited to play with a new toy.

How is this possible? Kelly thought. *Humans can't have powers.*

"She does," Dmitri commented.

Some of Embralia's power must have been transferred to her when she was struck. That must be what Marcos meant when he said it wasn't exactly 'electricity' that hit them.

Dmitri nodded. "Seems logical."

Kelly grabbed Dmitri's arm. "Wait a minute, I didn't say anything out loud!"

He furrowed his brow. "Huh? I heard you. You just said some of the power leaked from the mountain to Stephanie."

"No, I didn't say that. I *thought* it."

Dmitri gulped. "You mean...I read your mind?"

"What number am I thinking of right now?" she asked him. Before she could even think of a number the image of the teddy bear burning in the gauntlet popped into her mind.

His face fell. "You burnt my gift?"

"I had to."

By the next tree, Marcos clapped as Stephanie blasted it with lighting bolt after lightning bolt. As yet she showed no signs of tiring.

Being able to shoot deathly lightning bolts was a dangerous power, but it didn't make Kelly even a fraction as nervous as Dmitri's newfound ability to read minds. Thoughts should be private. *Can I block him?* she wondered.

"Why would you block me?" Dmitri asked innocently.

She gave him a *you've-got-to-be-kidding-me* look.

He laughed. "I guess I wouldn't want anyone to read my mind, either. Maybe I can learn how to shut it off."

"In the meantime, I have an idea." Kelly concentrated on fortifying the protective mental bubble around herself, just like she did with the whispers. "Can you hear what I'm thinking now?" She thought of the tacky cardboard cutouts from Marcos's gala.

Dmitri twisted his face with concentration. Finally, he shook his head. "No."

She breathed a sigh of relief. She would have been really

embarrassed if she'd been unable to block him and he'd heard some of the thoughts she tended to have about him. Her cheeks grew hot.

By now the second tree was just a pile of burnt ash. Stephanie and Marcos ran back over to Kelly and Dmitri. Stephanie talked a mile a minute. "Kelly, is this what doing magic feels like? It's so awesome! Lighting comes out of my hand, but it doesn't burn me. Marcos said he would teach me the other elements. This is just like my FSP visions. Blaine will be stoked."

Kelly's chest tightened. If Stephanie's FSP vision had just come true, did that mean hers would come true too? The one about the massive tidal wave hitting New York City? Weren't tsunamis triggered by earthquakes? Hadn't a very strong one just caused an entire cliff to fall into the ocean? "Um, we might have a problem," she said. She told them about her vision.

"A tsunami in the Big Apple seems unlikely," Marcos said. "But I can check." He pulled a phone from his jacket pocket.

"You have bars out here?" Stephanie asked.

"It's a satellite phone," he explained. He dialed a number. "Yes, Candice," he said into the phone. "Do you have access to the tsunami warning system? I need to know if there has been any activity." He waited. Then his eyes widened in shock. "What?" His voice cracked.

Kelly's stomach twisted in knots.

"That's not possible," Marcos continued. "A sixty-foot wave? When? Thirty minutes ago? Something like that should have taken at least eight or nine hours to travel across the ocean." Marcos listened as his assistant talked some more. "All right. Thank you, Candice. Have William start working on our first statement." He hung up and squeezed the phone like he was trying to strangle it. "Damn you, Father!" he yelled at the sky.

"It already happened, didn't it?" Kelly asked.

Marcos kicked the sand, in what Kelly thought was a futile

attempt to take his frustration out on it. "There wasn't any warning," he said. "Somehow the machines didn't pick up on anything."

They all shared worried, stunned looks. Kelly remembered the woman from her vision — her last moments of panic as the water rushed into her lungs. How many had suffered the same fate? And how many people had lost loved ones? Her chest clenched when she thought back to that morning, when Tommy had mentioned visiting his sister in New York City over the break. Was she one of the lucky ones? Or one of the unlucky ones?

"This is..." Kelly began, trying to find adequate words but not succeeding. "This is...awful."

"Like a bad dream," Dmitri said.

"Exactly," Stephanie agreed. "I keep thinking if I pinch myself it will end."

"It's far from over," Marcos said. His expression darkened as he stared into the distance. "Prepare yourselves, because this is just the beginning."

Kelly reached for Dmitri's hand. He squeezed it and gave her a brave smile. She found the strength inside to return it. Whatever was coming, at least they would face it together.